Ken Mitchell was born in Wellington, New Zealand, in 1964. He has worked a variety of jobs, including teaching, PR and local government. He is married with two sons and currently lives in Wellington. *Alternative 3* is his first novel.

GW00775626

KEN MITCHELL

ALTERNATIVE

3

HarperCollins*Publishers*

HarperCollins*Publishers*

First published in Australia in 2003
This edition published in 2004
by HarperCollins*Publishers* Pty Limited
ABN 36 009 913 517
A member of the HarperCollins*Publishers* (Australia) Pty Limited Group
www.harpercollins.com.au

HarperCollins*Publishers*
25 Ryde Road, Pymble, Sydney, NSW 2073, Australia
31 View Road, Glenfield, Auckland 10, New Zealand
77–85 Fulham Palace Road, London, W6 8JB, United Kingdom
2 Bloor Street East, 20th floor, Toronto, Ontario M4W 1A8, Canada
10 East 53rd Street, New York NY 10022, USA

National Library of Australia Cataloguing-in-Publication data:

Mitchell, Ken, 1964– .
    Alternative 3.
    ISBN 0 7322 7703 5.
    I. Title.
NZ823.3

Cover based on the original design by Antart
Typeset in 10.5/13 Sabon by HarperCollins
Printed and bound in Australia by Griffin Press on 50gsm Bulky News

5 4 3 2 1   04 05 06 07

For Finn

PROLOGUE

Berlin, April 1945

The Russian soldiers aren't taking any risks. Their progress into the heart of Berlin's central district is slow, deliberate and cautious. The final assault on Berlin is into its fourth long day, despite some of the heaviest air attacks of the war. The street combat has been savage as remnants of the Wehrmacht and SS fight for their very survival against an unstoppable Red tide.

To the few Berliners remaining in the beleaguered capital, their city is now largely unrecognisable from the one that had unleashed an iron empire stretching from North Africa to the Baltic. But the bombing has finally brought the reality of the war home to even the most complacent Berliner. The city is pounded relentlessly around the clock — even in broad daylight — such is the feeble resistance of the once mighty Luftwaffe. Almost every building has been shelled or burned out in the raging firestorms created by the incendiary bombing.

The city's infrastructure — from newspapers to public transport — has long since collapsed, and looting is widespread. Electricity, gas and sanitation have broken down, and food, a precious scarcity during the final few weeks, is now almost unobtainable. Broken hydrants are the only source of water but, as the Soviet grasp on the city tightens, it is no longer safe to venture even briefly onto the exposed, desolate streets.

Berlin's frightened civilian inhabitants have taken to their cellars — their sense of time distorted by the death and destruction around them. Glimpses of anxious faces at cellar windows are the only sign that inside, a family is clinging to the small hope that they will survive the Russian onslaught long enough to surrender to the Allies. But for most, those hopes are in vain, as the Russian juggernaut crushes all before it, unleashing with savage intensity the years of pent-up rage for the hell inflicted on them at Moscow, Leningrad and Stalingrad.

Two Russian armies of more than 2.5 million men and machines have Berlin circled in a vice-like grip. The Führer himself takes charge of the city's defences, and in a final radio broadcast to the few still listening, announces in a display of bravado that he will stay on in his capital to the last. Too late, he orders his beleaguered armies, retreating with alarming speed before the Western allies, to come to the rescue of his beloved city. But Russian troops have already shaken hands with the

Americans for photographers at the river Elbe, and the race has begun to be the first to march triumphantly into the very heart of the Nazi empire. Hastily thrown together divisions of defenders are rushed into position. But equipment and ammunition are scarce, and commanding officers are forced to use the civilian telephone network to arrange each line of defence, following numerous reports of Russian breakthroughs. Despite being outnumbered, outmanoeuvred and outgunned, the German commanders are ordered to 'set a shining example of devotion to duty unto death'.

The Russians have the Berlin garrison confined to a narrow east–west corridor less than 5 kilometres wide and 16 kilometres long. But soon it is penetrated in two places, leaving three small pockets of resistance. One of the pockets is to become the symbol of last-ditch resistance of the final days of the Nazi regime. At its centre stands the Reichstag building, the former home of Germany's National Assembly. For the Soviets it has special meaning — conquering it will symbolise total victory over Nazi Germany.

The assault on the Reichstag begins early. Artillery and howling 'Katyusha' rockets blast the huge grey monolith in the darkness, which lifts to reveal an overcast morning thick with smoke and the choking grit of battle. The Russian soldiers leading the assault are hardened combat veterans. But even they are unprepared for the fanaticism they face from the cornered Nazis, desperate to hold out until they can surrender to the Western Allies and avoid the terrible Soviet wrath. Every doorway and window must be cleared of snipers and anti-tank gunners before they can safely advance. It is slow, painstaking and dangerous work. Behind them a 4000-strong armada of Soviet tanks rolls into the heart of the city. Smoke and fumes already wreath the Brandenburg Gate. Once the scene of Germany's great military parades, it now stands as a silent monument to a dying city.

Up ahead of the advancing Russian infantry, the hulking grey outline of the Reichstag emerges from the smoke. Even with the end so near the Russian soldiers remain cautious, despite the urgent demands of their superiors to beat the Allies to the prize. They work in teams to clear side streets and bombed-out buildings of small pockets of brave but futile resistance. The defenders are mostly old men of the Volksturm — the German Home Guard — and boys of the Hitler Youth conscripted in the final few weeks of the war. Their equipment is limited and their training rudimentary. As they huddle in lonely doorways and foxholes, the ground beneath their feet vibrates as columns of Russian tanks inch towards them. The narrow streets amplify the growling of the monstrous engines and squealing metal tracks, as they lumber forward, spitting death at any sign of movement ahead.

The large square in front of the Reichstag is a ghastly battle zone strewn with rubble and debris from the intensive bombing. Abandoned 88-mm guns hastily set up by the defenders in the last few days stand silent, surrounded by bodies in bloody grey uniforms. Thick black smoke belches from gaping holes in the domed roof of the Reichstag, as inside, the defenders try to prevent the inevitable Russian assault. The lower storey windows, reinforced with steel and concrete, have turned the once grand building into a fortress. Small firing slits bristle with the barrels of weapons, forcing the Russians to take whatever cover they can find on the vast square below.

Eventually the Russian tanks take position and begin shelling the Reichstag with relentless precision. The ornate brickwork is blown apart, and one by one the concreted-up windows blown in. The small-arms fire from the building becomes sporadic. Through the lingering smoke, waves of hunched-over Soviets dive forward under cover as they advance steadily on the building. The long journey from Moscow is almost at an end.

Beneath the feet of the advancing Russians, a man stands alone in front of a cracked mirror. The faint light of a single bulb reveals a face swathed in bandages. Through the bandages two black, piercing eyes stare at their own dim reflection. The sounds of the battle above faintly penetrate the small concrete-lined bunker, each shell-burst showering the room with a fine layer of dust. The man's reverie is broken by a tentative knock on the door. He draws a long, deep breath, holding his gaze in the mirror. His hand moves to the Luger strapped to his waist, then abruptly jerks shut the zip on his black jumpsuit. It holds no insignia — no clue to the man's identity.

'*Kom.*' He turns from the mirror to a young oberleutnant standing at the door. There is desperation in the officer's bloodshot and black-ringed eyes, yet he is polite — almost reverent — towards the man in the bandages.

'It is time.'

The man with the bandaged face rests his hands on the officer's shoulders, squeezing them firmly, looking squarely into his eyes. The oberleutnant's heart races with the heavy burden of expectation. He nods that he is ready. The bandaged man begins stuffing a worn leather satchel with papers. Despite his exhaustion, the oberleutnant shuffles nervously, noticing that the papers include diagrams unlike anything he's ever seen before — circular designs annotated with complicated physics equations. He looks away as the bandaged man straps up the satchel, pretending he hasn't seen them.

Together they emerge from the room into a long concrete corridor bustling with soldiers, wireless operators and intelligence officers — some with their sleeves rolled up, shouting commands to men carrying piles of papers. The string of low-watt lightbulbs running along the arched ceiling begins to fade erratically as the bunker's generator sucks thirstily at the last precious drops of fuel. They fight their way up the corridor past a large room where filing cabinets are being ripped apart and their contents thrown into piles on the floor. Smoke is already starting to drift along the corridor ceiling, adding to the confusion being played out beneath the advancing Russians' feet.

The oberleutnant follows the bandaged man into another small room. It is dark, and at first the oberleutnant can only just make out the vague shape of a man sitting on a low cot, back straight, his hands placed on his knees. But as he rises to face the bandaged man, the face that moves out of the shadows is instantly recognisable. Before him in full uniform stands the Führer, the Third Reich's supreme leader. The two men silently examine one another. The oberleutnant, discretely moving back into the shadows, notices that the bandaged man is almost exactly the same height and build as the Führer. But the men appear oblivious to him, and to the sounds of the battle above. Time in the small room seems to stand still. Finally the bandaged man lifts his right arm in a tired Nazi salute, just as the oberleutnant raises his gun to the back of the Führer's head.

The sound of the pistol shot in the confined space is deafening, but even before it has died away the oberleutnant is gently lowering the lifeless body to the floor, placing his pistol into the Führer's own hand. For a moment he stands over the body, a thick pool of blood oozing across the concrete floor. His soft whisper is only just audible.

'Heil Hitler.'

But the bandaged man is impatient and the oberleutnant barely has time to give hurried orders to two dishevelled SS stormtroopers who have appeared at the door, before rushing back up the corridor after him. Fighting his way through the melee, he glances back to see the stormtroopers carry the blanket-draped body out of the room, and disappear into the dark smoky haze.

The bandaged man is no longer in the corridor, but the oberleutnant stops outside a door deep within the bowels of the cramped, underground complex. It is slightly ajar, and stealing a glance inside he sees the bandaged man standing over a woman sprawled across a small army cot against the wall. He is running his hand through the blonde hair spilling over her face, her eyes fixed in a glazed, faraway stare. On the dresser an empty bottle of whiskey — Yankee whiskey he notices — stands beside a few small black pills. The oberleutnant recognises the cyanide capsules with which he has also been issued, accompanied by orders to keep them on his person at all times, such is the fear of the Russians and the lack of information on their progress. He looks away, embarrassed to be witnessing this private moment, but his eyes are drawn back to the scene playing out in the tiny bedroom. The woman's head moves slightly at the bandaged man's touch. A pistol appears in the bandaged man's hand, and the oberleutnant closes the door as quietly as he can.

The sound of the shot from the room merges with a violent explosion directly overhead. Even as the smoke is clearing from the blast, the Russians are diving, running, ducking. But always advancing. Behind them a steel monster emerges over a pile of rubble with a furious growl of its engines. The massive Soviet T34 tank is now directly over the bunker, its forward machine gun hosing bullets into the black holes blasted into the side of the Reichstag. One of the Russian soldiers shielding behind it stops for an instant, his gaze held by a cleverly camouflaged pipe rising from the rubble. A few short sharp commands are shouted, and the rest of the soldiers fan out, eyes scanning the ground for any clues to the entrance of the underground bunker.

Just metres away in the relative shelter of the Reichstag garden, an SS officer is overseeing two stormtroopers emptying cans of gasoline over two crumpled figures wrapped in thick grey blankets. The soldiers are in a desperate hurry, wildly throwing the gasoline at the grisly pile, but the officer orders them to finish the job properly, to make sure the bodies are well doused. As soon as the cans are empty the soldiers pick up their weapons and run back to the door of the bunker, as the officer flicks a lighter and throws it onto the wet pile. The gasoline ignites instantly with a loud whoosh, and even though the officer feels the heat singeing his eyebrows, he waits to make sure the flames have taken hold. Finally, he too retrieves his machine gun and after taking one last look at the shelled remains of the Reichstag, retreats to the safety of the bunker, which is closed and locked.

At the far end of the underground complex, the bandaged man waits patiently as the oberleutnant struggles to slide a cabinet out from the wall. The room is used for storage only, since it is furthermost from the entrance and the last to receive air from the ducting system. The oberleutnant's brow drips with dirty sweat as he drags the solid Bavarian oak cabinet towards the centre of the room, revealing a cavity in the concrete wall behind it. It is a small gap, barely big enough for two men to squeeze into …

The defenders inside the bunker doors tense visibly in the darkness, as they hear frenzied shouts in Russian from just outside. The thick steel doors have been discovered. Now it is only a matter of time. They sit silently with their backs against the cold concrete walls, grasping their weapons tightly, as they listen to the sound of a tank manoeuvring into position. Some finger their small black capsules, but no one speaks. There is nothing left to say.

Inside the storeroom at the end of the bunker, the oberleutnant joins the bandaged man in the shallow cavity, kicking a steel pedal protruding from the wall at his feet. Immediately the room is filled with the heavy grating of concrete sliding on concrete, as the ceiling begins a slow descent towards the floor. They stiffen their backs against the wall, the bandaged man clutching his satchel tightly against his chest. The ceiling reaches the level of the large cabinet, which creaks for an instant before exploding in a spray of splinters. Still it descends, just inches from the faces of the two men. Their breathing comes hard as the thick concrete block appears to seal them into the cavity, but they remain silent and resolute.

Eventually the top of the ceiling block appears, and as soon as it comes to a stop the two men clamber awkwardly out of the cavity up on to it. It is pitch-black, and it takes the oberleutnant a few moments of fumbling about on his knees to locate the steel ladder lying on the ground. He struggles to lift it — it is hinged at one end to the floor, but with a loud ringing thud it soon stands erected, providing a stairway up into the darkness. At the top of the ladder the oberleutnant feels for a manhole in the wall, a smell of thick, wet decay emerging from the nothingness. As soon as the bandaged man has joined him inside the hole, he kicks the ladder back down to the floor, just as a huge explosion rocks the bunker ...

The moment the thick iron door is blown apart by a single well-aimed blast from the Soviet tank, the Russians rush the bunker in numbers. There is little resistance — the explosion within the tight concrete confines of the bunker rips through the corridor with devastating effect, instantly killing the German defenders, forcing the Russians to climb over their bodies to get inside. Each room off the central corridor is efficiently dealt with by a grenade and a wild spray of machine-gun bullets. The few surviving Germans, blood flowing freely from their shattered ear drums, deaf to the sound of their own voices mouthing 'Ich ergebe mich!', are executed summarily. The Russian progress through the maze of tunnels is surprisingly fast. Only one room thwarts all attempts to open it — a thick steel door at the very end of the complex. Holes blown in the door reveal a solid concrete wall behind it, impervious to the Russian onslaught. But the choking smoke in the bunker rapidly becomes unbearable, so the soldiers decide to look elsewhere in their search for any possible escape routes ...

The muffled explosions from the bunker gradually recede as the oberleutnant and the bandaged man moved down a narrow, wet tunnel. The men cling to a waist-high handrail as the tunnel undulates in the dark. The only sounds they can hear are their boots on the wet concrete floor, and the scurrying of rats at their feet.

Finally they arrive at the end of the tunnel, and in the dark the oberleutnant feels along the wall, soon finding what he is looking for. His fingers hit a hard steel rung, and after hauling himself up, he climbs a narrow shaft. A steel trapdoor seals the shaft from outside — identical to the watertight doors on German U-boats. An iron bar hangs from the top-most rung. The oberleutnant grasps the bar and thrusts it sharply upwards against the thick steel door, the noise echoing down the tunnel behind him. He can hear the steady breathing of the bandaged man below him as he waits anxiously for a reply. Finally he hears a single, faint knock. He swings the bar again — two sharp knocks on the door. This time the response follows immediately. Two knocks. The pilot.

He grunts in the darkness as he manhandles the wheel. At first it won't budge, but with a supreme effort it begins to turn. Soon the wheel is spinning freely until coming to a sudden stop, unlocked. As the door is slowly lifted open, a thin light filters down the shaft. There is a moment of recognition between the oberleutnant and the pilot, before he clambers out to join him inside a huge airship hangar. As they wait for the bandaged man to emerge, the oberleutnant anxiously scans the vast shadowy space, visibly relaxing when he realises that he has reached Templehof aerodrome — the Führer's own private military airport — ahead of the Russians.

'We must hurry.' The pilot is impatient.

They follow him towards a dark object squatting in the middle of the hangar, the soles of their boots echoing loudly in the silence.

The peculiar object is draped in a black shroud, which the oberleutnant recognises as parachute silk.

'The Russians have reached the far end of the runway. I'd say we've got five minutes, ten at most.' The pilot looks tense, but strangely confident. When neither of the men respond, he continues, 'Captain Schaeffer is waiting for us at Christiansand. Everything is ready.'

The bandaged man grunts an acknowledgment, but the oberleutnant is transfixed by the strange circular object in front of him — clearly some kind of advanced flying machine. The pilot of the strange vehicle barks at him, breaking off his curious gaze.

'Give me a hand with this.'

The oberleutnant helps him remove the cover, the light fabric bunching at their feet, as a sudden burst of machine-gun fire rips through the silence of the hangar. The men freeze. The hangar is quiet, their heavy breathing the only sound. The shots were close. Very close. In unison they begin seizing the cloth with renewed urgency.

As the last of the black cloth falls to the ground, the oberleutnant's jaw drops open in amazement. He marvels at the perfect symmetry and craftsmanship of the disc-shaped object, running his hand along the smooth, shiny steel fuselage.

'You did it!'

But the pilot of this strange machine is already running over to a large winch system against the near wall of the hangar.

'Quickly!'

The oberleutnant joins the pilot on the winch, setting in motion a complex system of geared pulleys. As they wind furiously, the roof of the hangar parts in the middle. A pale finger of light falls across the craft as two large sections of roof begin to slide down towards the hangar floor. After a minute of tremendous exertion, the hangar and craft are open to the sky. They run back to where the bandaged man waits patiently, the pilot diving under the low body of the craft and disappearing up a hatch underneath. The oberleutnant fails to notice the bandaged man standing directly behind him, his pistol drawn.

The bullet hits him in the back, dropping him to his knees. The pilot rushes back out from under the craft, startled, his weapon also drawn. But his angry confusion turns to dread as he watches the bandaged man stand over the oberleutnant, roll him over and coolly place a single shot through his forehead. The pilot stands motionless, silently questioning the dark, fathomless eyes under the thick bandages, before slowly wiping the sweaty dismay from his brow with his sleeve and ducking back under the craft.

'We have to get out of here!'

The bandaged man slowly holsters his gun. His eyes move from the lifeless figure at his feet to the craft beside him, to the darkening sky above, as he draws a slow, heavy breath. Then he too disappears underneath the craft and up the ladder.

Beyond the hangar and cratered runway, a Russian soldier ventures tentatively out onto the exposed grassy area from the thick bush on the fringes of the airfield. Silently, efficiently, more soldiers emerge, Tokarev rifles held tightly in both hands as they fan out into a wide arc. Incredibly, even more soldiers reveal themselves from the bush until the entire length of the airfield is a moving sea of infantry advancing towards the aerodrome hangars. But the men freeze almost simultaneously as a low-frequency humming begins to permeate the air around them, almost imperceptible at first, but rapidly growing louder. Several of them run and dive into large muddy craters, aiming their weapons wildly in the direction of the buildings as the noise continues to grow, the pitch rising with the volume. Other soldiers follow their lead, most falling flat onto their stomachs in a prone firing position. But they are unsure of any immediate threat — the strange noise appears to be emanating both from the aerodrome buildings, and from above them. Without a clear target they hold their fire.

As the noise grows to an unbearable shriek, a huge hangar at the far end of the complex suddenly illuminates from within. Brilliant white-orange light spills from cracks in the hangar's doorframes, the enormous doors shaking uncontrollably on their hinges. But what stuns the puzzled soldiers most is the searing white light shining into the low clouds directly above the hangar.

The soldiers are now more frightened than curious. They have heard stories of fantastic feats of Nazi engineering — rocket ships that can carry bombs from Germany to London by themselves, and planes with no propellers that can fly faster than any conventional design. But nothing has prepared them for the astonishing sight before them. A flat ball of orange fire hovers over the hangar. The noise and the dazzling, fiery light stuns the soldiers into a trance-like state of inertia. Some hold their arms in front of their faces to shield their eyes from the glare, others swap questioning glances with shoulder shrugs and blank shakes of the head. Too late, they realise that something is taking off from inside the building. Before they can react, it emits a series of blue-white flashes from its surface, instantly accelerating into the low cloud at phenomenal speed, and is gone.

Washington, October 1945

'I don't like this.' President Harry S. Truman stood at the White House window, hands on hips, as he always did when faced with a difficult decision. God knows he'd had a few of those. 'I don't like this one goddamn bit.'

The four other men in the room glanced at each other. From the looks on their faces they weren't enjoying themselves either.

Harry Truman had been in office only six months, but the former army captain had already presided over the end of World War II, dropped two atomic bombs on the Japanese to force a quick surrender, and begun supervising the rebuilding of post-war Europe. Thrust into office by the death of one of the century's most indispensable men, Franklin D. Roosevelt, Truman was far from prepared for his new responsibilities. Blunt, tough and plain-spoken, the second-term senator from Missouri had seen little of Roosevelt in his 12 weeks as Vice President, and had received no special briefings on the major issues facing the administration, such as the deteriorating relations with Soviet Russia, and the development of the A-bomb.

But the man was up to the task. In his first few weeks in office he had overseen the unconditional surrender of the German forces, ending the war in Europe while US troops were storming the beaches of Iwo Jima and Okinawa. The decision to drop the bomb on Hiroshima hadn't been particularly difficult to make. In his eyes it was purely a military weapon and he'd never had any doubt it should be used, when balanced against the heavy cost of life an invasion of the Japanese mainland would have incurred.

President Truman turned back to the men, loosening his tie as he closed a thick file on his desk. The words *Classified — Ultra Secret* shouted at him from the cover. 'OK,' he said finally, easing his tired body into his deep leather chair, 'let's work this through.'

The men shifted uncomfortably in their seats.

'I've read the file. Makes quite a read, I can tell you. How much do the Russians know?'

Again, the men shifted uneasily.

'That much, huh?' He flicked his pen thoughtfully on the desk. 'All right, then. If I have to make a call on this then we're going through it from top to bottom. Speak your minds. I've read the official line — now I want to make some sense of it, is that clear?' He leant forward to emphasise his point, looking each of the men in the eye.

The men nodded solemnly.

'Now, what can we make of the suicide?' he asked, leaning back into the chair. 'From what I can see we haven't been able to dig up one tangible bit of evidence.'

Secretary of War Henry L. Stimson cleared his throat. 'Our investigation was pretty thorough. Our men interviewed everyone from his personal waiter, valet, chauffeur, secretaries, pilots, top generals — the works. Their stories were remarkably consistent, even down to the details. All agreed he'd committed suicide. I don't think they could have agreed to a story like that without one of them slipping up. They're all convinced he topped himself in the bunker, so we have to assume they believe they were telling the truth.'

Truman looked sceptical. 'I put the question straight to Stalin at Potsdam,' he said, referring to the post-war conference where the victorious Allies carved up Germany and most of Europe. 'He didn't even have to think about it. Just shook his head with a big fat "*Nyet*". Seems to think he made it to Spain or Argentina.'

Stimson continued. 'We know they found a couple of bodies in the Reichstag garden, a man and a woman, burned beyond recognition. It fits with what we heard from everyone we interviewed, but it's certainly not conclusive. They couldn't find any dental records so they had his dentist draw them from memory —'

'And?' said Truman.

Stimson shook his head. 'They're close enough.'

Truman shook his head in disbelief. 'Gentlemen, from what I've just heard, and on the basis of present evidence, no insurance company in America would shell out on a claim on Adolf Hitler.'

The room was silent as each of the men digested this unassailable fact.

Truman was keen to move on. 'OK, let's look at the evidence for an escape. What have we got?'

This time Secretary of the Navy James Forrestal responded. 'I was with Zhukov when he described his entrance to Berlin.' Marshal Georgi Zhukov was in charge of the Soviets' final assault on the city. 'He says a whole division saw some type of advanced aircraft leaving Templehof airport as they stormed it. Apparently it scared the wits out of his men.'

'The flying disc,' said Truman emphatically.

'Well, actually they said they saw a bright orange object that looked like it was on fire.'

Truman grinned mirthlessly. 'Well so would I if I was a peasant Russkie straight from the Urals.'

Forrestal tilted his head and raised his eyebrows in reluctant agreement.

Truman continued. 'If you were Hitler — your empire's falling down around your ears, and the Russkies are right up your ass, where would you go?'

Stimson didn't hesitate. 'At the time we thought he'd fight it out at his Nordhausen base in the Bavarian Mountains. It's basically a fortress tunnelled from sheer rock. We figured if he left Berlin that's where he'd go. It's virtually impregnable to assault and conventional bombing, and we found it had enough provisions and armoury to sit out a siege for years. But there's no landing field close by, and the Russians had taken the road and train lines in, so —'

'So he didn't go there,' said Truman impatiently.

'No sign of him. They surrendered as soon the unconditional was announced. We searched it of course, from top to bottom. Hell of place — a real warren of tunnels and caves, but no A-dolf.'

'And now we have this submarine captain,' said Truman.

'Here's where it gets interesting, Mr President.' Chief of Naval Operations Chester Nimitz had been silent till now. He already knew most of what he'd just heard by heart, but the others knew very little of what he was about to tell them.

'I'm all ears, Chester,' said Truman.

Nimitz looked at the other men in the room for a minute, working out where to begin. Then, pulling a bundle of maps from his satchel, he stood up and placed them on the desk in front of the President. The other men joined him at the desk.

'Two months ago the Argentineans apprehended a German U-boat in the Mar del Plata. It was commanded by a Captain Schaeffer. We interrogated him in Argentina …' Nimitz unrolled the maps, twisting them round to face the President. 'If he's telling the truth, then this has to be one of the most remarkable voyages of the entire war.'

Now the others were all ears.

'He claims he left Kiel Harbor … here.' He pointed to the map. 'In the Baltic on 25 April … and stopped briefly … here.' He slid his finger across to the left. 'At Christiansand South for fuel the following day, arriving …' He pulled a second map out from the pile and splayed it out on top of the first. 'Here at Mar del Plata, Argentina, on 17 August. Nearly four months later.'

Truman looked puzzled. 'I've got two questions. Why, and why so long?'

'The second one's probably easier to answer. Schaeffer reckons he heard over his radio that the war had ended just a few days out from Christiansand, and decided to make for Argentina rather than staying on in Europe. Says he offered his crew the option of getting off along the Norwegian coast. That would explain why he was found with a skeleton crew, but — as you point out, Mr President — it doesn't tell us why.'

'You got that right,' said Truman.

'I have to say though, it's one hell of a naval feat.' Nimitz traced a route across the map with his finger. 'Through the North Sea and the Limey Channel, past Gibraltar and along the coast of Africa, to surface all of 66 days later in the middle of the South Atlantic Ocean.'

Truman looked sceptical. 'Could he do that?'

Nimitz nodded. 'I think he could. Says he evaded capture by diving and surfacing, and erecting imitation sails and even a funnel to look like a cargo steamer from a distance. It's definitely a possibility.'

They silently contemplated the map and the strange voyage for a moment, but the Fleet Admiral wasn't finished.

'What I don't understand is why you'd go to all that trouble, risking the lives of your men, when you could have turned the U-boat in to the Norwegians?'

Truman didn't like the way this was heading. 'OK Chester, what have you got? Let's hear it.'

'Well, Schaeffer still put in at Mar del Plata even though he would have heard over the radio that another fleeing U-boat, the U530, had just been captured by the Argentinean authorities.'

'What's your point?' said Truman quietly.

'My point is, sir, that if someone — someone important — wanted to get out of Europe without being caught, they'd take a U-boat. And this one was at sea long enough to —'

'To take a grand tour of German territories and friendlies,' Truman cut in. 'Did we find anything on board to suggest he was carrying a VIP?'

Nimitz shook his head. 'Nothing. The Argentineans went through it first of course, but according to them they didn't find anything either. They've been co-operating with us so we have no reason not to believe them.'

Neither did Truman.

'Remember the U530, the one that was caught just before Schaeffer? It was captained by a 25 year old, Commander Otto Welmut. The sub had a crew of 54 men.' Nimitz paused for effect. 'Usual U-boat crews are anywhere from 16 to 20. The cargo consisted of 540 barrels of cigarettes and unusually large stocks of food. The average age of the crew was 25. When they were questioned by the Argentineans they all claimed they had no living relatives.'

'All right,' said Truman, 'let's assume for a minute that Hitler somehow made it to Christiansand South and hitched a ride on the U-boat. If he didn't try to fight it out at Nordhausen, where did he go?'

'That's easy,' said Nimitz, rummaging through the pile of maps on the desk. He pulled out a map that Truman didn't immediately recognise. It was of a large continent — very large — surrounded by sea on all sides. The latitudinal lines — normally horizontal on the maps of Europe and the Pacific he had so carefully scrutinised since becoming President — were a series of concentric circles.

'Antarctica,' Truman whispered. He could feel the hairs on the back of his neck standing up as Nimitz straightened out the map.

'Fifty-six hundred miles from Africa, 1900 miles from the tip of South America, 4800 miles from Australia — and it's bigger than Europe.'

'It's colder than hell down there,' said Stimson. 'Nothing can survive an Antarctic winter.'

Nimitz shook his head. 'That's not entirely correct. It's not just a snow-covered ice pack like the Arctic. It's a real continent, with plains and valleys, and mountain peaks up to 15 000 feet. The temperature in the interior is around zero in summer, and never drops below 20 or 30°F below in winter.'

The other men looked at Nimitz blankly, so he explained, 'In other words, it's colder in parts of North Dakota or most of Canada than it is down there.'

Truman looked concerned. 'OK, Chester, I'm with you this far. But what evidence have we got for a base down there?'

Secretary of State Dean Acheson sat forward as Nimitz began rolling his maps up. 'Well, sir, quite a bit actually,' he said. 'And we didn't have to go down there to get it.' He took a seat. The room seemed smaller now. More humid. Perhaps it was because the men in the room were all breathing more heavily. Faster too.

'Throughout our interrogations of German Paperclip personnel, we've been digging for information on Nazi activities in the area.' Paperclip was the code name of the secret operation to bring the Nazis' top scientists to America to work for the US government on projects from jet engines to missile technology.

'Nothing obvious, just a bunch of general questions on a range of things. But when we put all the bits of information together, they added up to Antarctica.'

'How's that, Dean?' said Truman.

'Various scientific teams were moved down there — that's how we know all this. Seems scientists like to share their discoveries amongst one another. Anyway, they sent down the whole works: hunters, trappers, collectors, zoologists, botanists, agriculturists, plant specialists, mycologists, parasitologists, marine biologists ...'

'Lot of people to keep a secret,' said Truman.

'We know that once all the data was gathered, they shipped out some of their best deep-underground construction teams. These were the guys that built Nordhausen, so we know they had the technology to build an underground complex.'

'And they've been building it throughout the war?' asked Truman.

'It would explain why any ship that even came close to the shipping routes from South Africa to Antarctica was set upon by packs of U-boats.'

'To protect the secret,' finished the President.

'They'd need tractors, planes, sledges and gliders, and all kind of machinery and materials. By now they could have scooped out an entire mountain, and built a completely camouflaged base. A magic-mountain hideaway.'

Nimitz sat forward in his chair. 'That would explain some interesting comments from a Kraut navy admiral in '43. Apparently he and the rest of the submarine fleet took credit for having built something pretty special for the Führer. Called it a Shangri-la on land.'

'Not one for exaggeration, was he,' said Truman. He wasn't smiling now.

The men sat silent, each lost in his own private nightmare — that the man they all thought dead might not only be alive, but was probably well resourced in some hidden, impregnable fortress in the middle of the world's most isolated continent, plotting to continue the dream of the Third Reich.

Truman got up from his desk and returned to the window.

'I want him found, and I want the base A-bombed.'

'Mr President, if it were that easy, believe me …' Stimson shook his head in frustration.

'Of course it's easy. We fly over it and bomb the hell out of anything we find down there.'

'He's right, Harry,' said Acheson. He hardly ever called Truman by his first name, especially in front of others. But it made him listen when he did. 'If we dropped an atom bomb down there on the ice cap, it'd melt a hundred thousand tons of fresh water into the sea. Maybe more. That would raise the oceans by at least three inches overnight. Apart from some low-lying flooding in Asia and northern Africa, that's the good news. The bad news is that amount of fresh water would alter the salinity of the Southern Atlantic and Pacific Oceans. That means it would heat faster, and that would permanently change the mid-Atlantic current, triggering a series of super-storms right across the globe to Kentucky. In terms of American loss of life, we could drop one in the middle of Times Square and still not even come close.'

Truman looked thoughtful. 'So Antarctica's not such a crazy place to build his base after all.'

'There's another reason, sir,' said Forrestal. He paused, looking at Acheson. 'Technology — or more specifically, Nazi flying-disc technology.'

Truman's eyes narrowed, his brow creasing above his glasses. 'I had a feeling we'd be back with the flying discs soon enough.' He sighed. 'All right, James, take us through it.'

'We have good reason to believe the Krauts were more advanced in the area of military technology than we thought. Especially flight technology.' He pulled a thin file from a satchel at his feet and sat it on his lap. 'After the unconditional, we found that most of their experimental research bases were either blown up, or destroyed in the fighting. But over the next few months we discovered scientific papers hidden all over Germany — in tunnels, dry wells, ploughed fields, riverbeds, even in cesspits. We found evidence of things like heat-guided ground-to-air missiles, sonic-guidance torpedoes, highly advanced electrical submarines — over a hundred of which have apparently just disappeared into thin air I might add. But there were also plans of rocket planes that could fly even faster than the ME–262s and other vertical-rising jet aircraft, and even the beginnings of an atom-bomb project, and a manufacturing process for a metallic material that could withstand temperatures of about a thousand degrees. That's centigrade, Mr President.'

Truman nodded thoughtfully. 'How much did the Russians get?'

Forrestal pursed his lips. 'Probably as much as we have, possibly more.'

'How much more?'

'We think they got a wealth of documentation from German bases out east — including buzz bombs and V2s, surface-to-surface and surface-to-air missiles, a whole heap of technical equipment they found stranded on the docks at Lubeck and Magdeburg, and around 6000 technical specialists.'

'Six thousand!' Truman was astounded.

'But we think they have as little as we do on the flying-disc technology — perhaps even less,' Forrestal added helpfully.

'What's so special about the discs? Hell, the Russkies could start World War III with that lot!' No one laughed.

'Flying-disc technology, and its components — design, engines, principles of lift, materials — is about as far ahead of what we currently have as you can get. Imagine a flying fortress over Waterloo, and you're in the ballpark. This stuff is radical, even revolutionary, and probably constitutes the single biggest threat to American security ever. Period.'

'That's some claim, James,' said Truman. 'Care to elaborate for a simple infantryman?'

Forrestal pulled a thin sheaf of papers from the pile. The insignias looked unfamiliar to Truman, but he recognised the typing. It was German.

'A flying disc was test-flown sometime in February of this year near the underground complex at Kahla. It reached a height of 40 000 feet at a speed of approximately 1250 miles per hour. It was piloted, and seemed to have some form of radio that made it disappear off a radarscope, basically rendering it invisible. It could also have had electromagnetically or electroacoustically controlled weapons.'

'Twelve hundred miles an hour.' Truman winced. He knew the rough flight specifications of the new P–51 fighter. If what he'd just heard was true, the entire US airforce had just been rendered obsolete. 'Can we believe the documents? They're not some elaborate hoax?'

Forrestal shook his head. 'I don't think they are, Mr President.'

'So why don't you give me something I can get my head around. If Adolf Hitler is sitting down in some ice grotto on the South Pole, I need to know what sort of threat he presents to us. Your report doesn't explain why we're making such a fuss of this flying-disc business. Hell, he could probably hit us sitting here right now with a long range V2 carrying a mini A-bomb!'

None of the men thought this in the slightest bit funny. Or far-fetched.

'Ever heard of Foo-fighters, Mr President?' It was Stimson's turn.

'Well I'm sure I'm about to,' said Truman drily.

'In the closing stages of the war, our night-bomber boys started reporting strange flying objects — they called them Foo-fighters. Name kinda stuck. Anyway, we suspected they might be some type of new secret weapon. But the strange thing was, they didn't shoot our boys down — they just flew right alongside them. Soon we discovered a whole bunch of aircrews had seen them, but didn't include them in their flight reports in case the squadron commanders thought they'd been drinking.'

'Foo-fighters, huh?' said Truman. 'A radar-interference device?'

Stimson nodded. 'Seems they were not only invisible to radar, they could screw up the radar in our night bombers. Soon we had dozens of reports of the Foo-fighters being spotted just before malfunctions in the planes' radar systems forced them to return to base.'

'The Krauts called it the *Feuerball* — the Fireball. But it was actually circular and flat, kind of like two tortoise shells put together like this.' He clasped his fingers together into a clam-like position.

'I don't understand why our boys didn't just shoot the damn things out of the sky.'

'The pilots we talked to said the halo gave the impression of enormous size. It seemed to unnerve them long enough for the radar-jamming to occur. They were also worried that if the things exploded they'd take the plane down with it.'

Truman sat thinking to himself for a full minute, as though considering what he would have done if he'd been faced with a Foo-fighter. The men sat tight-lipped and serious. Finally he said, 'And now we know it didn't stop there, did it?'

'Goering had put together Luftwaffe engineers, rocket engineers, physicists and materials experts, and together they built an even larger, piloted version of the disc, complete with a domed pilot's cabin.'

'How big is larger?' asked Truman.

'They said it had a diameter of 138 feet, and a height of about 30 feet.'

Truman whistled. 'Was it destroyed as well, or do you think they took it to Shangri-la with them?'

Stimson drew a long sigh. 'No, Mr President. We believe it was seized by the Russians and taken to Siberia along with the technicians who developed it.'

Truman exploded. 'Goddammit, Henry!' he said, slamming his hands down hard on the thick file on his desk. 'You mean to tell me the Communists have got a factory going, turning these things out on a goddamn production line? Kind of shifts the balance of power, don't you think? We know they're already testing their own A-bombs up there. This is making my bowels move just thinking about it.' He could be real eloquent when he was annoyed. He stood and turned back to the window. 'What risk do these flying discs represent to us?'

There was a tight pause as the men collected their thoughts. Secretary of State Acheson was the first to respond.

'Mr President, I believe we are facing a very real national security threat. Not just from the Russkies once they've worked out the technology in the discs, but from the Nazis themselves.'

Truman nodded once. 'Go on.'

'It seems an incident over LA we put down to war jitters back in '42 now appears to have been a flyover of Nazi flying discs.'

Truman turned, his expression incredulous as Acheson elaborated.

'It happened in February '42. Only three months after Pearl, and the fear of a Japanese invasion was pretty real, so you can understand our scepticism at the time. But knowing what we know now ...' He trailed off for an instant. He too was having trouble coming to grips with the enormity of events unfolding in the quiet office.

The President seemed to have stopped listening. Perhaps he was back in '42. Before the death of F.D.R., before the bomb, and before this. The men sat patiently — this was how Truman made his decisions. He didn't hurry, and he liked to have his advisors' advice and opinions fresh in his mind.

When the President turned back from the window and leaned over his desk, they were in no doubt that the time for talking was over. 'Gentlemen,' he said softly, 'I don't have to remind you that we are on the verge of a war that could end up being more costly than the one we've just won. It's going to be a war without frontlines, but a war nonetheless. And that war is going to be fought by scientists and technicians, and physicists and mathematicians. It's going to be a technological war. And right now I feel like we're losing. We have the A-bomb and we're still losing. If I know Stalin he'll be working those Krauts around the clock.'

He turned back to the window. 'I don't care if that Kraut son-of-a-bitch is licking his wounds in some ice castle on the South Pole, this is a matter of national security. He's got what we need, and he's got one hell of a fight on his hands because we're going down there to get it.'

The men could sense the fire in the President's belly. This was fighting talk. They just needed to convince themselves he was right.

Bay of Whales, Antarctica, January 1947

Captain Charles 'Tommy' Thomson figured this must be what it was like to be seasick. He'd never been seasick in his entire life, which was all the more remarkable for the fact that he'd spent most of his life not just at sea, but in some of the roughest and most remote seas on the planet. In the process he'd probably broken more ice than any seagoing icebreaker skipper in the polar seas. But the uneasiness in his stomach just wouldn't settle.

He stood in the warmth of the bridge lighting a long puff on his home-made pipe as he surveyed the strange scene before him, and tried to pinpoint what it was that was wrong. Hell, if he was honest, there was plenty wrong about this whole operation. From the moment he'd received his orders from Navy Command back in late '46 about an expedition being led to Antarctica of all places, and by none other than Admiral Richard E. Byrd, the uneasiness had begun incubating in his gut. He'd been told that the expedition objective, code named Highjump by Nimitz, was to 'construct and establish a temporary base on the Ross Ice Shelf in order to extend the explored area of the continent and to test material under frigid conditions'.

Baloney, thought Thomson. Good old-fashioned navy baloney. But baloney for what? He couldn't for the life of him figure out what he was doing down here at the South Pole when the Soviet threat was at the other one. One thing was for sure though — someone was in a big hurry to get this circus up and running.

His own ship, the Navy Coast Guard Icebreaker *Northwind*, had been the first to leave its home port of Boston some two months ago, but preparations for the rest of the fleet hadn't gone smoothly, and his seadog's warning bell had started ringing loudly before he'd even lost sight of land.

Nevertheless, here he was. Moored in the Bay of Whales surveying the creation of Little America IV, just north of what had been Little America III — the west base of the 1939 US Antarctic Service Expedition.

It was a bizarre sight. A multitude of tents had sprung up in the middle of the white nothingness — enough to house the nearly 300 people stationed at the base — along with three compacted snow runways and a short airstrip of steel matting. Also moored in the bay were the rest of the vessels in his group, two cargo ships, the *Yancey* and *Merrick*, the submarine *Sennet*, and the expedition's flagship, *Mount Olympus*.

This group, imaginatively called Central, was to maintain the flight base for the aerial photography missions. The Eastern group was to head towards zero degrees longitude while the Western group was to circle the continent in a westerly direction until they met up with the Eastern group.

Even so, the sight of the 15 navy ships and an aircraft carrier of the full expeditionary force in the middle of the blue and white Antarctic landscape had cut a strange sight, even for someone of Thomson's polar experience.

As he relit his pipe and watched the little black fur-wrapped spots moving about on the ice, he pondered the reasons for his uneasiness. Throughout October and November '46, preparations had been quick, almost recklessly so. The expedition force had been drawn from both the Atlantic and Pacific fleets, and so both coasts had been busy ordering parkas, goggles, boots and thermal underwear, and the special tents and matting for Little America's new runway. Special dogsled trainers had been sent into the New Hampshire woods to work with the dogs. Caterpillar tractors, forklift trucks, powered sleds and other heavy machinery had been urgently manufactured and loaded onto railroad cars and shipped to docksides in California and Virginia. And yet, in all the haste, actual details of the operation were completely unknown.

The hasty preparation had been a concern, but that was minor compared with some of Thomson's other worries about the expedition. For a start, every vessel was steel-hulled. Sure, steel is stronger than wood, but in Thomson's experience, a wooden-hulled vessel caught in the vice-like grip of the pack ice tends to splinter slowly, whereas steel just rips apart. He knew that all but a handful of men — of which he was one — of the nearly 5000 military personnel involved, were totally lacking in adequate training for polar conditions.

Even the maps and charts had proven so unreliable they'd had to ask the British Admiralty to use theirs. Limey charts, for crying out loud. But they'd proven their usefulness as he'd relied on them almost exclusively to guide the ships of the Central group through the pack ice and into the Ross Sea. Not bad considering. In all it had taken him 15 days to negotiate the pack ice after which *Northwind* had broken a harbour out of the bay ice for the rest of the group.

But despite everyone's reservations, and Thomson's own uneasiness, things had gone reasonably well. The PBM flying boats had begun their long, hazardous photographic missions, which gave him plenty of time to chew on his pipe and mull over the real reasons for the expedition. Could be uranium, he thought. Apparently you need it for the bomb. But aerial photographs wouldn't show up mineral deposits, so he'd ruled that out some time ago. Anyways, he figured, without any reference points in the thousands upon thousands of square miles of ice, most photos of the interior would look exactly the same — white. Just didn't seem to make any sense. If he knew any better, he'd say the navy was looking for something. But what? And down here of all places ...

'Cap'n?' It was Thomson's XO.

'Yuh?' he said, breaking his train of thought, no closer to the answer.

'We're getting some interesting radio traffic from one of the PBMs. Thought you might want to listen in,' said the XO helpfully.

'Might as well,' said Thomson. 'Not as if I gotta helluva lot else to do anyways.'

Thomson followed his XO down to Ops, the room that handled all the sensors, such as radar, and the ship's communications.

'Not in trouble, are they?' asked Thomson as he swung through the bulkhead door and down an almost vertical ladder.

'Don't think so,' said the XO. 'Sounds like they've discovered something.'

Thomson gave another snort. 'Fly-boys probably discovered their second ass.'

The XO was grinning from ear to ear as they entered the communications nerve centre of the ship. The several navy personnel quietly and efficiently monitoring the equipment did not look up as their captain entered.

The XO passed Thomson a set of headphones and nodded to the radio operator as he pulled on another pair himself.

It took Thomson a few seconds to adjust to the thin static squawk of the radio channel. He leaned in front of the radio operator, tapped his headphones, and pointed to the sky. Instantly the static grew louder and he heard the radio officer on the USS *Mount Olympus*, the expedition's flagship just across the icy bay, coming in loud and clear.

'Say again *George One*, over?'

'We have a visual anomaly on the eastern horizon. Current position sector 0-2-1-2. Request permission to change course to investigate, over.'

Thomson shot a questioning look at his XO, who simply shrugged his shoulders and raised his eyebrows in response.

'Please describe the anomaly, *George One*, over,' came the response after a short pause.

'I can't believe this, *Olympus* ...' Thomson pressed his headphones closer to his ears. 'We've got some land up ahead with no ice ... repeat, no ice.'

'Copy that, *George One*, no ice,' came the response from *Olympus*.

'We got some lakes ... blue and green lakes ... ice free, but there's ice everywhere else ... can't explain it ... we're getting good pictures though ... visibility's good.'

Thomson could hear the steady hum of the engines in between the pilot's phrases. He could picture them, out in the middle of nowhere. All alone. Uncharted territory. Anxious.

'We got brown hills too ... Right out of nowhere ... Unbelievable.'

'Roger, *George One*,' came the response from *Olympus*. 'Any sign of human habitation ... repeat, any sign of human habitation, over.'

This peculiar question had Thomson really

intrigued. He didn't show any indication to his XO, who was also listening in.

'Negative, *Olympus* ... we have an ice-free lake big enough to land on ... we're gonna try and take her down.'

'Roger, *George One*, copy that. Permission to land but keep those cameras rolling,' came the reply.

'You have to see this, *Olympus*.' Thomson could sense the pilot's excitement. 'It's like an oasis ... must be warmed by some kind of underground heat source ... evidence of limited vegetation ... steam rising out of one of the lakes ...'

Thomson had a lifetime's experience in the Arctic, but even he was finding the pilot's report difficult to comprehend. He closed his eyes and tried to imagine the giant seaplane dropping out of the 20th century into an ice-age landscape, the crew's faces pressed to the windows as the pilot lined up on one of the lakes for a landing. He imagined that every other skipper listening in was trying to do the same.

'*George One* has touched down, *Olympus*. I want to keep the engines running so we're just going to examine the lake water and take some readings and we're out of here.'

'Copy that, *George One*.'

There was a long pause in the communications, so Thomson allowed himself the luxury of another pull on his pipe. He knew the radio operators hated the smell of his tobacco in the windowless room packed with electronic equipment, but he figured since he was skipper it was a luxury he'd earned.

'OK *Olympus*, we've got brackish water in the lake, so it must lead to the open sea somehow. That might suggest underwater access. Water's warm … we don't have a portable thermometer but I'd put it at about 80 to 90 degrees.'

That was warm for polar sea water, thought Thomson. Very warm.

'Surrounding hills completely ice free,' continued the pilot, 'and no evidence of recent ice or glacial movement.'

'Copy that, *George One*.'

Another short pause.

'*Olympus*, we're going to have to get moving … looks like we've got a front coming in fast.'

'OK, good work, *George One*. Set course back to base, we'll see you in a couple of hours. *Olympus* out.'

Thomson and the XO had already started removing their headphones to discuss this remarkable development, when one of the radio operators shot him a serious look.

'Cap'n, you'd better listen to this.'

Thomson threw his headphones back on and pushed them to his ears.

'Can't understand this at all …' the static was increasing, but through the white noise Thomson could pick the tension in the pilot's voice.

'This is freakish weather, *Olympus*, we're icing up badly … bow station plexiglass is frozen over … cockpit window's getting really bad.'

'*George One*, activate de-icing immediately, over.'

The time it took *George One* to respond wasn't

40

encouraging. 'Onboard de-icing operational, repeat, operational. Wings icing up now. We're getting too heavy ...' Urgency was creeping into the pilot's voice.

'*George One*, confirm your coordinates, over.'

Thomson could feel the uneasiness that had been brewing in his stomach for so long start to knot up.

'Instruments not operational, *Olympus*, repeat, instruments not operational ...' The pilot was starting to panic.

'*George One*, please confirm your coordinates ... Robbie, we need a reading to find you ... what's your position, over?'

'Compass and altimeters all showing different readings ... I don't like the look of this ... Let's get the hell out of here!'

Thomson could hear the roar of the flying boat's massive engines though the static.

The flight commander on *Olympus* was just as concerned. '*George One*, give me something to work with ... what was your last reading?'

Another disturbing static-filled pause, then, 'What the hell is that? Crash positions! We're gonna ...'

'Shit!' Thomson threw his headphones down and scrambled back to the bridge. He knew he was one of the few officers on the expedition who really knew what a polar climate would do to an exposed body. He figured it would only be a matter of hours before even the fittest men would succumb to the cold. If they were still alive. They had to act fast.

By the time he'd made it back to the bridge, his radio was buzzing with preparations to scramble another PBM into the air for a rescue mission. He could see men running along the decks of the *Olympus* across the bay, and already one of the PBMs was covered with technicians and aircrew in preparation for being lifted over the side and into the water for departure.

'*Olympus* to *Northwind*, come in, over.' His turn for receiving orders. He reached for his mike.

'This is *Northwind*.'

'Tommy, I want you and *Sennet* to set course for sector five. We're sending a PBM up now, but if the weather turns it'll be up to your boys to initiate a land-based rescue. We'll give you some clearer coordinates once we hear back from the PBM. And by the way, the force has been put on full battle-station alert. Do you copy that?'

Thomson wasn't sure he'd heard correctly. 'Copy sector five with *Sennet*, and full battle stations? Please confirm, over?'

The reply was instant. 'Confirm full battle-station alert. This applies to the entire fleet, over.'

Now he really was getting the jitters. A battle-station alert was the state of readiness in anticipation of an attack, not a sea rescue.

'Roger that, *Olympus*. *Northwind* out.'

Weird. Real weird. But hell, he'd learned to stop trying to figure out orders when he was still a swabbie. Some things don't change much, even when you're Captain. Nevertheless, even as an icebreaker, *Northwind* was armed to the teeth. He had two 5-inch guns mounted forward and aft, which were designed to be dual purpose — effective against surface targets and aircraft. They were big, each requiring a crew of 17 men, including seven inside the turret itself. And he also had three 40-mm Bofors guns, and six 20-mm Oerlikons, which, even though they'd proven too light to deal with dive bombers and kamikazes, still made things difficult for them.

The XO had been listening patiently, ready for Thomson's call to action.

'OK, Gordy, take us to battle stations and plot a course for sector five. Take us as far round the ice as you can before we go in — if those guys are out in the open, we've probably got about five hours before they start turning into ice cubes.'

The XO was moving even before he'd finished speaking, 'Aye aye, Cap'n.'

Thomson flicked an internal comms switch and grabbed a different mike. 'Pete, this is Tom. We're going to hightail it to the crash site, but we don't have exact coordinates at the moment. I don't know how far in we'll be able to get you, so you'd better get your boys kitted up now.'

The 'boys' were the ship's landing party, consisting of a platoon of Arctic-experienced marines. Probably the only marines with any polar experience in the entire expedition, thought Thomson wryly.

The *Northwind* made quick progress out of the bay and back through the gap it had broken just weeks before. It had iced over, but the ice layer was thin and Thomson was able to make steady headway without having to reverse and ram. Meanwhile, reports from the rescue PBM were not encouraging. The last given coordinates for *George One* were based upon a grid system within the huge sectors into which the expedition had divided the vast continent to assist with navigation and aerial photography. The USS *Sennet*, a brand new Balao class sub, followed close behind the icebreaker, which was ploughing through the pack ice at a steady rate of six knots. Slow going, thought Thomson, but going nonetheless. He looked at his watch. It had been three-and-a-half hours since the crash, and though every crunching lunge against the sheet ice brought them closer to their target, he knew the chances of finding the downed aircrew alive were diminishing rapidly.

Thomson was driving the *Northwind* hard, using all his experience and ability to keep the ship's momentum up, as the XO pored over the charts. The weather had started to deteriorate, and he knew that the high-altitude cloud formations sweeping across the sky up ahead meant some pretty rough squalls were on their way.

He was squinting into the white-grey blur of the horizon when a burst of static cut through the bridge.

'Come in, *Northwind*, this is *Olympus*, over.'

Thomson dived for the mike, desperate for news of the flight crew's location. 'Copy *Olympus*, what have you got for us?'

'*George Two* has reported bogeys, repeat, bogeys sighted by *George Two*.'

Thomson's initial alarm shifted to amazement. 'Are you guys serious?'

There was a long moment of nothing but static, as the *Northwind* rolled beneath his feet, then, 'Affirmative *Northwind*, *George Two* has a confirmed sighting of 11 bogeys. Currently taking evasive action. Move to high alert ... Tommy, they're heading towards your sector.'

'What the hell's going on here?' said Thomson out loud to himself. His XO, who had stopped working and looked up from his charts upon hearing the bizarre news, just shook his head. Thomson had been at sea too long, had endured a world war and the polar isolation only an icebreaker crew can know, to accept something like this at face value. But he couldn't take any chances.

'XO, sound the battle alarm, I want all crews in position and loaded. I want two-minute updates from radar, and get the chopper airborne ...'

The XO was already moving, punching the battle-station alarm button hard, and heading towards the operations centre.

'And I want all eyes skyward,' Thomson shouted after him over the alarm.

He lifted his binoculars and took a 360 of the horizon. It was clear at least, but he was acutely aware of how exposed his ship would be if it was caught in the ice from the air. Behind him he could see *Sennet*'s officers scrambling back down into the conning tower, its bow already sinking beneath the water.

He picked up his mike again, '*Olympus* …' He wasn't sure how to put this. 'Just who are we at war with? Are these Soviet bogeys, over?'

'Can't confirm that, *Northwind*,' came the response. More baloney. He had no idea what games were being played here, but he did know that he and his men were now the meat in this baloney sandwich. The gnawing in his stomach had climbed up into his chest. He wasn't afraid of combat. He'd survived everything the Krauts had thrown at him in the Arctic, and on more than one occasion the ice had saved him from a pack of hungry U-boats. But back then he knew who the enemy was, and he knew the game. Somehow he had a feeling the rules were changing on him, and no one was telling him why.

'Bogeys! I got bogeys at nine o'clock!' The shout from the tower jerked him back to reality. Snatching his binoculars, he scrambled to the starboard window and threw it open. The blast of polar air took his breath away, instantly dropping the temperature inside the bridge.

At first he couldn't see anything other than a glaring whiteness. He fumbled with the focus, and zoomed in on the horizon. There, sure enough, was a loose formation of black specks against the pale blue, racing across the pack ice towards them. The bastards had somehow circled round to come at them from the sea. How the hell did they do that, Thomson wondered. Unless this was a new set of bogeys. Already the huge gun turrets were rotating round to face them.

'All engines stop!' He couldn't afford to let the

motion of the ship screw around with the aiming mechanisms on the guns. He felt the vibrations of the engines through the deck subside, and within seconds the *Northwind* had stopped, surrounded in a sea of white right up against the hull.

'Radar, talk to me!'

The radar operator's voice was nervy. 'I've got one bogey, Captain, at heading 2-7-0.'

Thomson was starting to get pissed. 'What do you mean, *one* bogey? I'm looking at six or seven at least.'

But the radar operator was adamant. 'Only one bogey, Cap'n.'

Maybe they were flying in such close formation the radar couldn't pick them out. That's pretty risky flying in these conditions, but at least it would make for an easier target. He was glad they'd worked on their gunnery practice on the way down. They'd blasted a few icebergs to kingdom come. Thing was, 'bergs didn't fly at you or shoot back. But what really had him stumped was that, if these were aircraft, they needed to have taken off from somewhere. That meant a runway. And a base.

'Shit!' The ball in his gut dropped like a depth charge as it suddenly dawned on him why they were here. Damn Russkies had tried to claim Antarctica! And the brass had known all along. Someone's ass was going to get chewed out when this was over. Hell, his career was almost over anyway.

By now *Sennet* had completely submerged, with just a frothy blue swirl where the sub had been just moments before. But that just made

Thomson feel even more exposed. A giant steel sitting duck. He had to act fast.

'Radar, get a fix on your bogey to gunnery.'

'Already done, Cap'n,' came the reply.

'How far out is it?'

'I make it approximately 30 000 yards, altitude 2000 feet, sir.'

Thomson did some quick mental calculations. His big guns had a surface range of about 17 000 yards. They were still out of range. But an aircraft only flew this low when it had one thing in mind. Attack.

'It's slowing down, Captain,' said the radar operator.

Thomson threw his binoculars up again to confirm the report, but instead of slowing down, it appeared as though the bogeys were splitting up into attack formation. And they were still coming at him. Fast.

'Radar, I've got visual on about eight bogeys flying directly towards us. Tell me you've got them too.'

'Negative, Captain,' came the reply. 'Only one bogey now stationary at just under 30 000 yards.'

This wasn't making any sense at all. But self-preservation meant he would have to wonder what sort of radar-cloaking device the Russians were using later. And if they were radar cloaking, that meant they weren't dropping in for a vodka and a chat. There was only one sensible course of action to take, and he was going to take it.

'Captain to gunnery, all guns to optical, repeat, all guns to optical targeting. Fire when targets are in range. We've got at least eight hostile bogeys.'

By the time he had his binoculars back up there was only one small speck where a moment before he had counted eight. Where the hell had they gone? He swung his binoculars across the horizon, and to his horror realised the aircraft had almost completely circled his vessel, and were approaching at high speed. They were close enough now for him to pick up the glint of steel from their fuselages, and realised that they didn't seem to have any wings. Or a tailplane ...

Suddenly the ship rocked with the deafening impact of one of the 5-inchers opening up on a target. Their lead was immediately picked up by the rest of the guns, which were now firing at will, engaging each target as they came within range. They were closing in fast and low, changing direction erratically. Normal aircraft, well any that he knew of anyway, couldn't do that. One of the strange craft flew directly over the superstructure of the ship at an incredible speed, *Northwind*'s gun turrets spinning wildly to keep up. Another came in so low it was below deck level, and also below the arc of the guns. Some of the crew were leaning over the rails wildly firing rifles at it as it flew past. But it wasn't hit, and seemed to streak back out of range at phenomenal speed before turning back for another run. Now several of them were buzzing the ship at recklessly low altitude. Thomson couldn't believe what he was witnessing. These tiny, silver saucer-shaped aircraft were toying with him. Even with every single gun firing at almost point-blank range, none had been hit. The sound was deafening. And the men were panicking, their shouting becoming more desperate. The frustration at not being able to hit any of the bogeys was starting to take its toll on their aim. Some were firing randomly now, and within the huge circle of bullets and shells the *Northwind* had thrown up at them, the bogeys darted and streaked in low with almost reckless abandon.

Yet, Thomson suddenly realised, none of them had fired on his ship. Why not? They could easily have bombed him by now. But they hadn't. There had to be a reason.

Thomson screamed into the mike and loudspeaker together, 'Cease fire! This is the captain! Cease fire immediately!'

Gradually the firing dwindled to the odd rifle shot from the panicked crew on deck, and then stopped. Thomson watched to see how the craft responded. As if by command the objects slowed and settled onto the ice pack at distances of between 4000 and 5000 yards. What now, he wondered to himself.

'Captain?' It was radar.

'Go ahead.'

'My bogey is moving again. Directly for us!' The shooting had panicked the radar operator, and his voice was shaky.

'Speed and altitude, radar?' Thomson hadn't taken his eyes off the bogeys.

'Very low, probably a few feet. Speed six knots.'

Six knots. No aircraft he knew would attack at six knots. Hell, no aircraft he knew could stay in the air at six knots. 'Let me know the instant he changes speed, altitude or direction.'

'Aye aye, Cap'n.'

He could make the object out easily through his binoculars. For some reason this craft wasn't cloaked. The small attack craft that had buzzed the ship so brazenly were still grounded.

'Gunnery, hold fire unless fired upon. Is that clear?'

'Aye aye, Captain, holding fire …'

Every pair of binoculars was now trained on the large black circular craft approaching the ship. Time seemed to drag tortuously, after the rush of wild firing earlier.

As the huge craft hovered towards them over the ice, Thomson went out onto the external bridge, pulling his parka hood over his head. This didn't look like a Russian craft to him. He needed to know what it was up to. The big gun turrets swung slowly as it approached, keeping it square in their sights. Good on you boys, thought Thomson. If it so much as deviated slightly from its current speed or altitude it was history.

But it didn't do either. Thomson could see this craft was much larger than the little silver ones that had buzzed him. Shaped like a giant pancake, its edges seemed to spin. An amazing sight. Slowly, it circled round and began moving towards the rear of the *Northwind*. Every gun was trained on it now, as it came within 20 feet of the helideck at the rear of the ship. Then it stopped.

'Hold your fire,' Thomson called to his gun crews. All were watching. All were waiting. And everyone was as nervous as hell.

Then the craft hovered towards the flight deck. Jesus, it's going to land on our deck, Thomson realised. He didn't know what to do. This wasn't covered in the training manual. But the sight of the strange spherical craft hovering silently beside the icebreaker was mesmerising.

A stairway extended from underneath the craft, and stopped just short of the *Northwind*'s helipad. He could make out a pair of legs now, stepping down the ladder. They were booted legs. Wearing khaki green. US Airforce khaki green. Climbing awkwardly down the thin stairway came the entire flight crew of *George One*. The vessel was silent as the men walked out from under the craft and across the deck. Hell, even Thomson was speechless. After the eight men had emerged, some with bandages around their heads or arms, a figure in a black jumpsuit descended. He was young and pale, with a shock of blond hair. When he reached the end of the stairs, Thomson could see that he was speaking.

'What's he saying, Jim?' said Thomson into the intercom.

'Dunno, Cap'n. It ain't English. I've sent for one of the medics, he speaks Russian.'

Thomson watched as the medic walked out to the man at the bottom of the ladder, nodded a few times, and walked back to where the deck flight sergeant was waiting.

'You're not going to believe this, Cap'n.'

'Try me, Jim.'

'He's speaking German, sir. He's a Kraut.'

Thomson wasn't sure how to respond to this. Germans? Down here? 'What does he want?' he said, immediately suspicious.

'Well, Cap'n … he says he wants to talk to the expedition commander.'

'Tell him he either talks to me here and now, or he can kiss his flying saucer goodbye.'

'We did that, Captain.'

'And?'

'Well, Captain, he says he speaks on behalf of the Free German territory of Neuschwabenland. They must have a base down here somewhere!'

Thomson reeled inside. The world was just beginning to find its way back to some semblance of normality following the bloodiest and deadliest war in human history. And somehow the perpetrators had survived and escaped to Antarctica. And now they and their strange aircraft were on his ship. He felt a weariness envelope him. He was too old for this. Been through too much. He fought to hold back the cocktail of emotions unleashed inside him.

He heard himself say, 'So what does he want?'

'He's got a message for the President. And get this, Cap'n — he says they want to make a deal!'

1

Pittsburgh, present day

Curtis Hatch ran a hand through his hair and looked at the time. Two twenty-five a.m. Shit. But he couldn't exit. Not now. He'd paced himself well, taking time to organise and plan, to build a solid economic base using his industries, and his civilisation had just moved from the Dark Ages into the Feudal. He'd begun researching the technology required to support his rapidly advancing city, and building defences and a military capacity was now a priority.

And he was on a high. Curtis lifted the volume a notch on his MP3 player and adjusted his headphones. Bono was singing about the end of the world.

He knew he was good, and there were few others he'd met on the gaming site who could match the breathtaking speed at which he'd developed his civilisation. Technology was the key. Get your food, forestry and mining operations up instantly, create more villagers, and then develop sustainable agriculture and mining to work your way up the technology tree. Simple as that.

Curtis had no idea who he was playing tonight ... make that this morning. He presumed it was a he, since his nickname was Gonad. He didn't know of many chicks on the net who would name themselves after a set of genitals. But who knew anymore? What he did know, was that he was playing one of his best games ever, and Gonad was about to be whipped.

As he started amassing his military units — archers, infantry and cavalry — Curtis knew he had to attack Gonad early on, while he was still building his infrastructure, and hadn't yet reaped the huge technological and military advantages of advancing into the Imperial Age. He was focusing so closely on this he failed to notice Gonad's assault before it was too late. By the time he realised he was under attack, the assault had become an invasion. Curtis frantically assembled his growing, but still small and rudimentary, army, but it was too late. Gonad's armoured knights on horseback flew through his ranks, firing gunpowder-loaded hand cannons at point-blank range, dropping his soldiers where they stood. On they rode, chasing villagers and demolishing buildings. Curtis had never seen anything like it. He realised he'd just been beaten. Thrashed. And there was nothing he could do. By now his city was alight, and Gonad's troops were systematically destroying his civilisation, building by building. And then it was over. As quick as it was vicious. He pulled his headphones off and killed the music.

Curtis typed quickly into the chat frame to catch him before he logged off the site.

Good game, Gonad.
Thanks.

Came the reply. From somewhere in the world.

How'd you do it? I was still in the
early Feudal Age and you came at me
with hand cannons! You can't get
those until the late Imperial Age!
Easy.
Well I take my hat off to you, Gonad.
You're good. Real good.
Cheers, man.
Hey, care to throw me a few tips?
It's late here, and I'm beat. I've
got work in a few hours. But you're
the first person to beat me in ages.
Years actually.
Sure, what do you want to know?
Well for starters, how did you get to
Imperial so fast?
Basic, man. I cheated.

Curtis had to laugh at that. At least he was honest.

How?
I found the cheat codes for the game.

*You could be the best player in the
world and I'd still beat you.*

Curtis grinned in spite of himself. Cocky bastard!

Sure, but don't you want to win by
playing the game the way it was meant
to be played?
Why?

What did he mean, why? Curtis drew a deep sigh, and typed.

'Cos that's the POINT, man!

There was a pause. Either Gonad was thinking about this, or they'd hit a lag. The reply came eventually.

*WINNING'S the point, man. There ARE
no rules in war. THAT'S the point.
You use every means necessary to get
an advantage over your enemy. THAT'S
the game.*

Curtis took a minute to let his tired brain absorb Gonad's unique playing philosophy.

So you used cheat codes to short-cut
the play. How'd you get them?
Told you. I found them.

Curtis shook his head and smiled to himself as he typed.

Those codes are for the game
developers to test the game. They

don't advertise them on the net, man.
So I repeat, how'd you get them?

But Gonad wasn't going to reveal his secrets tonight.

They're there if you know where to look for them. And how.

OK, thought Curtis. Ladies and Gentlemen, we have a live hacker online.

You know, I could have attacked you with a '68 Cobra if I'd wanted to.

Curtis had to laugh at that. The thought of his medieval armies trying to attack a steel sports car moving several times faster than a horse with only swords and arrows would have been something to see.

Glad you went easy on me then!
Welcome to the game, enjoy the rules!
— Gonad
Hey it's late. Catch you here again sometime? Might not be so easy next time.

Curtis sat waiting for Gonad's reply, but he was gone. Just a flashing cursor. Weird, man. Curtis logged off and crawled into bed as the dim light from the computer monitor faded to black. As he lay in the darkness he thought about the game. Funny how even winning a computer game was based on the same principles of victory as warfare. Knowledge meant technical superiority.

Technical superiority meant military superiority. And military superiority meant that one civilisation could totally dominate another. What do they say? All's fair in love and war. Love? He wasn't going there tonight. Curtis set his alarm and drifted off to a fitful sleep.

The bus ride to work was excruciating because the painkillers hadn't kicked in yet, and even though he'd inhaled two double espressos on the way to the bus stop, his head still felt heavy, and his eyes felt like dead weights.

Curtis hung from the handrail, trying to keep his satchel between his legs as the bus driver experimented with the clutch. The atmosphere was claustrophobic as he watched the commuters around him, buried in their own little worlds. He flicked his headphones over his head with one hand and felt for the play button on his MP3 player with the other. He let out a breath of relief as The Edge filled his head with sublime guitar, instantly shutting out the commuter nightmare. The song was 'One'. The irony wasn't lost on Curtis, who hadn't been in anything resembling a relationship for longer than he cared to remember.

He thought about his strange conversation with Gonad last night as Bono teased him from the privacy of his headphones. It made him think. But not too hard. Not this morning. He felt his stomach tighten as he thought about the coding project due today — he was going to have to nail it fast if he was to meet the deadline. It wasn't hard, not even a challenge really, just a plug-in programme for the remote notification of firewall anomalies. That's a hacker-warning system. Few more espressos and a Pepsi should see it through by lunch.

Curtis's office at Trident Technologies Inc. was a joke. Open plan, with no windows. Security was tight, since the company prided itself on developing network security and encryption systems. That meant lots of card swiping, passwords and covert system searches which even the employees weren't supposed to know about. But Curtis wasn't your usual employee.

By the time his PC had fired up Curtis was feeling a little more sane. Caffeine injection number three and things were starting to look up. The secure work, like the programming he was finishing today, was done on a different computer. One hooked up to an independent network, isolated from email, phone lines and the internet. His 'workstation', as the company put it — his personal-use computer — wasn't much of a grunter compared with the turbo-charged monster he did his real work on. Probably couldn't even run a decent game on it. But it did the bizzo nonetheless. Curtis entered his username and password, and as the network came up the computer chimed at him. Email. Quite a few.

Curtis was starting to get psyched for the hours of concentrated programming ahead, so he quickly scanned the list of new mail for anything important. Or interesting. And he was lucky on both counts.

The first email he clicked open was from Terry Hay, his parole officer. Check-up time. Actually he got on pretty well with Terry now, despite the differences of opinion they'd had in the past over Curtis's previous 'indiscretions'. In some weird way they'd even become buddies — kind of. Terry had had some experience with computers in a previous life. What that was, Curtis had no idea, but Terry kinda connected with the wayward intelligent types like Curtis. Like he'd been there himself. It was Terry who'd gotten Curtis the job at Trident. The monthly check-ups were part of the conditions of his parole. If Curtis didn't respond the day he received his friendly email from Terry, there would be a good chance there'd be a polite knock on his door that night. It hadn't happened, of course. Yet. But they both knew the rules of the game, and as long as Curtis kept on the straight and narrow, that was the way it would stay.

He minimised Terry's email as a reminder to send him a reply later in the day. Then he spotted an email he really didn't expect to see. It was from none other than Turk. Turk the Dude. What the hell was he up to now? Curtis clicked it open.

Dear Dude
What's happenin', man? Long time no
see! I presume life and limb are safe
in the land of the free. Me? Same
old, same old. You should see some
of the gear I've got my hands on.
I get hard just thinking about it.

```
Anyway ... enough chitchat. Reason
for communication: Roly died, man.
Can you believe it? I sure as hell
can't. Apparently went for a swim in
the bay and just kept on swimming.
Cops haven't even found a body. His
mother's in a pretty bad way. She's
having a service tomorrow down where
he was last seen. Thought you might
want to know.
I think she'd be stoked if you could
make it. Be good to catch up again.
Sorry to be the bearer of bad news.
Life is short. LIVE HARD!
Turk
```

Curtis sat looking at the email, reading it over and over. Roly dead. Good-time, irrepressible Roly. Impossible. Turk used to be a huge practical joker, but even he wouldn't joke about something like this. Roly and Turk were the old gang. A life he'd left behind when he'd moved to Pittsburgh to take up his job at Trident. A life that used to include Roly's sister, Anna.

Roly's mother had always treated her son's group of young computer-dweeb friends like her own. The least he could do was turn up for the memorial service.

But Roly committing suicide was like Jordan missing a free throw. It just didn't happen. Things must have really changed after the bust. They say prison can do all kinds of things to you. And Roly wasn't your run-of-the-mill jailbird.

Curtis fired off a quick reply to Turk. Hi, how are you, and yes I'll be there kind of thing. He'd have to tell Terry, of course. Hell, he probably knew about Roly already. Associating with his old gang was one of the no-nos imposed by the sentencing judge. But Curtis was sure the judge didn't mean to include funerals in that. Compassionate leniency. You read about it all the time in the papers. Anyway, he'd kept his nose, and his hard drive, clean since the bust. Terry would understand. He'd have to. He took his time composing his reply to Terry, and explained that he'd be taking personal leave from work for a few days. Then he tried to put Roly, Turk and Anna out of his mind for the two-and-a-half hours it took to finish the coding.

By 2 p.m. he was shutting down and ready to leave for the airport via his flat for some clothes. He'd rung to tell his mother she'd be getting a visitor for a few days. At least someone was happy.

It seemed weird to finally be going back, especially under these circumstances. He was booked on stand-by, which meant a long wait in the airport lounge, and plenty of time to reminisce about the old days. And the mistakes. He'd sure made enough of those.

The bay was just as Curtis remembered. Four years was a lifetime in the computer world, but elsewhere life seemed to chug on regardless. The wind still blew, and cars and factories still competed with nature to turn the planet into a giant greenhouse. And his mother still cooked a mean spaghetti bolognaise.

The service was unusual, to say the least. No body, no clue as to why or how Roly had disappeared. Just a few belongings and clothes piled on the beach with his car keys tucked neatly underneath. And now just a group of people standing on the foreshore. Remembering Roly.

Curtis didn't recognise hardly any of them. He'd arrived late, and kept well to the back. But it was clear Roly's mother was pretty cut up by the whole thing. It wasn't the best occasion to catch up with people you hadn't seen for years. But Anna still looked great, despite the tears and grief. And Turk didn't seem to have changed that much at all. He just looked older.

As the service finished Roly's mother spread flower petals out onto the water. It was a touching gesture. Curtis paid his respects but managed to avoid Anna, even though he was acutely aware of her presence. What ifs.

Curtis decided he needed to be alone, and drifted away from the mourners. It wasn't a particularly cold morning, but it was kind of colourless. Perhaps it was just the mood he was in.

He zipped up his jacket, buried his hands in his pockets, and headed off up the beach. Sometimes it helps.

But Turk had other plans.

'Hey, dude!' Curtis turned to see Turk coming up behind him, looking genuinely pleased to see him, so maybe some company wouldn't hurt. In spite of it all, Curtis found himself grinning. He couldn't help it when Turk was around. That's why they called him Turk — because he was such a turkey.

'How's it going, Turk?' he said, waiting for him to catch up.

'Hey man, it's good to see you. Real good!' Turk punctuated his sentences by jumping onto Curtis's shoulders. Male bonding and all that. 'Look at you, man!' he said, appraising Curtis's threads. If you could call an old beige pair of trousers, a blue work shirt and a faded suede jacket threads. Curtis still didn't tuck his shirts in though. Just a little bit of the rebel left inside.

'Nice to see some things never change,' laughed Curtis, looking at Turk's old bomber jacket. Just as worn, just as faded, and just as many old airforce patches on it as he remembered. The guy must live in that thing.

Turk slapped him on the back. 'And not the least bit sarcastic, either.'

Curtis nodded towards the slowly dispersing group of mourners. 'Terrible, man. I can't believe he's gone.'

Turk became subdued. 'Yeah, I know. Things won't be the same around here.' They started walking up the beach together in silence. Funerals could be a bit of a conversation killer. Even for Turk.

Curtis sighed. 'What are you up to now anyway?'

'Bit of this, bit of that, you know how it is ...' said Turk. Curtis made a mental note: Turk's still unemployed. He didn't push it.

'Tell me about this new gear?' asked Curtis, changing the subject. Turk's eyes lit up. Computer gear was something he was passionate about. In fact it was probably one of the only things Turk was passionate about.

'Let's just say it took four-and-a-half minutes to load Windows,' he said proudly. Curtis nodded in appreciation. He had to hand it to him — that was fast. He asked the obvious question. 'How you paying for it?'

Turk smiled evasively. 'Oh I get by. Just got to know where to sniff out the good deals.' Curtis made another mental note: Turk was running either stolen or illegal imitation gear. He wasn't sure what Terry Hay would make of that if he ever found out.

'Hey, Roly's mother asked me to give you this. She said they were going through his things and found it.' Turk pulled a thick folded envelope from his jacket and handed it to Curtis. 'Must be a game you lent him sometime.'

Curtis took the envelope. He didn't remember lending Roly any games, but he took it anyway. Out of respect.

'How long you staying?' said Turk.

Curtis shrugged. 'Dunno. Couple of days maybe.'

'Let's catch up properly over a drink. Come down to Barney's about six. Then you can tell me about all those women you've scored since I saw you last.'

Curtis had to smile. 'OK, Turk. See you then.'

Turk stopped and looked at him. 'Damn, it's good to see you again.'

'You too, Turk. Catch ya.'

Curtis watched as Turk jogged back to the mourners. Hell of a nice guy — just a complete turkey sometimes. He shook his head as he thought of some of the more stupid things Turk had done in his time. Like rigging their parole officer's phone to a phone-sex service. Not the best way to impress someone. Turk had even pretended to be one of the callers so he could talk dirty to him. The cheek. Curtis caught sight of Roly's mother and Anna being ushered to the car by helpful relatives. He continued watching them for a minute, then headed back off up the beach alone.

Barney's wasn't what it used to be. They'd come here to drink when they were still underage, sitting at a back table planning their diabolical schemes. Roly was always the leader, but Curtis had provided the brains. Turk was just Turk. And Anna used to be Curtis's girl. But while Curtis had been away, Barney had sold out to someone with probably more business sense, but definitely less taste. What had once been a busy neighbourhood hangout run by an ex-hippie with a penchant for things nautical — and alcoholic it had to be said — now looked like an interior set from an old 'Miami Vice' rerun. Turk stuck out like a sore thumb. Even the music was plastic and modern. It was at Barney's that Curtis had developed his taste in music. The good stuff, with guitars, and guys who knew how to play them.

'Hey man,' said Turk, 'what you drinking these days?'

Curtis pulled up a chair. 'Bud'll do nicely, thanks.'

The Bud arrived and Curtis and Turk talked and drank. They talked about the old days, and the time in between. Seems Roly had cut a deal with the DA's office to offer his services to the government as a network-security consultant. According to Turk anyway. It sounded like things had been going pretty well for him, and though Roly didn't hang with Turk anymore — they weren't allowed to as part of the sentence — when they did catch up every now and then Roly had seemed happy enough. He never did tell Turk much about the job, but Curtis figured that probably wasn't surprising.

It was late into the night when Turk dangled the bait. 'Hey, you get up to any tricks back home?'

Curtis shook his head. 'Nah. Been a good boy. Pays the bills and keeps me out of prison.' Turk had timed his opening well. The beers were kicking in.

'Do you ever wish you could? Just once more. Just to see if we were as good as we thought we were?' Curtis didn't shake his head. But he didn't nod either. A tilt to the side was about as much as he was going to give away.

'Me too,' said Turk. Curtis looked at him sideways. He didn't like where this was going.

'What would you say if you had an opportunity to show how good you are — without even breaking the law?'

Curtis definitely didn't like where this was going. 'Turk, the answer is no. Whatever scam you've got cooking. Read my lips: N. O.' But Turk wasn't going to give up without a fight, and Curtis had had enough beers not to care.

'And if you were good enough, you could win yourself 50 000 smackeroonies along the way.' Turk waited for his reply. Curtis kept him waiting.

'Well, what do you say? You can't tell me you couldn't do with 50 K.'

Curtis had to admit, 50 thou' was a damn good argument. 'OK, Turk, spit it out, but I'm not saying yes to anything.'

Turk backed off. 'No way, man, no pressure. It's cool.' But he was on a roll, and Curtis had to smile when he leant forward on the table, and looked around to make sure no one was listening in. Maybe he thought Crockett might be standing behind him in a white-linen Armani. 'Ever heard of DefCon?' asked Turk.

'Sure,' said Curtis. 'Hackers' convention in Vegas. The hotels keep banning them because they get their systems hacked and cement poured down their toilets. Sounds like a giant dweeby frat party on steroids.'

Turk laughed. 'Yeah, sure there's all that. But there's also a competition. One I reckon we could win.'

Curtis shook his head. 'Forget it, Turk. I gave all that shit up a long time ago. I'm not going to risk it all for anyone — not even you, buddy.'

'I know that. And I would never ask you to. But I'm talking about 50 000 reasons to risk it. No one's ever gonna know, and you're not breaking the conditions of your parole 'cos you're not breaking the law — it's legal. You're actually doing people a favour, 'cos all these security companies put up their latest systems, and then it's a free-for-all to break in and walk away with the prize. You could do it, man, I'm telling you.'

Curtis wasn't giving anything away, but Turk could tell he had him hooked.

'I gotta work —' Curtis looked at his watch. 'Tomorrow!'

'You're on bereavement leave, man. They'll expect you to have a couple of days off. No one's gonna miss you.'

Curtis sat thinking. 'Vegas,' he said finally.

'Don't worry about that,' said Turk. 'Got us a couple of seats booked on Amtrak tomorrow. And I took the liberty of registering us yesterday.'

Curtis looked at Turk blankly. The cheek of this guy. 'What did that cost you?'

Turk smiled enigmatically. 'All expenses paid. And we're staying at the Oasis.'

Curtis smiled in spite of himself. 'You hacked them, didn't you.' It was a statement, not a question.

Turk grinned from ear to ear. 'Figured it was kinda poetic to hack in to register for a hackers' conference. The train and the hotel's just icing.'

Curtis got the feeling he was being talked into something he didn't really want to get involved in. But the lure of the money and the thought of competing against the world's best hackers sure was tempting. Of course it had nothing to do with the beers. But 50 thou' would go a long way to denting the huge amount he owed as part of his sentence. He'd followed all the conditions of release for so long. It hadn't been hard, considering the alternative was prison. But he missed the thrill. And the challenge.

'Come on, man. You're the best. You know it. Easy money for someone like you,' said Turk. Easy money, huh?

Curtis couldn't believe he was saying this. 'All right. Let's do it.'

Turk couldn't contain himself. 'You're the man! You won't regret this, Curtis. Just have to work out how we're going to spend the dolleros.'

'Who'd you register us as, Batman and Robin?'

Turk looked hurt. 'Hey man, you know I got more imagination than that. You're registered as Cyrus the Virus. I'm SuperCool,' he said proudly.

'Cyrus the Virus! Where'd you get that one?'

'Remember that movie where Nicolas Cage is this special-forces guy who's put away for accidentally killing a guy who was hitting on his wife? And he's on a prison transfer flight with all these bad dudes. Well, the worst one of the lot is John Malkovich — a.k.a. Cyrus the Virus.'

Curtis recalled the movie. 'You named me after the bad guy?'

Turk looked sheepish. 'Well you try to find something that rhymes with Curtis! Curtis the Tortoise just didn't cut it, man!'

Curtis laughed with him. 'OK, SuperCool. Let the games begin!'

Yep, he was pissed. But suddenly the world seemed a whole lot more interesting.

2

Curtis stowed his bag in the overhead locker and wormed his way into the seat next to Turk. If he waited long enough the train would be rolling, and any second thoughts would be hypothetical.

But the late night, the beers and the early morning hadn't dulled any of Turk's enthusiasm. He was having fun picking out the other guys on their way to DefCon, and he gave each one a time. The faster the time, the better the hacker. According to Turk anyway.

The highlight of his morning was when a cute chick boarded just before they left, and took the seat in front of them. She ignored Turk completely, but that didn't stop him nudging Curtis's elbow and nodding appreciatively in her direction. Curtis ignored Turk as well. Sleep. He opened the playlist on his MP3 player, and chose a song. Then he pulled on his headphones, rolled his jacket up under his head and shut the world out, leaving Turk to reconnoitre the buffet car for a few hours. The guy never stopped. Curtis smiled to himself as he settled back and let Adam Clayton's hypnotic bass take him to another place. But it was too good to last for long.

'Hey dude!' Turk was back, with some guys he'd met. Curtis tried to uncrumple his face and make sure he hadn't dribbled while he'd slept.

'Want to introduce you to some friends.' They were young. Curtis figured they were on their way to DefCon as well. One of them put out his hand.

'Hey,' was about all they were going to get out of Curtis right now.

'Turk's been telling us a lot about you. You're a legend, man!' Curtis looked suspiciously at Turk, who just gave him an innocent 'who me?' smile.

'What lies has SuperFool been telling you?'

'You're a legend,' said the guy. 'Wiring those phone lines to win that Mercedes!' Curtis shot Turk a look.

'Incredible, man!' The guy wasn't going to give up. 'Turk told us how you waited six days for the DJ to play the songs in the right order, and then you rigged it so each caller rang your phone once. All you had to do was count to 71, then casually ring in and collect the Merc. Brilliant!'

Curtis had to say something. It would have been rude not to. 'Thanks.'

The guy leant over further. 'And we heard how you got your name. Cyrus!'

Curtis looked at Turk again. He was pretending to avoid Curtis's glare, a big mischievous grin smeared across his mug. Well this would be interesting …

'Don't worry, man, we won't tell anyone. I read that virus cost over 140 mill. And it was benign! All it did was replicate! You could have snuck a bomb inside and brought down the entire net. Now that's power!'

This guy was starting to be a pain in the ass. 'No, that's illegal,' said Curtis flatly.

But the dickhead just wasn't getting the message. 'You'll kick some ass at DefCon, man. Turk told us you guys are going for the 50 K.'

The woman sitting in front of them turned in her seat and smiled sweetly at them. Curtis noticed she had a lappie open. It was on. 'Couldn't help overhearing you,' she said. 'You going to DefCon?'

Curtis nodded. 'Seems that way.'

'You sound pretty good. Cyrus, is it?'

'Uh, yeah,' said Curtis. Turk was really enjoying himself now. He'd keep.

But the dickhead leaning over Curtis just wouldn't give it a rest. 'This guy's a legend, man!'

The woman smiled. 'Yeah, I heard. And do you boys play as well?'

'Sure do,' came the quick reply.

'Then let's brighten up the trip,' she said. 'And let's make it interesting.'

'What you got in mind?' Dickhead was keen.

'Fifty bucks for the best hack. Here and now.' This was suddenly getting very interesting. Dickhead stood thinking for a second. The woman's confidence suggested she'd done this before. But he was game all the same.

'OK, you're on. Cyrus, you're the judge. Best hack gets 50.' Dickhead pulled a laptop and mobile from his backpack, and took an empty seat a few back from Curtis and Turk. The woman was also busy with her laptop.

But Curtis had to pee. On his way back from the john he took the opportunity to check out the woman more closely. She had short, dark hair, tomboyish looks. Not scruffy, though. Not scruffy at all. He couldn't see what she was doing on the screen. The guys were still at the back of the carriage, working intently on their hack. By the time Curtis had made his way through one dry muffin, courtesy of Turk, the competitors were ready to do battle.

'Let's get it on!' Curtis really hated people who said that. Where on earth did Turk find these guys?

'OK,' said Curtis, 'let's see what you've got.'

'Here,' said Dickhead, giving Curtis his mobile. 'Dial the number in there.' Curtis took the phone and dialed. He could hear it switch through a box. This was an untraceable call. That meant it was probably illegal. Uh oh. The phone rang, then someone picked up at the other end. Curtis listened closely.

'Hello.' A woman's voice. Strangely familiar.

Curtis played it cool. 'Hi, how's things?'

A pause. 'Who is this?'

'Sorry,' said Curtis, 'must have the wrong number.' He ended the call.

Dickhead was looking at him expectantly. 'Well?'

'Are you gonna tell me who I just called?' said Curtis.

'That was Madonna, man!' he said proudly. 'We found her private number!' Could have been. Possibly. But then it could have been anyone. Who knows? Curtis played along anyway.

'Pretty impressive, man.' Dickhead was beaming from ear to ear.

Curtis leant over the seat in front. 'OK, Miss Eavesdropper, you have to beat a call to Madonna. Show us what you got.'

The woman finished working on her lappie and turned to face Curtis and Turk. 'Here goes.' They sat there, waiting for her to do something. But she just sat there too.

Then Curtis noticed some cellphones ringing at the back of the carriage. The ringing was getting louder, and ring tones were changing. He looked back, and noticed that seat row by seat row, everyone was searching through handbags and satchels for the ringing phones. Then Curtis's own phone rang. And Turk's. And the guys' phones. All the way up to the front of the carriage. Now *that* was impressive.

Curtis looked back at the woman, who was looking pretty pleased with herself. The guys realised they'd just been beaten hands down. She'd somehow found the cellphone numbers of everyone on the carriage and then found out who was sitting in what seat. Then she'd rung every phone from the back of the carriage to the front. Dickhead looked pretty pissed as he handed over 50 to the woman. Curtis didn't hear much else from them after that. Probably went back to the buffet car to nurse their wounded egos.

'Well done. You're very good,' said Curtis. 'But I think you probably knew that already, huh?' The woman appraised him for a second. Then she stuck out her hand.

'Hi, I'm Gina.' Gina the hacker, huh, thought Curtis. He took her hand.

'Curtis,' he said, trying to give her his killer smile. Hard to do when you're sitting behind someone on a train. Hopefully she'd just think he was suffering from motion sickness. Which wasn't far wrong after last night.

But at least she smiled back. 'Might catch you at DefCon, Curtis.' Hey, things were looking up.

'Uh, yeah,' wasn't much of an intelligent reply. Apparently Gina thought so too because she turned back to her laptop and that was all Curtis heard from her for the rest of the journey. He pretended to ignore Turk's eyebrow problem, and the simultaneous nods of his head in Gina's direction. He couldn't believe this guy. Talk about trouble. If it hadn't been for the lure of some serious money, he would have been bailing at the next stop. Well, that and the mystery hacker-babe in front. Curtis pulled his headphones back on and hit the button. Time for some U2. 'The Real Thing'. Roll on, DefCon.

3

It was all it was cracked up to be. An outrageous event in an outrageous city, DefCon was bottled chaos. Hackers were no longer the skinny, nerdy white boys shown in the movies. These guys had attitude. And there were thousands of them. Of course, with all the music and cyber-talk, partying and showing off, it was hard to tell the show ponies from the real thing. DJs were spinning techno and Goth, and people were signing up for the recreational rifle shoot or the inflatable sumo-wrestling competition. If that wasn't your thing there was always the social-engineering competition, basically a game of celebrity deception and harassment. Go figure. The programme was topped off with a scavenger hunt, a ball and even a streaming radio station where everyone voted on what tracks to listen to. How's that for democracy? The place was supposed to be crawling with Feds. They even had a competition to spot one. As Turk discovered.

DefCon custom has it that when anyone spots someone suspiciously looking like an undercover Fed, they have to yell it out to the rest of the crowd and point him out. Turk did exactly that. Sure, the guy looked like a Fed, but so did half the dweebs there, and when the onlookers voted unanimously that he *was* a Fed, even though the guy protested his innocence, he was given an 'I am a Fed' T-shirt anyway. Poor bugger. Turk was happy though. He had his 'I spotted the Fed' T-shirt and some notoriety. Really suited his short peroxided hair and bulbous purple 'Bono' glasses.

Curtis and Turk wandered the exhibition hall. It was loud, brash and in-your-face. Turk fitted right in. Curtis looked at the schedule for the presentation sessions. Various 'experts' were doing sessions on everything from cryptography to cyber-forensics. Curtis knew that there were any number of security experts and cyber-police, and the odd federal agent, among the hackers. And then there were the corporate recruiters. All assembled to discuss the latest trends in security exploits. One of the break-out sessions even included a panel discussion with security officials from the Army and the National Security Council, with none other than the White House Security Director himself.

The conversation was all computers. Issues like high and low entropy, weak algorithms, credential checking and other techno-talk bounced around the convention. But the big talk was BO2K2.

A couple of years back a group of Californian hackers calling themselves The Cult of the Dead

Cow released a new programme that sent shockwaves through the computer underworld. Back Orifice, a typically hackeresque play on a popular Back Office software package, was a remote computer surveillance tool. And even better, it was, as hackers so delicately put it, 'self-installing'. The Cult had released the programme onto the web, where anyone could download and 'experiment' with it. That meant by now there were hundreds, possibly thousands, of dubious characters using it. The programme was loaded onto an unsuspecting victim's computer, either through email attachments or more subtle means. Once there, the 'remote user' could pretty much do anything the victim could do on their own computer, including controlling the full file system, grabbing video from any webcams they had hooked up, and seeing their screen and what they were doing on it in real time. Powerful stuff. And the new version was even better, depending on your point of view. That's progress for you. But Curtis was here for the competition, and so was the crowd.

'Good afternoon, ladies and gentlemen. Welcome to DefCon!' began some dude with a microphone on the stage. A tremendous roar went up from the crowd. They were hyped at the thought of seeing some of the planet's best hackers in action.

'We are DefCon!' screamed the announcer. Maybe his day job was preaching somewhere down the Bible Belt. The crowd loved it.

Curtis and Turk stood in the seething mass of

subversive subculture and waited for the show to begin. And begin it did.

'DefCon has been held every summer for eight years now,' began the Preacher. 'Over those years it has grown in size, and attracted people from all over the planet. People come to meet other hackers. People come to hang out with old friends. And people come to listen to new speeches and learn something, or just to hack on the network. That's what DefCon is all about!' More yelling. He had the crowd pumped.

'We are not trying to teach you how to hack in a weekend. We're creating an environment where you can hang out with people from all different backgrounds, all of them interested in one thing — computer security.'

The Preacher was on a roll now. No stopping him or the crowd. 'I'd like to extend a special welcome to our friends from the many law-enforcement agencies represented here today.' A big laugh. They liked that one.

'So to all you hackers, would-be hackers, security consultants and federal agents, now's the time for a good time! Now's your chance to share alcohol. Codes. Ideas. And for the lucky ones — casual sex!' That really struck a chord with the overwhelmingly young male audience. Dream on, thought Curtis, unless it was going to be with each other.

'But DefCon exists for many reasons. We want to spread knowledge and information to all who want to learn. Information about computers, telephones, the underground and technology in general. Hackers have undeservedly held a tarnished name for too long. And we plan to build that name back up. Instead of thinking criminal or vandal, we want the public to think of knowledge seekers and curious wanderers.' Curtis had to hand it to this guy. He was good.

'Destruction and unethical ignorance has plagued the underground for too long! Let's bring back the old-school ways of penetrating systems for the knowledge they hold. Not to destroy them. We're not going to change the hacking world, but we can do our part to help us to be better understood.'

The Preacher was starting to lose Curtis now. Just a little too full on. But it sounded great, and went down with the crowd even better. After several more minutes of preaching the underground gospel, he finally got round to what everyone was waiting for him to do — announce the competition. Curtis was more than ready.

'The Shield is a new security software system that its developers claim can't be breached. At the European Systems trade show in Munich, the Shield survived 1.4 million hacks from 360 000 anonymous ISP addresses. They've sold a lot of product since. In fact, they think it's so good that they've put up $50 000 in prize money for DefCon, because if one of us doesn't crack it, they're gonna sell a whole lot more. So don't get me wrong. This is a formidable foe. We are their litmus test. They know they can't model the collective genius of the hacker community in a lab. Only the best will have even a chance to bring it down.' Yeah, yeah, thought Curtis. Get on with it.

'This technology is aimed at protecting web servers from attacks that seek to alter data and web pages, or steal information and monetary assets. Contestants, you have a PC with your name on it somewhere in the hall. There are maps to find your way to your designated computer. Your challenge is to break into a fictitious e-commerce website we've set up. The only hitch is, the site is protected by the Shield. You have two hours to penetrate the system and to steal as many indices as you can. The winner is the person with the most indices. And they'll leave $50 000 richer for their efforts. Good luck to you all. Let the competition begin!'

OK, that's the challenge, thought Curtis. Stealing indices. Indices were merely groups of numbers. But to the uninitiated, they looked suspiciously like credit-card numbers. Turk was getting right into the interactive element of the Preacher's address. But Curtis was already thinking. Planning his hack.

'Come on, Turk,' said Curtis. 'We've gotta find the map and get to our PCs.'

'Yeah, OK man.' Turk followed Curtis through the crowd to a badly drawn map pinned to a wall. They found their PCs, Cyrus the Virus and SuperCool, right next to each other at the lobby end of the hall.

Beside their PCs, which were sectioned off from each other but with the monitors facing the crowd so people could watch the contestants at work,

Turk put out his hand. 'May the best man win!' he said chivalrously. Curtis smiled and shook.

'See you in two,' said Curtis.

The computer stations had been thrown together in a hurry. The bargain-basement desks and folding chairs were a give-away, but so too were the pre-installed software packages. Curtis did his best to shut out the noise and ignore the spectators wandering from competitor to competitor, assessing their chances, and probably taking bets too. He felt fidgety. Nervous.

He forced himself to concentrate. OK, he thought to himself as he logged onto the net, we've got a certified internet email delivery company. Time for some scouting. Curtis knew from experience that the more he knew about his target the better, even if it was going to take some time to find out. Time was the challenge — anyone could take down a system if they had long enough. But Curtis had two hours, and the clock was ticking. First things first.

He pulled his PocketPC from his bag — his small handheld computer organiser which could do anything from running his diary and some pretty nifty games, to sending and receiving email, surfing the net and playing music. It could also store programmes. And programmes were the tools of the trade.

He set the timer on it for two hours, and after a long search through his bag for a pen and pad, began his hack. He rubbed his hands together as he scanned the target website for partner affiliates, to find any corporate links to the target network. Nerves, dammit. The mouse felt familiar and comfortable in his hand. But he had to force himself to focus, to get into the zone. He pulled his MP3 player from his bag and wrapped the phones about his head. Time for some energy. Time for some Stones. As Keith Richards ripped into the first chords of 'Jumpin' Jack Flash', the bright lights and clamour from the hall began to fade away from his consciousness. Party time.

Curtis knew the weak link was often a fringe partner organisation that wasn't as secure as the main network. It was a possible way in. But he was disappointed — nothing stood out. Next, he clicked over to the InterNIC and ARIN registers, the services that assign and record domain information. Curtis keyed in a WHOIS command. Several seconds later he'd verified the domain name of the target and IP address. He scratched a note to himself on his pad — three servers. That meant three possible entry points.

He also now had the company nicknames, and the names and phone numbers of the site administrators. Not hugely useful in a short penetration exercise like this, but you never knew. Anyway, he had an overall picture of the target's network configuration.

The next step was to run a traceroute against the three IP addresses. Network administrators used tracerouting to track packets of data travelling between a source and its destination, similar to a sonar ping by a submarine. The traceroute told Curtis that a router was blocking his packets. A router sits as a sentry to a web server, which meant this router was doing its job. Shit. But Curtis was able to trace the outgoing traffic to a specified port number, which the target used to connect to its ISP. OK, ladies and gentlemen. Time for some hacker tools.

Curtis pulled a floppy disk from his bag and installed a host programme for his PocketPC into the computer, and while that was running, connected the device to the computer with a cable from his bag and selected his favourite tools for transfer. Soon his first programme was installed, and he was running a set of timed pings to a specified range of ports. The pings were slow and small enough to fall beneath the radar of intrusion-detection software. Of course, he could have gone for a full-blown assault on the network, but that would have brought the entire server down. While it would have given him a lot of information about the system, it would have been impossible to restore the system within the two-hour time period. He'd have to continue with the stealth attack.

Next he ran an IP network discovery tool, looking for an open port to use as a possible entry point. The software wasn't sophisticated. Just clever. Soon he had enough information to deduce which IP address was the router, and make an educated guess that the third IP address was the target's proxy server. An instant later he had the specs on the target's network software. Bingo. He fired off a few command lines in short, machine-gun blasts. This was familiar territory now.

He established a 'null' session with the target server, avoiding the need for user passwords or ID.

By logging on as 'null', Curtis was able to see everything and anything he wanted to on the target machine — password files, user accounts, network services, the works. And none of it was logged.

The only drawback was that he couldn't touch anything, but that didn't stop him from copying down a few user names on the notepad. Then he logged off, and logged on again using the user name 'backup'. He didn't have the password though. Time for an intelligent, scientific approach. He'd have to guess. Curtis couldn't help smiling in spite of himself. He had it with his first guess. It wasn't rocket science — the password was 'backup'. Doh! It still surprised Curtis at how slack people were with passwords. Even administrators running a simulated network they knew would be hacked. Go figure. He stole a glance at his timer. Forty minutes to go. It would be close. Real close. He wondered how Turk was getting on.

Soon Curtis had compiled a list of password hashes representing all the encoded passwords on the system. Now to decode them.

He installed a crack programme on the computer, and ran the coded passwords through it. In less than 15 minutes he'd cracked 70 per cent of them. More importantly, he had the one he was looking for: SuperUser. In minutes he was in, searching through the system files for databases of indices. The prized indices. But he'd have to work fast. It would take time to download them.

Curtis's hands were sweating now. He was close. He found the file he was looking for and initiated the download. The little grey bar began its long journey across the screen. Could it go any slower? He figured that by now most of the competitors would have some kind of access into the server. That would be slowing the system down. But there was nothing to do now but wait. He willed the little grey bar to grow — move, goddammit! Suddenly his monitor lit up with an access control list warning message. Curtis froze in horror.

The security system knew its doors were being rattled, and it was warning him, since he was logged on as SuperUser. That meant someone was launching an all-out assault against the entire range of ports — one through 65 334. Curtis shook his head in disgust. Someone was blitzing the machine. Too much 'noise'. He watched his transfer bar closely. It had stopped moving. The system was closing itself down. Shield was doing its job. If Curtis's approach had been a stealth operation with a few special-ops guys using knives, this was a full-blown airborne assault with B–1 bombers. He threw his hands up in disgust, just as the timer chimed. He was out of time. *Shit*.

It was over.

The network administrator closed the system and the computer terminated his session. Curtis wasn't pleased, but he'd given it his best shot. Now he had to wait along with everyone else for the results. He threw his PocketPC and notepad into his bag, cursing himself for even coming. He knew he shouldn't have listened to Turk. What the hell had he been thinking? He'd just have to hope he could get a flight back from Vegas that night so he wouldn't miss any more work. Terry Hay was probably starting to wonder where he was. He couldn't afford to risk his parole. Not for anything.

He'd been crazy to think he could still foot it with the best. There was probably a whole new generation of hackers now who could leave him for dead. And they probably had.

'Dude!' It was Turk. Didn't this guy ever give it a rest? 'How'd you go?'

Curtis shook his head. 'Bummed out.' An expression that could have been sympathy flickered across Turk's face.

'Too bad, man.' Then he was back to his old chipper self. 'Let's go see who got the dough. Only takes them a few minutes to get the results!' He was off.

Curtis had to scramble to keep up with him in the crowd hanging round to find out this year's winner of the competition. The Preacher was in a very serious-looking huddle on stage with some guys with long hair in ponytails and black T-shirts. The crowd was buzzing, and there was a current of excitement running through the hall. Amongst the bizarre collection of characters pressed together in front of the huge stage, Curtis spotted a face he recognised. Gina!

He watched her closely for a second. She was waiting for the results, and looked as though she was on her own as well. Curtis figured he had some time to kill, and since he was leaving later he should really be polite and at least say hello. He fought his way through the crowd to where she was standing, and casually stood beside her as though he hadn't spotted her yet.

He pretended to suddenly notice her. 'Hey, Gina!'

She looked around suspiciously. Heck, she was one of the few babes in the middle of this male madness, so she'd probably been hit on a hundred times before breakfast. Curtis was starting to think this was a bad idea, when her face broke into the most amazing smile he'd ever seen. A real traffic-stopper.

'Hi Curtis!' she shouted over the din.

Curtis leant closer to her ear to be heard. 'How'd you go?'

Gina shrugged her shoulders. 'Did my best. That's what matters, right?' Curtis couldn't tell whether she was serious or not, so he decided not to push it.

'Right.' He nodded casually.

'What about you?'

Curtis decided to play it cool as well. 'Not as well as I'd have liked.' Gina nodded her sympathy. He couldn't think of much else to say so he just stood beside her while they waited. But then she threw her bag over her shoulder and started to leave.

'Aren't you staying to hear the results?' Curtis tried not to sound too disappointed, but Gina shook her head.

'I'm not into crowds. And they're taking forever. Good luck, Curtis.'

The thought of losing Gina in the crowd sent a surge of bravado through him. Or was it desperation? Whatever the case, he surprised himself. 'What are you doing later? Want to catch up? I'll fill you in on how badly I did.'

Gina surprised him as well. 'Sure,' she said over her shoulder as she squeezed into the crowd, and disappeared. Great going, Curtis. No mobile number, no time or place. Just, 'Sure'. A real mystery babe.

This whole trip was turning into a lost cause. Curtis was still kicking himself and cursing Turk under his breath when the Preacher finally approached the microphone, looking very important. He was clearly taking his responsibilities very seriously.

'Ladies and gentlemen, hackers and hackettes!' The roar from the crowd was more from impatience than excitement. 'I have the final results of the competition.' Another roar and a few whistles.

'First of all, congratulations to all hackers who entered the competition. I can confirm that the system was breached, and we do have a winner!' Yeah, yeah, thought Curtis. Maybe it was time for him to bail as well. He looked about for Turk, but he was nowhere.

'I have the Chief Security Officer from the Shield with me to present the cheque for $50 000. Give him a big hand!' As several hundred hands were raised in mock salute, Curtis thought the Shield guy looked pretty sheepish. Their system had been penetrated. He'd be back to the drawing board on Monday, as well as answering some tough questions from his investors. But you had to hand it to him. It took balls to put his product on the line.

'The third place-getter, and winner of a year's free ISP membership, with 190 indices is ... SuperCool!' Everyone was craning their necks to see who SuperCool was. Curtis just shook his head in amazement. Turk had obviously spent some time on his trade since the old days. Perhaps there was a brain in there somewhere after all.

Curtis spotted Turk fighting his way up onto the stage. He was loving every minute of his notoriety, hamming it up for the audience. A born showman. Turk spotted Curtis in the crowd and gave him a wink. Cheeky bugger. Curtis was genuinely pleased for him though, and gave him the thumbs up and a big smile.

The Preacher was keen to move on, even though he had to wait for Turk to finish his antics for the audience. Soon the expectant hush was restored, as Turk made his way back through the crowd.

'Second place-getter!' shouted the Preacher into the mike. Like Pavlov's dogs, the roar followed. 'Winner of a rip-roaring eight gig computer ... with 455 indices ... Cyrus the Virus!' Curtis was dumbfounded. Confused even. He hadn't won, but he'd come second. Turk was going off, and of course it didn't take the crowd around them long to realise he was Cyrus. Turk was just as rapt for Curtis as he was for himself.

'Way to go, Cyrus!' he screamed, as he pushed him forward to the stage. Curtis felt his back slapped at least 20 times as he walked up to the stage through the path cleared for him by awed hackers.

'And here he is, folks!' There was no stopping the Preacher. Curtis felt exposed and self-conscious in front of such a large, crazy crowd. The guy from Shield shook his hand and slipped a voucher into it. He didn't look too thrilled though.

Curtis raised his voucher to the audience in appreciation. He had to admit, second wasn't too bad. Somewhere out there in the crowd was one hell of a good hacker. One he'd like to meet.

As Curtis made his way back through the crowd to Turk, the Preacher revved himself up for the big one.

'And now for the ultimate winner of this year's competition, the undisputed champion of the underground. And don't forget they'll be going home $50 000 richer, folks ...'

Curtis found his way to Turk, who was in the mood for more male bonding, as the Preacher continued. 'It looks like we have a new world record today folks ... with 2600 indices ... the legend lives on ... *Prometheus*!' By now the excitement was infectious. Curtis found himself screaming like a moron with the rest of them. Unbelievable. Totally unbelievable. He didn't feel so bad coming second to a legend.

The Preacher was shouting something into his mike over the yelling and screaming. It sounded like, 'Come forward and collect your prize, Prometheus!' He was scanning the crowd for the famous hacker. Despite a few goons pretending to walk up on stage, soon everyone was craning their necks, looking for the mystery man. But whoever he was, he was keeping to himself. The Shield dude was starting to look a little less stressed. He shouted a few words into the Preacher's ear, who nodded in agreement. It was obvious it was going to be a no-show. Curtis could just feel it.

But the Preacher wasn't about to give up on him. 'Prometheus, I must remind you that if you don't collect your prize now, you forfeit it forever!' No one promising emerged from the chaos.

Curtis tried to calm Turk down long enough to talk with him. 'Let's get outta here, Turk. He's not going to show today.' Turk looked as disappointed as Curtis felt. But he was wired and tired, and the urge to rid himself of the people and the noise and the bullshit was overwhelming.

Turk tagged along as Curtis ran block, pushing and elbowing his way through the mosh-pit to the lobby. The relief Curtis felt on exiting the exhibition hall was tangible. But he could also feel a headache coming on. Maybe a beer would help.

Turk must have been thinking the same thing. 'Hey dude, you thirsty?'

Curtis looked at Turk, still in his 'I spotted the Fed' T-shirt, and still wearing his silly sunglasses. 'Is the Pope a Catholic?' he said. 'But only a quick one. I'm heading back home tonight if I can get a flight.'

Turk tried unsuccessfully to hide his disappointment. 'Sure thing, dude. Just a quick one before you go … for old times.'

4

Three hours and even more Buds later, Curtis was still in Vegas, sitting in the lobby bar chewing the fat with Turk.

They'd gone over each other's hack in detail, comparing approaches and tools. Turk was impressed with Curtis's PocketPC. But neither of them could figure out how Prometheus had managed to win by so much. Turk had heard a few stories about him, but as far as he knew no one had ever seen him in the flesh. A few guys from the convention had recognised Cyrus and SuperCool, and had congratulated them on their efforts, but in the main they were left alone to reminisce and exaggerate about the good old days. Turk was just in the middle of explaining the ins and outs of one of his conquests to Root User when Curtis's mobile rang.

Surprise, surprise. It was Gina. Curtis raised his eyebrows at Turk.

'Hey congratulations, Cyrus the Virus!' She sounded genuinely impressed with Curtis's efforts in the comp. He figured he might as well make the most of his sudden fame, while trying to ignore Turk's suggestive antics.

'Yeah, thanks. Second's not too bad, I guess. Did you hear who won?'

'Yeah, I heard. Prometheus is about as good as it gets.'

'And about as shy as it gets,' said Curtis. 'Didn't even show for the prize money. Real weird.'

'Obviously likes his privacy. Anyway, weren't we going to catch up? Why don't you come over to my hotel? I'm at the Hilton. Come down to the pool.' The pool. Right. Curtis waved away Turk, who was still acting like a turkey, and weighed up his options. It didn't look like he was going to make a flight tonight anyway. One more night away from home wouldn't hurt. Surely.

'Um, yeah, OK.'

'Great. See you soon!'

When Curtis relayed the short conversation to Turk, he was beside himself with advice and suggestions. He'd obviously spent too much quality time with his computer in the past few years. He really had to get out more.

Curtis agreed to meet up with Turk later, and promised to fill him in on all the gruesome details. Yeah, right.

As Curtis headed out for a cab Turk managed to really embarrass him with a loud, 'Hey Cyrus, make sure you use a good anti-virus package!'

His idea of a very funny joke. Curtis couldn't help laughing as he hailed a cab and jumped in the back. A few hours away from this crazy place was just fine with him, and the thought of spending them with Gina by a pool was damn appealing indeed.

The Vegas Hilton was a monster. Probably designed by the same guy who built Cape Canaveral. Everything about the place was big, even the guests. But it all had a glossy, rich-club feel that Curtis just couldn't get into. So this was how the other half lived. How Gina could afford a room here was beyond him. He found a sign pointing to the pool and wound his way out into a little concrete paradise of pagodas, recliner deck chairs and martinis. It didn't take him long to spot Gina in one of the recliners. Black bikini, sunglasses and a pretty good tan. This was going to be a real chore. Somehow she'd managed to hide a small but toned bod under her day gear. Not that Curtis was looking, mind you. He did his best to swagger over to her as though he came here every day.

'Hey there,' he said casually. Probably too casually.

Gina raised her sunglasses with a smirk. 'So if it isn't Cyrus the Virus in the flesh.'

Curtis had to laugh at that. 'The one and only!'

Gina motioned to the recliner next to hers. 'Pull up a chair.' Curtis did as he was told. He didn't have his swimsuit with him, and anyway he wasn't about to blow his cool by letting Gina see his sun-starved body. He'd just have to sweat this one out.

Much to his relief, she didn't seem to care what he was wearing. She was easy to talk to, with a sharp sense of humour, and darn cute too. He could really get used to this life. It turned out Gina wasn't staying at the Hilton — she just wandered in as though she owned the place and used the pool. Curtis liked her style.

After some techno talk about Curtis's hack, they got on to their real lives. Gina was from San Diego, doing a Masters in Applied Computer Science or something. It was her third DefCon, and while she'd entered the competition only once, she'd decided it really wasn't her thing. She didn't appear to be a hardcore hacker though. She'd done a paper in network security and figured she could put it to some use in the comp.

But she appeared genuinely impressed with Curtis's efforts earlier that day, asking a lot of detailed questions on his approach, what tools he'd picked and why. The conversation led on to hacking in general.

To be honest Curtis had never really given the idea of hacking too much thought, other than actually doing it, of course. A criminal conviction was a damn good incentive for anyone to stop thinking about hacking, but Gina seemed to be interested, and so Curtis just followed along for the ride.

He also kept an eye on the pool-bar waiter, who seemed to have figured out that Curtis probably wasn't a paying customer.

'I just think the whole concept is interesting ...' said Gina. 'Hacking, why people hack, why people want to stop other people hacking. The whole net thing has exploded beyond anyone's wildest imagination.'

Curtis had to agree. 'Yeah, I guess so.'

'And although people don't realise it yet, it's changing the whole balance of power between people and governments. It's made it possible for them to come together and create virtual communities with more knowledge and influence on any issue you care to name than any single government could ever muster ...' Maybe they studied this in Applied Computer Science.

'Yeah, but it's brittle,' said Curtis.

'What do you mean?

'The entire net relies on electricity and dodgy software. Guess that makes it kind of amorphous.' Curtis got the feeling that disagreeing with her might not be the best move. 'But you're right,' he added quickly, 'people just seem to want to know stuff. Guess the faith in the establishment isn't what it used to be. There's so much spin on everything these days it's hard to know what the reality behind it all is. That's where the net's at its best.'

Gina nodded thoughtfully. 'Yeah, but consider this,' she said, 'food is regulated. Car safety is regulated. People even need licences to cut your hair. But you don't need a licence to write software. So our entire digital society is based on software built by people we don't know, who have no licences, who may not even have any quality control. And we rely on it so much. That's why hackers are so important to society. We're like astronauts pushing the edge of the envelope in a new frontier.'

Curtis hadn't heard it put like that before. Sounded like Gina was more into the hacker-hype than he'd thought. 'Well, in my experience some of them are more like graffiti artists than astronauts. They're not exactly making giant steps for mankind.'

Gina thought about that for a bit. 'Yeah, I suppose.' She thought for a minute. 'So how vulnerable do you think we are? What's a reasonable scenario of what could happen?'

It was Curtis's turn to think for a bit. If Terry could hear him talking like this he'd be nailed. 'I suppose if you really wanted to expose the vulnerability, you'd have to consider both a physical infrastructure attack as well as a computing or electronic attack. But I guess it would be relatively simple. You could start by taking out the Barking Sands time antenna in Hawaii, the one that synchronises computers. Then you could take out the global positioning system antennae playing a similar role. You might go for the Federal Reserve computer for good measure. And even though it's got a hot and cold backup, it's more than likely you'd cause chaos on Wall Street.'

Gina seemed captivated. 'Go on, what else would you do?'

Curtis racked his brain. Hard to do when you're horizontal next to a hotel pool. Gina wasn't making things any easier either for that matter.

'I guess you could explode the Alaska pipeline and the Panama Canal, maybe take out the seven bridges across the Mississippi that carry all our food. Just look for the nodes and target those. All hypothetically speaking, of course.'

Gina smiled. 'Of course! But it's scary. Really scary when you put it like that. Kind of like an aeroplane wing. The more advanced it gets the more brittle it becomes. Your average disaster suddenly becomes calamitous. Welcome to the digital age Mr ... what *is* your last name?'

Curtis hesitated. This was taking things to the next level. 'Hatch.'

'OK, Mr Hatch, nice to meet you.' She held her hand out to shake, accompanied by her killer smile.

'And nice to meet you, Gina —'

It was her turn to squirm. '... MacIntosh. But you can call me G.' Curtis wasn't sure what to smirk about first. The obviously conjured-on-the-spur-of-the-moment surname, or the Spice Girl nickname. G Spice — it had a ring to it, you had to admit.

He decided to play along. 'Nice to meet you, G. You can call me Curtis.' That got a laugh from her. 'And I'll call you Gina, if you don't mind.' That brought another laugh. And an invitation.

'Let's do dinner. You know, a real Vegas three-course special. We can hire dresses and suits here. It'd be a scream.'

Curtis wasn't so sure. 'Me in a suit would be a scream.'

But Gina had made up her mind.

'Nonsense. I'll meet you over in the lobby at seven. I'll be the one in the little black dress.' Ouch. Curtis usually couldn't spot a come-on if it held up a sign that said 'Come-On'. And the thought of Gina in an LBD wasn't helping any chance he had of him spotting one now. By the time he'd put aside the visual, he realised Gina was sliding her bottom back into a pair of jeans.

'You're going?' Talk about stating the obvious.

Gina demonstrated her multi-tasking skills by talking without a single pause in her pack-up routine. 'Girl's gotta take time to prepare for a night out in Vegas.'

Curtis smiled. It would be worth the wait. 'I might just sit here and grab some Zs. Catch you at seven.'

Gina smiled that smile again. 'Play your cards right, anything could happen! See you, Mr Virus!' Curtis squirmed. Turk would pay for that later.

Then he got it. Cards. Vegas. Badaboom, crash. He smiled in spite of himself, and stretched out on the recliner. In a final 'I dare you' to the pool-bar waiter, he pulled on his headphones, adjusted his sunglasses, and folding his hands behind his head, closed his eyes as The Edge worked his magic. *Achtung Baby* indeed.

At seven o'clock, Curtis realised he'd been conned. Not only did he look like a bad Frank Sinatra impersonator, but he'd paid to look that way. Even the pockets were false, something Curtis discovered when he'd tried to put his hand into one in a vain attempt to inject some cool back into the suit. It didn't stop him checking his hair in the reflection of a lobby shop window though.

He spotted Gina before she saw him, and a wave of nerves broke in his stomach. Not only was she beautiful, the black dress was a stunner. Talk about a make-over. She'd obviously put the preparation time to good use.

Curtis did his best to pretend he wasn't intimidated by the whole thing. 'Hey, you look fantastic!' Well, he never was much good at pretending.

'Thanks, you scrub up pretty well yourself.'

'What's the plan?' he asked. 'Fancy a cocktail before dinner, madam?'

Gina curled her arm around his. This must be a date, he thought. A real live date. He hadn't had one of those in … well, longer than he cared to remember.

Gina looked up at Curtis. She was very close. 'You read my mind,' she said mischievously.

He hooked his arm inside hers, and wheeled her round in the direction of the hotel bar. 'Come with me, Ginger!' he said.

Gina gave him that smile again, 'I'm all yours, Fred!' This was going to be a blast.

And to Curtis's pleasant surprise, it really was. It had been a while since he'd last taken a girl out and not talked computers all night. Not even once. It felt good. Gina even laughed at his jokes. They cocktailed and dined, gambled and danced. That was two firsts for Curtis in one night. He'd never gambled before. Well, not with money. And he couldn't remember the last time he'd danced, but he felt comfortable enough with Gina not to care how goofy he looked. Gina made him look good anyway.

Even a late-night thunderstorm didn't affect the mood. In fact, it seemed to help things. After a mad dash for a cab, and some dripping and laughing in the back, Gina invited herself up to Curtis's hotel room. Well, it was sort of an unspoken mutual invitation. But one thing led to another and before Curtis realised it, they were in the sack, doing the wild thing. And wild it was, too.

It was somewhere around midnight when he realised he really did miss having a life. It was probably about time he threw all this computer stuff in and got a proper job. In the real world. But that was about as far as his thinking got, as he got distracted. Gina. She was really something.

Curtis woke alone in his king-sized hotel bed. The curtains were still open, and it looked late. But that didn't seem to matter so much this morning. Like remembering a dream, he tried to recall the night before. Lots of fun, lots of laughter, and lots of sex. Oh yeah.

He scanned the room from his pillow. Even her things were gone. But while he was searching for his watch on the bedside cabinet, he found a note from her. Short, but touching: *Best night I ever had. You're something else, Mr Hatch! XX*

Couple of Xs — a good sign. He leaned back on the pillows and put his hands behind his head.

Time for some music. He fumbled with the buttons and threw the MP3 player down beside him on the bed. 'Mysterious Ways', all right. A few hours more sleep and then a flight back home. Back to the grindstone.

But first he had to pee.

He ran the gauntlet of carelessly thrown clothes from the night before to the small bathroom, and it wasn't till he was on his way back that he noticed the envelope under his door. Maybe another note from Gina. He tried to pretend he wasn't excited about opening it, leaving it on the bedside table for a few minutes while he perused the breakfast room-service menu. But curiosity won over appetite, and it wasn't long before he was ripping it open. A single page. Typed.

Dear Cyrus the Virus
Congratulations on your achievement
yesterday.
You are now eligible to compete in
the BlackHat competition.
Please do not discuss this invitation
with anyone. The BlackHat competition
is for selected competitors only. The
prize money is $1 million.
Should you wish to participate in the
BlackHat, come to the lobby of the
Orion Hotel at 2 p.m. today.
You will be met.

Um, OK. One million, huh? Curtis had to think about that for a bit. A million fucking dollars. If they were asking him, the second place-getter, that probably meant they had asked Prometheus as well. He'd love to have another go at Prometheus, million or no million. But the fact it was called BlackHat, and the secretive note, meant that it was probably an illegal hack. A live one. One in which you could get caught. And imprisoned. High stakes.

But hey, he was in Vegas. And if he hung round here long enough he might be able to see Gina again. Maybe for another night.

Curtis dialled Turk on his mobile, but he wasn't answering. Turk had probably had a harder night than he had. He left a message, 'Hi there, SuperCool, this is Cyrus. Great night, feeling lousy this morning. Got an invite to another comp. Big money this time. Might check it out. Give me a ring when you're back in the land of the living.' Two o'clock, huh? Curtis looked at the time. Room service, a couple of hours more sleep and an hour in the shower. Plenty of time.

He'd be there.

5

The Orion was a new hotel, not one Curtis had heard of before. He was feeling pretty pleased with himself as he paid the cab driver and wandered though the outer lobby. What was it with hotel developers in Vegas? They were really into big. Probably drove big red convertibles too.

The Orion was a monster. Like a giant alien mothership decked out in neon. Very swish, and probably even more expensive. The lobby was the size of an aircraft hangar, complete with a tropical rainforest and waterfall. Amazing. Curtis looked around for someone. Anyone. But company was limited to hotel workers and large, rich guests. He found a newspaper, ordered a latte at the lobby café, and stretched out in a deep leather seat in the sun. He punched the MP3 player and chose some sounds. Something loud. Time for some Tom Petty. He could wait. They'd have to find him.

They did. At five minutes past two a big guy in a suit tapped him on the shoulder. 'Mr Cyrus?'

It took Curtis a moment to realise the large guy in the expensive shiny suit was talking to him. 'Ah, yeah. And you are?' he said, pulling his headphones off.

'A friend of someone who is very keen to meet you.' Very cryptic.

Curtis rose from his seat. 'OK, then. Let's go meet him.' He followed the man to the elevators. The large man didn't say anything else — just stood there filling up the elevator. Curtis noticed that his shoes and watch were shiny, just like the suit. Even his hair was shiny, pulled back in a tight little ponytail. And his knuckles were shiny too. Shiny with old scars. Uh oh, thought Curtis to himself. Shiny Man must be someone's bag man.

He watched the elevator floor numbers flick up into the twenties. At 24 the doors opened. Curtis found himself releasing a breath he didn't realise he was holding, and drew in another deep one once he was out in the corridor.

'After you!' Curtis smiled cheekily. But Mr Shiny had left his manners down at the lobby. No smile, no talk, just walk. Eventually he stopped to knock softly on a door, then scanned the corridor before he opened it with his own key. Very mysterious. He held the door open, so Curtis accepted the invitation and walked through to find a hand thrust in his direction. He took it and checked out the guy on the other end.

Tall, very tall. Cheap watch, scuffed shoes and a suit desperately in need of a dry-clean. The goatee and the messy blond ponytail somehow seemed to fit, though.

'Cyrus! Thanks for accepting the invitation. It's great to meet you. I was hugely impressed with your efforts yesterday. And congratulations. That was one helluva hack, I'm telling you!'

Very friendly. Maybe just a little too friendly. Curtis's radar was in overdrive.

Cyrus rescued his hand. 'Not good enough to win, though.'

'Yes, yes. Prometheus is something else. Please, come in, have a seat.' The guy gestured to a giant black leather sofa in the middle of the largest hotel room Curtis had ever seen. The bar alone was bigger than his entire apartment. Curtis remained standing.

'Oh, I'm sorry. Name's Oliver Branton. But mostly people call me Ollie.' Ollie launched himself at a king-size lounger, which threatened to swallow him whole, and again waved his arm in the direction of the sofa. 'Make yourself comfortable. I'm sure you're keen to find out about the project. Can I get you a drink?' he said, waving his arm towards the bar this time. Curtis studied Ollie for a moment, and then shook his head and sat.

'Look Mr Ollie —'

Ollie looked hurt. 'Please, just Ollie.'

'OK, Ollie. I got your note. I'm here. But I haven't agreed to anything. I'm just curious. It's in my nature.' Judging by Ollie's look, Curtis figured he'd peeled off the first layer of Ollie's schmooze. In fact it seemed to make him relax. Just a little.

'Of course. Let's get down to business, shall we?' Nothing like a rhetorical question to get the ball rolling. Curtis heard a faint shuffle behind him, and turned to find Mr Shiny sitting in a chair he'd pulled up, his jacket hung over the back. Curtis was surprised he wasn't packing. Paranoia. He'd seen too many Robert de Niro movies. Focus, Curtis. Ollie began his pitch.

'I'm one of the original organisers of DefCon. Eight years ago we were about as popular as an A-rab at a KKK convention. The Feds were at war with hackers, and well … we had to go underground to survive. All because a few idiots were dumb enough to get caught. But I'm sure you know all about that. Anyway, what started out as DefCon soon became a circus. Now it's a joke. Most of them are script kiddies who come for the partying. Nothing more than vandals and graffiti artists. A few, like yourself, are serious hackers who come for the prize money. You're the ones we invented DefCon for. So a few years back, we developed BlackHat. It's not advertised, and entry is by invitation only. We usually only take the top two. We use the comp to weed out the fakes, and each year we're approached by various sponsors to put up the prize money. Real money. You with me, Curtis?'

Curtis nodded. 'I'm with you.'

Ollie nodded back. 'Good.' He paused to collect his train of thought. 'So this year we have a very special sponsor, who's kindly offered a million bucks to the winner. It's the most we've ever had put up.'

'What's the catch?' Curtis figured there had to be one.

'Catch?' Ollie was playing dumb, so Curtis decided to help him out.

'Well, no sponsor I know of has a million bucks to throw around on testing their software. Maybe the government, but they're hardly going to let a bunch of nobodies loose on their systems. Financial institutions perhaps. But they'd employ a full-time security tech to monitor and patch it for a fraction of that. So my guess is it's a live network. Is that the catch?' Curtis heard Mr Shiny shift in his seat. Still, Ollie didn't look rattled in the slightest.

'You're a bright young man, Cyrus. Let's just say that before I can tell you anymore about BlackHat, I need to be as sure of your integrity as I am of your intelligence.' Ollie nodded at Mr Shiny, who thrust a sheet of paper and pen under Curtis's nose.

'We can't go any further unless you agree to sign a confidentiality agreement. I'm sure you've signed these things before. Just gives us some security. After all, you could be a Fed, for all I know.' Curtis had to smile at that. So did Ollie. 'Have a good read. If you decide you don't want to sign, you'll be escorted back to your hotel. This meeting never happened. This conversation never took place. Take your time.'

Wunderbar, thought Curtis. He read the agreement. No letterhead. No company name or file reference. Just a standard, everyday confidentiality agreement not to divulge anything to anyone else. Of course some lawyer had been paid a shitload of money to say that in five long paragraphs, which most spellchecks would highlight as ungrammatically long.

Curtis realised he wasn't going to find out anymore about BlackHat unless he signed. And he needed to know more before he could make a decision. Even if he bailed, as long as he didn't reveal the nature of the project, he wasn't going to be in breach of the contract. He had to wonder, though — if BlackHat involved hacking a live network, which was clearly illegal unless it belonged to the sponsor, just how legally binding was this confidentiality agreement going to be? Still, play the game and learn the rules as you go. That's Hacking 101. He signed on the dotted line: Cyrus V. Let's see how legally binding that was.

Curtis lifted the agreement over his shoulder to Mr Shiny. 'I'd like a copy of that, if you don't mind,' he said.

Ollie seemed to relax, and began waving his hands in front of him like an honest politician. 'So tell me, Cyrus, what would you like to know? I'll try to answer your questions as fully as possible, within the bounds of *my* confidentiality agreement, of course.' Yeah, right.

Curtis focused for a moment. 'OK, Ollie. For starters, who's the sponsor?'

Ollie smiled apologetically. 'I'm sorry, I'm not at liberty to reveal the identity of the sponsor.' Surprise, surprise. 'But I can tell you that your identity won't be revealed to the sponsor either. Goes both ways.' Fair enough.

'Who's the target?' asked Curtis nonchalantly.

Ollie was obviously expecting this one, and started waving his hands again on cue.

'If you don't mind, I'd like to brief you and Prometheus on the project together. It's quite detailed, and to be fair to both of you, I'd like to make sure you both get exactly the same information at exactly the same time.'

Made sense, Curtis figured. OK, another question. 'How long have we got?'

'As long as it takes. BlackHat is goal-oriented, not time-specific.' Curtis had to fight back a wry smile. Ollie had missed his calling as a college counsellor. 'But don't forget you're competing against one another. And Prometheus comes with a pretty awesome rep.' Yeah, yeah. Drop the 'Survivor' show-host routine, Ollie.

'So back to my earlier question. It's a live network?'

This time Ollie nodded seriously. 'Yes it is, Cyrus.' Curtis shifted in his seat and stole a look at Mr Shiny, who was intently picking one of his fingernails. He turned back to Ollie, who was still studying him, waiting for some response to the revelation he was going to be doing something unlawful.

Curtis took his time. This was it. The moment of truth. Everything up until now he could explain away. Terry would give him the benefit of the doubt, in view of his emotional state following Roly's funeral. He and Turk could head back home and their parole officers would be none the wiser. The thing was, he and Turk would be none the richer. A cool mill. It would turn around his screwed-up life, and he could start over, with a clean slate. Sure it was a risk. But hey, this was Vegas.

'All right,' said Curtis slowly. Meaningfully. 'I'm in.'

Ollie slapped his knees in appreciation and pulled himself out of the sofa. 'Great!' Even Mr Shiny looked up, the first sign of interest crossing his prize-fighter face.

Ollie stood, waiting expectantly for Curtis to follow. 'I know you're going to do real well, man. Real well!' Curtis stood to find Ollie's hand on his shoulder, leading him through the vast hotel room.

'Let's get down to business, shall we? I know you're keen to find out what this is all about, and Prometheus is waiting for us in the boardroom. We're all keen to get this show on the road!'

If it hadn't been for Ollie's schmoozey routine, it would all have been too weird. Somehow, the former hacker turned DefCon organiser and hacking agent made the surreal seem normal. Ollie, Curtis and Mr Shiny followed the ceiling-to-floor windows around the corner of the room to another door, where Ollie proceeded to punch in a security PIN.

OK folks, here we go.

It was another atmosphere entirely inside the room that Ollie so euphemistically called a boardroom. The tasteless trappings of easy Vegas money had been replaced by something Curtis felt more closely resembled digital-corporate cool.

The room had probably been designed by an advertising exec with too much money. Dark, with lots of black, dark blues and purples, and a shiny black boardroom table. Mr Shiny would feel right at home in here. Banks of monitors and televisions, all silent and black. But the most striking thing were the chairs. Black elliptical half-spheres, which actually hung from the ceiling. Really out there. So unless the chair was facing you directly, you couldn't see if anyone was in it, let alone who they were. Maybe that's how these guys preferred to do business.

Ollie gestured towards one of the spheres. 'Please, Cyrus. Have a seat and we'll begin.' Curtis chose a chair at the back of the table. He had to admit though, it was damn comfortable. He wondered if one of these would fit in his apartment back in the Pitts. Probably not. Oh well.

Ollie had ensconced himself in the chair that the board chairman probably used. Either him or the Mafioso don. He paused, making sure he had Curtis's full attention.

'First of all, thank you for agreeing to participate in BlackHat. This is a unique competition, for the best of the best. You two have proven yourselves worthy of that title.' Curtis did a double take around the darkened room.

Two? Prometheus was in the room with him? He searched each of the spherical chairs, most of which he couldn't see into, but none of them had moved since he'd entered the room. Curtis's confusion wasn't going to stop Ollie's little routine though.

'Cyrus, meet Prometheus!'

Curtis was excited. There was no denying that. For the past few years he'd been reading about the exploits of the legendary Prometheus. His hacks weren't necessarily bad or disruptive. It was just that they were so well executed, and his targets were often high-profile organisations and companies who had a reputation for boasting about their security systems. Like the FBI, the State Department and the Air Force. Risky hacks, you had to admit, but Prometheus had somehow pulled them off without getting caught. And as Prometheus's reputation had grown, so had his penchant for anonymity. As far as Curtis knew, no one knew what he looked like, or where he worked or lived. The only contact he had with other hackers was via the net. Anonymously.

So here he was in the same room as Prometheus. Now that was something. Maybe it wasn't worth a million bucks, but even if he lost he might learn something along the way. One of the chairs began to swivel round to face Curtis, and in the darkness he did a double take. A real are-my-eyes-working-properly double take. Because sitting in the chair across the table from him was … Gina!

For a moment Curtis's brain let him down. 'Gina! What are you doing …' Then the smile from across the table and his own brain caught up with each other. Curtis wasn't amused.

'What the fuck is this?' he said, getting up from his chair. This obviously wasn't what Ollie had planned and even Mr Shiny was starting to look interested. In the wrong sort of way.

'What's the problem, Cyrus?' asked Ollie.

'She's the fucking problem. If that's Prometheus then I'm the President!'

Ollie was clearly getting rattled by the unexpected turn of events. 'Cyrus, please sit down! I have every reason to believe the person sitting across from you is, in actual fact, the one and only Prometheus.'

His sentence was punctuated by the ruffle of a shiny suit and the gagging odour of overcooked cologne. Curtis decided to sit, and Gina spoke for the first time since she'd been lying naked in bed with him.

'I wanted to tell you. You have to believe me, Cyrus.'

Curtis examined her closely, trying to work out two things — whether or not she was telling the truth, and whether or not he still wanted to spend another night with her.

'You won the comp,' said Curtis. It was more of a statement than a question.

Gina nodded.

'So why didn't you stay to collect your prize money?' Gina smiled the way women sometimes do when a man asks a dumb question but they don't want to make him feel dumb with the answer.

'I'm here for the BlackHat. That was just pocket money compared to this. I was invited to compete, and the comp was the test. Now they know I'm Prometheus, and like you, I'm here to find out why we're here.' Made sense, Curtis had to admit. But he couldn't help feeling bitter. And he was going to enjoy it while it lasted. He decided to ignore her.

Curtis returned to Ollie, who was clearly surprised by his outburst, but looking even more convinced he had the real Prometheus sitting in front of him.

'I wasn't aware that you two knew each other …'

'We don't,' interrupted Curtis. 'Just get on with it.'

If Ollie didn't like being spoken to that way, he didn't show it. He went right on as though nothing had happened. 'Now, if we can return to why we're here. I'm going to show you some video. I should add that what I'm about to show you is not confidential, stolen or in breach of copyright in any way. In fact it is currently available on the net. There are two short clips. They're black and white, so please excuse the quality.'

While Ollie shuffled about with a remote and aimed it at one of the screens, Curtis turned his attention back to Gina. She seemed so unruffled by the whole thing, staring intently at the monitor, waiting for it to come to life. He couldn't believe it. And she was so beautiful. He couldn't help it, but she was.

Curtis's reverie was broken by the first real light that had entered the room since he'd come in. Ollie had got the monitor working. Curtis swivelled his chair back to watch, but just enough so that he could still keep an eye on Gina.

'Here we go,' said Ollie enthusiastically. 'As I said, the quality is terrible, but I'll just let you watch it the first time and we can go over it frame by frame if we need to.' As the monitor flickered to life, a grainy picture of black, white and grey burst onto the screen. The camera that had taken the shots was being shaken, and then trained on something in the distance. The focus was adjusted and the picture became clearer. As clear as a snowstorm in Alaska.

Curtis had to squint to make anything out at all. It looked like rows of large buildings. Aircraft hangars. Huge ones, like the sort NASA used for the shuttle. But he could also make out, as the camera zoomed in, a Nazi swastika over one of the buildings. A swastika? Weird.

Curtis kept watching, trying to make out more of the picture, but whoever was holding the camera was having trouble focusing, because the screen kept going white. Then the camera zoomed right back, and Curtis could see that the whiteout wasn't the fault of the cameraman. In fact, it was what was making it impossible for him. Because the white seemed to be emanating from one of the hangar buildings. It was shining so brightly that at times the whole screen was white. Curtis could tell the camera was being shaken by whoever was holding it. If what he was seeing was real it would probably make him shake too.

It was right out of an 'X-Files' episode. Curtis forgot about Gina and Ollie completely. Leaning forward, he watched as a black disc-shaped object rose from the top of the hangar building and seemed to hover in midair. The camera was really jerking around now, and Curtis sensed that this footage was something special. Then the monitor went black. The short movie had finished.

The room was silent as the occupants tried to grasp what they had just seen. Ollie was the first to speak. 'You know every time I see that — and I've seen it a few times now I can tell you — it just seems to get weirder and weirder.'

'What did we just see?' asked Curtis.

Ollie shook his head in amazement. 'Well, as far as I can make out, we just saw some footage of what looked like a UFO over a German World War II aircraft hangar. Did you see the swastika?'

Curtis nodded. 'Yeah, I got that. What I meant was, what did we just see? What's the significance?'

Ollie nodded seriously, as though fully understanding Curtis's question the first time, and placed the remote down carefully on the board table. 'What you just saw was an mpeg downloaded from a website three weeks ago. The webmaster claims this footage is a copy of an original, which was sent to him anonymously over the net. He just put it out there for the rest of the world to see. You know how the story goes ...'

Gina spoke up for the first time. 'What sort of website?'

'Well, the people who traffic in this sort of stuff aren't your usual tax-paying citizens. This was downloaded from a website dealing primarily with conspiracy theories. You know, wacko versions of history. Everything's part of a cover-up. But the nature of this footage has got our sponsor really interested. He's a keen collector of historical military information — if it's real, that is. Anyway, the website we found this on claims the sender said it was actual footage of the Führer himself leaving

Berlin as the walls came tumbling down. He even claimed it was shot by a Russian infantryman, no less.' Curtis was damn curious now.

'OK. So you've got some mpeg of what's supposed to be some actual footage from World War II. What's that got to do with us?'

'Our sponsor wants you to find out where the mpeg came from. Who sent it to him, that sort of thing. He wants to find out if it's a fake. And he can only do that by going back to the original footage. Finding who turned the original footage into an mpeg and sent it anonymously over the net to this weirdo's website is going to be your job.'

Gina's turn now. 'Is that it? Your sponsor's going to fork out a million dollars for that? I don't get it. Seems way too much for a simple job like that. What's the catch?' Curtis wanted to shout 'Yeah, that's right! You go girl!' Instead he just nodded thoughtfully. Ollie looked pained, as though he wasn't being trusted as being straight with them.

'Look. Think about this. Something that appears to be ancient historical film appears anonymously on the net. And the website claims the person who sent it believes it to be proof that Adolf Hitler didn't die in Berlin, as everyone knows he was supposed to — as we've always been taught in school and in the history books. The catch is the significance of the footage. It would change modern history completely. And that's worth a million dollars to our sponsor. Now if he's got the money, I'm not going to argue with how he wants to spend it. I'm just telling you what you two have to do to earn it. One of you, that is — this is a competition, remember.'

Curtis looked at Gina, and found she was looking squarely back at him. Sizing up the competition. Now they were competing against each other with a million at stake. Curtis wasn't entirely sure how he felt about that.

'Now before you rush off and start planning your strategies, there's a second piece of footage I need to show you as well.' Curtis and Gina both turned back to Ollie. 'This is off the same website, also an mpeg, and also claimed by the webmaster to be a copy of authentic footage. And this one's really interesting, I can tell you …'

Ollie swung back to the monitor and aimed the remote at it. This time the picture was clearer, but again, there was lots of white. But the hangars were no longer there. Just lots of white. A hell of a lot of white. Then Curtis realised he was looking at ice. He established a horizon where the white turned to grey, and picked out the little black dots that whoever was holding the camera was trying to capture. But to do this the cameraman had to swing in wild arcs. The horizon would roll over and back, causing the picture to focus off into the distance.

The picture then cut to one of the most bizarre sights Curtis had ever seen. The camera was now held still, and focused on what appeared to be the back of a ship. A military ship. Curtis could make out the barrels of anti-aircraft guns and a large helideck. All around the ship was white. Ice. But that wasn't what was freaking him. Above the helideck on the ship was the same sort of UFO thing that had hovered briefly over the hangar in Berlin. A ladder was extended from under the UFO, and men in some sort of uniform were climbing down it onto the deck of the ship. Before Curtis could identify anything else the mpeg ended, and the monitor resumed its now comforting blackness.

'Wow,' said Curtis, impressed. 'Is that for real? Have you had it analysed?'

Ollie nodded. 'The sponsor has had some of the best people in their field examine the mpegs, and without access to the originals the footage appears to be authentic. They can find no signs of doctoring, or any evidence that they're hoaxes. The sponsor will only know for sure once he's had access to the original footage. And if they're not a sophisticated hoax, history will never be the same.'

Curtis had been absorbing all this, while still thinking about the second mpeg. 'Where's the second one shot? That looks like ice to me.'

Ollie nodded again. 'Yes it does. As far as the sponsor can figure, it's a polar ice cap, or somewhere very close to it. And we don't really have much on the ship at all — the uniforms appear to be US Air Force, and of a World War II vintage, but the expedition badges are pretty pixellated, and don't resemble anything we could find on record.'

'What did your sponsor say about the UFO thing?' asked Gina.

But Ollie wasn't forthcoming. 'Not much at all. That's part of the mystery. Fantastic, isn't it?' Ollie was starting to annoy Curtis, but since a million dollars was at stake here, he decided not to show it.

'So let me get this straight, Ollie. You have someone who will pay either of us a million dollars, and all we have to do is track down where these mpegs came from? Is that it?'

Ollie did the hand thing again and smiled. 'That just about sums it up, Cyrus. Whichever of you is the first to bring back proof of origin of the mpegs, so that we have access to the originals, will leave a million bucks richer. Not bad for a day's work, huh?'

But Curtis still wasn't completely convinced. 'Why don't you just hire a private detective?'

'In a sense we've hired two private detectives, with specialist skills in cyber-forensics. But don't think that this is just a job you can do from your desktop. There may be demand for some of your other skills, such as what we now call social engineering. In fact, your ability to succeed may depend upon a flexible approach to problem-solving. This isn't a simulation, this is the real world.' Thanks for the moral lesson, Ollie two hands, thought Curtis. He looked across at Gina, who was sitting thoughtfully, taking it all in. Curtis couldn't figure her out. If that was Prometheus then there was one hell of a brain inside that pretty head. Cutest hacker he'd ever met. So why the hell hadn't she been straight with him last night? Curtis could spot a game player when he saw one. And he didn't like being played.

He forced his rising anger down, and turned his attention back to the dark room. And the million dollars. 'I'll need clean access to the net, and an anonymously routed ISP. I don't care how that's organised, but it's non- negotiable. I'm not going to jail for this. Even for a million dollars. Got that, Ollie?'

'It's all been taken care of. You have a room each here at the Oasis. You can collect your keys on the way out. We've arranged to have the video-surveillance cameras on a one-minute loop, so there'll be no record of your being here. There are a couple of other small inconveniences to secure your privacy, but I'm sure you won't find them too obstructive. You'll find you have everything you need waiting for you in the room, including the URL of the website in question. If you have any problems, call Mr Styles here, and he will see to it. As for the project, I'd appreciate your keeping me posted on your progress. I'm sure you can understand that the sponsor is very keen for some good news.'

Curtis turned his chair to look at Mr Styles. The name fit like a hand in a boxing glove. At least he wasn't called Mr Yellow or Mr Pink, but Curtis was getting the feeling this situation was getting uncannily close to a Tarantino movie. Minus the blood. Shiny Styles returned Curtis's once-over with a steady, expressionless gaze. Tough guy.

But Ollie wasn't finished yet. 'If you need to travel, you'll have to make your own arrangements. As a measure of good faith, our sponsor has provided you with $5000 each.' He pulled out two thick envelopes, and sent them spinning across the table towards them. 'Of course we won't require receipts, but you will be expected to account for every dollar upon completion of the project.'

Ollie got up and stretched. 'So that just about wraps this up. I'm really looking forward to hearing how you get on. Good luck, and may the best hacker win!' He smiled at his own joke. What a funny guy. And with that, the briefing was over.

Shiny Styles escorted them back down to the hotel lobby with the same level of polite chitchat he'd shown on the way up. None. But this time Gina — Prometheus — was with them. Curtis showed her the same courtesy as Shiny.

Shiny handed them a key each, and returned to the stratosphere of the upper floors. Curtis and Gina stood looking at each other, a key in their hot little hands, but he didn't have anything to say to her. He turned his back and left her standing by the elevator.

Out in the lobby things hadn't changed at all. Just Curtis's whole world. Hitler and UFOs. This was way too much. Even if he got busted and had to explain all this to Terry or the Feds, no one would believe him. And the woman he'd just fallen for wasn't who he thought she was. He wasn't sure what was upsetting him the most. All of it. He needed some fresh air and some thinking time. Outside.

'Hey Curtis …' It was Gina. So what. 'Curtis! Will you hold on!' For you? Sorry, darling.

'For God's sake, Curtis. Will you just stop and let me explain? Explain what? That you strung me a line and hooked me like a stunned mullet?'

Well fuck you, Miss Prometheus. Curtis walked out into the dry heat of the Nevada sun, threw on his shades, and considered his options. He wasn't ready to do the business yet.

'Where are you going?' Jesus, she was still following him.

'Somewhere you aren't.'

'Listen Curtis, I couldn't tell you who I was. But my real name is Gina. This is me. The real me. All that stuff is just something I do. And I didn't tell you about it 'cos I wanted to protect you. The less you know about that the better. I knew Ollie from DefCon a few years back. He contacted me to ask if I was interested in a BlackHat. All he said was that it was a big one. But I had to go through the comp just like you. That's why I didn't stay for the money — I sure didn't need the publicity you and your friend got on stage. I was watching from the back of the hall. You have to learn to be more inconspicuous. Your friend just attracts attention —'

'You leave Turk out of this. I owe him more than you'll ever know. But you probably wouldn't know a lot about friendship and trust, would you?' Hope that hurts.

'That's not fair.' Yep, bull's-eye.

'Maybe not, but from where I'm standing it's the truth. You were shitting me, and I don't like being shat on. Go find someone else to play your little games on.'

'Oh for God's sake, Curtis,' said Gina angrily. 'Will you stop behaving like a sulky little boy and grow up? Everything that happened between us was real. It wasn't a game. Do you think I sleep with people just for fun?'

If she was waiting for an answer she wasn't going to get one.

'I see,' she said, finally. 'Well, if you're going to let your ego get in the way of a million dollars you're not the person I thought you were. I had a wonderful time last night. But business is business, Curtis. Opportunities like this don't come along every day. Shit, they hardly ever come along at all.'

Curtis had reached the roadway. He had the choice of keeping walking, with Gina half-running, half-walking alongside him, or sitting on the edge of a fountain pool. He chose the latter. Gina took this as a sign he was thawing, and sat down beside him.

'What do I have to do to prove to you that I'm for real? You want me to walk away from a million dollars? Are you scared I'm going to beat you? You afraid of being beaten by a woman? Again?' Whoa girl, you're pushing it now.

'Of course not. I know you're better than me. You proved it yesterday. The only reason I'm still in is more out of curiosity than anything else. It's one for my memoirs, that's for sure.'

Gina allowed herself a smile. 'Do you believe all this? Mpegs of old forgotten film posted on a website that could change history?'

Curtis tilted his head and shrugged his shoulders. 'All we have to do is find them. What Ollie's sponsor does with them is his business. As long as he pays up, I don't care.'

'A million dollars is a lot of money just to find some old movies,' said Gina.

Curtis shrugged again. 'Some people have more money than sense. I'd love to know what that feels like.'

Gina suddenly got a faraway look in her eye. The same look she had when she asked him to go to dinner with her. 'Why don't we split it?' she said. What?

'What do you mean, split?' asked Curtis, suspicious again.

'Well, you're right. It's more than enough money for both of us. So why don't we cooperate instead of competing. If we're still together after all this then we come out equal. We go in as partners and combine our talents. What do you say, Cyrus?'

Curtis's head said no, but his heart was screaming, 'Go for it, my boy!' He had to admit, she was meeting him halfway on this. Maybe she was for real after all. Half a million, one million. It all fell in the category of a shitload of money. More than enough. More importantly, it improved his chances of seeing any of it.

'You haven't seen my talents, how do you know they're worth partnering?'

Gina unleashed one of those killer smiles again. 'I saw enough last night.'

That got Curtis grinning. 'OK, OK! Enough already.' Damn it if she hadn't found his weak spot. The male ego. Must be like stealing candy from a baby. Let's just hope the job was as easy. 'OK, Ginger, you're on,' he said finally.

'You won't regret it. Fred.' They shared a laugh and one of those looks that said they were trusting each other again. It felt good.

'God, I've got to get out of this heat,' said Gina, fanning her shirt against her chest. It might have been a felony in some states.

Curtis jumped at the excuse for some space. 'Yeah, I've got some things I need to do before we join the millionaire's club. Why don't you go and see what you can find out about the target? I'll probably be a couple of hours — can you manage that long without me?'

She laughed at that. 'It'll be tough! Anyway, I need a long shower and some Zs before I can look at another computer screen. Wake me when you get in.'

Uh oh. That look again. She waved her key in front of Curtis's face. Her room number was instantly inscribed on his memory.

'You got it. Take care, Miss iMac. I'll see you soon.'

'Bye Curtis … and thanks … for listening to me.'

'Forget it. Let's start thinking about how we're going to spend the prize money.'

As he watched those jeans make their way back into the lobby, Curtis couldn't help thinking that maybe things really were looking up. He put his headphones on and punched up a song. U2. There was a spring in his step as he left Gina, and a million dollars, waiting for him at the Orion. He fought back a silly grin. It felt good to finally have something to smile about. Light my way Miss Prometheus.

6

On his way back to the hotel, Curtis tried Turk a couple of times on his cellphone. There was no answer when he buzzed Turk's room either. Curtis wasn't bothered — his main concern was that Turk was up to something on the wrong side of right somewhere, and that he'd somehow be implicated. But his first priority was to find an internet café and check his emails. He'd been away from his life too long for Terry Hay not to notice.

Curtis found a seedy coffee house with a couple of old Macs out back, doing its best to look like a place people would actually want to sit down and eat. The coffee was weak and lukewarm — nearly as bad as airline coffee. But for a dollar an hour he could surf the web and check his emails. He was glad he did. Just one new mail. From Terry. He'd received Curtis's email about going on leave for a few days to attend the funeral of a close friend. Somehow Terry had found out it was Roly's memorial — he dropped it into his reply ever-so-casually, but it hit home like a brick. Terry was still keeping a close eye on him, and this was a gentle reminder. Hell, it wouldn't have surprised him if Terry had watched the service through some binos somewhere. It wasn't that Terry was overly suspicious of Curtis. It was more of a paternal role. Maybe Terry wasn't loved enough as a kid, and had taken Curtis under his wing as therapy. Hell knows.

But Curtis owed him for going in to bat for him when he was facing a prison sentence, and for helping him back onto the straight and narrow with the job at Trident. And Terry never let Curtis forget it. Maybe it was time to come clean. Well, semi-clean at least.

Curtis's fingers punched the filthy keyboard hard. Most of the keys had a coating of what Curtis was hoping was just coffee, and they stuck like superglue ...

```
Terry
So you heard about Roly. Thanks for
the kind words. I need a few days to
myself. I'll stay in touch via email,
same day return as agreed. Can't
understand things at the moment. Need
to try and figure out why. Cut me
some slack. I'm OK.
Curtis
```

Curtis hoped he sounded suitably cut up over the whole Roly thing for Terry to give him a few days' grace. He figured the less Terry knew about where he was the better, and the web-based email would be virtually impossible to trace. He sat in front of the screen for a while, lost in thought. His mind kept turning back to Roly. He'd been a big part of his life. He was going to miss him. He remembered the envelope Turk had given him. He'd said his mother had wanted Curtis to have it. It must have been a mistake. But when he pulled the envelope open he found a CD ROM game with a label on it. The label said RETURN TO CURTIS HATCH in thick red ink. It wasn't his writing though. Not his game either.

It was an empire-building strategy game, the kind Curtis had been playing a lot online recently. He lifted the disk out of the container and shoved it into the D: drive. The auto-start kicked in and the game loaded. Up came the familiar load-up screenshots. The pre-game movie started, and Curtis clicked it through. But when the main menu screen came up, in the player-name space, the words didn't say Player One as they were supposed to. Instead, it said: *Welcome to the game — Enjoy the rules! — Gonad.*

Curtis felt the hair on the back of his neck stand up. He was being played. This game had been out less than a year, and he hadn't lain eyes on Roly for at least four. Something was going on here. If the game was Roly's, then Roly was Gonad. He was sure it wasn't coincidental. And if Roly was Gonad and he didn't tell Curtis who he was, then Curtis wanted to know what the *fuck* was going on.

He started up the game. It ran normally. He played a few scenarios, using different combinations of civilisations and periods of history. It was just a game. A game. With rules. That got Curtis thinking. He clicked out of the game, and brought up the net browser. Then he did a search using an underground search engine he'd heard of a few years ago. It was still operating. Eventually he found what he was looking for. Cheat codes. He downloaded a screenshot and sent it to the printer. Curtis noticed that fat had soaked through onto both pages he'd printed out. Then he loaded up the game again, and started a single player.

When the game was underway, Curtis typed in the cheat code for more wood. Instantly the game froze. The screen went black, and suddenly a list in DOS appeared. Lists of ISP numbers, access codes, Federal and State computer network numbers, user names and passwords. It was hot property. Curtis realised why Roly had put his name on the CD, even though it wasn't his. He knew Curtis would be able to recognise it as his blacklist and deal with it responsibly. Like destroying it as fast as possible. Curtis killed the disk and put the game back in his pocket.

Not here. Not now.

He logged off and searched for a toilet to wash the scum and grease off his fingers. When he discovered the state of the basin in the john he decided he risked less chance of infection by wiping his hands on his shirt. But he couldn't help himself as he left the café. As he passed the counter he served one at the FUB'er behind the counter. That's Fat Ugly Bastard for the uninitiated. The guy was smoking and reading a magazine, stopping now and then to wipe the ash off the page and wipe his brow with his stained apron.

'You ever clean this place, man?' said Curtis. The FUB'er looked up from his magazine, which Curtis noticed had a lot more pictures than words. He didn't even bat an eyelid.

'Not since the wife left. That was her job.' Go figure. The flip side of Vegas. Don't see that in the brochures.

Back at his hotel room, Curtis noticed with the pleasant surprise of someone who doesn't spend a lot of time in hotels that his room had been made up. He made a mental note: top of the list after getting the money was a maid.

He changed shirts and washed his hands a dozen times to get the smell of the sticky keyboard off them, then packed a few essentials into his backpack — clean shirt and underwear, toothbrush, condoms — and made his way to Turk's room. He thumped on the door a few times, but there was no sound of movement from the other side. Probably still comaed from the night before. Curtis figured he should at least check with reception. He knew he shouldn't be expecting Turk to behave like a normal human being by leaving him a message somewhere, but he could at least give him the benefit of the doubt.

The woman at reception was no use. Polite, yes, but useful, no. No messages, not checked out, and hadn't seen anyone resembling Mr Turk at all. Wonderful. But on his way out the revolving doors of the lobby one of the concierge dudes ran over with an expression of 'man have I got some news for you' on his face.

'You looking for your friend? The guy with the blond hair and glasses?'

Curtis hesitated. 'Yeah, you seen him?' He could feel a tip coming on here.

The concierge nodded enthusiastically. 'Try the roof. He's been up there all night!' The roof! What the hell?

Curtis nodded. 'OK, thanks. How do I get up there?'

'There's a health spa and swimming pool up there. Just take the elevator to the top floor. You can't miss him.' Curtis folded a five-dollar note into the concierge's pink little hand and headed for the elevators, shaking his head as he went. The roof?

'Hey Turk! What the hell's going on?' Turk was mid-stroke, uncoiling the driver from behind his head, and he didn't look up or register Curtis's arrival as he sent the white ball screaming off the hotel roof in a wide arcing slice. He watched the ball disappear into a hotel carpark some 18 storeys below, before turning to Curtis.

'Hey dude, look what you did! That was a 250-yard shot if you hadn't put me off!' He pulled another ball from his pocket, placed it on the tee and lined up another shot. Curtis noticed that the tee Turk was using was actually a woman's bra, with the tip pushed in to hold the ball. He looked around for the owner of the bra, and found not one but three women, all in various states of undress, sleeping around the pool in the hotel deck chairs. Turk whacked another shot, watching the arc of the ball as it disappeared after bouncing off the roof of a laundry truck.

Curtis lost it. Big time. 'What the fuck's going on, Turk? You lost your fucking mind?'

Turk just lined up another shot. 'Nice to see you too, man. Just having a little fun! I can't seem to stop slicing my three wood. Maybe I'm moving my head too much.'

'Maybe you're losing your fucking head!' Curtis grabbed the driver off Turk. 'You could kill someone doing that! Think about that for a second!' Turk wobbled on his feet. He was out of it.

'Sure, man. Anything you say.'

'What have you been doing? I tried ringing you. Did you get my message?'

Turk just smiled. Curtis could tell there was a connection problem here. He motioned towards the women. 'And who are they?'

Turk's mind meandered in slow motion. 'Oh, yeah … they're just some friends I met last night.' Curtis wasn't impressed.

'You paying for friends now, Turk?' Turk didn't respond, and Curtis lost it again. 'You fucking idiot, Turk. We're not even supposed to be here, remember? And we didn't pay for our rooms, remember? And in case you've forgotten, we're both still on parole, remember?'

'Hey chill out, dude!' Turk threw his ball over the side of the building. 'I'm just having some fun. We used to do that too, remember?'

'Yeah, right. Getting arrested by the FBI is great fun! I had a ball being interviewed for 48 hours straight and going to court and bankrupting my parents with lawyers' fees. I know Roly had a great time in prison. Man, I was so disappointed when I only got parole and missed out on all the fun he had inside! So why don't we just turn ourselves in now and really start enjoying ourselves. And maybe we won't have to 'cos if the hotel doesn't, then one of your "friends" probably will!' The angry silence between them was palpable. But Turk wasn't backing down, so Curtis tried reason.

'Listen, man! I'm onto something big. Really big. I'll tell you more about it in a few days, but when it's over I'll buy you enough friends to screw yourself silly. But I need a low profile right now. That means you too. I don't know how you paid for all this, and I don't want to know. Just keep your head down. Please.' Turk eyed him suspiciously, weighing up Curtis's argument against his own. Slowly Turk's face spread into the all-too-familiar mischievous grin.

'Sure, man — you only had to ask.' Curtis smiled too, in spite of himself.

'It's just for a few days. I might not be reachable for a while, but I'll contact you as soon as I can.'

Turk suddenly looked interested. 'Yeah? Where you going?'

Curtis shook his head. 'I don't know yet. Maybe nowhere. Just make sure you leave your cellphone on. I might need some help, and if I do, I'll need you sober, OK?

'OK, man.' Turk shook Curtis's hand like the homeboys in the movies, the way they used to do before the bust. 'You got it.'

But Curtis still had his doubts. 'I'm trusting you, man.'

Turk smiled back at him. 'Hey, I need a few days' sleep anyway. Besides, this game is impossible, it's much easier on Playstation!'

By the time Curtis got back to the Oasis, he was hanging out for another dose of Gina. Soon he was bounding down the hotel corridors like a love-sick puppy, and knocking on Gina's door with a stupid grin. Sickening really.

'Honey, I'm home!' he said, as Gina opened the door for him. Curtis laughed at his own joke, but it fell kinda flat when he noticed he was the only one who found it funny. She was wearing a hotel robe, with her hair wrapped up in a towel, but he could tell by the look on her face that she was in work mode, not play mode. Damn.

'Hey, come and have a look at this,' she said, turning back into the room. 'This is the website Ollie was talking about. The stuff on here is incredible.'

Curtis followed her inside and closed the door. Gina had well and truly moved in. There was girl stuff all over the bathroom, and she was sitting at a computer set up on the desk. Curtis leant over her shoulder to look at the screen, as much to smell her freshly showered scent as to look at the website. He read out the name of the site.

'ConspiracyWatch-dot-com,' he said sarcastically. 'Now that's original. I hope we're surfing anonymously, Prometheus?'

Gina nodded impatiently. 'I'm using a modified version of FreeSurf. We're undetectable. Even our local ISP can't trace us.'

He read aloud the text immediately below the title.

```
The Truth is In Here. America has a
long history of deceiving,
manipulating and exploiting the
mindstate of its own people.
Information you need to know and will
not be told about via the mainstream
media can be found here.
```

Curtis threw his pack onto the bed, sat down and kicked his shoes off. 'I don't know how these guys sleep at night with all these conspiracies going on. Most of us call it collective paranoia. You don't want to join me in the shower first? I'm sure ConspiracyWatch will still be there when we get back.'

But Gina wasn't in the mood for romance. Or even a quickie for that matter. 'Pick an event,' she said excitedly. 'You know, some major significant event of the last century. Don't go for the obvious. Pick something really obscure — it's got a take on everything in here!' Curtis lay back on the bed and thought for a second.

OK, something obscure. 'How about the sinking of the *Lusitania*?'

Gina turned back to him, looking confused. 'The sinking of the what?'

Curtis rolled over on one elbow to face her. 'The *Lusitania*. It was a passenger liner sunk just before we got into World War I. Sunk off the coast of Ireland, I think, by a German U-boat. It basically turned the tide of public opinion in the States and led to us declaring war on the Kaiser a couple of years later.' Gina was already entering *Lusitania* into the keyword search engine on the website.

'How do you spell *Lusit* —'

'L-U-S-I-T-A-N-I-A' Curtis was guessing, but he wasn't letting that on to Gina.

'Here we go … got it! Check this out!' She'd found something. Curtis got up and leant over her again to look at the screen. His face was just inches from Gina's ear lobe. A dozen thoughts crossed his mind, but Gina's curiosity was infectious. He focused on the web article — the story looked convincing. And its detail was disturbing. It alleged that the *Lusitania* was carrying a large cargo of munitions that was the ultimate cause of her demise. It said that the British Admiralty, and in particular First Lord Winston Churchill, had deliberately put the ship in harm's way to encourage an incident that might bring the United States into the war, even though the German government had taken out advertisements in all its newspapers advising Germans not to sail on her.

It claimed that the *Lusitania* was sent at a considerably reduced speed into an area where a U-boat was known to be waiting, and her escorts withdrawn, despite the fact that the liner received a series of warnings in the two days before her sinking — warnings which were ignored. According to supposed eyewitnesses, several messages between the *Lusitania* and the British Admiralty were missing from the official investigation records, and they included urgent requests from the captain to divert from the planned route. The requests were refused, and the *Lusitania* steamed on into the annals of history, with the loss of over 1000 lives, and significantly (according to the author), 123 Americans. The rest, as they say, is history.

Curtis shook his head in disbelief. Sure it made for convincing reading. But he'd seen enough crackpot websites not to take a story like this without a large grain of salt. But one thing he found really interesting was that soon after the ship went down, actors were hired to portray drowning passengers for a newsreel, which was shown repeatedly around the US for the following two years. According to the story, the newsreel was presented to the public as authentic. The real enchilada. No one at the time questioned how a cameraman had been able to film a sinking passenger liner in the middle of the ocean. Curtis decided he'd read enough.

'Come on, Gina, we're here to crack this site,

not read it. We've got better things to do, like planning how we're gonna spend a million dollars, right?' He nudged Gina's ear with his nose for effect.

'Come on, stop fooling around.' Gina wasn't having any of it. 'You might get offers like this every day, but I sure as hell don't. Why don't you try keeping it in your pants long enough to finish the job, and then you'll have the rest of your life to seduce me.' Sounded like a fair deal.

'That a promise?' He might as well get some commitment while the going was good.

But Gina's mind was already back on the screen. 'Look, there's some stuff here about Pearl Harbor.' Curtis did his best to focus, and pulled a face. He could see his chances of some nookie fading rapidly.

'I saw the movie. Think I prefer Hollywood's version of history, but what's ConspiracyWatch got to say for itself on that one?' Gina clicked through to the Pearl Harbor Conspiracy Page. Yes, it had its own page, can you believe it, and Gina was right into it.

'It's called the Mother of all Conspiracies!'

Oh shit. Here we go. And the list of so-called evidence was exhaustive, claiming to prove that F.D.R. had planned the attack.

Maybe exhausting would be a better description. Talk about paranoia run wild. F.D.R. provoked the attack, so the story went. He knew about it in advance and covered up his failure to warn the Hawaiian commanders. He needed the attack to sucker America into declaring war, since the public and Congress were overwhelmingly against entering the war in Europe. It was his backdoor to war. So he blinded the commanders at Pearl Harbor by denying them any intelligence reports, suckering them into thinking negotiations with Japan were continuing to prevent them from realising a war was on the cards. To the point of having false information sent to Hawaii about the location of the Japanese carrier fleet. Of course it listed not one, or two or three, but 61 separate occasions that could have constituted an early warning. From the message from the Peruvian envoy in Tokyo 11 months before the fateful day, right up to the morning of the attack, when warnings from both the British Admiralty, and the Navy's own Japanese code breakers were ignored, and all evidence of the messages deleted.

But it didn't stop there. Oh no. It was overkill. Every scrap of possible evidence: secret documents since discovered, F.D.R.'s diaries and those of his wife and Chiefs of Staff, every urgent secret message between Churchill and the President, and every broken Japanese code and intercepted message were itemised, detailed, listed and explained. Ad nauseum.

Curtis lost interest almost immediately. Unfortunately, Gina didn't.

'Can you believe this stuff? Would an American president really sacrifice his own countrymen for politics?'

Curtis shook his head and smiled in frustration. 'Come on, Gina. You're an intelligent woman. Don't tell me you're falling for this crap?'

Gina was indignant, despite the compliment. 'What do you mean? You've got to have an open mind about these things. Who's to say we haven't been fed some enormous lie all these years? This is where the web is at its best. Freedom of speech — it's in the Constitution, remember?'

But Curtis wasn't buying that one. 'Of course it's credible — that's the whole point! But don't you think that if the whole Pearl Harbor thing really was a huge conspiracy by F.D.R. to get us into the war, we'd actually know about it? We wouldn't have to read about it on some crackpot's obscure little website 50 years later?'

Gina's turn to shrug her shoulders in frustration. 'Possibly, I suppose.'

But Curtis wasn't finished. 'And that's precisely because we live in a country with a Constitution that enshrines freedom of speech as one of its basic principles.' He was starting to find the whole conversation ironic. If only his American studies teacher could hear him now. He was definitely on a roll. 'If all this was true, why would ConspiracyWatch and all the other Sculder and Mully weirdos claim it's all some big secret cover-up? It's not covered up. There is no secrecy. I think it's time we started focusing on the job, huh?'

But Gina hadn't even been listening. She was now reading the 'truth' behind Diana's death. Bloody hell! Curtis shook his head in disgust and threw himself back on the bed. 'I don't think an impressionable young mind like yours should be reading this stuff. It'll rot your brain.'

Gina didn't even look up, but her response was caustic. 'Compared to some of the stuff you've probably inhaled, sniffed or snorted, I think my brain is doing just fine, thank you very much.' Ouch. Curtis decided tactical withdrawal was the best option. He closed his eyes and pulled his cap over his head.

'Wake me when you've discovered who the mystery Fiat driver is, and I'll ring the Secret Service.' Silence. Double ouch. Oh well. He never was much good at knowing when to quit.

Eventually Gina spoke. Her voice was soft and brittle. Curtis looked up at her from behind his cap, and noticed that she was crying silently. What was it with women? Why couldn't they just take a joke and laugh it off? Curtis decided she probably needed some male company and support. Maybe even an apology.

'Hey, I'm sorry. I was only kidding ...'

Gina shook her head and wiped her eyes, interrupting him mid-sentence.

'It's not you, you idiot!' A half-smile escaped her frown for a moment. Curtis realised during her laugh/cry combo, that she was still reading the Diana cover-up conspiracy.

'I can't read any more of this ...' A racking sob shook her body, and Curtis went over and cradled her into his arms. The sobbing continued. It was wet and snotty against his T-shirt, but he felt that it was important that she let out whatever pain the website had uncovered in her. As he held her, Curtis read the article that had triggered the reaction. His anger at the story became as tangible as the emotion he was beginning to feel towards Gina.

He scanned the story quickly for its key allegations. This one wasn't just intriguing with its baseless interpretation of the tragic event, it was downright disturbing. According to the author, Diana was still very much alive after the car crash. She was also three months pregnant, the likely father being Dodi Al Fayed. Stunned, Diana exited the car and walked around, and was photographed by the paparazzi who were soon on the scene. An ambulance arrived and she was assisted into it, but it took over an hour for the ambulance to get her to a nearby hospital. And this was where Curtis felt his anger turn to revulsion.

The ambulance carrying Diana parked itself on a side street where a deliberately botched abortion was performed, which ensured that the princess would be delivered to the hospital on the verge of death.

Curtis shook his head in silent disbelief. How could anyone even think this stuff. He read on.

According to the remarkably well-informed author, the story suggested that Al Fayed's Mercedes limo had recently been stolen and returned with tampered electronics. A 'source' told the author that the car had been rebuilt to respond to external radio controls. On the fateful night, every single one of the 17 close-circuit cameras on the route from the Ritz to the Pont l'Alma tunnel was malfunctioning. This had never happened before. Simultaneous to the camera system failure, all police communications frequencies in central Paris went down. Of course they did.

Gina had finished sobbing, but was content to just sit in Curtis's arms, as he scrolled down the page with his free hand, behind her back.

The bizarre story continued. Contrary to media reports, the driver wasn't drunk when he drove the car away from the Ritz, because the hotel surveillance videos didn't show him as being obviously intoxicated. Two days prior to the car crash, he had supposedly taken an extensive medical exam to renew his pilot's licence, and according to the extraordinarily well-informed author, the results of the medical showed no alcohol-related problems.

So somewhere between the Ritz and the Pont l'Alma crash, the driver was poisoned with a toxic substance, since an abnormally high level of carbon monoxide was found in his blood during the autopsy. And then the author entered the realms of pure speculation as he/she recounted the events of the night in more detail than any other account Curtis had ever seen.

As the Mercedes sped through the Parisian night, unknown motorcyclists blocked a series of off ramps, forcing the car to enter the Pont l'Alma tunnel. Inside, a flash of light (and *not* a 'paparazzi' camera flashbulb the author stressed) from an extremely powerful 'anti-personnel device' momentarily blinded the driver. So a blinded and poisoned driver lost control of a vehicle that was now being controlled remotely, and it crashed into the pillar. Right.

Curtis lifted Gina's face to his and kissed her gently. He could taste the salt of her tears and the warmth of her lips on his.

'I'm sorry, Curtis,' she whispered.

'Hey, it's OK.' See, he could be the kind understanding type if he tried.

'It's just so … awful. To even begin to think that any of it might be true. The baby …'

'Don't even imagine for a minute that any of that crap is true. You gotta see this stuff objectively. There are some really twisted people out there.'

Gina nodded. 'Yeah I know …'

'But what's even more scary is how many gullible people there are. This Diana stuff is the *Lusitania* newsreel of the 21st century. Just because they read it on a website, and it has a whole heap of footnotes which refer to other websites, they take it as proof of a conspiracy.' Curtis shook his head. 'The web at its worst.'

Gina wiped her nose with the arm of her robe. Now *that* was a good look. 'I need to clean up,' she sniffed into Curtis's chest, getting up from the computer and disappearing into the bathroom.

Curtis examined the website more closely. He wasn't entirely sure why Gina had been so disturbed by the story. Sure it was pretty ugly, but he'd pegged Gina to be a little less squeamish than that. Not at all the Prometheus he had imagined. As he heard the shower start up inside the bathroom, he clicked back to the front page and sat thinking for a minute. Something had been bugging him since the meeting with Ollie and Shiny Styles. He went through the meeting again in his mind. Damn if he could pinpoint what it was. Maybe all this paranoia was getting to him. He pulled his cellphone out of his backpack and dialled a number.

The voice on the other end was groggy. 'Yeah?'

Curtis talked softly but urgently into the phone, 'Turk, it's me. Where are you?'

'I'm in bed. Like I said, man, got no sleep last night. I'm wasted.'

'I need you to do something for me when you wake up. Got a pen?' Curtis heard a rustling and banging followed by a loud groan from the other end of the line.

'Uh, yeah, sure. What do you want?'

'Write this name down. I want you to find out as much as you can about him — credit-card transactions, dates for the last month, ISP logs, cellphone logs, web finger, emails, sites visited, driver's licence, social-security number, the works.' There was silence at the other end. 'Turk! You got that?'

'Yeah, yeah. Sure. What's the name?'

'Oliver Branton. That's one "l" in Oliver, and Branton's with one "t", I think.'

Another moment of silence.

'You got that, Turk?'

'Got it,' came the response. Eventually.

'Email the results to my webmail address.'

'You got it. Everything OK?' Turk sounded concerned. That was one for the books.

'Yeah. Great. Might be nothing. I'm just being paranoid. Lot of it about at the moment.'

'Got that right.' Turk used to love the cloak-and-dagger stuff. Hell, he probably even visited sites like ConspiracyWatch when he wasn't actually hacking them. Curtis heard the shower turn off.

'I gotta go.' He ended the call. Just as he was putting the cellphone back in his backpack, Gina emerged from the bathroom, looking in a considerably better state than when she went in.

'Watchya doing?' she said, drying her face with a towel.

'Nothing, why?' Curtis wished he was a better liar.

'Thought I heard you talking.'

Curtis shrugged it off. 'Just singing to myself. About time I had the real thing, I reckon.' He pulled his MP3 player from his pack and sat down in front of the computer, as Gina turned back to the bathroom.

'Just gotta dry my hair. Won't be a minute.' Curtis let out a quiet breath.

He searched through the playlist until he found the song he was after. Something good. Something old. He wrapped the headphones around his head, adjusted the volume to loud/extra bass, and hit the play button. As the first beats of the song shook his world, Curtis rubbed his hands together and cracked his fingers. And as his fingers punched the keyboard, Roger Daltrey and Pete Townshend echoed his very thoughts: 'Who are you?' 'Cos Curtis really wanted to know.

This was familiar territory for Curtis. The easiest million bucks he'd ever make. Since most web addresses in the world were registered with the INTERNIC — the Internet Network Information Centre — all he had to do was telnet into the INTERNIC website, and enter ConspiracyWatch's URL into the search facility. Instantly Curtis had what he was looking for. ConspiracyWatch's physical address — a post box in some town in Nevada he'd never heard of. But he also had the site administrator's name and email address. Bingo. James Maze. Gotcha. Then Curtis ran a traceroute on the site, which showed him which road on the information superhighway he was using to connect with the site. The last ISP address on the list was the site's domain server. Curtis ran a WHOIS command on the ISP, and verified it as a local hosting service also run out of Nevada. Practically up the road. This was looking better all the time. A local set-up would provide far less of a challenge than a national domain server. Security would come second to running a low-cost service to compete with the biggies.

From another site, he downloaded a special programme he would use to penetrate the ConspiracyWatch site, and made a few adjustments to the coding. This was the most time-consuming part of the whole exercise. But once installed, it would enable him to ferret around inside the administrator's computer and identify the source of the mpegs. When he was finished, Curtis drafted an email to Mr James Maze, attaching a small black-and-white picture of a UFO he'd found on the website. But hidden behind the picture, his programme lay waiting to install itself onto the administrator's computer next time he updated the website. Simple as that. He was just putting the last touches to his email when Gina emerged from the bathroom. He could see her eyes light up when she saw him sitting at the computer. The hack had begun.

Whatever emotions the Diana story had unleashed earlier were now packed up and back in the suitcase.

'How's it going?' she asked cheerfully.

Curtis sat back, looking mighty pleased with himself. 'Done. Just need some help with the email.' It was Gina's turn to lean over Curtis's shoulder as she read his attempt at imitating an email from an admiring fan to the site administrator.

```
Dear ConspiracyWatch
Yours is the best site I've ever seen.
I'm glad there's a few of us with the
guts to tell it like it is. I found
this photo on your site and thought I
might be able to shed some light on it
for you. My wife took that about four
years ago from our back porch while I
was ploughing the field.
```

Gina looked at Curtis. 'Come on — ploughing a field?' Curtis shrugged as he pulled a face, meaning if you can do better, go for it. She didn't, choosing to read on instead.

```
This was the craft containing four
aliens that abducted me, and over the
```

```
period of two days, performed all
sorts of humiliating sexual
experiments on me.
```

Gina snorted. 'You've been watching way too much 'X-Files' Mr Hatch!' She finished reading the email, preferring to ignore Curtis's imitation of a mutant alien about to abduct her.

```
If you enlarge the photo you can see
the marks my shotgun left on the side
of the UFO as it landed. I've never
told anyone about this, but my wife
showed the photo to some men who
turned up a few days later, asking
all sorts of questions. They said
they were with the FBI, but I never
saw them or the photo again. Until I
saw it on your website, that is.
Yours, Charlie Rumbleton
```

Gina gave him a sceptical look. 'Now that's convincing!' Her sarcasm was actually quite funny.

Curtis weighed up his chances. 'Well we won't lose anything if it doesn't work, but we've got to get the guy to open the image. Figured a story like that might just make him curious enough to have a closer look.'

It was Gina's turn to weigh things up. 'It might just work, you know. It's stupid enough to be convincing.'

Curtis hit the send button, and got up and threw his player and phones back onto the bed.

'So now we just have to wait — got any preferences on how you'd like to kill some time?'

Gina looked up from the screen, and caught the suggestive look in Curtis's eye. An 'I know what you're thinking and you might be able to talk me into it' smile gradually spread across her face. Now this was more like it, thought Curtis, as he lurked by the bed with intent. He didn't tell her that he'd rigged the new mail message not to activate for at least two hours.

And a tough two hours it was. Their blossoming relationship was becoming more than physical. More than just good fun. Curtis could feel it, and he knew Gina could feel it too. Their lovemaking was softer this time. Gentler and less rushed. But neither of them spoke about it. Nothing needed to be said.

Gina fell asleep in his arms, but try as he might Curtis just couldn't sleep. There was way too much going on in his mind. The events of the last couple of days needed some catching up on. He slid his headphones on without waking her, and flicked the volume down low. He needed something slow, and introspective. He chose 'So Cruel', and just hoped the lyrics weren't an omen. Bono reckoned in love there were no rules.

No rules. His mind went back to Gonad. And Roly's disappearance. 'Suicide' just didn't stack up — not if you knew Roly. He thought about DefCon, the hacking comp and the BlackHat invitation, but always his mind kept coming back to the million dollars. The chance. The possibility.

He was still struggling with the fact that Gina was actually Prometheus. Certainly had a few secrets, this girl. And Curtis was sure he hardly knew any of them. Not that it really mattered. What mattered was that he was feeling more alive now than he ever had during his most daring hacks. Gina was starting to fill a void in his life he hadn't known existed. And he was getting kinda used to having her around. Curtis looked at his watch.

Two hours was nearly up, and he couldn't resist sliding out from Gina's embrace and checking the computer for new mail. And he wasn't disappointed. Curtis clicked open the email and sat to read it.

```
Dear Mr Rumbleton
Your email contains a predatory virus
specifically designed to compromise
the integrity of ConspiracyWatch.
IF YOU FEDS DON'T LIKE WHAT YOU SEE
AT CONSPIRACYWATCH THEN CHECK THE
CONSTITUTION. YOUR ACTIONS ARE
ILLEGAL AND A DIRECT CONTRAVENTION OF
THE US BILL OF RIGHTS.
FUCK YOU AND YOURS,
James Maze
```

Shit! 'Gina, wake up!' Curtis ran the message through a scanning programme to check whether he was the one being tracked. Gina had stirred, but was still in la-la land. 'Gina! The bastard's on to us!'

Gina lifted her head. 'What do you mean? Did you get a response?'

Curtis nodded as he finished the scan. Nothing. He breathed a little easier. 'The guy must be so paranoid he's running some kind of super virus detector.'

Gina was up and reading the message now. 'He thinks we're the Feds?'

Curtis nodded. 'Looks that way. This guy must know a thing or two about computers to have found my bug. Shit!'

Gina didn't seem too worried though. 'So what do we do now, Einstein? Launch a denial of service attack and crash his system? That'd fix him for speaking to us like that!'

Curtis looked up at her, amazed. 'You're kidding, right?'

Gina burst out laughing. 'You should see your face right now!' Curtis allowed himself to lighten up. He kinda liked the way her breasts jiggled when she laughed like that. Focus, Curtis.

'OK. Time for Plan B.'

Gina was one step ahead. 'You got his address, didn't you? So we have to access his machine.'

'Well, at least it's in Nevada. Never heard of the place though. Rachel, Lincoln County. Probably some tiny desert town. Figures.'

But that didn't put Gina off. 'So we have to go for a road trip. Could be fun. I had a feeling this was all a bit too easy. You still in?'

Curtis studied her for a moment. God, she was so beautiful she took his breath away. Even after a couple of hours in the sack. 'Of course I'm in. I'm not giving up a million bucks that easily.'

'At least we'll feel like we're earning our pay!' said Gina. But Curtis was sitting her down on the bed. He had a very serious look on his face.

'Listen, Gina. This changes things big time. It's one thing to hack a site from the safety of the net. But this is completely different. If the site isn't run off a network, we could be looking at some serious breaking and entering. We're going to have to watch the target and learn everything we can about him before we even attempt to access his machine. You ready for that?'

Gina wasn't laughing now. 'Look, it's not as if I haven't done any of that stuff before, you know. I'm not some naïve little girl who wandered in off the street —'

'I didn't say you were,' said Curtis.

'Well, save the patronising advice for your other women.'

Curtis smiled. 'I do. That's why they're no longer around.' To her credit, Gina managed to see the funny side of that one. 'Look, all I'm saying is that we're getting into unknown territory here. I'm not saying it will be dangerous, but there has to be a reason this guy is running such sophisticated security on a crackpot website.'

Gina looked at him. 'So?'

'So the chances are he's probably as paranoid in real life as he is on the net. And probably taking as many precautions.' Curtis could tell Gina had got the point, because she sat silently for a moment. Maybe he'd overcooked it. 'Hey, maybe I'm being too cautious. I could be totally wrong. But it doesn't hurt to stay one step ahead. And that means using this,' he said, pointing to her head.

'Well, Mr Smarty Pants,' said Gina, suddenly grabbing his crotch, 'you sure used enough of this ...' Curtis's shout could probably have been heard down in the lobby, as they both fell back onto the bed laughing.

Then it was Gina's turn to be serious. 'Don't worry, Curtis. I don't have any illusions about what we're getting into here. This is serious stuff. But so's the money. I think we should at least try.'

Curtis found himself agreeing with her. 'Well, we can check him out. See what sort of challenge he'll present. We can make a call then. Agreed?'

Gina nodded. 'Agreed.'

But Curtis was already planning his next move. 'We'll need a rental car. And a map. We should also tell Ollie our plans. I'd hate to think no one would miss us if we disappeared out in the desert somewhere.'

'I'll take care of Ollie if you like, while you get the car.' Curtis didn't see any problem with that. 'When do we leave?'

Curtis looked at his watch. It was getting late, and it would soon be dark. 'Could be a long drive. You up to sharing the driving?'

Gina nodded again. 'Of course, I wouldn't have it any other way. I'm happy to leave now.'

Curtis didn't see any problem with that either. 'OK, but I've gotta eat something first. Why don't you cook us up some beans?'

Gina screwed up her face in dismay. 'Beans! Cook your own bloody beans, mister!' Then she realised Curtis had just got one back on her.

'Just asking!' said Curtis mischievously.

Gina pretended to be unimpressed. 'Go put some clothes on before we end up back in bed.' Now there was a thought. But before he could act on it, he found Gina was already putting her legs back into her jeans. Damn.

'OK, then,' he said hauling himself up off the bed. 'Let's go to work.'

Rachel, Nevada, here we come.

7

Curtis had to admit there was something intensely liberating about pushing 60 in a convertible at night in the desert.

When he found a no-dent car hire off the main boulevard with a salesman who looked sufficiently shifty, his main plan had been to find some wheels. Period.

He'd pretended he hadn't noticed the Hummer soft-top sitting on the pavement, and made it clear to the dirtbag holding the fort that he was after a reliable, inconspicuous form of transport. But boys will be boys, and there is always something uncomfortably seductive about anyone selling or hiring a car sexier than they are. Especially when it was a 6.5 litre turbo diesel beast of a thing like a Hummer.

Anyway, the upshot of it was that Curtis ended up pulling in to the Oasis in the car he planned to own when the job was over. Gina almost had to pick her jaw up off the floor when she saw it, but under the bright lights of the hotel entrance, it somehow seemed appropriate. She got right into it, much to Curtis's relief. He didn't mind being accused of most things — hell, he had already been accused of more stuff than most guys his age — but being called irresponsible by a woman he was trying to impress was one thing he wasn't looking forward to.

'Mr Hatch, you never cease to amaze me.' Yep, she was cool, this chick.

'Well, we *are* heading into the desert!' he said. 'All aboard the million-dollar express.' Curtis tried to sound confident about his choice of transport, as Gina threw her things into the back and jumped in beside him. Yep — she looked good in a convertible. Even a Hummer convertible. The jeans had gone, and her thin floral dress complemented the car perfectly. Curtis didn't have to look, but he knew the doormen were green.

Dream away, boys.

As Curtis pulled into the traffic, he resisted the temptation to gun the engine and instead focused on the business at hand. 'How was Ollie?'

'No problem. But that guy he has with him gives me the creeps. He was disappointed we couldn't crack the site from here. But he seemed happy with our approach.'

'So the money's still up.' It was more a statement than a question.

Gina nodded. 'We're still in the hunt.'

'Music to my ears.' And with that, Curtis couldn't resist letting a few hundred horses under the bonnet out of the stable as he accelerated the beast into the traffic.

Once they'd left behind the technicolour-shotgun lights of Vegas, the night seemed to take on a life of its own. The cool scent of the desert air combined with Gina's perfume and the smell of leather upholstery. Guy heaven. Curtis flicked the Hummer into cruise control, and tried to ignore what the wind was doing to Gina's hair. And her skirt.

As Gina fiddled with the radio, Curtis got to thinking. 'What do you reckon is so important about some old movies posted on a website that someone wants to pay a million bucks for them?'

Gina didn't look up. 'You heard the man. He's a history nut with more money than sense.'

'Yeah, I know what he said. But think about it for a second. What have we got? Some old black-and-white footage of some sort of UFO leaving a building with a swastika on it. And then we've got another UFO landing on a US warship somewhere with lots of ice. If I didn't think Ollie was for real, I'd think he'd ripped it from an old "X-Files" programme.'

'Well, he thinks it's for real. And so does the sponsor.'

Curtis thought for a second. 'Yeah, well that's another thing. Who do you think this mysterious sponsor is?'

'Money doesn't mean sanity — think of all those guys who stand for the presidency with more money than sense. As long as he's paying, I'm not asking any questions.' Gina found a station she decided was worth listening to, and kicked up the volume. It was some sort of middle-of-the-road country rock. Curtis cringed. There would be a limit to his tolerance for that stuff. He decided to give it a go and not say anything. The compromises one makes in a relationship.

Gina sat back in her seat. 'So once we find out where the video came from, our job's done and we're out of it.'

Curtis wasn't convinced yet. Not by a long shot. 'Since we've got some time, let's do some what-ifs. What if the video is for real? It's some long hidden footage of a UFO leaving a Nazi airfield. That would put it at World War II. That's pre-1945.'

Gina wasn't following him. 'So?'

'So it also means either of two things. One — the thing is being piloted by Germans, or two — there was some sort of alien contact. What do they call it? Close encounters of the fourth kind or something. But the point is, there might have been some sort of contact with alien life-forms. And it was over 50 years ago.'

Gina was looking him over, not sure whether he was joking. Curtis felt it necessary to explain his point further. 'Don't you see? That must be why it's worth a million dollars. Hell, it would probably be worth ten times that if it could be proven. Think about it. Proof that mankind has had contact with a life-form from another planet. Kinda changes your perspective on things, doesn't it?'

Gina thought about it, and continued on the line of thinking. 'And the second movie. It's got

American soldiers in it. That means our own government has had some sort of contact as well.'

'Exactly,' he said.

That just got Gina thinking some more. 'But what makes this footage different from the dozens of other videos they show on those UFO programmes? How do you tell the hoaxes from the real thing?'

'Yeah,' said Curtis, 'every drunk farmer and paranoid reporter has been photographing those sorts of things for years. But as far as I know, I've never seen any photos of military craft alongside them. Not that I'm an expert in this stuff.'

'So you think we might be on to something here?' Gina studied him for a moment. The possibility was more than either of them wished to imagine.

'Let's just say there's a reason this guy wants to pay a million dollars to prove their authenticity. I don't think we should just walk into this whole thing blind. That's all.'

Gina looked sceptical. 'Well, we won't know until we get into this guy's machine, right?'

They sat silently, the implications of what they were about to do not lost on either of them. Curtis needed a break.

'What's this we're listening to? You like this stuff?' he asked innocently.

'All I could find on the radio. Want me to change it?'

She didn't look too upset, so Curtis took his chance. 'I've got some old CDs in my bag. Feel like some real music?'

'Sure.' Gina passed him his bag from the back seat, and with one hand on the wheel he pulled a CD from its holder and inserted it into the car stereo.

By way of introduction, he added, 'I love this stuff.'

Gina was curious. 'What is it?'

Achtung Baby. U2 at their finest. The last of the great rock-and-roll bands.'

And with that Curtis flicked the volume up dangerously loud, and sat back as the unearthly intro to 'Ultra Violet' split the Nevada night.

Rachel wasn't really a town, or even a village. More like a claim in the desert, unsure if it's permanent or not. But after the monotony of the 'ET Highway', it seemed like a caravan of lights around an oasis.

The night was getting cool, and Curtis had lifted the roof a while back, as Gina continued her beauty sleep uninterrupted. But when he lowered the window as he pulled the Hummer off the road into a parking lot to park his horses at the OK Corral, he was surprised at the silence of the place. Like a campsite after dark, when everyone is being polite and hushed. Even the clicking noises of the engine cooling down seemed loud.

The silence woke Gina too. 'Where the hell are we?'

'Welcome to Rachel,' said Curtis. 'Let's check out the bar — how do you say that — A-Lee-Inn?'

That got Gina curious. 'It's "alien" — just spelled with an I instead of an E.'

Curtis looked at Gina. 'You mean there's an E in alien?'

Gina realised he wasn't serious and hit him in the arm. Hard.

'Come on you idiot, let's go camping.'

Stepping inside the 'A-Lee-Inn' was like taking a step back in time. Not sure which time, but definitely pre-Beatles. The sign on the door said *No Vacancy* very proudly, as though this was something to tell people about. And much to Curtis's surprise, the place was quite busy. Curtis ordered a beer, and a water for Gina, and asked the motherly looking large woman behind the bar where they might get a bed for the night. She told him there wasn't anywhere else other than the 'Inn, and they were full since the hike was on and all. The hike. Go figure. But he did get a nod in the direction of a skinny old guy sitting at one of the tables eating beans. Yep, beans.

Curtis wandered over with his most charming smile. 'Hi there, we're in town for the night and just need —'

The guy held his hand up for him to stop. 'Manners to wait until a person has finished eating.'

Curtis stopped mid-sentence, flabbergasted. Manners was also to wait until a person had finished speaking. Had to admit, though, it stopped Curtis in his tracks. Not entirely sure what to make of this, he retreated to the bar, and waited with Gina for the guy to finish his goddamn beans. Which he eventually did.

Curtis was starting to feel distinctly uneasy. The mood had changed since his manners blunder, and even the old girl behind the bar was very busy keeping herself to herself. The old guy stood up and stretched out, very tall and very denim, and finally wandered over to where Curtis and Gina were sitting.

'You looking for a bed, right?' he said, scratching his head before covering it with a sweat-stained trucker's cap.

Curtis nodded. 'Yeah, motel's full up. Lady behind the bar said to talk to you. Can you help us out? It's just one night,' he added helpfully.

'Well that depends,' came the reply. Curtis sure as hell wasn't in the mood for games. The guy gave Curtis and Gina the once-over. 'You here for the hike?' Hike? Yeah right.

'No, just passing through and thought we'd drop in on someone we were hoping to meet. Left it kinda late leaving Vegas, so we'll track him down in the morning.'

The guy was instantly suspicious. Curtis could see it in his eyes. 'Who you looking for?' Curtis wasn't sure how to play this, but decided the less this guy knew about what they were up to, the better.

'Just a friend. Haven't seen him in ages. Thought we'd surprise him and say hello,' Curtis lied. Badly. The guy looked at the woman behind the bar, who was doing a bad job of pretending not to listen in on the conversation. 'So we just need somewhere to camp for the night. Anything you got, we'll take it. We'll be outta there in the morning.'

'Eighty bucks,' said the old guy, in a take-it-or-leave-it kind of way. Curtis did a double take, and Gina nearly spat out her water.

'That's a little more than we were planning on spending. What's the cheap option?'

'Ain't one. Eighty bucks is the package. A bed and the hike. Take it or leave it.' So there it was. They were both tired, and money really wasn't the issue. But he could forget the hike.

'Look, we'll just take the bed. Thanks for the offer anyway,' said Curtis.

The guy shook his head. 'Still cost you 80.' This was bloody extortion. Highway robbery.

Curtis forced a smile. 'Sure. No problem.' He started to make for the door, assuming the deal had been done, but the guy just stood there waiting. 'There something wrong?'

'Money up front, if you don't mind.' Maybe not weird, just a heister. Curtis dug into his pocket and flicked the guy the money. He buried it in his denim. 'All right, where you parked?' This was more like it.

Curtis nodded out the window. 'Just out front.' The guy started walking out the door, so it was hard for Curtis to hear him. But it sounded like, 'I'm the white pick-up. Follow me.'

As Curtis started the Hummer, he saw a pair of tail-lights across the park. White wasn't the word, even in the red glow of the lights he could see that soon the only thing this pick-up was going to pick up was rust.

'What do you think?' said Gina, asking the obvious.

Curtis shrugged. 'Well you weren't expecting Pleasantville, were you? A bed's a bed, even at 80 bucks at night. Bet the room service sucks.'

Gina looked a little more comfortable. 'Well, we're not going to find Mr Maze tonight, so let's just crash.' Curtis couldn't have agreed more.

The white pick-up stopped at the edge of town. The word 'town' was a metaphor in this place. Even in the dark. The trailer home was the last one on the road, where it turned back into desert. Curtis parked the Hummer in front of a second trailer. As he got out he noticed the forest of aerials and satellite dishes on top of the guy's trailer. It looked creepy in the light of the moon. *Blair Witch Project* stuff. But the guy went straight into his trailer without acknowledging his guests at all. He emerged moments later with two faded sleeping bags. If he hadn't been so tired, the whole experience would have been straight out of *Deliverance*, what with the warm hospitality and all.

The guy nodded his head at the second trailer. 'There's your bed for the night, and those are your bags.'

Curtis took the bags. 'Thanks very much.' Just when he was starting to think they'd made a mistake by accepting the bed, and wondered if they shouldn't camp out in the Hummer, the guy softened a little.

'I'll be up for a while, and I usually light a campfire at night, if you want to join me later. Can get kinda cold out here.'

A crack in the ice. Curtis jumped at it. 'Sure.

Just grab a shower and unpack, and we'll be there.' The guy fought down a half-smile. Curtis took it as a friendly gesture, and smiled back. 'Later.'

With that the guy disappeared into his trailer, the only movement the shadows from his windows on the desert floor. Curtis and Gina surveyed their bed for the night. Even in the dark it was underwhelming. The trailer wasn't one star. It was no star. Basic in the extreme. And Curtis realised the guy had been laughing *at* him, not with him, when Gina discovered to her horror that there was no shower. The joke was on them.

They spent a few minutes unloading their things from the back of the Hummer, and Gina set the bags out on the double bed. They were both aware of how far every sound carried in the desert, and acted as though it was completely natural to unpack without talking to each other. Eventually they ended up on top of the bags. It was Curtis who started the whispering first.

'Fancy a hike as well? We paid for it already. Might be fun.'

Gina missed the sarcasm completely. 'Curtis, there is no way, and I mean no way, that I am going on a hike with that man. Anywhere.'

Curtis couldn't help but smile. 'I thought you liked the great outdoors?'

'I mean it, Curtis. If you think I'm about to hike in the desert dressed like this then you're on your own here. I'd rather sleep in the car.' Curtis got the message. Don't mess with me.

'Hey, I'm only kidding!' He noticed how much more relaxed she was, now they'd established she wasn't going to be hiking in the Nevada desert at night without her make-up. It wasn't long before they heard their host–extortionist rustling around outside. Gina peeked through the torn curtain and discovered him preparing a real live wild-west campfire, complete with a small kettle and logs for seats. They decided to join the party.

As they approached, the guy didn't look up. Uh oh, thought Curtis. Here we go again. Do the manners rules still apply out here? At least he wasn't eating beans this time, but Curtis was pleased he wasn't sharing a trailer with him. No wonder he left his windows open at night.

'Enjoy the shower?' Very funny. But Curtis saw the humour. Unlike Gina.

'Even had time to shave my legs,' she said. The sarcasm just dripped off that one. Curtis was wondering if he was going to have to referee the two of them, but the guy responded with the first proper smile they'd seen since meeting him. Surprise, surprise. He didn't suffer from paralysis of the facial muscles after all.

He motioned towards the log. 'Have a seat, I'm just brewing a coffee. Want some?' Coffee. The magic word. The aroma seemed to make things ordinary again, as though it was completely natural to be sharing a coffee with a complete stranger over a campfire in the middle of the Nevada desert at night.

The bloke brewed a wicked cup of coffee — strong, black and beany. Curtis pointed to the array of aerials and dishes sprouting from the roof of his trailer. 'That's a serious set of equipment you got there, by the look of it. What's it for?'

The guy shrugged. 'I'm a bit of an electronics nut. Comes in handy around here.'

Curtis offered the hand of friendship. 'I'm Curtis, and this is Gina.' She waved at him from behind her steel coffee mug.

The guy responded with a shake. 'Jim Maze.' He said it so matter-of-factly that it took a second for Curtis to realise what he'd just heard. It wasn't lost on Gina, either, judging by the sharp dig in his ribs. Curtis couldn't believe his luck. They were sitting right beside the guy they'd come to find.

Suddenly the conversation became meaningful. One million dollars worth of meaningful. 'You're not the guy with the website, are you? I'm sure I've heard your name before.'

'That's me. Darned thing costs me an arm and a leg to run. But it's my baby. And my insurance.'

'Insurance?' said Curtis. 'Not sure I follow you.' Jim Maze laughed. Curtis figured it was probably at his expense.

'Well, the little hike I'm going on in the morning is pushing the limits of legal, you know. So as long as I keep running some of the far-out stuff on the web, people think I'm harmless. Keeps them guessing, anyway.'

Curtis's confusion shifted to suspicion. 'What people?'

Jim looked away. 'The sort of people who keep secrets, and don't want anyone else to know about them.' Very mysterious. Curtis didn't have the foggiest as to what the guy was on about. He didn't push it.

'So tell me some about the hike. Where are you hiking to?'

Jim spat into the fire. It sizzled loudly. 'Out near where we shouldn't be.' Not particularly forthcoming was Mr Jim Maze.

'You do a lot of hiking out here, then?'

Jim shook his head. 'Only when I get some paying customers. I'm just the tour guide.' This wasn't making any sense at all. Jim must have sensed Curtis's frustration, because after a few seconds staring into the flames, he said, 'I advertise on the website. When I get me enough paying customers, I organise a hike for them. Usually only about twice a year or so. Don't want to get too familiar with the security guys.'

'So it's not a nature walk then?' asked Curtis.

Jim laughed at that one. 'I wouldn't call it that. Some kind of interesting wildlife though!'

Curtis wasn't sure he got the joke. But he laughed along with him anyway. So he was some kind of hiking guide. Sure as hell didn't look like one.

'So how long is the hike? You go from here?'

Jim nodded. 'We go most of the route in the pick-up. Just the snakes you gotta watch.' Snakes. He could sense Gina stiffen beside him, and carefully check the ground around her.

Jim must have noticed too. 'Oh, we're all right here. All the beans I've eaten tonight there won't be a snake for miles.' Funny guy — he must have seen *Blazing Saddles* too.

'So how long you been running the site?' Curtis wanted to know more about Jim Maze. Lots more.

'Oh, I don't know. About three years, I guess. The Feds shut me down a couple of times when I posted some government stuff they didn't like. Turns out whoever sent it to me had hacked it from their computers. They hate to think people might see their dirty laundry.' Wow. This was serious wacko territory.

Curtis decided to cut straight to the chase. The game-playing was getting tiresome. He knew what he wanted — what he needed. 'I was really blown away by those two mpegs of UFOs you got on the site. You know — Hitler escaping Berlin and the one over the ice? Pretty amazing stuff if it's true.'

Curtis watched Jim closely, as he nodded thoughtfully. 'Say that again. It's the best evidence I've seen yet. There's no way anyone could fake those. And if they did they wouldn't have done such a bad job.'

'Where'd you get them?' Curtis asked innocently.

Jim shrugged. 'They just arrived by email. Totally anonymous. And that's another thing. If someone was going to take the trouble to fake them, they'd sure as hell want some credit for the effort. But these just arrived one day out of the blue. No return address, nothing.' Curtis nodded silently. Shit. But he didn't want to let the subject slip.

'You said they're the best evidence. Evidence of what?'

Jim shook his head knowingly. 'Well, let's just say it's a bigger jigsaw puzzle than you or I could ever imagine. They're just two small pieces. Hard to tell what the picture is of, until you see more. But it doesn't stop us guessing, and when we get a reaction we know we're getting close to something worth hiding. That's kinda the way it works.' But the question brought a change in Jim along with the answer. He looked Curtis and Gina over for a second. The same way he'd done back at the A-Lee-Inn.

'Tell me about yourselves. What brings a nice couple like you out here in the middle of the night to go hiking to a secret military installation?' Curtis caught himself before he gave the game away. He certainly wasn't expecting that one. Did he say secret military installation? So that was what all this cloak and dagger was about. Luckily for Curtis, Gina had her wits about her.

'We're both computer-studies students. We met at DefCon — it's a convention for … for internet-security consultants. We saw your website and here we are.'

Jim didn't look all that convinced. Curtis wouldn't have been either, but it was all he was going to get at short notice. Jim gave them the once-over again. He even checked out the Hummer this time. What the hell was he thinking?

'You look like a couple of undercover Feds to me.' Curtis was dumbfounded. He and Gina looked at each other, and couldn't help smiling a little at the thought of them, of all people, being considered Feds.

'Mr Maze, I can assure you that we are not Feds,' said Curtis, as straight-faced as he could.

'How?' came the reply. Straight-faced and serious.

Curtis didn't understand. 'How, what?'

'How are you going to assure me that you're not Feds? Because until you do, our conversation is limited to how-d'you-dos and excuse-mes.'

Shit. Curtis hadn't been expecting this at all. He'd never had to prove he *wasn't* a good guy. Usually it was the other way round. It was time for him to get creative.

'I have a criminal record, and I'm on parole for accessing computer systems without the owners' knowledge. Will that do?'

Jim shrugged. 'Not unless you can prove it. So you're a hacker. Heard about them. You good?'

Gina came in on cue. 'He's very good, Mr Maze. One of the best.'

Another shrug. 'Not good enough, sounds like.'

Curtis smiled self-consciously. 'That was a long time ago. I was just a kid.'

'What did you do?' It was Jim's turn to get curious. But Curtis wasn't ready to get into details. Besides, he had an idea.

'Look, Mr Maze, if you let me use your computer I can prove it to you. Right here, right now.' Jim thought about that for a second, staring hard into Curtis's eyes. Curtis eyeballed him back to show that he was serious.

Finally he said, 'OK, let's go into the Palace and you can strut your stuff. But I don't have all night, you know.'

Curtis jumped at the opportunity. 'Won't take 20 minutes. If you leave me alone to work on it for a bit, I'll call you when I've got the proof on screen. How's that?' He only needed a few minutes to locate and copy the email.

But Jim wasn't having any of that. 'No way, mister. I'll be watching every move you make the whole time.'

Curtis saw the chance to access Jim's emails vaporise before him. So he went with the play. 'OK, no problem.'

Jim got up from the campfire. 'This way.' Gina threw Curtis an urgent look as they followed him. Curtis shrugged. It said he was just playing this as it went, and they might as well just go with it. She didn't look like she approved.

Jim Maze's trailer took after its owner's name. It was truly something to behold. A maze of maps, photos and documents on the walls, table, bed and floor. Computer equipment, satellite stuff and what looked like some high-tech electronic radio gear all crammed into a single room. In the dim light of one wall lamp and a single computer screen, it even looked kinda spooky.

The computer was the cockpit, the screen proudly displaying the ConspiracyWatch homepage. Jim pulled back the chair and made Curtis some space. 'Not much room in here for three, but it's home for me so excuse the mess.' Curtis settled into the chair and started typing and clicking. He could sense Jim and Gina watching him closely. Better make this good. Curtis exited from the homepage and telnetted into a backdoor entry of a site he knew already existed. He knew that because he'd done this once before. Just after he'd been sentenced.

He'd done it more out of spite than anything else. And anger — though mostly at himself for getting caught, he had to admit. Just to prove to himself he was better than that. Soon he had a request for a username and password up on the screen. He typed in a name — Terry Hay. Sorry Terry, but what you don't know won't hurt you. Curtis rattled off the password quickly, to make sure Jim couldn't see what buttons he was hitting. He wanted to be safe even in the dim light of the trailer.

Bingo. He was in. Now Jim could see exactly what system he was accessing.

'This is the FBI investigations database.' So he could read.

Curtis didn't look up, 'Uh huh.' He clicked on the national search facility and entered his own name. Curtis Hatch. And hit the search button.

Instantly the screen filled with a profile sheet displaying his own stats and the mugshot they'd taken when they took him in for questioning. And arrest. He was younger then, but there was no mistaking the good-looking dude peering out at them from the screen. Curtis felt mildly embarrassed at the picture. Not one of his prouder moments, that was for sure. He didn't know what Gina was going to make of this.

He got out of the seat so Jim could read the screen. He already had a pair of frameless glasses on his nose, as he squinted at the picture.

'Is that proof enough?' Curtis asked, looking at Gina for a reaction to the news she'd been sleeping with a criminal. She didn't seem to care, or perhaps she was doing a very good job of pretending not to.

Jim took his glasses off, and extended his hand. 'That will do nicely, thank you, Curtis. Hope I didn't offend you. But I've learned from experience that it pays to be safe than sorry.' Curtis took his hand. It was the second time he'd shaken Jim's hand, but he felt it was the first time it was actually meant.

Gina still hadn't said a word. Curtis logged out and Jim's familiar homepage returned to the screen. It seemed that Curtis was now a member of some sort of club, because Jim's demeanour changed noticeably for the better.

'I could sure use another coffee, and judging by the way you emptied the last cup, you're probably itching for another one too, right?' He was looking at Gina now.

'Yes, please,' she said. 'Tastes much better than some of the filter we got in Vegas.'

Jim smiled warmly as he ushered them out of his 'palace'. 'Well that would be the desert dust and bugs at the bottom of the kettle. Haven't washed it out for at least two months.' The icebreaker was welcome after the earlier awkwardness. Jim even seemed slightly human now.

'You play chess?' he asked out of the blue. Chess! Curtis figured this must be Jim's version of the olive branch.

'Umm … sure. I downloaded a learner programme once. Beat me every time.'

Jim shook his head in disgust. 'A programme! Chess is a game to be played by people, not bloody computers.'

Curtis pulled a face. He half-agreed. 'It's just a case of computing all the possible combinations of moves and choosing the best one. That needs computing power, so a chess computer would beat a human every time. The human brain doesn't have the capacity to calculate that much information at once.'

Jim snorted a laugh in mock disgust. 'You kids. Computers are the answer to everything.' Curtis didn't appreciate either implication — that he was a kid, or that he was a member of the computer holy-grail club.

But Jim wasn't finished. 'Chess is an art form, not a science. No software designer can interpret the subtleties and nuances of chess. It's not the moves that make the game, it's the people. The human factor. Strategies, gambits, aggression, defence — it's the players that make it, not some super calculator.'

Jim was obviously very passionate about his chess.

Curtis decided not to push it. 'OK, I take your point.' Jim rummaged around in a dusty leather bag behind him and pulled out an old scratched chessboard. The pieces were loose in the bag, and they emerged in handfuls. Curtis tried to remember how to set them up. When he'd finished, there were two pieces missing. He was about to mention it, when Jim pulled two bottle tops out from the bag, and placed them in the empty squares.

'Jim Beam is my queen,' he said matter-of-factly, as he placed the top onto the board. Curtis couldn't help feeling there was a metaphor in there somewhere.

'Your pawn is Jack Daniels.' Curtis had to smile and shake his head. Jack Daniels, huh.

'You're white. Your move,' said Jim. As Curtis opened with a pawn — a real one — Jim kept the conversation going. Maybe it was a ploy to distract him. Maybe he was lonely. Who knew.

'You know, I belong to this internet chess club. Mostly I play people over the net. Between that and the website, don't have time for much else.' Curtis moved a knight in response to Jim's move. Let's try and make this as short and painless as possible. He figured that if this was the way he was going to have to win Jim Maze's trust to get to the email, then he'd have to humour the guy. So chess it was.

'Anyways, we been talking about the same thing. Debating would be more accurate.' Jim came back at him with a knight as well. 'So the club is organising a challenge to settle it once and for all. You ever hear of Bobby Fischer?' he asked without looking up from the board.

'Can't say I have.' Curtis winced as Jim casually removed one of his knights with a bishop that came from nowhere.

'Best player that ever lived. Genius. But he disappeared when he was at the top. Beat anyone who mattered hands down ... But he never played a computer.' Curtis went back to some serious pawn-shuffling.

'So a friend of mine says he reckons he's been playing this guy over the net for a few months who never says who he is. And he does the strangest openings. Like he's handicapping himself to make the game more interesting.' Jim took Curtis's remaining knight with one of his own. He was going down in flames.

'And after a while he starts to recognise the style of play. And some of the comments the mystery guy drops makes him think. You understand me?'

Curtis nodded. 'Yeah, sure.' He didn't have a clue what Jim was going on about.

'Now my friend is no amateur — he's a Grand Master. And here's someone who won't give his name, beating him with one hand tied behind his back.'

The penny dropped. 'Bobby Fischer,' said Curtis.

'You got it,' said Jim, as he unleashed his Jim Beam on Curtis's exposed rook. 'So this guy comes straight out one day and asks him. They'd been playing on and off for months. And you know what?' Curtis shook his head as he examined the chaos on the board in front of him. 'He didn't deny it.' Well that proved everything.

'So time goes by, and they get to talking about computers. And this mystery guy says he's never played a computer before. So you know what my friend does?' More guessing games. Curtis shook his head.

'He convinces him to play against a computer!' Jim paused for a while to let this significant fact sink in. 'Except we don't have access to them fancy computers like Deep Blue, or whatever they call it. So we came up with an idea. My friend and I set up a different kind of computer. What do you think we did?'

The guessing games were really starting to test Curtis's patience. 'I have no idea. Your move.'

'Well, all we need is computing power, right? So we organised through my friend's website for all the club members to go online at one time. Been planning this for months. We're gonna create a supercomputer using 1800 desktops!' Now Curtis was genuinely impressed. No mean feat, even for someone of Curtis's computer skills.

'Oh, check, by the way.' Shit. Curtis was on the wrong side of a good old-fashioned thrashing.

'That's pretty amazing,' said Curtis. 'When's the big game?'

'Tomorrow night,' said Jim proudly.

'Best of luck, then. Hope you do better than me.'

'We're making history. The best player that ever lived against a supercomputer for the first time. Incredible! And we can watch it live right on our computers from the luxury of our own homes.' Now there was an exaggeration. But Curtis had to admit, it was a neat idea. It might even work. He was still thinking about it when Jim delivered his coup de grâce. 'That's checkmate, son.' The torture was finally over.

'You need to play more,' said Jim, as he returned his chess pieces to the old bag.

'Say that again,' said Curtis, embarrassed at his lack of chess prowess. He'd had enough anyway. He liked to play to win. Jim pulled out a bottle of something from his bag of tricks beside the fire and offered them a drink.

'Say, you like a wee nightcap before turning in?'

Curtis accepted the offer, and so did Gina. But it was time for a change of conversation. He wanted to get back to the email.

As Jim poured the stuff into his mug, Gina asked what they were drinking.

'Just a little something I brew for myself. Probably illegal, but it keeps me warm on these cold desert nights.' Jim poured himself twice what he'd given Curtis and Gina. It tasted like lighter fluid. Real desert firewater.

But after the first few disgusting swallows, the firewater started taking effect, and it wasn't so bad after all. Obviously an acquired taste.

'So tell us about the hike, Jim,' asked Gina. 'What's that all about?'

That's right. Keep him talking. Bring him round slowly.

Jim didn't seem to mind the question. 'I've been doing these hikes for about a year now. Always people around who want to see what the government's getting up to. I'm just a businessman meeting a demand, that's all.'

'You mentioned something about a military installation. What's that all about?' Gina was on a roll. So was Jim now he'd had a few. He paused for a second before answering. They could tell that what he was about to tell them was important to him.

'You ever heard of Area 51? The Ranch, Dreamland, Groom Lake? It's got a dozen names. The Government denies it even exists. But it exists all right.'

Curtis nodded. 'Sure — isn't that where the Air Force develops all their secret hardware? You know, stealth bombers and stuff?'

Jim smiled knowingly. 'That's what they'd have you believe. It's the excuse for roping off half the Nevada desert anyways.'

'What's so special about this one? There's dozens of military bases all over the country.'

'Because the secrecy surrounding this place is unbelievable. They're not just hiding what goes on here from the enemy. They're hiding it from the American public.' Curtis shot Gina a quick look. This was the first feeble step into serious wacko territory.

'So what do *you* think goes on here?' she asked.

Jim gave them a look as if to say, you have no idea. 'What I think isn't as important as why they're hiding it,' he said, pouring himself another top-up. They sat watching the flames for a while. Even Curtis wasn't sure how to proceed from here. Maybe the firewater wasn't helping as much as he thought. But Gina did a great impression of being fascinated by the whole thing.

'Wow, this is really exciting! I love this secret stuff.' It brought Jim out of his reverie and back to the conversation.

'Everything I'm gonna tell you is fact. When I leave fact I'll tell you, OK?'

Curtis nodded along with Gina. 'Sure, Jim.' Right, Jim.

'What I've pieced together over time goes something like this. Area 51 is some sort of military base that was set up next to the Nevada test site, where the Government experimented with nuclear bombs and shit in the early 50s. Even though it never appeared on aviation charts or US geological survey maps, a base appeared in the mid-50s alongside Groom Lake. That's when they were developing the U2 spy plane, but the place has been a test site for Black Budget intelligence and defence projects ever since.'

Jim sat thinking for a bit. So did Curtis and Gina.

'Anyways, in '84 they started getting publicity shy, and simply grabbed about 90 thousand acres of public land around the base to stop people from coming near it. Just like that. Fortunately for us, they forgot to take White Sides Mountain, which gives a pretty unobstructed view from just outside the border.'

'Is that where you're going?' asked Curtis.

Jim nodded. 'That's where we're going. Me, and about six others who want to see the place bad enough to pay 80 dollars for the privilege.'

'Don't they run any surveillance out there? If the place is that secret, it must be crawling with security.'

Jim shook his head. 'They don't need guards when they got eyes in the sky.' He looked upward. 'They got all sorts of hardware protecting this place. Only time I ever see real live people is when they send out a four-wheel drive 'cos they think we're getting too close. They just sit in the distance watching us through their binos. People usually get the hint and leave. I heard all the security guys they got here are ex-special forces. Real tough nuts. And they've been deputised by the local county sheriff's department, which means they can hold you legally any time they want. But that hardly ever happens.'

Jim continued as though this sort of conversation was entirely normal. 'But they know what's going on most of the time. Pretty hard to hide from a satellite. Probably got people just monitoring and filing and logging everything we do out here. Kinda like trainspotters. Except when the shit hits the fan. That's when all the info they're busy collecting comes in handy.'

Curtis was starting to feel uneasy. 'So how good are these satellites? Can they see us here now?'

Jim shrugged, which Curtis took as a yes. 'I think they use infrared at night — so they can see heat signatures. This fire's probably like a beacon. I'm sure they're used to it. But some of the stuff I've seen on the net is pretty detailed. They'll know exactly who's here and who isn't. And who's taking a crap right now.' Funny.

'They probably got your licence plate when you drove into town.' Not funny at all. Curtis looked at the Hummer, rented under his own name. At least it was paid for with cash. But he didn't feel so confident about this whole thing if what Jim was saying was true.

Enough beating around the bush. 'So what's your take on the UFO videos? You talked about them being part of a jigsaw — what did you mean by that?'

'You really want to know more about what's in those movies?'

'You got that right. More than you know. Curtis nodded. 'Yeah, sure.' Jim hesitated for a moment, as though deciding whether Curtis had earned the right to be privy to his suspicions.

'Wait here a second.' And with that he got up and disappeared into the Palace.

Gina looked at Curtis as they listened to him digging around in the maze, clearly looking for something.

'So it looks like you have some secrets too, huh?' Gina smiled as she whispered sweetly into his ear. Curtis knew she was referring to his conviction. Touché. Curtis was still trying to think up something appropriate to whisper back, when Jim returned clutching a worn ring-binder under his arm. His mug hadn't left his other hand the whole time.

'I'm gonna show you some stuff I've collected over the years. They're pretty old, and don't ask how I got them. But they've stood up to every authentication check me and smarter people than me could do on them.'

As he sat down he passed the folder to Curtis, along with a tiny flashlight. Curtis opened the folder to find it full of plastic sleeves containing copies of photocopied black-and-white photos and well-fingered, official-looking documents. Curtis flicked through them. They all seemed to be official in some sort of way, stamped with TOP SECRET or ABOVE TOP SECRET. But they were hard to make out under torchlight. He was grateful that Jim provided a running commentary. It was just like going through someone's photo album.

Almost.

'That's a memo from President Truman setting up something called Majestic–12. Ever heard of it?' Curtis shook his head. 'That was when they realised there was something they needed worse than the bomb.' He paused for effect. 'German flying-disc technology!' he said finally.

'Flying saucers?' said Curtis. Uh oh.

Jim nodded. 'Got that right.'

'So you're saying UFOs aren't really about aliens and science fiction. They were invented by the Germans 50 years ago?'

'Right again, Curtis.' This was becoming too much. But it was entertaining stuff, especially the way Jim told it, what with his conspiracy paranoia in overdrive.

'It's plain fact that our boys found designs for the flying discs when they invaded Germany and took over their scientific bases. Hell, we even brought some of their top brains back here to work on our own space programme. Ever hear of Operation Paperclip?' Curtis shook his head.

'Well, that's another story. But there's always been rumours that Hitler survived the bunkers.

That he somehow escaped. Of course there's never been any proof. Doesn't really matter now, anyways. But the Nazis had invented this technology so superior to our own, even though we'd just won the war, that it blew our defence programme out of the water. Big time.'

'They had this stuff *after* the war?' asked Curtis. The men in white coats were gathering.

'Got that right,' repeated Jim, dead serious. 'While Berlin was going up in flames, Plan B was put into effect. Tactical withdrawal. And where do you reckon they went?'

Curtis shrugged. 'I have no idea.'

Jim leant over to whisper in Curtis's ear. The fumes smelled highly flammable. 'The South Pole!' He sat back smugly to let his words sink in. This was getting weirder every minute. It was Curtis's turn to shake his head in disbelief.

'You're kidding, right?' Jim shook his head. Curtis could tell from his eyes that he was very serious. It sobered him up a little.

'It gets better,' Jim continued, 'because somehow we found out about their base and we invaded it in '47!'

Curtis was mock-shocked. 'No way!' Then the penny dropped. Loud and clear. 'So that's what you think that second video is of,' he said. 'A German flying disc attacking one of our ships down in Antarctica!'

'Got that right.' Jim punctuated his sentence with an impressive spit into the embers, which sizzled with a similarly impressive hiss of steam. Curtis sat and thought for a moment. The firewater was really dulling his brain, but he had to wonder. He had to think … what if?

'So what's this Majestic thing you were talking about — was that our own flying-disc project? That would explain all the UFO sightings around the country since the war. Fly them where you like because if anyone sees you they're gonna think it's the neighbourhood aliens buzzing in for a close encounter.' Jim sat there for a moment. He looked tired now. Maybe passing-out time wasn't too far away after all.

But he was just gathering his thoughts. 'Not as simple as that, Curtis. You see, back then they thought the real threat was the Commies. We needed every edge over the Russians, and so when the Nazis offered us a deal, we didn't turn them down.'

Curtis was gobsmacked. 'A deal? What kind of deal? Money in return for a flying saucer?'

Jim shook his head. 'We agreed to leave them alone in return for the disc technology.'

Curtis was blown away. 'No shit!'

Jim nodded firmly. 'No shit.'

'But how d'you know all this? I mean, if it's such a big secret, how'd you find out?'

Jim stared into the darkness. 'The clues are there if you know what you're looking for. And how to look for them.'

Curtis had just about had enough conspiracy theories for one night. 'Man, this is too much. If you know all this is true, and you've got the proof, why don't you just tell everyone about it? If the evidence stacks up, they'll believe you.'

Jim looked at Curtis through a pair of red, watery eyes. 'You've got a lot to learn, Curtis.'

Curtis didn't like the way Jim was looking at him. It wasn't aggressive or anything like that. It was the sadness in his eyes. Curtis had a feeling it was directed at him.

Gina decided she'd had enough. Curtis couldn't blame her.

'Well if you don't mind, I might hit the sack,' she said, getting up and dusting off her backside. She caught Curtis watching. 'Good night, gentlemen. This girl needs her beauty sleep.'

'I'll be in soon,' said Curtis. Gina smiled and disappeared into the trailer, leaving Curtis and Jim staring into the embers. He needed to get Jim talking again.

'It's getting late,' said Jim finally. 'If you come on the hike tomorrow you'll find out a whole lot more. You might as well tag along. You paid for it already.'

The invitation gave Curtis an idea. 'How long will we be gone?'

'Oh, leave at four, back around nine. That's a.m.,' said Jim.

'Yeah, OK. Sure. Count me in.' Plenty of time for what Curtis had in mind. But a 4 a.m. start? Definitely time for bed in that case. 'Well, Jim, if I'm getting up at 4 a.m. I'm gonna have to get some sleep. Been real interesting talking to you.'

'Night, Curtis. I'll wake you.'

Curtis left the old guy sitting there deep in thought as the embers died, and the night slowly swallowed him up.

'Gina, you awake?' Curtis whispered as he climbed into his bag beside her.

'Yeah, kinda,' came the reply. Gradually a ruffled head of hair emerged from the bag. He could just make out her face in the pale moonlight.

'Can you believe this guy? The website's just the tip of the iceberg. We've had UFOs, Nazis and flying discs tonight.'

Gina yawned. 'Yeah, I know. And I can't believe you drank that stuff. Talk about dog vomit.'

'Come on, it wasn't that bad after the first swallow. Hey, I've got an idea. But you need to focus.' Curtis could tell she was still halfway between sleep and listening to him. 'How 'bout some wild sex? Right here, right now.'

That sure got her attention. 'Curtis Hatch, I sincerely hope you're joking.'

'OK, OK. Listen, I'm going on this hike to Area 51 tomorrow morning. We leave at 4 a.m., and he said we'll be back around nine. You notice he doesn't lock his trailer?'

Gina looked as though she was nodding. 'Yeah, I noticed.'

'Think you could find those emails and download them onto a disk while we're gone?'

'Yeah, sure,' came the tired reply.

'Knew I could count on you.' Curtis kissed her on the lips. 'If we come back early I'll make sure I'm shouting and hollering. Give you plenty of time to get out. But you won't need five hours, that's for sure.'

'OK, James Bond. But right now I need some sleep.' And with that she disappeared back under the bag, leaving Curtis to think about his plan. It just might work. He tried to think of any reasons why it wouldn't, but at that hour, after that much homebrew, he wasn't up to the task. He was asleep before his head hit the pillow.

8

Curtis froze in his bag, instantly awake. Something had grabbed his foot. He was sure of it. He lay dead-still for a moment, too scared to breathe. The thing grabbed his foot again, and this time he jumped out of his skin.

'Sorry, Curtis. Didn't mean to scare you.' It was Jim. But it had only been five minutes since he hit the sack. It didn't make any sense. Slowly Curtis realised the night sounded different. It was colder too. He looked out the window. The fire was out and Jim was packed and ready to go.

'Yeah, uh … I'll just be a minute.' Fucking hell. Curtis got up and wandered around the trailer in a sleepy, firewater daze. Cap, shirt, MP3 player. He was vaguely aware there were people outside.

He emerged half-dressed from the trailer to find a group of heavily clothed people sitting in the back of Jim's pick-up, waiting in stony silence for him. He could tell they didn't approve of his tardiness. He climbed into the back with the rest of them, and forced his brain to catch up with his body. Jim's driving didn't help. He only hoped the old rust bucket would hold together under all this weight. After a while he started to get used to the obscenely uncomfortable ride, the darkness, and the closeness of sitting next to people he didn't know.

The chubby guy with the beard was the first to break the ice. 'I'm glad I took the expensive option!' He followed it up with a well-timed smile. Even in the darkness Curtis could make out the teeth emerging briefly from the beard.

'If it was easy, everyone would be doing it.' That was the intense Greek-looking woman opposite.

'Do you ever ask yourself, why am I doing this?' said the blonde woman down in the corner. All American apple pie. Stuck out like a sore thumb amongst this lot. Curtis dug into his bag for some music. Anything was better than this. He found what he was looking for. A remedy to this weirdness. He lifted his phones over his head and The Edge invaded his consciousness. 'Zoo Station' all right.

By the time the song had finished, a group-bonding session was well underway. Curtis sat listening to the talk with his headphones on, pretending he was still tuned out. They were a pretty sorry bunch if this was the best ConspiracyWatch could throw at the establishment. Young nerds, nervy alcoholics and the truly weird. And the blonde woman over in the other corner, keeping the conversation going. These people clearly weren't used to saying more in public than 'Yes, I'll have fries with that', but she was stringing them along with clever lines of questioning. They were basically spilling their guts out to her. Curtis could see the handicam she kept waving around like an accessory. It only stopped waving around when someone was getting personal. Painfully personal. Curtis removed his phones and she was on him in an instant, looking for a new angle on paranoia. Maybe she figured he was weirder than the rest.

'Hi there! Glad you could join us!' she shouted across the jumble of feet and backpacks. Curtis could tell it was more for everyone else's benefit than his.

'Just listening to the last episode of the "X-Files" — you know, getting into the zone! Woohoo!' OK, maybe the firewater had something to do with it, but it shut her up nicely. Shut the whole bunch of them up, as a matter of fact.

Blondie was the first to react, and her reaction said more about her than him. 'So you're not a believer, then?' Curtis looked at the faces around him. They were serious, earnest faces, questioning Curtis's integrity. Either he was a believer — whatever that was — or he was an outcast. He looked at the camera, which had stopped waving and even though the woman never once looked at it, it was trained straight from her hip to where Curtis was sitting. He was sure the record light had been taped over.

'I believe what I can see. That's why I'm here.' He pulled his cap down low, and shrunk into the corner of the pick-up.

'Ain't that the truth.' It was beardy man. Al from 'Home Improvement'.

'Yeah, man.' That was from one of the dweebiest guys Curtis had ever seen. This place was a dweeb-magnet. Abductees Anonymous. Time to exit this conversation. Curtis pulled his headphones back on, and pretended to hit the play button. He sat back and listened to the strangest bunch of people he'd ever shared a ride with, while Blondie tickled their paranoia bones.

'So what brings you all here? I mean, it's a pretty odd thing to do on your day off, isn't it?' she asked innocently.

'Not if you know some of the stuff we know,' said Al.

'I'm not going anywhere. Fill me in, I love a good conspiracy theory,' said Blondie. Yep. She was fishing.

'It's not theory. It's fact. Just gotta have an open mind, and put all the pieces together.' The Greek woman was deadpan as she spoke. Sad, emotionless eyes.

'I'm sorry, but you're going to have to help me out here. I'm really not up with the latest on this,' said Blondie, surreptitiously turning her camera in the direction of whoever was speaking. 'What do you think is *really* going on at this place? Is the government hiding something you think we should know about?'

'Oh it's bigger than that!' said the Dweeb on Curtis's right. 'It's much, much bigger than one single government.' This sounded like his special topic. 'You can't possibly begin to understand the

scope of this thing. Not in five minutes, anyway.'
Blondie's eyes lit up. This looked like just what
she'd come to hear. Wacko conspiracy theories.
Alive and well in Nevada.

'Give me the short version. Is it really that
bad?' she asked.

'It's probably worse, actually,' said Al, matter-
of-factly. There was a moment's pause in the
weirdness. They looked like they were
contemplating the end of the world. 'How much
do you know about Area 51?' he asked.

'Not much … top-secret air-force base for
developing secret weapons. Like the stealth
bomber and all that.'

Al shook his head knowingly. 'Then you're not
ready for the truth, I'm afraid. But don't worry,
it'll be ready for you soon enough.' They passed
around knowing looks at Blondie's expense.

Finally the Greek woman took pity on her. 'We
have reason to believe that much more goes on
there than that. That's what the government
wants us to believe. It's a cover story.'

'A cover story? For what?' asked Blondie.

'For the biggest conspiracy ever known. The
big one. The conspiracy to end all conspiracies.'

Blondie shook her head in confusion. 'You
mean like who killed J.F.K.? That sort of thing?'

The Dweeb shook his head. 'That's small-time
compared to this.'

'So what's it all about? Come on, I really want to
know this stuff.' Blondie was getting desperate.
They were clamming up on her. 'I really admire you
guys. I really do. You're like freedom fighters for

the truth. Why don't you share the burden? Tell me what you've learned and open my eyes to this stuff. That's why you do it, right? To warn everyone?' A few coy looks were exchanged. Curtis was impressed. She was working them like a pro.

Al was the first to take the bait. 'We have to be careful about who we talk to about this stuff. Not everyone's ready for the truth. Can't blame them though. Kinda upsets your view of things.'

'Outta the comfort zone, huh?' said Blondie.

'Well, when you find out that just about everything you take for granted, you know, freedom of speech, democracy, the Constitution … when you find out they're all just part of the façade, well that can rock your boat some.'

'Yeah,' said the Dweeb, 'we're just pawns, man. Just pawns.'

'What do you mean?' said Blondie. 'Just how big is this thing? Give me an idea, at least.'

'Well there's the bases, like the one we're having a look at now. They're all over. But they're pretty well hidden.'

'Bases for what?' Blondie was losing her patience. So was Curtis. This was getting ridiculous.

'All sorts of things. But mainly they're where they develop and launch the spacecraft.'

'Spacecraft?'

'For colonising the human race.' Colonising. The human race. Curtis fought back a smile.

'They're all over the world. Quite a few here in the States. Places like Mountauk Point in Long Island, Dulce, New Mexico …'

'And there's that new one beneath Denver International Airport. It's supposed to be massive!' It was the Greek woman. She'd suddenly come alive again.

'She's right,' said Al. 'The biggest and oldest one is Base 211. It's under UN control now, but it was originally built by the Nazis during the war. Down at Antarctica somewhere.' Blondie looked lost for words. Finally.

But she'd started the ball rolling. Now she just had to sit back and keep up with it.

'You see, *they* developed the original flying saucers. They were so advanced they kept them secret after the war. But we ended up making a deal with them to leave them alone in return for their hyper-advanced technology. That's when the whole thing started.'

'What about the space race? And the space shuttle? How's that connected?' asked Blondie. Fair question.

'Oh that's just a front,' said Al, waving her off. 'That's just the excuse to siphon trillions of dollars into the colonisation project. The Apollo missions were all for show. They weren't the first people to set foot on the moon, that's for sure!'

'Damn right!' said the Dweeb emphatically. 'Oh they all knew about it. But it must have given them a hell of a fright to see flying discs and a moonbase back then. Of course, they censored all that stuff out of the transmissions they made available to the public.'

'OK … so where's the colony, then?' asked Blondie. 'On the moon?'

The Dweeb shook his head. 'Mars. The moon's just a half-way station, to store supplies, refuel and do the serious business away from prying eyes.'

'Mars,' said Blondie slowly. Like Curtis, she was having trouble with all this.

Luckily the Dweeb explained it for her. 'See, they exploded an atom bomb in the atmosphere around '63, which released all the oxygen in the planet's soil. It was frozen into the subterranean ice. It's breathable now.'

'And who's "they"?' Blondie asked.

The Dweeb pulled a face. 'A bunch of high-powered military from about a dozen countries. Started off with just us, the Nazis, the Russians and the Brits. Now I think there's more than that involved. Like a top-secret United Nations.'

'OK ...' said Blondie sceptically, 'but you haven't told me why. If this is all true, why are they doing it?'

'To save the human race. That's what they believe anyway. Only their version of what's worth saving is probably a little different from ours.'

'Save us from what? Ourselves?'

'Global warming. The next Ice Age. Scientists have known for decades we're entering a period of acute global warming. Greenhouse gases are just speeding up what nature's doing anyway. Around every 25 000 years, the planet heats up, and the poles melt. That screws up the weather and eventually you get apocalyptic floods, and then another Ice Age. Exactly what happened to the dinosaurs. Noah lived through the last one. But I'm not so sure we're going to be as lucky this time.' Now that was a real conversation stopper. Curtis sat as spellbound as the rest of them. Just for different reasons. A psychiatrist would have a field day with this lot.

'Anyway,' continued Al, 'during the fifties they held a scientific summit to come up with ways of surviving the catastrophe. Came down to three options.'

'And they were?' asked Blondie, less convincingly now.

'The first one was to explode a nuclear device in the atmosphere, to punch a giant hole in it and release all the greenhouse gases. But that raised the problem of atmospheric radiation. Next they came up with the idea of trying to survive the Ice Age underground. You know, to develop vast subterranean cities. They'd already proven that crops can grow faster underground than they do on the surface, but they wouldn't fit the earth's whole population down there — they'd only have room for the world's elite. But that one hit a snag too, when they realised the heat from the earth's crust would eventually make life impossible. Even underground. And of course, they would have had surface flooding of biblical proportions to contend with. So they came up with Alternative 3.'

'Alternative 3?'

Al nodded. 'Evacuation of planet earth.' Curtis couldn't believe what he was hearing. They made it all sound so matter of fact, like they discussed this stuff every other day. Probably did for that matter.

'It was the only option left. Colonise Mars. Of course, they'd still only have room for the elite, so it had to be done in absolute secrecy. Otherwise civilisation would just fall apart. And they don't want that to happen until they're good and ready.'

Blondie whistled thinly. 'That's some conspiracy. I'm assuming you guys have some good reasons for believing this stuff?'

'Evidence is everywhere,' said the Greek woman. 'Everywhere you look. But it really only started to come together after a British documentary cottoned on to it in the 70s. They started doing a story on the scientific brain-drain in the UK during the 60s. Seemed that several top scientists they were investigating vanished into thin air. Then they realised it was just the tip of the iceberg. It was happening over here as well. They had accidentally discovered evidence of an ultra-secret interplanetary project.'

'Yep,' said Al, 'and when it went to air, it frightened the bejesus out of everyone. The TV station was swamped with tens of thousands of calls. Then the TV network came out with a statement saying the whole thing was an April Fool's joke. Seems someone else got spooked by the documentary too ... Except it wasn't shown on April first.' They all shared Al's little in-the-know laugh. 'But they must have been on to something. The documentary got pulled from schedules all around the world. It never got shown here. A few of the reporters who'd put it together got fired, I think. They wrote a book about it a while later. No one ever heard from them after that. They just disappeared like the scientists they'd been investigating in the programme.'

'Alternative 3, huh?' said Blondie after a while. She'd run out of questions. Curtis breathed a quiet sigh of relief. He'd run out of patience. They looked odd enough, but what he'd just heard was downright scary. Now he knew how the Chief must have felt in *One Flew Over the Cuckoo's Nest*.

Eventually the torture subsided when Jim pulled the pick-up into a large crevasse at the base of some serious rock. Curtis couldn't see the top in the dark. Jim obviously knew where he was going, though, judging by the way he swung in to park. Without lights on. Must eat a lot of carrots, as well as beans. The motley group piled out of the back. It wasn't a pretty sight, and Curtis was glad it was dark. The tension had risen substantially since Jim turned off the engine. This was radical stuff for most of them. Peering into the mouth of the volcano. Something to tell the grandchildren.

But for Jim this was just another guided tour. 'All right, stick close, follow the person in front, with your left hand on their shoulder. It's gonna be dark and we're not using flashlights. Keep the noise to a minimum. Let's go, folks.'

With that he vanished into the black as the group gradually got their wits about them and hurriedly formed a line to catch up with their guide.

Curtis found he had Blondie with the camera behind him. Her hand on his shoulder felt surprisingly strong. Or suprisingly scared. They were climbing, and the stillness of the desert air was refreshing after the pick-up ride. It was also very intimidating. Following the person in front in pitch-black over ground he'd never seen, knowing that the chances were good they were already being watched.

'Come on, why are you really here? You don't fit in with this lot. You look far too sane.' It was Blondie. Curtis decided to ignore her. They kept walking. But a while later she had another go.

'You know, this is so exciting! Kinda like playing searchlight in third grade!'

Curtis couldn't resist shutting her down before she got started on him. 'We'll be playing searchlight with a helicopter if you don't keep your bloody voice down.' She obviously decided Curtis wasn't going to give her a sound bite for the vidcam, because she didn't try again. Much to his relief.

They gathered around Jim, who'd finally stopped. 'The point's up ahead. Hands and knees from here till you feel the tip of the cliff. That's a good time to stop. No lights or cigarettes. And no flashbulbs either. When you get tapped on the shoulder it's time to go. Remember that could be any time. Show time, folks.' He disappeared up the hill on his belly.

Curtis joined the rest of them at the tip of the hill, and waited for dawn to arrive. As he lay on his stomach on the cold dirt in the darkness, he started to forget the dull ache in his head and the bruising on his butt, and revelled in the freshness of the morning air. He heard Jim slide in next to him, but he wasn't in a conversational mood. A couple of thermos flasks got handed down the line. Curtis declined the offer. He didn't want to get too familiar with this lot. But as he lay there, the ground got harder. And colder. He just hoped Gina was doing the business back at the trailer.

Gradually the blackness washed into the steely grey of dawn, and Curtis could see for the first time some of the features ahead of him. A long valley. Huge. More hills. Some incredibly high. As the light increased he could make out a long white strip down one of the bigger valleys. It turned into a runway. Then the first buildings appeared through the haze in the distance. A loose collection of featureless military-style buildings. But the size of some of them was remarkable. As the sun started to assert itself over the night, the valley was laid bare before them. Curtis could tell that some of the group were in a state bordering on arousal as the runway and buildings came fully into view. These guys had to get out more. Curtis wasn't sure what they were expecting the buildings to reveal. They were probably disappointed the buildings didn't morph into UFOs and try to abduct them.

Curtis indulged in a quiet smile to himself. Jim didn't show any expression at all. He'd probably seen it a dozen times. And probably been a hell of a lot closer than this.

It wasn't much longer after daybreak that the tapping on shoulders began, and the group pulled back to the meeting point.

'That's it, folks. Let's hightail it back.' Jim wasn't keen to hang around.

Some of them looked a little disappointed it was over. Eighty bucks worth. But mostly they kept to themselves on the way down. Lost in their own paranoid little worlds.

Except Blondie. 'That turn you into a believer?' She wouldn't let it rest.

'Well, I believe there's a bunch of buildings down there. What about you?' Let's focus on her for a change.

'I find the social phenomenon of the whole thing more interesting. You know, what makes people travel all this way out here and pay 80 bucks to walk through the desert at night to spy on some government base?' Sounded like a reporter to Curtis.

'So why did *you* come?' she asked, finally. Curtis had been waiting for that one. He needed to think fast.

'Why not?' Well, that was thinking on your feet for you at this ungodly hour. It would have to do.

'What's your name, if you don't mind me asking?' She was walking right beside him now. Curtis kept an eye on the camera. It didn't seem to be switched on. That was the last thing he needed right now.

'Neo,' he said, offhandedly. Let's see if she guesses where that one came from.

'So you see yourself as a bit of a Keanu Reeves, do you?' Shit. So she'd seen *The Matrix* too.

'I see myself getting tired of your questions. You didn't tell me your name either.' Time to exit this conversation.

'Sam. Pleased to meet you, Neo.'

She put out her hand, which Curtis reluctantly took without missing a step.

'Ditto.' It was at that moment, when they were descending down the last hill to the pick-up, that Jim raised the alarm.

'Look's like we got company, folks. Put your camera gear out of sight and make straight for the pick-up. They won't bother us if we don't bother them.'

Jim was looking at a ridge-top in the distance. At the very tip was what appeared to be dark-coloured four-wheel drive with blacked-out windows. The group of conspiracy hunters suddenly became hyped. The first sign of movement all morning. They passed hushed comments between themselves about 'cammo dudes', whoever they were. Sounded like some nickname for the security guys in the four-wheel drive. The pace picked up, and soon they were back at the pick-up. The two guys who'd shared the cab with Jim took it upon themselves to sit with the great unwashed in the back. They made a show of graciously offering 'their' seats to the others. One of them looked at Curtis, and he had to be honest, after the punishing his butt took on the way in, a seat was damn inviting. And he wasn't sure he could handle another conspiracy group-session at this hour. He suppressed his desire to launch himself at the door, and did the honourable thing by offering the invitation to the Greek woman. She turned him down flat, obviously having too much fun in the back. Either that or she had a higher pain threshold than Curtis. But he wasn't going to be too generous with the offer, and dived into the cab next to Jim, hunting for a seatbelt. There wasn't one. That was when Sam jumped in, squeezing uncomfortably close next to him. Shit. He shook his head in disgust.

The conversation in the front wasn't much heading back to Rachel. Jim was probably as tired as Curtis after the late night and early morning. Thankfully Sam the Reporter seemed to have run out of questions. But it looked as though most of them in the back had got their money's worth. He could hear the excited chitchat through the cab's rear window. Sighting the 'cammo dudes' had changed everything. It would probably keep them in bulletin-board posts for years.

As the pick-up bounced its way across the desert, winding between the incongruous-looking Joshua trees, Curtis started to doze.

But Sam pulled him out of it. She had a question. Here we go again. 'Hey Jim, if you really wanted to sneak into one of these places, could you do it? How well guarded are they really? Didn't see any barbed wire or fences.'

Curtis could tell Jim was thinking — either that or he was pretending not to show he'd already asked himself that exact same question.

'Well, let's see. A lot of the perimeter seems to be marked with roads. I reckon they've got all kinds of sensors and stuff. I've heard it called the electronic fenceline. They got these orange posts every couple of hundred feet or so. Not sure what they're for.' Curtis noticed Sam was showing a very keen interest in this line of discussion. He also noticed the camera was off. Maybe her battery was dead.

'The stuff that's known about includes some sort of magnetic sensors. They're supposed to detect large metal objects. No prizes for guessing what they're designed to pick up. Then there's the ground-vibration sensors. Probably got them all over the place. But they'd have to be set so they didn't get triggered by all the wildlife around here. Otherwise they'd go off every time a rabbit farted.' Jim obviously liked that one, because he allowed himself a good laugh. 'And they're supposed to have these electro-optical trip sensors, like laser beams that go off when the beam is broken. But they'd have to be about waist-height or they'd have the same problem with the wildlife.'

Curtis was surprised. Jim had obviously studied this sort of stuff.

'And then you got your ammonia sensors. They reckon they can tell the difference between human and animal sweat. Amazing, huh?' The only thing Curtis was amazed at was that Jim hadn't set them off already.

'So when one or two of these sensors goes off, they send out these black helicopters. Hate to think what sort of detection equipment they have on those. Probably infrared cameras — they read heat signatures — and night-vision cameras. That and the usual array of top-secret weaponry.' Curtis was impressed. With both Jim's knowledge *and* the extent of the security measures. The ones Jim knew about, anyway.

'Wow,' was Sam's summation of the whole thing. Curtis's too. Certainly made you think.

Jim dropped the tourists off back at the motel. A few polite goodbyes and a sarcastic 'nice meeting you, Neo' from Sam, then it was just Curtis left in the cab as Jim returned to the trailer. Curtis was keen to find out how Gina had got on. He made some lame excuse to Jim about catching up on some sleep for a few hours and dragged his exhausted body back to his no-star motel. But as soon as he entered the trailer he could tell something was wrong. The sleeping bags were empty, and it was dead quiet. He called Gina's name softly, so that Jim wouldn't hear the concern in his voice. No answer. Maybe she'd gone out to pee. He called out her name for a second time. This time he heard something. It was muffled, but it sounded like Gina. And she didn't sound happy. Actually, she sounded terrified.

'Where are you?' Curtis couldn't see her anywhere. But her voice sounded close. It wasn't as though there was anywhere to hide in this closet on wheels.

Curtis noticed one of the sofa cushions lifting up, and the door to the compartment underneath as well. It was Gina. What the hell was she up to?

'Help me outta here, goddammit!' Curtis grabbed one of her arms and pulled her out.

'Funny time to play hide and seek!' he said. His alarm had shifted to amusement at finding her safe and well. But it soon faded when he saw how pale she was. It looked like she'd been crying too.

'What the hell happened? What are you doing in there?'

But Gina wasn't kidding around. 'I want to get out of here. This place gives me the creeps.'

Curtis was dumbstruck. 'What's wrong? Did you get into his machine?'

To her credit, Gina pulled herself together remarkably well. But Curtis could tell she was really freaked. With a sniff and a nod, and a long breath to compose herself, Gina recounted for Curtis what had happened since he'd been gone.

As soon as the noise of Jim's pick-up had faded into the night, Gina had sneaked across into his trailer. She'd easily managed to find the email on his machine. He hadn't even deleted it. She'd been able to download it onto a disk, and remove all trace of her activities within 15 minutes. But after she'd gone back to sleep, while it was still dark, she'd woken thinking Curtis had returned. She couldn't see or hear anyone in the trailer, so she figured she must have been imagining things. As she lay in the dark in her sleeping bag, she heard the trailer suspension squeak. Just slightly. But enough to make her lie very still. That was when she lost it, because, as she explained to Curtis, she could just make out a black shape *inside* the trailer.

Not moving. Just watching her. And she could make out two bright green eyes staring at her.

Curtis had to wonder what drugs she'd been on while he was experiencing the great Area 51 adventure. Gina continued her story. As she lay frozen with fear, her heart racing, she noticed the thing was waving a thin red light over the whole trailer, as though it was looking for something. Or someone. She said she felt, more than saw, the light hesitate over her head for a second, then she sensed the thing stiffen, as though it had just noticed her head sticking out from the pile of sleeping bags. For an instant she thought it was going to approach her. And for an instant Curtis thought she might be making the whole thing up. But no one could have acted that genuinely scared out of their wits. Not for any amount of money.

But whoever — or whatever — it was, disappeared out of the trailer as silently as it had appeared. She waited for as long as she dared in the darkness, straining to hear if it had gone. Then she searched for somewhere to hide — there was nowhere outside, apart from the car, and Curtis had the keys. So she found the storage space under the seat and managed to worm her way in, where she stayed till he found her, two hours later.

Curtis couldn't believe it. No wonder she was hysterical when he'd pulled her out. But retelling the story had calmed her down, and in the cold light of the desert morning the trailer looked harmless enough. But Gina was sure something had been in the trailer last night. And Curtis had no way of knowing who. There wasn't much else he could do, except console her. He was getting good at that.

'I'm not spending another night here. We've got the emails. Let's just check them out back in Vegas. We've got what we came for. After what I went through last night, I reckon I've earned that money fair and square.'

Curtis nodded. 'Yeah, sure. Let's get out of here. I've had enough of this place too.'

'How was the hike?' asked Gina.

Curtis shrugged. 'Pretty boring really. Bunch of buildings way off in the distance. The best part was listening to all the crazies talking about these really out-there conspiracy theories as though they were fact. You shoulda heard some of the stuff they were going on about.' He shook his head in amazement. No matter how hard he tried he would never be able to convey the weirdness of the whole experience.

It was about then that Jim Maze burst into the trailer, complete with a rifle aimed squarely at the two of them. 'I believe you have something of mine.' He said it so politely, that if it wasn't for the rifle Curtis would have been really impressed with his manners. But it was too much for Gina after her 'visitation', and she was starting to panic. He needed to calm things down. For her sake.

'What's the problem, Jim? And what's with the gun? You outta your mind?'

Jim wasn't in the mood for chitchat. 'Don't fuck about with me, kid. This isn't a toy. The trailer might not be locked, but that don't mean I don't take precautions.' Curtis was thinking fast. What did he mean, precautions?! Ammonia sensors?

'What you do mean, Jim? I'm not following you.'

Jim waved the rifle at Gina as he spoke. 'Caught your little woman here going through my computer on the surveillance camera. Didn't really think I'd leave the place unprotected, did you? You two must be dumber than you look.' Surveillance camera. Right. Time to panic. Curtis couldn't see a way out of this.

'So just hand over the disk, and whatever else you took, and you can wait here until I call the county sheriff's department. It'll take a while for them to get here though.'

Did Jim say sheriff? Definitely time to panic. Curtis thought hard. There was only one way out of this. The truth. Hell, he didn't have many other options. 'OK, listen, Jim. I'll tell you what we're really doing here. But you gotta put the gun down first. You're scaring the daylights outta Gina.'

Jim shrugged and lowered the rifle.

'OK. I'm all ears.' Curtis let out a long slow breath, and tried to work out where to begin.

'Well, we're not really here for the hike.'

'Had that figured,' Jim snorted.

'We actually came to meet you.' That stopped him in his tracks.

'Whaddaya mean?' He was instantly suspicious. Maybe he thought they really were Feds this time.

217

'And we're not Feds, so relax, OK?' said Curtis.

'I'll be the judge of that.' This was going to take some convincing.

'Gina and I really did meet at DefCon. Just days ago. We won a computer-security competition. And then someone asked us if we could do them a favour.'

'What kind of favour?' Jim's voice was starting to lose some of its edge. Thank goodness.

'To find out who sent you those mpegs. You know — the flying-disc videos. Apparently the guy's a historian. Gets off on this stuff.'

Jim looked sceptical. He nodded in Gina's direction. 'Is he telling the truth?'

Gina nodded. She was clearly still freaked out. Curtis wasn't sure whether it was the visitation in the night or Jim's rifle that was scaring her most.

Jim must have noticed she looked pretty shaken up. 'What's wrong with you?'

Gina looked at Curtis. He could tell she wasn't sure whether to tell him or not. Curtis decided to make up her mind for her. 'Someone broke into our trailer last night. While we were out having fun with all the wackos. Scared the shit out of her.'

Jim was instantly curious. And suspicious. 'Who?'

'I don't know who,' said Gina adamantly. 'They didn't leave a business card, OK?' It was slowly dawning on Jim that neither of them were joking around. His earlier aggro was turning to concern. He sat down. Slowly.

'All right. Tell me what happened.' Gina recounted her story. Jim sat silently the whole time. No questions. Just listening. Hearing it for a second time, Curtis realised just how unnerving the whole thing was. Real spooky.

When she'd finished, Jim sat silently for a few more moments. He looked like he was having trouble coming to grips with what had happened. Either that or he was deciding whether to believe her, what with the green eyes and red light and all.

'I know who it was,' he said finally. OK, thought Curtis. This was going to be interesting. 'They sometimes send out some of their security guys to check up on us. Think you just met one of them.'

Gina looked confused. 'You mean that was some security guard? Didn't look like any guard I ever met.'

Jim smiled. 'Well, that's probably because they're not. These are specialists. They probably knew I was out taking a few people to see the base. Probably been monitoring the website. Guess they figured they'd have a little peek at what I'm up to while I peeked on them.'

'But what about the eyes? And the red-light thing?' asked Curtis.

'Night-vision goggles. Makes night as clear as day. And the red light was most likely the laser-scope of his gun.'

Gina went white. Curtis couldn't really blame her.

'You're fucking joking!' she said. Curtis thought she was going to break down. Delayed shock. He put his arm around her to comfort her, and to make himself feel better for putting her through this. Jim got up and went outside. He held the trailer door open as he studied the ground around the doorstep. When he came back in he was grimacing.

'Yep. There's a boot mark out there, all right.' When he sat down again no one was sure what to say next.

'At least it wasn't an alien,' said Gina eventually. Somehow she'd managed to see a funny side to the whole thing. They all found the joke funnier than it really was.

'At least my gun wasn't loaded!' said Jim. That one really set them off. They were all laughing harder than the joke deserved.

'Look,' said Jim in between laughs, 'you want to know where the movies came from?'

Curtis nodded. 'That's all. I swear.'

'Well, why didn't you just ask me?' said Jim. Curtis looked at Gina, and together they realised what idiots they'd been. Gina just started laughing again. And soon all three of them were laughing and shaking their heads.

'So why don't you give me the disk you took, and we can find out where these things came from together, OK?' Gina nodded, still laughing sheepishly, as she pulled an unmarked disk from her jacket pocket and handed it back to Jim.

One million dollars. And they just had to ask.

9

Back inside Jim's trailer, Curtis spotted the inconspicuous-looking surveillance camera straight away. But this time he was looking for it. He couldn't believe he hadn't guessed that someone as paranoid as Jim might take some pretty unusual security measures. Leaving the trailer unlocked had fooled him all right. But soon all that was forgotten, as Jim proved he was as keen to find out who had sent him the mystery footage as they were. Except he was just curious. Curtis was doing this for the money, make no mistake about that. Soon the email was up on Jim's screen. Sure enough, it was from Anonymous. Very original. Soon Curtis was analysing its footprints, providing a commentary more for Jim's sake than anything else.

'This is basic stuff really, once you know how. See, every email gets a header right?' Curtis brought up a list of long phrases containing abbreviated names and sets of numbers onto the screen.

'Now the sender usually only controls the receiver line and the subject line.' Jim nodded. He understood this much.

'But the mail software adds heaps more stuff as it gets routed to the receiver.' Curtis clicked to reveal a long, complicated-looking set of numbers and abbreviations.

'See, when you send an email, it passes through a series of gateways, like post offices in the old days. And just like the old postmarks you used to get on your snail mail, it picks up the postmarks of all the servers it goes through.' Curtis pointed at a line on the screen. 'Each computer that receives this message adds a field with its complete address and time stamp on it.'

Jim shook his head. 'Amazing. I didn't know that.'

'So we can track the message back to the sender's server if we have to. But it can take a while because you have to check with all the logs on the servers. I'm just hoping this one has only been cloaked, and not totally falsified.'

For the first time, Curtis could feel the million bucks getting closer.

'The first line tells all the other computers which one really sent the email, so they can send error messages back to it if it gets bounced somewhere. Now this line here,' Curtis pointed to the top line, 'that's the message ID — basically a unique identifier for this specific message. That will help us trace it if we need to. But first I'm just going to check the name and email address of the message ID with the return path. If they're different this is going to take a while. If it's not, then we're in the money.' So to speak. Curtis was in luck. He tried to control his excitement, and keep his voice steady.

'See here, the return path is different to the sender line, but it's the same server as the message ID line. So the sender line's been faked. But we've got them with the ID.' They all peered at the line on the screen above Curtis's finger. Hello sroberts@news2U2day.com.

Jim read the address out loud. 'News2U2day-dot-com. Never heard of it.'

'Neither have I,' said Gina. 'Let's check it out, Curtis.' She was getting impatient. So was Curtis. He opened Jim's web browser and keyed in a popular search engine. Instantly they had a URL address for News2U2day.com. Curtis clicked on the hyperlink and there it was. News2U2day.com in all its glory. It was an internet news agency. It looked like it sourced a lot of its stories from other news organisations, but also had its own small staff of reporters based out of LA.

'OK,' said Curtis, 'let's find out if Mr Roberts is here.' He clicked onto the staff pages, and brought up the profiles of their reporters, most of whom had their own niche-market columns. As he scrolled to the bottom of the page, Curtis saw the name he was after. And a face he recognised. The 'S' stood for Samantha. Samantha Roberts, Junior Staff Writer.

'Well I'll be …' Jim recognised her too. Hell, they'd only been sitting next to her an hour ago. Curtis looked at Jim with an expression that told him he couldn't believe it either.

'No wonder she was asking so many questions,' said Curtis.

'Who is she?' asked Gina.

'This woman was on the hike this morning,' said Jim shaking his head. 'She's a reporter, and she sent me the videos and must have come on the hike for a story.' He didn't look happy. 'Goddamn!' Yep. He was very unhappy. There was something very weird about this, thought Curtis. Very weird indeed.

He looked at Gina. When she saw him watching her, she nodded her head towards the door. Let's get out of here, it meant. Curtis nodded so Jim couldn't see. They had what they were after. Time to go. But Jim had other ideas.

'I think I'm going to have to pay Miss Roberts a visit before she leaves town.'

Curtis had to admit, he was suspicious at the coincidence. In fact he was sure it wasn't one. But he also had a feeling gnawing at his gut that going back to the sponsor with the name of a reporter from an internet news organisation wasn't exactly what he'd been asked to deliver. In fact, he felt deflated. The whole thing was probably a hoax to cook up a story for her column. Gina just wanted to make tracks, though.

'Look, Curtis and I have to get back to Vegas. We've got what we came for. And we're very grateful to you, Mr Maze.' She really was keen to leave. Curtis couldn't blame her after her episode in the night. But he needed to know, just like Jim did, where the footage came from.

'Don't you want to find out why she sent them here? Or where *she* got them from?' asked Curtis.

Gina nodded impatiently. 'Well sure, but that's not what we were asked to do. I need a hot shower and — no offence, Jim — a decent night's sleep. I want to go back, Curtis. Please.'

Curtis looked at Jim. 'You going to see her now?'

Jim nodded. 'Yep. Before she leaves the motel. Have to leave now if we're gonna catch her though.'

'Just give me an hour, OK?' said Curtis. He could tell she wasn't impressed, but Jim's presence was keeping her from serving one at Curtis.

'I'll be in the car ... with the engine running,' she said abruptly, and promptly got up and left the trailer. Jim smiled.

'You got a feisty one there, my boy!' Curtis gave him a half-smile back. He didn't know the half of it.

'OK, let's do it. We've got an hour,' said Curtis, getting up.

'Women,' said Jim as they climbed into the pick-up. Sounded like there was some history there. Curtis decided not to ask. It was a short drive back to the A-Lee-Inn, and Jim went straight in to the woman behind the bar, who was now serving meals to a number of hungry conspiracy hikers. Curtis tagged along behind, since Jim seemed to know what he was doing.

'Maggie, I need to get into one of your rooms. It's important.' Maggie gave Curtis the once-over, no doubt wondering what the hell they were up to. But she seemed to know Jim well enough to do as she was asked without asking why.

'Which one?'

'The young blonde woman. The reporter.' Curtis could see a flash of understanding cross her face. She reached under the bar and pulled out a key.

'Room three, down the hall.' Jim thanked her and they made their way through the tightly packed dining tables out to the motel section of the 'Inn. It wasn't luxury by any stretch of the imagination, but it looked clean and comfortable enough.

Outside room three, Jim and Curtis looked at each other. They were unsure whether to knock or not, so Jim decided for both of them. He jammed the key into the lock and swung the door open a few inches. From where Curtis was standing, he could see Blondie — a.k.a. Samantha Roberts — sitting on the bed, wearing a towelling robe. Her hair was wet, and she looked freshly showered. She was busy typing on a laptop she had set up on her bed. He also noticed the video camera beside it. It was plugged into the lappie.

She looked up as they entered her room. 'Hey! What do you think you're doing?'

'We need to speak to you for a moment. It's important,' said Jim.

Sam got up from the bed and came to the door. She didn't look too pleased about the short notice.

'Well, where I come from people knock before they go barging into someone's room.'

But Jim came back at her, with interest. 'And where I come from people don't pretend to be something they're not.' Curtis saw a moment of doubt in her eyes, instantly suspicious. Suspicious that they were on to her little scheme.

'Give me a couple of moments, will you?' And she closed the door on them. Jim's manners returned, and the two of them waited silently out in the motel hallway for the door to re-open. When it did, Curtis saw the lappie was gone. Only the camera remained.

'Now what can I do for you two gentlemen?' she said, inviting them in.

Jim came straight to the point. 'You sent me some video footage. I want to know why.' Sam instantly dropped the charm and poise she had collected while they were waiting out in the hall.

'I don't know what you're talking about. What video footage?' She was good. Curtis decided to have a go.

'We know you work for News2U2day. We traced the email you sent Jim back to your address.'

To her credit, she took this revelation completely in her stride. Didn't even bat an eyelid. 'There must be some kind of mistake. Look, I have to get back to LA. I'm sorry to disappoint you both, but I really don't know what you're talking about. Now would you mind ...' She walked back to the door and held it open. They'd outstayed their welcome. Curtis looked at Jim. This wasn't working out as planned. Time to get creative.

Curtis sat down on the vinyl sofa and made himself comfortable. He had a feeling this was going to get awkward. 'Well, we're not leaving until you tell us why you sent the video to Jim,' he said. He was pushing it now, but the fact that he *knew* the emails came from her gave him the confidence to call her bluff. Then Jim walked over and gently closed the door, and really upped the ante.

'And neither are you, Miss Roberts.'

Sam eyed both of them warily, sizing them up. Jim did a convincing job of looking like he meant business.

'Look, I haven't got time for this. Yes, I sent you the video footage. But that's all I'm saying. You want anything else you're shit out of luck.' It was a small victory for Curtis and Jim. Curtis tried to bring the tension down a notch.

'We just want to know why, that's all. Is that why you're here? You've been waving that video camera around all morning. Is this some sort of undercover exposé? Wacko alien-hunters alive and well in Nevada?' But Sam wasn't playing ball.

'If I don't call my editor at 11 a.m. on the dot, he's gonna call the local sheriff's department. You understand what I'm saying? You're already up for breaking and entering. And this could easily be mistaken for kidnapping. Is that what this is?' Curtis shook his head and tried to brush off the insinuation.

'Hey, we're just curious. We want to find out where the stuff came from. How did you get it? Or were they made up? Is it some sort of hoax to get a good story out here?' Curtis looked at his watch. It was two minutes to eleven. He wasn't prepared to play this bluff, even if Jim was. 'All right, make your call. We got what we came for. Just wanted to know, that's all.'

'Give me a minute,' said Sam. And with that she scrimmaged through her bag and pulled out some clothes, a mobile phone and a packet of cigarettes, and went into the bathroom, locking the door behind her. Curtis looked at Jim. He appeared very relaxed about all this.

'You think she's shitting us?'

Jim shook his head. 'She sent it all right. Could see it in her eyes.' They sat listening to Sam's voice coming from the bathroom. It was muffled, so they couldn't make out what she was saying, but there was a lot of talking going on. Occasionally she raised her voice, as though she was arguing with someone. Eventually the talking stopped, and the bathroom door opened again. She was dressed now, like a blonde Lara Croft, ready for action.

'I managed to talk my editor out of calling the cops. But if I don't ring him in 15 minutes he's on the phone, OK?'

'That was gracious of you,' said Jim sarcastically.

Sam sat back down on the bed. 'We discussed your request. I'm prepared to answer any questions you have.'

Things were starting to look up.

But she hadn't finished. 'And no, the stuff isn't a hoax. Not by us anyway. We got it sent to us a while back. There was no way we could find out where it came from, or who sent it. It got passed to me because no one else knew what to do with it. My editor decided it was too far "out there" to make a decent story. But I do have access to the email, and I'm prepared to show it to you.' Curtis couldn't help thinking that somehow this all seemed just a little too easy.

'On one condition. You let me film everything.' Yep. Way too easy.

So those were the terms. Curtis smiled wryly. There wasn't a snowball's chance in hell she was going to be doing any filming while he was in the room. She was a hardball reporter, though, that's for sure. Probably had a good future ahead of her. He had to admire her spunk.

'OK by me,' said Jim. Uh oh. Curtis decided enough was enough.

'Hey, there's no way I want myself on your website. With your cellphone and lappie you could have it posted before we even got back to Jim's trailer.' Curtis sat back. End of negotiations. But Sam had another card up her sleeve.

'All right. How about I only use the old analogue camera. No digital. No wiring to the website. Not until you say so. What do you say?' Curtis shook his head. Forget it, girl. Sam could see this wasn't working for Curtis. So she tried her last trump card on Jim.

'Look, if I get a story we can use, our company will pay you. Twenty-thousand dollars if we use it. And I won't identify either of you if you don't want me to. That's my final offer.' So that was what it was worth to them. If it ran.

Curtis could see Jim was giving the offer serious consideration. Twenty thousand was a lot in anyone's language. He was probably thinking about all the hardware he could buy for 20 grand to stick on top of his trailer with all the other stuff. But Curtis found it hard to believe all this was worth that much to anyone.

'No website I know would pay that for a story like this. Why's it worth that much to you? It's just some old black-and-white UFO movies. Hundreds of those around already. What's so special about these ones?'

Sam flicked her hair back self-consciously. 'The website is only offering five. I'm putting up the rest as part of a deal if it runs. I know some current-affairs' producers who'll pay that if it's good enough. I've already got enough footage for background and context. I need a hard angle. You're it.' A real businesswoman.

So it was worth 20 grand to her. Curtis wondered what she'd actually sell it to a TV network for. Probably heaps more than that. Jim was watching Curtis carefully. Eventually he said, 'I could sure use the money, Curtis. And all we're doing is the same thing to this email as we did to hers. Just find out who sent it.'

Curtis found himself wanting to help, since Jim had been so accommodating to him, helping him earn his million-dollar pay cheque and all. But every bone in his body said this wasn't a good idea. 'How can we be sure you'll protect our identities?' he asked.

'You'll just have to take my word,' said Sam. 'But I'm not about to start revealing my sources this early in my career. It'd be over before it had begun. You can use any pseudonym you like. You could be Deep Throat for all I care.' Yep. A real live Woodward and Bernstein. Except much better looking.

'All right,' said Curtis. 'You got yourself a deal. No digital. Keep our identities hidden. We get a look at the email, and the 20 goes to Jim. OK?' What the hell. Jim looked like he needed the cash more than him. And he didn't have a million waiting for him back in Vegas. But even as he said it, Curtis had a feeling he was doing something he was really going to regret.

'You gentlemen have got yourselves a deal. Let me just call my editor back.' She went back into the bathroom with her phone.

'That was a hell of a nice gesture, Curtis. You sure about that?' asked Jim as soon as the door closed.

'Yeah. No problem, Jim. Told you I'm not in this for the money.' Not that kind of money, anyway.

Jim nodded. 'Thank you. Mighty decent of you.'

Curtis waved it off. 'Don't mention it.'

Sam was back moments later. Obviously an easier conversation than the last one. 'Just give me a moment to load the camera,' she said. 'My laptop's under the bed. If you pull it out and switch it on for me, I'll bring up the email in a second.' Curtis did as he was told, while Sam busied herself loading a film cartridge into a large, chipped camera with stickers all over it. It looked heavy.

Once the lappie was firing on all cylinders,

Curtis let her at it to dig out the email in question. Once it was up on the screen, she stood back and heaved the camera up onto her shoulder.

'OK, boys, it's all yours.' Curtis stood looking at Jim. They were now being filmed. He could tell Jim felt as uncomfortable about that as he did. He knew Gina was waiting for him back at the car, and she wasn't going to be impressed if he was late. So Curtis flicked the lappie round on the bed, and kneeled in front of it. Jim stood just behind him, watching. On screen was the $1 020 000 email. Curtis felt like Indiana Jones standing in front of the gold idol. Time to go to work.

The text of the email was exactly the same as the one Jim had received from Sam. She hadn't altered it at all. He played the two mpegs attached to it. Exactly the same as the footage he'd seen back in Vegas with Ollie. Next he brought up the header. That was the real surprise. If Sam was good enough — or had access to someone who was good enough — to cloak her email to Jim, this was something else entirely. The whole header list was a jumble of letters and numbers unlike any he'd ever seen before.

He brought Jim up to speed. 'OK, same email. Same text. And same mpegs. But the header looks like it's been encoded. Or encrypted. Never seen anything like it.'

Jim leant closer to have a look. 'Doesn't make any sense to me.' Sam was still filming.

'I need to download some programmes off the net to see if I can make sense of this. You have web access on this?' Sam shook her head.

'Only for emails. I send them through my mobile.'

Curtis looked at Jim. 'Reckon we take it back to your place for a closer look?'

'Sure,' said Jim. Curtis turned to Samantha, trying to ignore the camera lens.

'I need a disk,' he said. She fumbled around inside her bag, filming the whole time, and pulled a disk out and threw it at Curtis. He downloaded the email onto the A: drive and tucked the disk into his pocket.

'We need to go and use Jim's computer. You coming?'

Sam nodded, lifting the camera off her shoulder. 'You betcha.' Curtis couldn't help smiling to himself as they left the room. Was this girl desperate for a story or what?

When they pulled up in Jim's pick-up back at the trailer, Gina was sitting on the hood of the Hummer, waiting. Curtis could tell she wasn't impressed by the blonde holding a camera in the back.

'Curtis, can I talk to you for a minute?' Uh oh. She walked him away from the others, who were still climbing out of the pick-up.

'Curtis, we're leaving. Why is there a camerawoman in the pick-up?' The whispering was worse than if she'd been shouting at him. 'Look, I don't know what the hell's going on, but she's going straight back to whatever Barbie-doll box she climbed out of, and we are heading back to Vegas.'

Curtis was tired, and it started to show. 'Do you

want a million bucks, or not? If you do, then just go along with it for a bit. We'll be 15 minutes.'

'I'm not going on camera, Curtis. No way.'

'Then stay in the Hummer. Put the roof up and we'll leave you out of shot.' Gina looked at him even harder. Man, she was furious. But she stormed off back to the car and pouted. It was very sexy. Curtis turned back to Jim and Sam. She was asking him about all the aerials and shit on his trailer roof. He was pretty much giving her the guided tour. The one they didn't get earlier this morning. Curtis decided to get this over and done with.

'OK people. Let's do this,' he said as he herded them into Jim's trailer. He switched on the machine, and watched while Jim checked a video-surveillance camera in the roof.

'Nope. Been no one here,' he said, adding quickly, 'but I knew that 'cos Gina was here the whole time.' Shut up Jim, thought Curtis to himself. Stop while you're ahead. Soon the email was up on screen, and Curtis was running a sample of header text through several programmes he'd downloaded from the net. After his third attempt with the third programme, Curtis turned to Jim.

'It's encrypted. That's for sure.'

'What do you mean?' asked Sam, a little too quickly.

'Well, whoever sent this has a programme that doesn't just play hide and seek. It literally turns it into something else. This must be that 128-bit encryption I've read about.'

'Can you crack it?' asked Jim.

Curtis nodded. 'Sure. But cracking it isn't the problem. It's how long it would take. Try three years.'

'What do you mean?' Another open-ended question from Sam.

Curtis sat back and sighed in frustration. 'To calculate all the possible variations to unlock this code would take a super-computer. Like one of those Kray computers. Raw computing power.'

'Hold on,' said Jim. He looked like he was thinking. First time Curtis had seen him do it actually. 'You mean like a chess computer?' Curtis understood him instantly.

'Like 1800 chess computers!' Man. It might actually be possible.

Sam was confused. 'Would someone mind telling me what you're talking about?' Jim and Curtis eyed each other. They were on to something. And it might just work.

'Tonight there's a chess game on the net,' said Curtis, 'One of the players is human, the other is a supercomputer. That supercomputer will be made up of 1800 desktops and lappies from around the world.' Sam looked stunned, as she realised the audacity of what he was proposing to do.

'This is great. This is *great*!' She was getting hyped. She might have a programme after all.

'There's just one problem,' said Curtis.

Jim threw him a knowing look. 'I'll have a talk to her.' That made Curtis blink. This was Jim, getting in touch with his feminine side.

'Sure,' was all Curtis could muster. And Jim left him alone with Sam, who was still filming.

'So who do you think sent it?' she asked Curtis as soon as Jim had left. This was for the viewers at home. 'Who would encrypt something like that. Someone who doesn't want to be found?' Curtis shrugged. The camera was pointed directly at him.

'I have no idea,' he mumbled. Curtis could see Jim and Gina talking by the car. They were having an animated discussion by the look of it, but it seemed like they were getting on OK. A good sign. That meant she might be coming around. Soon Jim was back, with Gina in tow.

'She's agreed to stay one more night, as long as she can get a hot shower.'

Curtis smiled. Excellent news. He looked at Gina. Jim sure had a way with women. He wondered what his secret was.

'You can use my room. Don't mind the mess.' Sam was extending the hand of friendship, with a hot-shower carrot.

'Thanks,' said Gina, smiling for the first time in quite a while.

Jim looked at Curtis. 'You think you can pull this off?' Shrugtime.

'Won't know till we try. I just hope your chess is good enough to keep the game going long enough for me to crack it.'

'How long do you need?'

'Two hours, I guess.' Maybe more. But there was another thing to consider. 'You'll have to keep the game interesting enough to keep everyone online for the whole game. As soon as they start logging off it'll slow down big time.'

'This is incredible. It's fantastic. Great drama!' said Sam.

'I better start practising then,' said Jim. That wasn't really what Curtis wanted to hear at that point.

'Why don't we meet back here around 6.30. That'll give me enough time to set things up before we start. I need some sleep.' It seemed to go down like a plan.

As Curtis climbed onto his sleeping bag, he heard Jim taking the girls back to the motel. As the quiet descended he could feel the tiredness pulsing in his head. He was instantly asleep.

10

By the time 6.30 had rolled around, Gina had showered, Curtis had slept, and they had all eaten dinner at the A-Lee-Inn. Conversation was tense during dinner, although Maggie had warmed to them, now they were sitting with Jim. And the food was all the better for it. Curtis was glad Sam hadn't brought her camera with her, because he hadn't been looking forward to telling her she couldn't. They ate quickly, and Sam put the dinner on her work Visa. Nice gesture. Curtis figured she probably saw it as an advance payment. Back at Jim's trailer, Curtis spent 30 minutes preparing for the crack. He'd rigged up three of Jim's screens so they could keep track of everything. One for Jim to make his moves on, the second for the de-encryption programme. The third, an old 14-inch monitor Curtis had found stacked away underneath a pile of computer equipment, was to keep track of the number of users that were logged on. He needed to know how much computing power he had while the crack was underway. If it dropped too much, the de-encryption would slow down. Too much more and it would choke the supercomputer. And if things got really heavy, there was a chance he could crash all the connected computers. A worst-case scenario. But possible. By seven o'clock — the time for the game to start, Curtis was ready. Jim logged on to the site, and the pre-game chitchat over the bulletin board was underway. Jim's friend — the one who ran the site — was introducing his mystery friend, possibly the world's worst-kept secret. Curtis watched as the graph showing the number of users connecting and running the special programme to form the supercomputer began gradually sliding upwards. Party time. Jim looked psyched.

'You OK?' asked Curtis.

Jim nodded grimly. 'Just make sure you crack it. Leave the chess to me.'

He looked wired at the thought of playing his childhood idol. Pity he'd never be able to tell anyone about it.

'You sound pretty confident. I thought he was the best?' said Curtis.

Jim eyeballed him. 'He is. But I've got an advantage. And I'm going to use it to psyche him out.'

'What kind of advantage?' Curtis didn't follow.

'He thinks I'm a computer. So he thinks I'm calculating every possible combination of moves and choosing my moves based on the calculations. And that's how he'll respond. He'll assume that

because I'm a computer, I know what I'm doing.'
Jim looked at Curtis and smiled. So that was his
advantage. A real confidence booster. Curtis went
back to the screen, following the conversation
online. They were almost ready. Sam was filming
now. Gina was stationed on the user graph down
on the floor.

'How many we got online?' asked Curtis.

'About 1200. Still climbing.' It would have to
do.

Fischer was white. He opened with a pawn. But
the instant his pawn settled on a new square, Jim
responded with a similar opening. There was a
pause, and then Fischer moved again. This time
Jim's response was even quicker. He threw another
pawn out into battle. Curtis wondered what the
hell he was up to, but refrained from questioning
Jim's technique, as he launched the de-encryption
programme, and instantly the sets of numbers and
letters in the boxes in front of him began spinning,
like roulette on speed. The crack had begun.

Curtis could now only sit back and watch. Jim
was focusing intently on the game in front of him.
It was weird to think so many other people from
all over the planet were watching his moves at
exactly the same moment. Jim wasn't wasting any
time making his moves, but Curtis noticed Fischer
was taking longer and longer to make his.

As he watched, Curtis finally realised what Jim
was up to. He was moving the split second Fischer
had finished his move. He was demonstrating the
supercomputer's raw computing power, trying to
intimidate his opponent.

Curtis knew from memory, and basic math, that early on in a game of chess, there were zillions of possible moves and combinations to calculate. That would normally be the time when the drain on the computer was at its highest. But by moving the second Fischer finished his moves, Jim was making him think this was one hell of a supercomputer. And he was sure Fischer was starting to question his strategy, as several of Jim's moves had made no sense at all. It must have been driving him wild.

But it was early days. And as the game progressed, Jim started to lose more pieces, despite his 'strategy'. This guy was good. Whoever he was.

Curtis looked at the de-encryption screen. Only one of the dials had stopped spinning. One number. About 56 to go.

Gina read out the user graph. 'We've peaked at just over 1500.'

The tension was mounting. This was going to be close. As the game wore on, Curtis found his breathing starting to quicken. The trailer was getting warm, and as the numbers spun on his programme, and the number of chess pieces on screen fell, he was beginning to doubt whether they'd do it.

If that wasn't enough, as the game entered its final stages the level of interest in it started to drop off. People were getting bored and logging off the system. And Jim was now fighting for his life. He was making some pretty un-computerlike moves, trying to stay out of trouble.

'OK, we're halfway there,' said Curtis. He willed the numbers to spin faster, but Jim wasn't going to be able to hold out much longer.

'We're down to 1100,' said Gina, her voice rising. Curtis was starting to get worried.

'We need to stop them logging off, Jim. Can you liven it up a bit?'

Jim made a couple of ridiculous sacrifices. The user graph slowed its rapid descent. Easy as that. Curtis breathed a little easier. Slowly but surely, more and more numbers and letters on the email header began to stop spinning. They were nearly there. But Jim was desperately trying to avoid checkmate. He was spending most of his time just moving out of check. The end wasn't far away. Curtis willed the programme to work faster.

'Down to 900 now. We're slowing down again,' said Gina.

Curtis looked at his watch. Jim had kept the game going for over an hour and a half. Not bad considering. There were only a few letters left to crack. But everything was slowing down. Big time.

Suddenly Jim sat back and wiped his brow. 'I'm done.' Curtis looked over at the screen. He'd been checkmated. Game over.

'We're falling right off now,' said Gina. 'That's us for the evening.' But even as she spoke Curtis saw the second-to-last letter drop into place. The programme stopped. Completely. They'd probably crashed every computer left on line, cooked them with too many calculations, too little processing power. Real shame. But the ploy had worked. They'd cracked the code. Unbelievable.

'Did we do it?' asked Samantha nervously. Curtis tried to contain his excitement and relief, acutely aware of the camera pointing at him.

'Houston, we have lift-off,' he said, as emotionlessly as he could under the circumstances. He saw Gina's eyes light up. So did Jim's. They were really hyped now.

'So what does it say?' Sam was keeping up the pace. Probably didn't want to waste too much film. Curtis read it out. It didn't appear to be cloaked.

'It's from somewhere called Aurora-dot-UNA3,' he said. 'Mean anything to you, Jim?'

Jim pulled a face. 'Never heard of it. Aurora …' He sat in thought for a moment. 'I recall reading about some controversy over something called Aurora a while back. Something to do with a line that appeared in a Federal budget. Sixty-one billion was going to some project called Aurora. No other description or explanation. A few people tried to make a stink, from what I recall, and tried to find out where it was all going. That's how I heard of it. Don't think anything ever came of it, though. Never heard from them after that.'

Government, huh. This wasn't turning out the way he'd expected. Not at all.

But Sam wasn't going to let that get in the way of a good story. 'Can we do a search or something? Find out anything about it? I've never seen a domain name like that before.' But Curtis had. A long time ago. When he and Turk had been up to their old tricks. Before they were caught. Turk had downloaded a whole bunch of URLs from a website somewhere. They were secret government URLs. Ones people weren't supposed to know existed. Curtis remembered a whole list of URLs with the UNA3 domain name. They hadn't given it any further thought at the time, because they were too busy getting up to other mischief. It wasn't much later that they were busted. Curtis decided to keep that to himself.

'Me neither,' he said offhandedly.

But Sam was getting impatient. 'Well, we can do a search, can't we? We're not going to leave it here? Surely.' Curtis looked at Gina. She looked nearly as hyped as Sam.

'Can't hurt to take a look-see,' she said. 'Not as if we're going anywhere, is it?' Ouch. That was aimed at Curtis.

'OK,' said Curtis, unconvinced. 'I can do a quick search, but that's as far as it goes.' That was final. He turned back to the computer and launched some search software he downloaded from the net. Basically a WHOIS on steroids, because it put a whole bunch of domain-name databases together before it searched them, since Curtis figured a URL like this wasn't about to be listed on somewhere like INTERNIC. No way. But he came up with nothing. He used every search engine for every database he could remember. Still nothing. There was no way he was going to be able to track down this address legally. Then he remembered Roly's CD ROM game. The one with the lists of confidential and top-secret government access numbers. It was still in the envelope Turk had given him. And it was still in his bag. But he wasn't about to try anything like that with the camera rolling. No way.

'I can't do it,' he said finally, sitting back in the chair. The faces watching him dropped in unison. It was over. Curtis clicked out of the search engines and put the PC to sleep. Sam dropped the camera and took a breather. Jim wiped his brow and went out for a walk. Curtis got up and followed Gina outside and over to the car. She looked pissed off. Curtis couldn't believe it. He'd done his best. Which hadn't been half bad, considering.

'Look,' he said, 'I can do it. But I'm not doing it on camera, that's all. We're going to have to leave this for another time.'

Gina looked impatient. A flash of irritation showed briefly in her eyes. 'Come on, Curtis. Let's do it now. We're so close. Then we can get out of here. Leave all this behind. The comp, Vegas, everything.'

Curtis shook his head. 'I don't trust her with a camera. She's going to end up turning us into a digital Bonnie and Clyde.'

'Let me talk to her. If I can get her to turn it off and leave it outside, we'll do it, right?'

Curtis looked into her eyes. They weren't giving much away.

'OK,' he said, 'but her camera's going to turn into space junk if it comes anywhere near me while I'm doing it. Make sure she understands that.'

Gina touched Curtis's cheek as she turned away. 'Leave it to me,' she said. Leave it to her. Yeah, right. But Curtis had something else to worry about. This thing was becoming less about money, and more about something else. Maybe something more important. Because if Roly's game held the access numbers for UNA3, then Curtis had a nagging suspicion it wasn't going to be a coincidence.

Which meant there was some serious shit going on. And Curtis didn't know what. It was time find out what the fuck it was. As he watched Gina talking to Samantha, Jim walked over.

'Can't believe we could be so close. You really out of tricks?' Jim was eyeing him curiously, as though he could be straight with him now that the men were alone. Curtis was more abrupt than he meant to be.

'I can do it, Jim. I'm not going to do it on camera, that's all.'

'Then what the hell we waiting for, boy?' said Jim, patting Curtis on the back. 'Don't worry, Curtis, if Gina can't sort Sam out, I sure as hell will.' Some consolation. Curtis decided he'd had enough. Enough games and bullshit. He just wanted to know if Roly's list had a UNA3 address in it. Because if it did, it meant there was definitely something going on. He was starting to get pissed off. Pissed off at Roly for giving him the game, and for not telling him he was Gonad. Pissed off at Sam for waving her bloody camera around all over the place. And he was pissed off at Gina too. It was almost like she had completely changed her mind. One moment she wanted to go back, the next she was urging him on.

Curtis dug into his backpack for Roly's game, and went back into Jim's trailer without a word. Soon the others were gathering round. Sam didn't have her camera with her. He started up the game. As the graphics loaded, he could tell they were getting impatient. He took his time.

Once he had a game underway, he punched in one of the cheat codes from the web-page printout from the internet café. Instantly he was in DOS, and a list had appeared that was growing larger and larger by the second. He could see the scrollbar handles shrinking as the page numbers spun wildly upwards. Curtis scrolled down to U.

He found a single number and access code. Hiding in thousands. What a coincidence. He was angry now, but he wasn't sure at what. Somehow Roly knew he would be attempting this. Roly had given him the codes. Before he needed them. That meant he knew about the project. And the sponsor. And the million dollars. What was he up to?

Curtis highlighted the row and saved it in a small window. Then he typed in the access number and let his programme do its stuff. The modems took a long time to connect. Jim's satellite dish was slowing things down, instead of speeding them up — must have been all the electromagnetic sensors from the base screwing with the radiowaves. Suddenly a window bounced open in the centre of the screen.

Username and Password.

Curtis punched in the name and password from the list. Instantly he was in at a main menu. And there was no mistaking the name at the top of the page. Same as the URL address domain name: UNA3.

But it was the subtitle that drew everyone's attention. Curtis heard a sharp intake of breath. It was Jim. He'd heard of UNA3 as well. But Curtis had only learned of its existence this very morning, from a bunch of people he'd written off as nutters. The words he was looking at on the screen said *United Nations Alternative 3*.

'What is this? Some sort of UN site?' asked Sam. No one answered. Curtis saw the word Aurora under the American flag, one of a whole number of flags linked off the front page. At least five different languages, including Russian, German and Japanese. As much as he wanted to check the network out further, Curtis knew he had just seconds to upload a worm programme before the intrusion was noticed. Any decent security technician would have seen the activity burst and checked it out immediately. If it was short enough, it might just get under their warning system. In five clicks, his worm was inserted. He logged off and closed down the browser. Done.

'Now, we wait,' he said, turning in the chair.

'How long?' asked Samantha. She was having trouble hiding her disappointment.

'Two hours should do it — we need a long-enough gap so no one sits up and takes notice. The worm I've just inserted will do some scouting around for us and copy anything interesting. Just keeps the profile low. Nice and safe.'

'Must be time for beans and coffee,' said Jim. The old guy needed a break from all the excitement. The thought of another campfire evening was kind of appealing after all the drama. But the waiting wasn't. Curtis sat back from the computer and shook his head in amazement. He couldn't quite believe what he'd just done. Inserting a worm into a government computer was about as illegal as illegal could get. Nothing he could do about it now. Nevertheless, his internal radar was working overtime, even though there was nothing on the screen he could point at. Something was going on. He just wanted to know what.

They were the longest two hours Curtis had ever experienced. He kept to himself, not yet ready to share his doubts with Gina. He wasn't really sure about them himself. Jim didn't say a lot either. This was about as close as he'd come to 'The Big One', as he called it. But Gina and Sam had warmed to each other, and they were chewing the fat as only women can. Curtis was happy to let them do all the talking. He sipped on his Jim-brew coffee, and tried to make some sense of it all, running the events of the past few days over in his head. Again. He was starting to feel like he was on a roller-coaster, and someone else was steering. Not a good feeling at all. Maybe he was just thinking too much.

He got up and moved over to where Jim was lost in thought, his hand wrapped around his tin coffee mug. He didn't even look up when Curtis sat down.

'You thinking what I'm thinking?' said Curtis. Jim looked up at him. He seemed kinda far away.

'You know, Curtis, we should really be getting this on camera. It's uncharted territory. Probably the closest anyone's ever come to uncovering this thing. Or at least finding out what the hell is going on with all this Alternative 3 stuff.' Curtis shuffled uneasily in his seat, and said nothing.

'Maybe Samantha's going to be more useful than we thought,' added Jim.

'Tell me what you know about Alternative 3,' said Curtis. It was time to get this thing straight in his head. 'I heard your hikers talking about it on the way out this morning. Thought it was a load of crap at the time — real "Twilight-Zone" stuff.' Jim eyed Curtis closely. There wasn't a lot of humour in his eyes.

'Kinda spooks ya, don't it?' said Jim. 'It's one thing to find out about this kind of stuff half a century later. It's another thing completely to chance on it while it's happening.' He spat into the fire to punctuate his sentence, much to Sam's disgust.

'You see, Jim, that's my point,' said Curtis, quieter now. 'I'm not sure how much chance has got to play in all this.'

Jim looked at him sideways. 'What d'you mean, son?' Curtis poked the fire with a stick, not sure where to begin. In fact, the more he thought about it, the sillier his suspicions felt.

'I'm not sure what I mean. It's just a feeling, that's all.'

'Sometimes that's all you have to go on,' said Jim. 'Sometimes that's all you got ...' He trailed off, lost in thought for a moment. 'That's why this is so important. This is the first time I ever had much more to go on than my gut. We could be on to something big here, Curtis. Bigger than you, bigger than me. Did you think of that?' Curtis shook his head, not entirely sure what Jim was referring to. Must be the colonisation thing. Alternative 3. The Big One. He decided to leave Jim alone to his thoughts. He had enough of his own to worry about, that was for sure.

By the time two hours was up, Curtis had worked himself up into a real state. He needed to know what was in the UNA3 network system, but the cold, heavy feeling in his stomach was a constant reminder that downloading the worm was not only illegal — and probably punishable with a prison sentence for a parole violator — but there was also a chance he could get caught. Connecting long enough to download whatever his worm had decided to copy and send him was risky. Just how risky depended upon the level of system security UNA3 were using. It was a gamble, Curtis had no doubts about that. He wasn't even sure why he was doing it. They had their mil' in the bag. Hell, Jim would probably even get his 20 at this rate. Curtis looked at his watch.

'It's time. Let's do this,' he said to the others. 'Bring your camera, Samantha.' Sam did a double take, not sure she'd heard him correctly.

'This isn't for the programme,' Curtis explained. 'It's for Jim. According to him we could be making history.' Well, that sure raised the tension by about 100 per cent, as if it wasn't high enough already. Soon Curtis was back in the Palace cockpit, firing up Jim's computer and logging onto the net.

'So what's this worm of yours supposed to find?' asked Sam. She couldn't help herself. If she was holding a camera, she just *had* to ask questions.

'I set it to search for video,' said Curtis, opening up the worm programme. 'We came looking for video, and we know someone who'll pay to see some more.' He chanced a look at Gina, as he clicked the mouse button to connect again with UNA3, and then clicked 'Get' to start the downloading. She wasn't letting on what she thought of what he was doing. Curtis figured he probably didn't want to know.

Surprise, surprise. It was working.

The computer icons signalled they were flat out downloading some damn big files. The little blue bar told Curtis that the worm was working correctly. He opened up a new file on Jim's desktop to save the goodies in, and started timing the download.

Two minutes went by. No one spoke. All eyes were on the blue bar. Things were going OK. Five minutes. Curtis was surprised at the size of the files he was downloading. They didn't usually take this long. Eight minutes. It should have finished downloading by now. Ten minutes passed, and Curtis decided enough was enough. He clicked on the 'Abort Transfer' button and pulled the plug. They had plenty downloaded they could look at. Better to be safe than sorry, as Jim had said to Curtis yesterday.

With a sharp panic, Curtis realised that the programme was overriding his command. He clicked the 'Abort' button a few more times. The programme was ignoring him completely. He checked the computer network icons. They were still furiously downloading. Downloading what?

'What's wrong?' asked Gina.

Curtis shook his head. 'I don't know. The programme's not responding … it's really weird.' He checked his task list. The programme was still running correctly. Jim's entire system was running correctly. Only the worm was not responding.

Curtis clicked open the network-connection menu and killed the connection. Nothing happened. Now Curtis was starting to sweat. This wasn't supposed to happen. It couldn't happen. Time to get serious. Curtis jumped out of his seat and scrambled round behind the computer. He was looking for the modem cable.

'What's happening?' asked Jim.

'Computer's frozen! It won't stop downloading. I can't disconnect,' said Curtis.

'I'll turn off the satellite,' said Jim, spinning round all sorts of equipment on the small bench in front of him.

'It's OK,' said Curtis, breathing a little easier. 'I got the modem cord. It's out.' He sat back down at the computer. The download icons had stopped flashing. Good news. But when he tried to close the worm programme, it denied him access again. System crash, thought Curtis. A reboot is round the corner. Nothing to worry about, though. But Jim was still examining the back of the satellite-connection hardware.

'This thing's still connected, Curtis. I can't shut it down.' The alarm in his voice was disturbing.

'Pull the bloody cord out from the wall,' said Curtis, louder than he intended. This was really starting to freak him out.

'I've done that,' said Jim grimly.

'Can someone please explain what's going on here?' demanded Sam. She was getting some great drama.

'The satellite dish is still downloading,' said Gina helpfully. 'But it can't be 'cos we've killed the connection.'

Jim was getting edgy. 'I don't like this, Curtis. Tell me what's happening here.'

Curtis shook his head. 'I don't know! Let me think for a second!' He tried to make sense of it in his head. Still downloading. Via the satellite dish on Jim's roof. No connection. Not from this end anyway. That meant whatever was being downloaded was overriding his commands. It had frozen up the satellite dish so it could keep downloading. It had frozen open the link. The question was, *why*? Curtis forced his mind to think. Fast. There was a reason he was getting so panicky, he just couldn't put his finger on it.

Then his stomach dropped, as he suddenly realised what was happening. They were being traced. The UNA3 network had frozen open the download link, so it could trace them. So it could find them. *Fuck!* Curtis looked at his watch. They'd been online for over 12 minutes. Easily long enough for a trace.

'We're being traced!' shouted Curtis. 'Jim! Do whatever you have to, but shut *everything* down. Anything you can find, turn it off. Even the generator. *Now!*' Jim didn't need to be told twice. He scrambled around under the bench, furiously flicking switches and pulling cords. Gina joined in. Sam kept the camera rolling.

'It's no use!' said Jim. 'It's jammed!'

'Keep trying!' urged Curtis. He should save the files. Now.

Curtis searched the desk for a CD ROM, sweeping off electrical gear and food wrappers off the desk with his arm. He found what looked like an empty disk, jammed it into the D: drive, and began saving the worm files. But it was taking forever. Big files.

As he watched the Save bar inch across the screen, Curtis thought he could hear something. An unusual sound. An engine, maybe. In the distance, but definitely becoming more distinct. Jim could hear it too. He'd stopped what he was doing, and was listening hard. He looked up at Curtis from the floor. He couldn't make the noise out either, but they shared a look that said they'd sure heard something.

'What *is* that?' asked Sam, lifting the camera off her shoulder.

'It's a chopper,' said Jim. 'Heard them fly over us one night when we were getting close to the base. They use them on stealth mode. I don't like this. We should really finish up here.' But before anyone could react, the noise suddenly burst around them into a high-pitched whine. Sure didn't sound like any helicopter he'd ever heard. Curtis looked at the Save bar. It was nearly finished.

Just then the trailer was rocked by a thousand tornadoes coming from every direction. Curtis grabbed the desk and tried to stop the computer from sliding onto the floor. The curtains blew in as desert dust and grit entered the trailer from every open window. Maps, photos and papers began swirling crazily around them in the chaos. A helicopter was hovering directly over the trailer! The trace. They'd found them.

Curtis freaked. Totally. So did Gina and Sam, their screams lost in the thunder of the buffeted trailer. Just when things couldn't get any more bizarre, the whole trailer was bathed in a searing white light. It seemed to be shining down from directly above them. They freaked in unison now.

It was the most terrifying thing Curtis had ever experienced. The entire trailer, and everything in it — including the air — was vibrating violently. Suddenly an emotionless electric voice boomed at them through the roof.

'James Maze! Exit the vehicle immediately. Lie down on the ground with your hands behind your head. You have five seconds to comply.'

It was a loudspeaker from the chopper. The whole scene was fast becoming surreal. Curtis forced himself to think. To think *hard*, dammit. He checked the Save. It was finished. He punched the eject button and pocketed the disk. Jim was coming to his senses, and was slowly climbing up from the floor. He leant into Curtis's ear and screamed to make himself heard above the din.

'You saved the files?'

Curtis nodded and pointed to his pocket, tapping the disk. Jim nodded back, his face grim and taut. He didn't look unused to being in situations like this. It helped settle Curtis's nerves a little.

'I'm gonna do a decoy!' shouted Jim. 'Give me five minutes and then you get the hell outta here! The Cammos won't be far away now. Email me when you're safe!' Before Curtis could say anything, he grabbed a set of keys off a hook and shouldered the door open against the blast. Curtis lifted his sweater over his face as the turbulence blew the desert floor into the trailer. When the door slammed shut, Jim was gone.

Curtis grabbed Gina and Samantha and pulled them to the floor, signalling for them to stay put. They heard the rough growl of Jim kicking his pick-up into life, and a spray of dust spat in through a window as Jim floored it.

Then the light was gone. The deafening whine started to fade as well. They'd taken the bait.

Curtis poked his head tentatively out the door. A brilliant white cone of light was following Jim's pick-up out into the desert. He was zigzagging over the rough desert floor for all he was worth, but the light stuck to him like glue. He could just make out the bottom of a black chopper above the apex of the beam. Something long and narrow was rotating wildly from beneath it.

Curtis turned back to the girls. 'We've got about two minutes before the security guys arrive. We need to get out of here! Now!' Gina and Sam didn't need any encouragement. Curtis ran to the Hummer and climbed in, keying the ignition and kicking it into gear in one smooth movement. Sam clambered into the back seat, and hunkered down sideways, her camera up and rolling. Gina had grabbed her bag and lappie from the second trailer and was climbing into the passenger seat as Curtis rolled the car backwards.

'Let's go!' she shouted. Curtis floored the accelerator and sent the Hummer into a tight U-turn. He left his lights off, and tried to avoid touching the brake pedal. It was a wild ride in the dark along the makeshift desert road.

'I need my things from the motel!' shouted Sam from the back seat.

'What makes you think you're coming with us?' Curtis shouted back, as he wrestled with the spinning steering wheel.

Gina threw him a look as he flung the Hummer into another dark corner. 'We're not going to leave her here, Curtis. And slow down! You'll kill us driving like this!' Curtis lifted his foot slightly, and the car slowed. Much as he hated to admit it, it was easier to follow the road at a slower speed.

He was just about to respond to Gina when the desert night erupted into a violent orange fireball. It was an awesome sight in the darkness. Curtis felt the explosion rock the Hummer ... in the same instant he realised that the blast had come from the direction where Jim had just disappeared with the chopper in hot pursuit.

'What the fuck was *that*?' shouted Sam. They all peered into the night in the direction of the explosion.

'My God!' cried Gina, 'that was Jim's truck! The bastards shot him!' She looked hysterical. Curtis couldn't believe it. It was one thing to trace and harass them. It was another thing entirely to shoot to kill. Curtis felt himself losing it. Big time.

'We can't just leave him,' said Curtis, sliding the car to a skidding halt. Fuck the brake lights. 'We have to go back. He could still be alive!'

'You've got to be kidding!' screamed Sam. 'You think they're gonna think twice about shooting us as well?'

Gina grabbed Curtis's arm. 'She's right, Curtis. He gave us a chance to escape. Don't waste it. We can't do anything for him now.' Curtis knew she was making sense. But it didn't stop every fibre in his body wanting to turn around and go back. He sat behind the wheel, his chest heaving, fighting the emotions churning inside. He felt nauseous, and fought to control it. Think, dammit.

After a few moments, he put the car into gear and drove it as fast as he dared towards the lights of the A-Lee-Inn. As he slowed to a stop out the back, he turned to Sam. 'You've got 30 seconds. If you're not back by then we're going without you.'

Sam was already clambering out of the back. 'I'll be here!' Curtis looked at Gina. She was sickly pale. He figured he couldn't have looked too hot either.

'Wait here. I'll be back in a second,' he said as he climbed out the door. He didn't plan on giving Gina a chance to debate this one. Curtis followed Sam in the back, and as she disappeared into her room, Curtis followed the hall around to the bar. Maggie was behind the counter. Most of the hiker group seemed to still be hanging around, playing cards and stuff. But he could tell they'd heard the explosion as well. They were hushed and apprehensive as he ran in.

'Maggie, I need to speak to you. It's urgent,' he said. Maggie looked at him, puzzled. 'It's about Jim,' he added. She still wasn't getting it.

'*Now*, Maggie!' She wiped her hands and threw her cloth onto the counter. Curtis followed her out the back.

'Listen, Maggie, something's happened to Jim. We got buzzed by one of the black choppers from the base. Jim took off to let us slip away, but we heard an explosion as we were leaving. A big one. I think they got him.'

Maggie's mouth dropped as the colour drained from her face. She said nothing, but the way she leaned against the kitchen bench said enough.

'We have to leave,' said Curtis. 'Sam's coming too. We'll fix you up later, OK? If anyone comes asking, you never saw us.' Slowly Maggie got her wits about her.

'You kids be careful. This isn't a game.'

'Thanks Maggie,' said Curtis, 'I know we can count on you.'

He left her leaning against the kitchen bench. She looked pretty shaken. Maybe Jim was more than just a regular customer. As Curtis screamed back through the motel, Sam appeared from her room, dragging a few small bags and a laptop.

'Let me take those,' said Curtis, ripping the bags from her grasp and throwing them in the back.

'Come on!' yelled Gina, her patience stretched to the limit. Curtis couldn't blame her. He jumped into the car and fastened his seatbelt. Showtime.

'Belt up, folks, we're outta here.' Curtis gunned the engine and kicked the clutch. In a few short seconds they were off the desert road and back on the highway. No one spoke. When the lights of Rachel had faded from the rear-view mirror, Curtis hit the headlights, and let the roar of the Hummer's engine take them away from the madness, back to Vegas. To civilisation. And sanity.

11

As the Hummer ate up the road in the dark, Curtis kept the needle pointed at 60. He fought the urge to really see what the big diesel could do. He noticed his hands were sweating on the wheel. He wiped them on his thighs and wound the window down, the cold breeze stinging his ears, but it helped him to focus. Gina and Sam were silent as well, each of them trying to come to grips with what had just happened. Curtis still couldn't believe it. They had shot at Jim. This wasn't a game any longer. He was in it up to his neck now. He checked the rear-view mirror again, half-expecting the white beam to appear over the Hummer as he chased the white line along the desert highway. Gina and Sam were also peering back into the darkness. Maybe they were thinking the same thing too.

'Does this thing go any faster?' said Sam from the back.

Curtis shook his head. 'We're already doing the limit.' Gina looked over at him. She looked shaken, but seemed to be holding up well, considering. Maybe better than Curtis.

'You think they got him, don't you?' she said finally. Curtis didn't answer. That was an answer in itself.

'What do we do now?' said Sam, leaning forward between the front seats.

Curtis had been asking himself the same question.

'We disappear,' he said, 'but first we need to get rid of the Hummer. They've probably got our licence plate off the satellite.' With one hand firmly on the wheel, Curtis pulled his bag out from behind his seat and dug through it for his cellphone.

'Who're you calling?' asked Gina.

'Turk,' said Curtis. 'I've got an idea. And we need to call Ollie to tell him we're on the way ... and that we won't be hanging around.' Gina nodded that she understood.

'Who's Turk?' asked Sam. 'And who the hell's Ollie?'

Curtis waved her off as he dialled. 'Just a couple of friends in Vegas. We might need some help to get outta this.' Curtis put the phone to his ear as it dialled Turk's number.

Pick up, dammit. But it cut to Turk's voicemail. Shit.

'Turk, it's Curtis. We've got a problem and I need your help. We're on our way back to Vegas. I think we're being followed, and we need to swap vehicles, so I need you to pick up a rental and meet us on the way in. This is important,

Turk. They've already shot at a friend's car. I don't think he made it. Ring me back as soon as you get this. I'm relying on you, buddy.'

He ended the call. Fucking great. Turk was never there when he needed him. But it was the only thing he could think of. And the longer they were in the Hummer, the more chance they had of being caught.

'Curtis! There's someone following us!' shouted Sam. Curtis checked the mirror. He couldn't see any headlights.

'Where? I can't see anything!'

'They've got their lights off. And they're catching us fast. Speed up, Curtis!'

Curtis peered into the rear-view mirror. Nothing. He checked again. Then he spotted it. A dark shape against the night behind them. And it was growing fast. Curtis punched the accelerator to the floor, the Hummer kicking them back into their seats. 'Do your belts up,' he shouted above the roaring diesel and singing tyres.

Curtis watched the needle jumped up to 80. He checked the rear-view mirror, but he could only see black.

'They still there?' he asked grimly. He could see Sam staring intently out the back, searching for them. She suddenly leant forward again. 'Got them! They're still gaining, Curtis. Faster!' Curtis leaned on the accelerator again. The needle climbed to 90. The engine was nearly at full throttle. But it was as fast as he dared take the giant vehicle in the dark on a road he didn't know. This was getting out of hand.

'Bloody hell!' screamed Sam, 'they're right behind us!' Curtis felt a wave of panic wash over him. He looked in the rear-view mirror for as long as he dared. But in that split second he could definitely make out the black shape of something following them. Close. He could even hear the scream of an engine over the noise of the Hummer. They must be really pushing that thing, he thought.

Gina shot him a look. 'Curtis! Do something!'

Curtis kept his eyes on the road. 'Like what?'

'Anything!' screamed Gina. He chanced another look in the mirror. They were close now. Very close. He could make out a black four-wheel drive. Blacked-out windows. The headlights were off. Must be driving using those night-vision goggles Jim talked about. Jim. Curtis realised that these guys probably meant business. If they shot at Jim trying to escape, they probably weren't going to ask him nicely to stop. Suddenly Curtis felt the Hummer lurch under him.

'They hit us!' yelled Sam. 'They're trying to run us off the road!' OK, time to panic.

'Have you got a light on your camera?' Curtis shouted to Sam.

'Yeah, why?'

'How bright is it?'

'Pretty bright. Eats the battery though!' said Sam. Curtis had an idea. 'Rig it up! Don't turn it on until I tell you!' Curtis could hear Sam digging frantically around in her gear.

'Here they come again!' she yelled suddenly. Curtis braced himself for the impact. It was harder this time, but the size of the Hummer absorbed some of the violence of the shove. Maybe it wasn't such a bad choice of vehicle after all, thought Curtis.

'OK, listen!' he shouted over his shoulder to Sam. 'Keep the camera down until I say. Then I want you to turn it on as bright as you can and aim at the driver's eyes. You got that?'

'Got it!' said Sam.

Curtis looked at Gina for a moment. 'Brace yourself! Grab anything you can hold. Put your feet up on the dash!' She did as he suggested.

'Sam!' he yelled. 'When I say, you have to blind the driver; I'm going to hit the brakes so brace yourself! Can you do it?'

'Just do it!' screamed Sam. 'I'll be OK!' Curtis checked the mirror. They had pulled back and were starting to accelerate for another shove. Curtis waited for them to get close. Real close. And prepared himself for the crash.

Ready. The four-wheel drive pulled closer …

'Now!' shouted Curtis. He watched in the mirror as Sam yanked the camera out onto the back of her seat, and flicked it on. The light was dazzlingly bright. The grille and hood of the black four-wheel drive lit up like a Christmas tree. He got a brief glimpse of the driver covering his eyes with his arm. He was wearing goggles all right. In that instant Curtis kicked the brake pedal for all he was worth. The Hummer's wheels locked up tight, sending it into a tyre-shredding skid. A split second later, the four-wheel drive hit the Hummer from behind. Hard.

Curtis thought he'd bitten off his tongue. He could taste blood in his mouth. His head had just missed the steering wheel. He shot a look at Gina. She was pale and grim, but she looked OK. The skid seemed to last forever. Curtis fought to keep the Hummer on the road, but it was starting to skew. Uh oh.

Then something passed his window. It was the four-wheel drive, spinning past them in a wide slow skid. As if in slow motion, Curtis watched it leave the asphalt, and hit the sandy road edge. Then as the driver lost control of it completely, it arced into a wild spin, and began to roll. Curtis lifted his foot off the brake and tried to take the Hummer out of its skid. But it was too late. It was already aiming for the opposite side of the road from the four-wheel drive. Only its low body weight kept it upright.

Eventually it ground to halt in a cloud of sand and dust. The smell of diesel and burnt tyres filled his nostrils.

'Everyone all right?' he yelled. He killed the engine. She was still white-knuckling the handles though, her feet still firmly wedged against the dash.

'You OK?' said Curtis. Gina didn't look up. She just nodded. She was OK.

Curtis breathed a little easier. 'What about you, Sam?' he said, turning in his seat. A shock of blonde hair appeared from behind him.

'I'll live,' she said shakily, climbing back up onto the seat. 'Lost the camera, though.' Curtis looked over to the four-wheel drive on the opposite side of the road. It was on its side. Smoke was pouring from the hood.

'We better check to see they're all right,' he said, unbuckling his belt. 'Wait here.' He opened the door and started walking warily over to the upturned vehicle. Didn't look like there was any movement inside. He heard a door open behind him. It was Sam.

'Just getting my camera! It's got all my film in it!' she said, breaking into a run back down the highway, searching for the camera. Just as Curtis was crossing onto the other side of the road, a door opened on the four-wheel drive. He could hear a radio squawking from inside. Lots of static. He stopped and waited, not sure whether this was a good sign or not. An arm and head appeared. It was the driver. He was climbing out the top.

Curtis quickly looked back to the Hummer, and judged the distance. Just in case. In the dim light, Curtis could just make out the guy reaching back into the four-wheel drive. Maybe he was pulling his friend out. But the thing he pulled out wasn't a person. It was too long and skinny.

It was a gun. Curtis spun and sprinted back to the Hummer.

'Sam! Get back in the car! Now!' he shouted, climbing into the seat and slamming the door. But Sam was too far back down the road to make it in time. He'd have to go back for her. Curtis started the Hummer and slammed it into reverse. The wheels spun crazily in the sand as he floored the accelerator. The guy was clambering across the top of the four-wheel drive now, the gun clearly visible in his grasp.

As soon as the Hummer hit the asphalt it jerked violently and picked up speed. Backwards. Curtis craned his neck round and did his best to keep the Hummer straight. He could see Sam further down the road. She had her camera, and was running back towards him. As he neared her, he hit the brakes. The Hummer stopped hard. Sam threw the camera over the back and climbed in after it.

'The bastards broke my camera!' she said. She looked more upset about the camera than being nearly killed by the guys in the four-wheel drive. Curtis worked the gear lever and got the Hummer up and moving again, forwards this time. But in the beam of the headlights he could see the guy was now standing squarely in the middle of the road. He had the gun up on his shoulder and was aiming it at them. He briefly saw a red spot of light dance across the windscreen. He hit the brakes again and killed the lights.

'Hold on!' he shouted, as he swung the Hummer off road. It dipped and bucked as it hit the edge of the highway, and then became a wild thing as he took it out into the desert in a wide arc away from the gunman. It was terrifying stuff. Curtis clutched the wheel hard, fighting it as the Hummer heaved and kicked under him. He just hoped Sam and Gina were holding on.

A muffled thud reverberated through the Hummer. Curtis thought he must have hit something. He was having a hard enough job dodging the Joshua trees which kept appearing out of nowhere in the darkness. But the Hummer seemed to be still going OK. Then he heard the noise again.

So had Gina. 'Curtis, he's shooting at us!' The bastard was taking pot shots at them. He must have been using a silencer because Curtis couldn't hear the shots being fired. Not above the lurching Hummer, anyway.

'Get down!' shouted Curtis. He tried to lower his profile as much as he could, but the bucking made it impossible. Suddenly a shot cracked into the windscreen, right in front of Gina's face. She totally freaked, screaming hysterically and climbing all over the seat in terror.

'Just go, Curtis!' screamed Sam from the back.

He urged the Hummer on. It was almost out of control. They were a long way from the highway. Curtis wrestled the bucking wheel around to point the Hummer back towards the road. Gina was still freaking out in the front. Her hysterical screaming wasn't helping his concentration. Another bullet thudded into the Hummer. Somewhere. No one said anything this time. Curtis was focusing on keeping the Hummer moving, away from the nut with the gun. Eventually the giant wheels of the Hummer bumped up onto the highway again. It felt like home. He floored the pedal and shifted quickly through the gears. Soon they were racing back along the highway.

'Is anyone following us?' he yelled back to Sam.

'Don't think so!' she said. Her voice was calmer now. Curtis brought the Hummer back to a respectable speed, but he left the lights off all the same. Not taking any chances this time.

Curtis felt his arms begin to shake like crazy, and he realised he was still squeezing the life out of the steering wheel. He forced himself to relax. Take a deep breath. But his heart was still racing outrageously. The delayed shock was starting to kick in. He was drained, but he didn't dare slow down. He rubbed his eyes and forced himself to focus on the road ahead. They weren't out of this yet.

That was when Curtis noticed something up ahead. He could just make it out against the night sky. Something big. Directly in front of them. He lifted his foot a little. It seemed to have just appeared there. It covered the highway easily, hovering over the road. And it didn't look friendly. Curtis slowed the Hummer to a stop. It had to have come from the base. Time to exit. Backwards again.

But when he looked in his side rear-view mirror he got the shock of his life. A similar sort of huge object had appeared right behind them. Out of nowhere. It was so close Curtis could see his brake lights reflected on its side. Curtis froze.

Suddenly the one in front shot a powerful beam of light at them. It was a penetrating white glare. Curtis reached into the door compartment, pulled out his Randolphs and stood up behind the wheel. They were serious sunglasses. But even with them on, all he could make out was a huge, black silhouette against the night. He held his arm over his eyes and tried to stare it down. That's how scared he was. Then the light stopped. And nothing.

'I can't believe I'm seeing this shit and my camera's busted. Fuck!' It was Sam. She was annoyed she wasn't filming this. Talk about a pro. It must have been like a journo's Holy Grail to see this stuff.

The Hummer began to vibrate rapidly. Curtis heard the electrics go off at the exact same time as the motor died. But as quickly as it had started, the vibrating stopped. Dead silence. Curtis remembered how Richard Dreyfuss got buzzed like this when he was sitting in his pick-up in *Close Encounters*. They were supposed to be aliens. But there was definitely nothing alien about this shit. Curtis knew what a bitch it was for aliens to coordinate their busy schedules to fit in a quickie to earth to scare the shit out of some people who just happened to be getting chased by security goons from a military installation. It was working though. He put his arm on Gina's shoulder to comfort her. And himself. Just as the vehicle in front started slowly lifting up. Vertically. Into the air. It just seemed to sit there, hovering high enough for the Hummer to pass underneath.

This was his cue. He lifted his arm back from Gina's neck to start the Hummer. But as he did the motor started again before he'd even got his hand to the key. The electrics came on too. Fucking weird. Curtis looked up at the hovering object. It seemed to be letting them go. He slowly inched the Hummer forward. He looked up but there was no reaction from the craft, so he just kept going, edging the Hummer towards it.

Then Curtis's cellphone rang. It had been kicking around his feet the whole time, underneath the pedals. The ringing was strangely comforting in all this weirdness. He reached down and picked the phone up off the floor as he drove. It was Turk. About fucking time.

'Turk!' whispered Curtis as the Hummer passed directly under the object.

From underneath it appeared to be circular. And it was black — a thick, military kind of black. He kept driving, chancing it a little faster now.

'Where you been, man?' said Turk impatiently, oblivious to what was going on at the other end of the call. 'I've left you about twelve messages! How d'you expect me to ring you back if you turn your phone off!' Curtis blinked.

He hadn't turned his phone off. Or back on. Something had interfered with the signal. They could even be tracking his phone right now too.

'Turk, shut up and listen to me!' said Curtis. 'I need you to go and rent some kind of car, and meet up with us somewhere on the way back to Vegas. You're gonna have to pretend you're us for a while, and drive around in the Hummer. All over the place. Then I need you to return it for me. Think you can do that?' There was a hesitation as Turk paused to let it all sink in.

'Yeah, man. Sure. Where do I meet you?' Curtis tried to think of somewhere with lots of people at this time of night.

'What about one of those all-night truck stops?' said Turk. 'Gotta be one along there somewhere.' Curtis tried to recall whether he'd passed any on the way out.

'Yeah, I'm sure there is!' said Turk. 'It's on your side too. I'm leaving now. Ring you when I'm there.'

'Thanks buddy.'

'Hey Curtis?'

'Yeah?'

'Did you say Hummer?' asked Turk. Curtis couldn't believe this guy sometimes.

'It's a real live Hummer, Turk,' said Curtis. 'Even got bullet holes in it.'

There was silence at the other end for a second. Sometimes Turk's brain needed some catch-up time. 'I'm leaving now …' The call ended, to leave Curtis trying to figure out a way of getting himself, the girls and the Hummer back to the truck stop without any more excitement. It was way more than he could handle already.

'What the hell were they?' asked Gina incredulously. Curtis shook his head as he drove. Hard one to answer. He looked back in the mirror and they were still sitting there. Hovering actually.

'Must be some sort of stealth craft from the base, I guess,' he said.

He felt Sam lean forward behind him. 'Why did they just let us go like that?'

'Want me to go back and ask them?' said Curtis, just a little sarcastically.

Sam, to her credit, didn't bite back.

'Where are we meeting Turk?' asked Gina. 'We swapping cars or something?' Curtis nodded.

'Jim said they probably got our plate on satellite photo when we arrived. And this thing's just too conspicuous. I don't want to risk it.' He'd risked far too much already. 'How's the camera?' he asked Sam over his shoulder.

'A mess! I just hope the film cartridge is OK.'

'Handy weapon you got there!' said Curtis.

'How did you know it would blind him?' asked Sam.

'No one can drive that fast at night without headlights. Not unless they're wearing night-vision goggles.'

Gina clicked. 'The green eyes! The guy in the trailer!'

'I saw it on a movie once,' said Curtis. 'They just magnify existing light, so when you shine a torch or something at them they get blinded.' Seemed to work, anyway.

As the strange, silent black objects faded back into the night behind them, it suddenly seemed to get very cold. Curtis wound his window up and concentrated on driving. And on calming down. They didn't say much at all on the way back in to Vegas. What do you say after something like that? The bullet mark on the windscreen was a constant reminder of what they'd just been through. That it wasn't a dream. Nightmare was probably more accurate.

At least he still had the disk. He felt for it in his pocket. It was still there. He wondered what sort of goodies it had — they'd sure downloaded something from the UNA3 network. Soon the truck stop Turk had mentioned came into view in the distance. The bright lights of the truck park and fast-food joints lit up the desert night.

Curtis drove right past it the first time, checking for black four-wheel drives. There were none that he could see. No bloody alien motherships either. He swung the Hummer back around and drove back to the truck stop. This time he pulled in off the road and took it round the back. He found a park out among the trucks, pulled into it and killed the engine.

'I need some coffee,' he said, unbuckling his seat belt.

'I need a bourbon,' said Sam, like she meant it. She climbed out the back and lit a cigarette. Her hands were shaking. Curtis couldn't blame her. He checked the body of the Hummer. Sure enough, there were two small holes. Right next to the petrol tank. That was a sobering thought.

'We'll see you inside,' said Curtis, following Gina towards the coffee-house. She hadn't said much lately. Not a good sign.

Inside the truck stop life appeared so amazingly normal that Curtis wondered if they'd all been hallucinating. Truckers were reading magazines and scoffing huge servings of deep-fried stuff. Waitresses in aprons were doing the rounds of bottomless coffees.

'I need to use the bathroom,' said Gina. Curtis decided it wasn't a bad idea, and followed her out to the rest rooms. While he was washing his hands he examined his reflection in the mirror. He'd looked better. He could feel his whole body starting to shake uncontrollably. Delayed shock. He threw some cold water over his face. It seemed to help. The face in the reflection looked pale, like he'd just had the shit scared out of him. Not far wrong.

As he towelled his face on the dispenser, he decided two things. First, he was going to collect the pay cheque, thank you very much. Second, he was on the next plane out of there. No matter what. He went back out into the restaurant and ordered two coffees and some pastries while he waited for Gina. She was gone a long time. When she got back they sat down in a corner furthest away from the other customers.

'You OK?' said Curtis.

'I'll be all right,' she said quietly. 'Last time I go on a road trip with you.' She was going to be OK. Curtis reached across the Formica table and held her hand.

'I'm sorry, babe,' he said gently. 'I still can't believe how this whole thing just turned to shit. Jim ...' He shook his head in disbelief.

'Have you still got the disk?' asked Gina. Curtis tapped his shirt pocket. Gina looked like she approved. It made the whole experience somehow less meaningless.

'Let's check it when Sam's not around,' he said.

'I don't think I can take much more of this. I want to go home,' said Gina, picking at her pastry. 'This wasn't exactly what I had in mind when I signed up.'

'Gina, something's going on. I don't know what, but there's a hell of a lot that's not making sense. Even without the UFOs. That disk with the access codes on it — it was from a friend of mine. I was at his funeral a couple of days ago. Turk said his mother gave it to me, thinking it was mine.' Gina didn't say anything, waiting for him to continue. 'I figured he put my name on it so it wouldn't be found — by who, I don't know. Guess he knew I'd know what it was and get rid of it.' Gina was still giving him a weird kind of look, so he tried to explain. 'Gina, I was playing the game on the net, just days ago. I'm sure it was him I was playing. Very sure.'

Gina looked confused. 'What are you saying, Curtis?'

'It just seems too coincidental, that's all,' he said. 'He disappears — they never found his body — but here he is playing me on the net. And he doesn't let on who he is. Then I get his game disk, which just happens to have the UNA3 codes on it. Which we just happen to be trying to access. How much do you know about Ollie and his shiny sidekick? You sure there's nothing you're holding back from me, Prometheus?'

Curtis couldn't work out what Gina was thinking. He could tell the reference to Prometheus had upset her. Too bad. She hadn't trusted him once. He had to make sure it wasn't going to happen a second time. Just as she seemed to be about to answer him, Sam joined them at the table. Curtis slid along to make room for her.

'You guys OK?' she asked. Curtis was sure she could sense the awkwardness between them.

Gina gave a hint of a smile. 'Definitely been better!'

Sam looked at Curtis. 'When's your friend turning up?'

'As soon as he gets here, I guess,' shrugged Curtis. 'He'll ring me.' Sam got stuck into her burger, stopping only to ask them questions as she ate.

'So what do you guys do when you're not being chased by guys with guns?'

Gina shot a quick look at Curtis. It said, say nothing. But he had to say something.

'We're network-security consultants. Also do a few other odd and ends,' he said offhandedly.

'Yeah, I noticed you know your way around a PC. That trick with the chess game was something else. But you still haven't told me why you wanted to find out where that email came from so badly.'

'Just doing a favour for someone,' said Curtis. That was all she was going to get. She didn't push it.

'So what do you reckon those things were back there?' she said, changing the subject.

Curtis shrugged. 'What do *you* think they were?'

Sam stopped chewing for a second. 'You saw the mpegs. If they weren't the same kind of flying-saucer things then I'm the next President.' That was what Curtis had been thinking as well.

'And what about that light? What was that all about?' she asked. 'Can't believe I didn't get them on camera.'

'Don't know about the light,' said Curtis, 'but I think they buzzed us with some sort of electromagnetic pulse. Knocked out the engine. All the electrics too. Even killed my cellphone. That's why Turk couldn't get through.'

'This is way past weird,' said Gina.

'We have to tell people about this,' said Sam. 'We can't just let them get away with this shit.'

Curtis shook his head. 'No way, Sam. You'll be on your own.'

Sam looked at Curtis. Then Gina.

'You can't tell me you guys aren't going to do something about this! We've been shot at for Christ's sake!'

'Because we hacked their computer network!' said Curtis angrily. 'We've probably broken a dozen laws. Like I said, you want to go public with this, then you can leave us out of it.'

Sam realised she was fighting a losing battle. She let out a long sigh. 'Just be our word against theirs without video, anyway.'

'You got it,' said Curtis, relieved.

'But did you see the way those things just hovered there?' said Sam. 'Why do you reckon they let us go like that? They had us. Doesn't make sense!'

She was right. It didn't make sense to Curtis either. It was like they'd been ordered to let them go. Maybe they were tailing them, to see who they were involved with. Curtis slowly eyed each of the diners. Then the restaurant staff. No one was paying them any attention at all. That was why they had to change vehicles. He looked at his watch. Turk would be a while off yet.

'So what do we do now? I need to get back to LA,' said Sam.

'We wait,' said Curtis. 'I saw an internet service booth on the way in.' He looked at Gina. 'Can I use your lappie for a while? Got something I need to do. You two be OK here?'

Gina pulled a can't-see-why-not face. 'Yeah, sure.' Somehow she didn't seem entirely comfortable with him using it.

'I'll be over there if you need me. I'll let you know as soon as Turk calls. When he does, we're outta here. Keep an eye out. For anything.'

Curtis slid out from the table and made his way to the Hummer. This time he saw the dents in the back, where the four-wheel drive had hit them. It was a sobering moment. He grabbed Gina's laptop, leaving the keys under the wheel arch this time, and went back inside, checking for anything suspicious on the way in. Nothing that he could see.

The internet connection was five dollars per hour. Pure extortion, but out here at this time, that was the going rate. As soon as Gina's lappie had powered up, he pulled out the disk from Jim's computer and plugged it in. First he went to the file manager, and explored the contents. Mpegs. A whole bunch of them. The worm was working after all. It had just found so much to send it had probably decided to send them all. No wonder it had taken so long to download. It had kept the connection open while they traced them. Long enough for them to get a fix, anyway. The sort of thing he would do if he was asked to programme a Firewall Anomaly Beacon. F.A.B. — it was something Curtis had worked on a few years back, when he'd first joined Trident. It was based on the venus-flytrap principle. Let them in to where you want them, and kill them with kindness. Or goodies. The ones you didn't mind them having — lower security stuff. Long enough to establish a trace.

Curtis looked around. No one was paying him any attention. He clicked open one of the mpegs, a smaller one. Time to see what he'd got. The viewer software came up, and the video started. It had sound. Curtis plugged his headphones into the jack on the lappie. A picture formed out of a window of solid static. It was colour, but a faded colour. Like an old black-and-white movie that's been colourised, and not quite true. When the picture cleared, the camera seemed to be skimming low over a desert at very high speed. Then Curtis realised this wasn't just a desert. It was a whole planet. He could see the desert stretching out in the distance to a wide arcing horizon. It was a red tortured landscape. No vegetation, no suggestion of life. Mars. Then he picked up some static on the headphones. Another sound coming through. Men cheering. Then a voice cut through loud and strong.

'OK ... scan initiating. Three, two, one ...'

'Scanning now,' came another voice.

'Readings stabilising. We'll punch them up on screen as soon as we're through, gentlemen.' The first voice again.

The word 'Temp' appeared on the lower left. And almost instantaneously, a word was duplicated below it. In Russian. Curtis was sure of it.

'*Just a few more seconds now ...*' said the second voice. Then a number appeared alongside the word Temp. It said four degrees. Centigrade. More words appeared on screen, first in English, then with what looked like a Russian translation below it. Wind Speed, Barometer, Humidity, Gravity — all followed by numbers that didn't make any sense to Curtis. He shook his head in wonder. What the fuck was this all about, he thought to himself.

'*OK, looking good,*' said the voice again. Curtis saw more stats appearing on screen. H_2O, Hydrogen, Oxygen. They were analysing the atmosphere. Mars's atmosphere. Must have been one of the early Mars explorers, decided Curtis. Old news. But as the Oxygen reading came up, the American announcer changed Curtis's mind entirely on that score.

'*That's it, folks. We have a confirmed reading. We have air. Repeat, we have air on Mars.*'

Say what? In the background Curtis heard cheering and yelling as the guy spoke.

Then the second dude cut in again. '*We've done it! Air on Mars! If they ever take the wraps off this thing, it'll be the biggest date in history. 22 May 1962. We're on the planet Mars, and we've got air ...*'

The video finished, leaving Curtis staring at the empty viewer window. He played it again. He hadn't been hearing things — the guy said 1962. Air on Mars. Must be a hoax. He closed the viewer down and went back to the file manager. This time he paid more attention to the file names. Sure enough, what he'd thought were just random numbers were actually dates. The one he'd opened was called 620522. 22 May 1962. He closed the file manager, and sat in thought for a second. He needed to save the files somewhere. Anywhere. Just for insurance. But before he could decide where to save them, his phone rang. Turk had arrived. Curtis pulled off his headphones and answered it.

'I'm here,' said Turk.

'Where?'

'Out front. Where are you guys parked?' asked Turk. He sounded nervous.

'We're round the back. Park as far away as you can from the Hummer. I've left the keys under the front driver's wheel arch. Just leave yours in the ignition. What sort of car have you got?'

'I'm coming round now. I'm in a black Camaro,' said Turk.

'When we see you drive out, we'll see if anyone's following you. If they are, you need to keep them following you. You understand?' said Curtis.

'You ring me if you see anything, dude. I don't like surprises,' said Turk. 'OK, I got the Hummer. Call me if you see anything.' Turk ended the call. Curtis looked back at the screen. Now that Turk was here, he knew he didn't have time to email such a large bunch of files to his webmail address.

It would take forever. The only alternative he could think of was Gina's laptop. He quickly saved the files to her hard drive. Then he opened up her mail, clicking open a new message. He attached the files and clicked 'Send to Outbox'. Next time she connected the message would send. Whenever that would be. Curtis closed out of her mail, and ended the session. He put her lappie inside his bag and went over to where the girls were waiting. Sam was puffing away on a Marlboro Light. Gina had her head in her hands.

'He's here,' said Curtis. 'We need to watch to see if anyone follows him out …' The girls looked at each other. Time for the nightmare to continue. They got up and followed Curtis over to a front window table. But just as they were sitting down, the whole restaurant complex suddenly shuddered. The sound that immediately followed was deafening. An explosion. Out back. A few people screamed, but everyone seemed all right. The truckers were all leaving their food and heading out back to check it wasn't their truck. Curtis, Gina and Sam looked at each other. What the fuck was that?

'You guys wait here,' said Curtis. 'If you see the Hummer stop out front, then I'm driving it. That means we'll be leaving in it, OK?'

'Be careful, Curtis,' said Gina. She looked like she meant it too. As he started to leave, Sam got up behind him.

'Where are you going?' asked Curtis.

'You think I'm just gonna sit there and miss out on all the action while you play Bruce Willis?' For fuck's sake. Curtis looked at Gina.

'Let's all go,' she said. Great. They worked their way through a throng of men who hadn't showered for a day or two. When they got outside, they found the carpark lit up by the flames from a car parked in between two trucks. It was the Hummer. Curtis's mind turned immediately to Turk.

'Turk's in there!' he said. He pushed through a wall of the truckers and ran. But it was already an inferno of white-hot flames and orange heat. Someone had bombed it. He couldn't believe his eyes. The Hummer they'd just been driving was now a melting fireball. And Turk was in there. This was too terrible to be true. No way.

Gina and Sam appeared at Curtis's side. Gina was urging them to go. To get out of here.

'Turk's in there,' he said for the second time. There was nothing he could do.

'Curtis, we have to leave. That was meant for us. Where's Turk's car?' asked Gina.

Curtis shook his head. 'I can't fucking believe this.' Gina grabbed his arm. Hard.

'Curtis, where's the car?' she said. 'Where's the Camaro?' Curtis slowly came back to the here and now. They had to get out of here. Fast. Now they knew for sure their lives were in danger.

He walked away as inconspicuously as he could, finally turning away from the flames. Then with Sam and Gina in tow, circled round through the trailers. They spotted the Camaro parked on its own at the far edge. Curtis willed himself not to run. Not because he thought he might be caught. Just because he felt like running. Anywhere.

He half-expected Turk to climb out of the driver's seat as they got near. But it was empty. Keys still in the ignition. They threw their things in the Camaro and climbed in. Curtis reversed out of the park, and drove the car as sedately as he could across the apron and out the exitway. There were still people running around, but most were out back watching the Hummer, waiting for the fire brigade to arrive. Curtis felt like he was going to pass out. He cried instead. Just a couple of tears. He merged with the highway and continued the journey back to Vegas. This wasn't worth a million dollars. No way. It was worth way more, thought Curtis. Way, way more.

12

No one said anything as they drove away. Everyone was focused on who or what was going to pull in behind them as they left. Curtis kept his eye on the flames as they receded into the distance. He picked up his cellphone and speed-dialled Turk's number. It cut straight to his voicemail. As he listened to Turk's final tasteless voicemail greeting, Sam interrupted him. 'Uh oh, they're here already.' A sheriff's car sped past them in the opposite direction, lights flashing. Curtis pocketed his phone.

'You guys should really go to the cops, you know,' said Sam. 'You can bring prosecutions against the government for stuff like this. It's outrageous. It'd be bigger than the Iran–Contra story.'

Curtis wiped his brow. And his eyes. 'What we should really do is drop you off on the way into town. Then you're going to forget about us. Please.'

'Are you kidding?' said Sam. 'You guys are on to something. I don't know what the hell it is, or why these people are chasing you, but there's a reason.'

Curtis sat fuming. Sam didn't have to say 'and you'd better tell it to me or else'. It was kind of inferred in the way she said it.

'Tell her, Gina,' said Curtis. 'This isn't for print, OK. This is just us, to you.' Sam nodded. She must have been wondering what the hell she was going to hear.

'We aren't computer-studies students,' said Gina. 'Not in the conventional sense. We're hackers.' Well, that wasn't putting too fine an edge on it. Sam just nodded silently.

Gina continued. 'We were invited to enter a competition to source those mpegs. That's all there is to it.'

'OK,' said Sam, thinking hard. 'How many people are trying to track these mpegs?' Gina looked at Curtis. She had to tell her something.

'Just us two.' Sam nodded again. Curtis almost heard the penny drop.

'So how much are you two being paid to find out where these mpegs came from?'

'One million dollars — but actually only half that 'cos we've teamed up and we'll split the money,' said Gina helpfully.

'A million dollars?' said Sam. Gina didn't answer, but the look said all Sam needed to hear.

'So how does Jim fit into all this?'

'We traced the mpegs to his website. That's how we tracked them to you.'

'So you only just met Jim?' asked Sam curiously.

Gina nodded. 'He offered us a place to stay for the night, and we realised he was the guy we'd come to see.'

'I see,' said Sam. Curtis wasn't entirely sure what she was seeing, but the way she said it sounded like she'd thought something was up, she just needed the pieces in place.

'So this whole guys-with-helicopter-and-guns thing is just over our wee foray to see where the email came from?' said Sam, rather incredulously.

Curtis didn't answer. It sounded too ridiculous. Two people dead because of what? Some old documentary footage. Not your garden-variety documentary footage he had to admit, but it was old stuff. History. What could be so precious about it now?

He was still trying to figure it out when he spotted sharp slivers of silver moving erratically up ahead. Reflective tape. Being worn by someone. Curtis slowed the Camaro and tried to work out what was happening. Too late, he realised it was a roadblock. The truck ahead of him had blocked out the lights. A sheriff's deputy was already signalling them to slow down with long swings of a torch. There was nothing any of them could do. They just had to sit there, and go with it. If he reversed they'd be spotted, and Curtis didn't fancy taking the Camaro off-road. Not after the last experience with the Hummer. He sat and sweated. Eventually the truck moved ahead, and Curtis pulled up to a uniform shining his torch at the licence plates and registration stickers.

'Evening, sir. Can I see your driver's licence, please? We've had an explosion back aways, d'ya see it?'

Curtis was caught off guard by the question. 'I, no, didn't see anything, but I've been pretty much focusing on the road. In the dark and all …' The cop flicked his torch onto Curtis's face while he spoke.

'Can I ask you to wait here for a moment while I check this? Won't be too long, sir.' The cop went over to his vehicle parked just off the road, angled ready to go at a moment's notice in case they got a runner. He spoke into his radio for a while. After a short moment, he was back.

'Sir, I'm going to have to wait my place in the queue, I'm sorry. Lot of requests coming through tonight. Can I ask you to park your vehicle over against the curb, and I'll let you know as soon as it's through.' It was asked very politely, but Curtis understood. Go over there and wait. He pulled the Camaro off the road, and they sat and waited as the deputy stopped a couple of other cars, then let them go straight through. What the hell was going on? He must be on to something. When the cop eventually got off his radio for the third time, he sauntered over to the Camaro. Curtis wound down the window as the cop leaned in.

'Curtis Hatch?' Curtis nodded.

'Yeah?' The cop suddenly reached in and grabbed the keys from out of the ignition. It looked like he'd practised that a few times before.

'You're under arrest for parole violation. As soon as I'm finished here, I want you to follow me back to the station so I can process your papers. And I'll keep these in the meantime. How's that?' He dangled the keys for a second then pocketed them.

'All right,' was all Curtis could manage. The cop went back to his traffic-stopping. He asked some of them a few questions. He checked the licences of a few, like he'd done to Curtis. All were let through.

About an hour later Curtis was following a sheriff's department car into the desert town of Fairey. Right up to the station. The deputy waited for them to get out of the car, then took the keys again after Curtis had locked it. As they entered the station, he turned to Gina and Sam.

'You two ladies mind waiting here, this'll just take a few minutes.' Gina and Sam sat on the hard steel bench seats in the reception area, as the deputy ushered Curtis through a maze of desks to an office out back. It looked like an empty office. Apart from the person sitting at the desk.

'Hello, Curtis. Have a seat and tell me about your adventures.'

It was Terry Hay. That was why the deputy had kept them waiting — so Terry would have time to get here. Curtis sat down in the only other chair in the room. Terry looked real pissed.

'What you doing out here, Terry?' said Curtis, keeping things positive.

'Seeing you, Curtis. Figured you must have forgotten you were on parole. What with all the grief over Roly's death and all. So I was going to ask you the same thing. What you doing out here, Curtis?' Curtis felt the world on his shoulders.

'Just sightseeing. Enjoying the company, that sort of thing.'

Terry looked at him. 'Been seeing any sights on the net lately?' Curtis couldn't hold Terry's gaze.

'Just one or two,' said Curtis into his chest.

'Would that include the FBI investigations database?'

Curtis nodded. 'How'd you trace me?'

'Didn't have to,' smiled Terry. 'Only person who's ever accessed your file in the last four years was you. When they told me about the breach, and showed me the photo that had been accessed, I figured you must be up to something. Of course, disappearing like this is a bit of a giveaway too.' Curtis decided enough was enough.

'OK, Terry, you can drop the bullshit. Yes, it was me. And no one got hurt, so let's drop it.'

'Well then why don't you start by telling me what you've been up to? We can overlook a peek at your mugshot for a minute.'

'Terry, Turk's dead.'

Terry suddenly dropped the niceties. 'What do you mean? Is he out here with you?'

Curtis nodded reluctantly. 'Terry, something's going on. I don't know what, but we're right in the middle of it.'

'Why don't you start at the top? I'm not going anywhere. Neither are you for that matter. What happened?'

Curtis drew a deep sigh. Begin at the top. So much had happened in such a short space of time.

'I met up with Turk at Roly's funeral.'

Terry nodded. 'Yeah. Real shame. He had a lot of trouble adjusting after he got out. Not really sure he learned anything.'

'Well, Turk talked me into going to DefCon. I just needed to get away for a few days. We entered the comp — it's a simulated network so I figured it was OK. Anyway, we almost won it.'

'Was that Shield system?' Curtis nodded. 'Yeah I heard it got busted wide open by a few hotshots at DefCon. Wasn't Prometheus one of those?'

'Yeah, think so,' said Curtis.

'Not a very good way to keep a low profile, Curtis,' said Terry.

'Yeah well, someone else noticed us as well. They offered us a million bucks to source a couple of mpeg videos. Real far-out stuff — UFO footage or something.'

Now Terry was interested. 'Tell me about that.'

'We traced them to a website run out of a trailer town in the desert. I went out there to see what we could find.' He stopped for a moment to gauge Terry's reaction to this, but he seemed to be digesting it all, so he continued. 'We traced the email — with the guy's permission — to a really odd network system. Something I'd never seen before. I thought I'd have a quick look around, but we got traced. That's when they blew up the guy's car.'

Terry did a double take. 'Who blew up what guy's car?'

'The choppers from Area 51,' said Curtis. 'The website must have been linked to them somehow. They were on to us in a second. He didn't stand a chance.'

Terry had pulled out a notebook and was busy writing. 'What's the name of the town, and the guy?'

'Rachel,' said Curtis. 'And the guy's name is Jim Maze.'

'Where was Turk in all this?' asked Terry. Where to start? Curtis decided to give him a brief rundown of what happened.

'We managed to escape the choppers, but a four-wheel drive followed us and tried to run us off the road. They crashed, and when I went over to help them out one of them started shooting at us.'

For some reason, Terry didn't look as surprised as Curtis thought he would be at that news.

'You OK?' he said.

Curtis nodded. 'So I got Turk to hire a car and meet up with us somewhere. I figured they'd already spotted the Hummer. We needed to change cars quickly.'

'This would be the truck stop back a few miles?' Curtis nodded again.

'I left my keys for him to take our car, and waited inside. That's when the car blew up. I think Turk was in it.' Curtis couldn't believe it himself. But Terry seemed to be giving him the benefit of the doubt.

'You have to believe me, Terry,' said Curtis. 'They shot at Jim. His pick-up just exploded.' He didn't look too upset. Probably just another day in the life of a parole officer. Who knew?

'So now you think someone planted a bomb in your car while you were waiting inside the truck stop?' said Terry.

Curtis shook his head in disbelief. 'Must have,' he said. 'I can't think of any other way they could do it. It must have been rigged to the ignition. Turk didn't stand a chance. They were after me, Terry. These guys kill people and ask questions later.' Terry sat looking at his notes for a moment. Then he sat back in his chair.

'That's quite a story you got there, Curtis. Give me a few minutes to check some things.' He got up and left the room. Curtis heard him lock the door behind him as he closed it.

Terry was gone longer than a few minutes. When he got back Curtis was going nuts. He wasn't good at waiting. They'd only pulled him in for the parole violation. Or so it appeared. No one had even asked about Turk or Jim. Yet.

'I've talked to your friends — Gina and Sam?' Curtis waited for him to say something he didn't know. 'I've taken a statement from them. They're free to go. Sam's taken a ride back into Vegas, Gina's waiting for you out front.'

'Have you heard anything about Turk?' asked Curtis hopefully.

Terry shook his head. 'Not a thing. Local sheriff got called to a car fire at the place you mentioned. No sign of any bodies, though. They've put it down to faulty electrics, and since there were no casualties they're not in any real hurry to get it investigated.'

'This doesn't make sense, Terry, I'm telling you. Turk rang me just before the Hummer blew up, he was going to take it back to Vegas for us. I looked for him everywhere but he wasn't even answering his phone. Something's happened to him, Terry.'

Terry sighed. 'Well, until we find a body, or he's officially declared missing, there's not much else they're gonna do. I can run a check on him. Leave it with me. If he's around, we'll find him.'

'And if he's not?' asked Curtis. Terry didn't answer that one. Instead he changed the subject.

'So tell me about this Jim Maze. Where did he get blown up?' Curtis recounted the how and where of Jim's last few moments alive.

Terry took a few notes and thought for a second. 'I'm going to have to check this with the base authorities. Local sheriff hasn't had any reports of a pick-up being fired on though.' Curtis didn't find that all that surprising.

'What do you expect?' he said. This was complete bullshit. 'They shot and killed someone. For what? It doesn't make any sense. They're just covering the whole thing up.' But Terry wasn't convinced. Curtis couldn't blame him really. He just figured Terry would give him the benefit of the doubt.

'You're going to have to let me go through the proper channels on this, Curtis,' said Terry. 'Now at the moment you're on parole violation. I might be able to get that reduced to a suspended sentence, but if you're in any way implicated in this other stuff, you're going to have more to worry about than that. You with me?' Curtis nodded. He was with him.

'Now I'm going to make some calls,' said Terry. 'I'll bring you back a coffee.'

He left Curtis alone for a second time. And the waiting wasn't getting any easier. When Terry returned with a hot filter coffee Curtis had just about had enough. He was being as straight as he could with Terry, without getting himself or Gina in deeper shit.

'All right,' said Terry as he sat back down. 'Here's where we're at. The sheriff has ID'd the Hummer as being rented to you. I told them to check again for a body, but they're convinced there was no one in it. They've got a scene investigator coming out from Vegas, but until he arrives, I've asked them to keep it low key.'

'Thanks Terry.' Curtis wasn't sure what he was thanking Terry for, but it sounded like he was trying to do him a favour.

'Now normally they'd hold you,' continued Terry, 'but I've told them you're under my jurisdiction while you're being held for a parole violation. But the way I figure it, you've got until Turk is notified as missing. Then yours is gonna be the first door they come knocking on. You know that car you're in is rented out in Turk's name? He got it just a few hours ago.' Curtis nodded silently. Yes he fucking knew.

'What about Jim?' he said. 'Did they find him?'

'Nothing. Spoke to the base duty commander, says they've had a quiet night. No incidents logged. And no helicopters shooting at private motor vehicles in the desert. That one's not holding water, Curtis.'

Curtis gave him an I-don't-believe-this smile. 'Terry I can prove it. It happened. Did you ask Gina?'

Terry shook his head. 'She's not saying much. But she's not under arrest for anything, and I can't make her talk. It's just your word, Curtis.' He sat looking at Terry across the desk.

'So what are you saying? You're gonna bust me for parole violation if I can't prove I was shot at and Turk was killed?'

Terry shook his head in sympathy. 'Curtis, if I didn't know you I'd be holding you for a hell of a lot more than just a parole violation. You're basically admitting to being involved in two shootings. They take that kinda stuff pretty seriously out here.'

'They weren't shootings, they were explosions,' said Curtis angrily. 'And *they* were firing at *us* from helicopters. Come on Terry, you gotta believe me!'

'Curtis, there are no bodies. Show me a body, and I'll show you a warrant to search the place. But until you have some proof it's just your word against theirs. And a judge is likely to believe the party that doesn't have a prior. You know what I'm saying?'

Curtis gave up in frustration. 'You're saying *fuck all*! That's what you're saying. You know I wouldn't make this shit up. Terry, people are dead. And now it's being covered up. This is *bullshit*!' Under the circumstances, Terry took the outburst pretty well.

'Calm down,' he said. 'It's not bullshit, it's the law. Unless you've got some proof that someone's been shooting at you, and you can show me a body, then you're looking at 6 to 12 months' minimum. That's just for the parole violation. But if it turns out you've been holding back on me, if you're more than a spectator in any of this — in any way at all — you're going to be looking at a damn sight more than that. Am I making myself clear?'

Curtis was fuming. But he kept his trap shut. He was wasting his time on Terry. So there it was. Either he was in the shit, or he proved that he wasn't just hallucinating and making it all up, which would put him in even deeper shit. So be it.

'I can get proof, Terry. I just need some time. And I can't do it from here.'

Terry weighed up Curtis's implicit suggestion. He was asking Terry to let him go.

'I can give you 24 hours, Curtis. No more.' Curtis looked at Terry. Frustration and despair. Not a good mix.

'OK,' he said. Twenty-four it was.

Terry walked Curtis back to the waiting room. Gina was alone, waiting for him. She looked half-asleep, but she got up when she saw Curtis arrive. He figured she could probably tell from the look on his face that things weren't hunky dory. Far from it.

'Come on, we're outta here,' he said. Gina grabbed her bag and followed Curtis out to the rental. When she saw him get in and start the engine, she jumped in as well.

'Is it over?' she asked.

'For us it is,' he said. Gina was on her way home, wherever that was.

'What do you mean, for us?'

'We're going straight back to Ollie to give him the disk. Then we're taking our mil' and getting the fuck outta here,' said Curtis. 'Give him a call and tell him we're on the way in.' Gina shot him a you've-got-to-be-kidding look.

'Curtis, I'm tired, we've been shot at, and it's nearly four in the morning. The disk can wait. So can Ollie. I need some sleep.'

Curtis wasn't happy, but he didn't argue. He just wanted to finish this. Now. The million had become a second priority. It needed to be sorted so he could focus on something way more important.

'OK,' he said finally, 'but we're getting up at nine. Where you go is up to you, but I'm on a plane by noon.'

'Yeah, fine,' said Gina. 'I just need some sleep first. And a shower.'

She rested her head back on the seat and sighed. 'I'm so glad it's over.' Over? Not by a long shot. She reached into her backpack and pulled out a cigarette and lighter. It was a Marlboro Light. Same as Sam had been smoking. She wound down her window and lit the smoke with a deep inhale.

'I didn't know you smoked?' said Curtis. Gina looked over at him as she puffed out a breath of smoke.

'There's plenty you don't know about me, mister.' Wow. This was another side to Gina. Curtis could definitely see something in her eyes he hadn't seen before. Maybe this was what being shot at did to people. Curtis decided to play the game.

'How much plenty are we talking about here?' Gina gave him a smile that didn't say a lot.

'Enough to keep you busy for at least a few years.' Nice comeback. Curtis let it drop. When she finished the smoke she threw the butt out the window and wound it back up. As she curled up and went to sleep, Curtis felt himself getting tired as well. His eyes were getting heavy and he was finding it hard to focus on keeping the Camaro aiming where it should be. Trust Turk to rent a getaway car. He should have known it. Even Gina knew it.

He remembered Gina yelling at him to find the Camaro. But the thing was, Turk had only just told *him* what sort of car he'd rented over his cellphone. She couldn't have known what sort of car to look for. Not unless someone told her. Curtis remembered she'd also spent a long time in the toilets. Long enough to make a few phone calls.

That's when it clicked into place. Curtis suddenly realised what an idiot he'd been — he'd fallen for it hook, line and sinker. Gina had to be an undercover Fed. He'd had his suspicions about her being Prometheus. She knew fuck all about the stuff *he* should know about. But she did know about as much as any bright young FBI field agent might pick up on a course at Quantico. It was a big piece of the puzzle, but it still didn't fit together. What the hell was she doing? And who the hell was she after? Curtis knew the FBI wasn't after him, because he hadn't done anything wrong. Well certainly not enough to start an undercover FBI investigation. Terry hadn't given any suggestion that he knew about it — maybe it was too secret even for him. Curtis tried to work it out. Gina must have been using him to get close to someone. But everyone they'd got close to had been shot at or blown up. He racked his brain for something. Anything at all. But unless she was just chancing a meeting with a hacker like Curtis at DefCon, it didn't make any sense.

Curtis shook his head as he drove. This was getting way too complicated. So maybe it wasn't a *who*, he thought. Maybe it was a *what*. Maybe it was something Curtis was getting close to. Something like a website. Or a black-budget project that had gotten out of hand.

'Fuck!' he said under his breath. Was that what this was all about?

Gina lifted her head. 'Did you say something?' Curtis looked over at her. She was beautiful. But that didn't make her any less of a Fed.

'Nothing, babe. Go back to sleep. I'll wake you when we get to Vegas.'

Gina gave Curtis a tired, sexy smile, and went back to sleep. He went back to driving, his mind spinning. His heart wasn't much better. Music. He pulled his MP3 player out of his bag and flicked the headphones on with a well-practised rhythm. Larry clicked the band into a ballad. 'One'. He was back where he started. As he listened to Bono walk all over his emotions, he found it easier to stay awake for some strange reason. But there was no getting away from the fact that Gina was a cop. Curtis shook his head in wonder. They'd even slept together. Is that what they did now? Sleep with their targets? Curtis felt the emotion of the hours of adrenaline they'd just gone through wash over him. He'd figured Gina was too good to be true. When he looked back without the love goggles on, there had definitely been something in her eyes. That was why he was so sure of her real identity now. And why he was so sure he had to get rid of her. As soon as they'd collected the money.

13

Curtis took the rental back to the Oasis, figuring he'd return it in the morning. Turk had left the receipt in the glove box, and Curtis noticed he'd paid for it with cash. He had no idea where Turk had found the money, but that was the least of his problems. The Oasis was where they'd last slept together. Where she'd slept as she lay in his arms.

He got the car valet-parked and they headed up to the room. They leant against the elevator walls and looked at each other as it ascended. Curtis couldn't suppress a wry smile. They'd been through a lot since they were last here. A fucking lot. He still couldn't quite believe she was a Fed, but in his heart he knew. As Gina headed straight for the bathroom, Curtis noticed the computer that had previously been set up on the desk was gone.

'I'm gonna take a quick shower,' she said. 'You might want to think about one too.'

Thanks for the tip, thought Curtis. Compared with Jim and the truckers, he didn't think he was *that* bad.

'Hey, d'you mind if I use your lappie while you're in there?' shouted Curtis through the bathroom door. 'I just have to check my mail. Didn't get time back at the ...' Back where Turk got killed.

'Sure,' shouted Gina from the bathroom as the shower started up.

Curtis threw his things on one of the beds and pulled Gina's laptop out of his bag. He searched through his pack for a cord to connect it to the phone socket. In an instant it was up and running. Curtis opened Gina's mail and sent the message he'd stored in her outbox earlier. As it was sending he realised it was going to be too large for his webmail address. He'd have to log on and increase his storage capacity. That meant going from spam free to spam hell. As he was clicking his options, Curtis remembered Turk was going to send him an email, the one Curtis had asked him to send once he'd done a check on Mr Ollie Branton. He opened the inbox and sure enough, there was one message. From Turk.

Hey dude. Finished the search on your buddy Oliver H. Branton. Here's the highlights on the attached. What's going on, man?
Turk

Curtis read the email a few times. It was the last message he'd get from Turk. He'd written this just before his death. It was probably one of the last things he did. Like hiring the rental and driving out to the desert. All because Curtis asked him to. And he'd done it without question. And now he was dead. Curtis punched up a song. He needed some time out. Some time for Turk. The song was somehow fitting, as Turk had always been trying to throw his arms around the world. Curtis rubbed his eyes as he listened. It was all his fault. Turk would be alive right now if …

But what ifs weren't good enough. Not for him. Not after this. Curtis vowed on Turk's memory to find out who'd done it and why. This wasn't just about clearing his own name now. It was for Turk as well.

When the song finished, Curtis opened the document Turk had attached. It was a list of all the stuff he'd asked Turk to find. First thing Curtis looked for was the list of credit-card transactions, around the date he'd met with Ollie. He found them all right. But the descriptions and locations were not quite what he'd been expecting. After buying a woman's fur coat in New York, Ollie Branton had paid for an outrageously expensive meal at some restaurant called Manhattan. Only problem was, Ollie was supposed to have been sitting with Curtis and Gina in Vegas at the time. Feds. It hit him like a cold shower. Oliver Branton's identity must have been a cover for an agent as well. The Ollie that Curtis had met had to have been part of the operation. Whatever *that* was. The million — the whole 'project' — was part of an FBI investigation. No wonder they'd been shot at.

While the mail finished sending, Curtis looked up News2U2day.com on the web browser. An idea was forming in the back of his brain, and Sam was a big part of it. When he found Sam's profile, he wrote down her mobile number on the hotel pad, and pocketed it. He closed the mail as soon as it was finished, and shut down the computer. He still had time to strip, brush his teeth, and fiddle with the aircon by the time Gina had finished her 'quick' shower. Then it was his turn. Curtis was in and out of the bathroom in two minutes flat. He was nervous about getting back into bed with Gina, now that he knew who she really was. He decided to sleep with his boxers on. They didn't touch much as they got into bed, but Curtis was asleep before it became too much of an issue.

He was woken by the sounds of Gina moving round the room in the half-light of the bathroom wall-lamp. Curtis had no idea what time it was — there wasn't any daylight spilling out from the curtains. Must have been early.

'Hey, whatcha doing?' he said. He lifted his head off the pillow, and at the same moment realised he still felt like shit.

'I'm meeting Ollie,' said Gina, brushing her hair as she leant out the bathroom door. She was dressed. 'He's really nervous. About the project *and* all the attention.' She ducked back inside the bathroom as she spoke. 'I couldn't sleep so I rang him from the bathroom. The sponsor's rattled too. Ollie wants me to meet with him to settle him down. He just needs reassuring.'

Curtis started getting out of bed and reached for his clothes.

'I'm going alone, Curtis,' said Gina. 'He just wants to see me.' Of course.

'You knew him from some time ago, didn't you?' said Curtis. As offhandedly as he could. Just a wee poke to see if he got a bite.

'I'll ring you as soon as it's over,' she said. He heard her open the door and close it behind her. No bite.

Curtis lay back on the bed. She'd ring him, huh? As he lay in the soft dark of the hotel room he worked on the idea he'd been mulling over since last night. It was becoming more of a plan than an idea. He closed his eyes and waited for Gina to ring. Moments later he was dead to the world.

It seemed like he'd only just put his head back on the pillow when his cellphone rang. He fumbled around on the dresser in the dark, and felt for the call button.

'Hello,' he said.

'Curtis, it's me.' It was Gina. Now she was coming at him with the 'it's me' thing.

'What is it? Everything OK?' He checked the clock on the dresser. It was 8.34 a.m.

'Curtis, listen to me,' she said. 'I'm leaving.' Curtis's mind scrambled into consciousness.

'What?'

'The deal's on, but I'm through with it. Ollie doesn't know I'm ringing you. He's expecting us to make the drop at the hotel at 10. You take it, Curtis. You've earned it.'

Curtis screwed his face up as he tried to make some sense of what she was saying. 'You're leaving? Where to?' was the best he could do under the circumstances.

'I'm at the airport. My flight leaves in under an hour. Don't worry about me. I'll catch up with you soon. I just need to get out of here. This whole thing has gone ballistic.' Curtis sat trying to think what to say next. His mind was in a turmoil. His heart wasn't in a good state either.

'I — will I see you again? Where?' he said.

'I think you should just let me find you. It's been fun, Curtis. The you and me bit, anyway.' Curtis was still searching for words when she killed the call. He sat dazed. The money was still on, but she didn't want any part of it. She was at the airport. Leaving in an hour. He tried to make sense of her leaving. Now of all times. He was sure she didn't know she'd blown her cover with him. It must have been something else. It was clear they were taking her off the case. Either that or the operation — whatever it was — was over.

Curtis showered and got dressed, and went down to the hotel lobby. He got some directions from the front desk on how to get to the business centre, and sat down at one of the computers in the guest internet lounge. He spent a few minutes taking the machine off its 'guest' profile, and logged back on using one of the trainee manager's names he'd seen behind the desk. Next he searched the web to pull together all the airlines with flights departing Las Vegas within the hour, and went data-mining for the passenger lists. One by one, he pulled together the passenger manifestos for each flight. She had to be on there somewhere. He looked through each of the lists for a first name starting with G. There were about 12. Then he went through the last names, one by one. There was no MacIntosh, not that he expected to find one. He kept looking. There *was* a G. Rogers. Curtis almost smiled. He checked the flight and gate number. It was going to San Diego. He clicked off and ran back through the lobby to the taxi rank. In seconds, F. Astaire was on his way to the airport.

As soon as the cab pulled up outside the terminal, Curtis flicked the driver a note and jumped out. He searched for a floor diagram, and looked for Gina's gate. It was boarding. Curtis moved into a gentle jog as he threaded through the terminal to her gate, where people were lining up to wave their pass and go through security onto the flight. He worked backwards through the queue. She wasn't there. His heart sank. He'd missed her. He leant back against a wall and watched the passenger queue shrink before his eyes. But as the queue filed past him, he noticed someone sitting by themselves in the gate lounge with her back to him. It was her. Gina Rogers. Curtis walked over. She didn't look like she was in a big hurry to board. In fact she didn't look like she was interested in boarding at all. She was sitting in a trance, her eyes bloodshot and red, like she'd been crying for a while.

'Plane's boarding,' he said. Gina looked up, coming out of her trance.

'What are you doing here, Curtis?' she asked, wiping her eyes with the back of her hand.

'Came to ask you the same question,' he said, sitting down beside her.

The flight attendant came over to them, reminding them that the final boarding call had been given. Gina looked at Curtis. So much to say, so little time.

'Look, I don't care who are, or who you work for. I want to see you again.' Curtis looked into her eyes. They said, how did you know? There was guilt maybe, and some embarrassment, but there was a toughness there as well. She wasn't going to admit to anything. But Curtis thought he could see something else in those eyes too. He'd seen it the night they partied like Fred and Ginger. A million dollars from now.

'Be careful, Curtis,' said Gina, getting up and lifting her bag over her shoulder. 'Jim was right. This thing is bigger than you, and it's sure as hell bigger than me. Goodbye.'

Curtis sat and watched her turn her back, wave her pass at the attendant, and disappear down the bridge. Then she was gone. As the plane was pushed back from the gate, he stood close to the huge windows in front of him, opening out onto to a dry desert apron of asphalt. He put his headphones on and punched up a song as the gleam of the sun on the fuselages of wide-bodied jets reflected off the windows. He drew a deep sigh. He decided that Bono had this one all wrong. She was dangerous, because she wasn't honest. A real wild horse all the same. The guitar merged with the sound of the jet as it pulled back from the gate. Sha la la.

The next song on his playlist jarred him out of his reverie. 'The Fly.' Like a cold slap in the face. Enough feeling sorry for himself. He had things to do. He walked back through the terminal, in step with the beat of the song. It helped him focus, the chorus steeling within him a reckless determination. He had things to do. When he was outside he pulled out his cellphone and dialled Sam's number. She answered on the second ring.

'Hello?'

'Sam, it's Curtis. I need your help.'

There was a pause while she thought. 'What sort of help?'

'The kind with a camera,' said Curtis.

'When?' Curtis looked at his watch. His Wenger had been knocked. It had a tiny crack running across the glass. Half-past nine.

'I'm meeting someone at 10 at the Orion. Can you meet me there?'

'Who?' said Sam quickly. 'The history nut?'

'Not quite. The guy who did the deal on his behalf.' Curtis stood against a column while he talked. He didn't want anyone overhearing. 'Sam, I'm going to have to prove these people killed Jim and Turk. And if I can't get proof, I'm going to make them own up. Even my parole officer doesn't know anything about it. He says they've told him they didn't find any bodies. It's a cover-up, Sam. It's a fucking government security fuck-up, and they've erased the evidence. As soon as Jim and Turk are reported missing, I'm the first person they're going to come after. A fucking frame job.'

'Whoa! Calm down, mister. Take a deep breath and let it go. Now I know a lot of weird stuff's been happening, but it's happened, Curtis. It's history. You won't change that.'

'It's history, all right. More than you'd ever know.'

'What do you mean?'

'Sam, I think whatever's going on out there is somehow related to those videos. I'm beginning to think there's more to them than meets the eye. They could be real. Think about that. You saw them. And you heard those people talking about Alternative 3.' He let it hang. It didn't seem so silly once he'd said it.

'Curtis, I'm booked to go back to LA. The tape was ruined, I don't have any video, and my editor's on my back.'

Curtis felt his frustration rising. 'You'll get way more than some hacking footage and some old UFO sightings, I promise you that.'

Sam didn't answer immediately. She was thinking over his offer. 'All right,' she said finally. 'One more day. But I can't make the Orion by 10. I'll meet you in the lobby at 10.30. That long enough for you to meet your historian?'

'Perfect. I'll bring the disk with the stuff we downloaded onto Jim's computer.'

'You still got it? Have you checked it? What's on it?' She was hooked now.

'Yes, I've got it. And there's stuff on here that leaves the mpegs you've got for dead.'

'OK,' said Sam. 'Bring the disk and show me. Where are you now?'

'I'm at the airport. Gina's gone back home.'

'Oh,' was all she said to that. Her mind was on the story. 'Are you giving your historian the disk? Can you make a copy?' Did she think he was born yesterday?

'No, I don't have a copy. But don't worry. You'll get to see it.' There was another pause. Shorter this time.

'All right. The Orion at 10.30.' She ended the call. Curtis grabbed a cab off the stand and headed back to the Orion. Once he'd collected the money he could start the real game. He rested his head back on the rest and went over the plan again. It wasn't going to be easy. That was for sure.

The cab pulled into the Orion at five minutes to ten. Curtis checked the lobby foyer for anything suspicious. Nothing out of the ordinary. For Vegas anyway. And no UFOs or aliens either. He figured Shiny Styles would come for him again, so he sat down in the same chair as last time. *Déjà vu*. Except everything else had changed. He kept his shades on, checking out everyone exiting the elevators. Lots of people, but no Mr Shiny. He was late. At 10.10, Curtis decided he wasn't going to wait any longer. He got up and went over to the elevators. When one arrived, he pushed the button for the 24th floor and waited. The doors opened to an empty corridor. He walked down the soft carpet to the room he remembered, the corner suite with the boardroom. He waited outside the door and listened. There was no sound coming from inside, so he put his ear to the door and held his breath. Still nothing. Not a good sign. He knocked, and stood back waiting for the door to open, feeling for the disk in his pocket. Just to make sure. It was still there. The door stayed shut, so he knocked again, louder this time. But there was no one home.

Curtis felt his anger growing. Where were they? Gina had said 10. The Feds were his chance to find out what was going on and clear his name. He had the feeling he was being played. Big time. He stood in front of the door, fuming. So these were the rules. There weren't any. He was on his own. So be it. He focused his anger. It was time he did some playing himself. The money was irrelevant. It just proved that Ollie was a Fed. The whole damn thing must have been a set-up.

Curtis put his shades back on and walked back to the elevator and pressed the call button. Time to meet Sam and get on with the real business. With or without the Feds, he was committed. It was up to him now.

The elevator button lit up, signalling a lift was coming. But as the doors opened, two men got out on the same floor. He passed them as he entered the elevator. They were dressed in nondescript black suits, but they had military written all over them. Curtis quickly pressed the lobby button and willed the doors to shut before they saw him. But just as they were almost shut, an arm shot in and held them open. The two men got back in the elevator. Uh oh. As the doors shut again, one of the men turned to him.

'Curtis Hatch?' Curtis looked at him through his shades. Who the fuck are you? He shook his head and pulled a face.

'Sorry, wrong guy,' said Curtis. Suddenly the other suit grabbed Curtis from behind, wrapping a hand around his mouth and twisting his arm up behind his back with the other, slamming him against the elevator wall. The other dude hit the emergency stop button.

'We'd like you to come with us. Car's waiting out front. This'll be easier for you if you cooperate.' Curtis's face was jammed up against the wall, pushing his shades halfway up his forehead. He didn't really have much choice. He was sure they weren't Feds — they'd have shown him some identification by now. They had to be Cammos. But if these turkeys thought they were going to take him anywhere, they had another thing coming. There was no way he was going to end up like Turk and Jim.

'Fuck you!' said Curtis, trying to pull away. The guy holding him threw him against the elevator wall again. Harder this time. The guy doing the talking leant closer.

'Don't make this any harder than it has to be. I don't want to hurt you, but I'm authorised to use whatever force I have to to get your cooperation.'

'Does that include blowing up innocent people? Is that what you do if you don't get your way?' said Curtis.

The guy holding him began frisking his body with one hand, while he leant against him with his arm twisted up his back. It wasn't a lot of fun. He frisked all the places someone might conceal a weapon. Or a disk.

'I think you've been watching too many movies, Curtis,' said the guy. 'You have in your possession some highly classified data. Where is it?'

'I don't know what you're talking about,' said Curtis. The guy nodded to the one frisking him. Suddenly he was rammed back up against the wall, his arm jammed up between his shoulder blades. Curtis couldn't help yelling out in pain.

'I'm not saying anything until you tell me who you are. Who are you working for?' The guy smiled in a humourless way.

'You're not really in a position to be making demands, Curtis. I don't think you realise the seriousness of your situation.'

'What situation?' said Curtis. He tried to sound tough, but it wasn't convincing. Actually he was shitting himself.

'It doesn't matter who I am.' Curtis felt the guy's hand stop as he felt the hard plastic of the disk cover. Then he pulled it out slowly, and gave it to the talking turkey, who pocketed it.

'I don't believe that's your property.' Curtis just eyeballed him. Well, fuck you too.

'Whose property is it, then?' demanded Curtis.

'That information is classified. You're a clever kid, Curtis. I don't know how you managed to compromise our security systems, but if I find out you're more than some dumb punk hacker who just got lucky, you're gonna get more than a suspended sentence this time.' He paused for effect. 'Now there's two ways we can do this. Either you can walk through the lobby with us like a stroll in the park, or we can carry you out. Which is it?'

Curtis shook himself loose from the other guy's grip, and straightened his shades and jacket.

'I'll walk,' he said. The mystery man hit the stop button again and the elevator jerked back to life. They stood silently as the elevator slowed to a halt on the ground floor. The doors opened and Curtis just stood there. He was desperately thinking how to get out of this. There was no way he was getting in any car with these nuts. No way. He had to think. Fast. After a sharp jab in his back, he began making his way across the marble floor of the hotel lobby. As he did, he spotted a concierge pushing a trolley full of bags coming his way. He figured the Suits were pretty much right behind him. Worth a shot.

As the concierge approached, Curtis moved as if to make way for him, and as he did, he grabbed the trolley from the surprised concierge, and swung it round behind him as hard as he could. The Suit behind him didn't jump away in time, and the trolley met him square on the shin. It had to hurt. But Curtis didn't stay around to watch — the instant the trolley hit home he was sprinting for the doors. He heard the other guy yell '*Hey!*' followed by the pounding of his shoes on the marble. Curtis headed for the revolving doors, the Suit only moments behind him. He pushed the doors hard and jumped into a revolving section that closed before the guy could join him. He'd have to take the next revolving section. The doors kept swinging. Curtis waited until the doors had revolved enough for the Suit to be enclosed where Curtis was a second ago. Then he shoved his foot under the door, stopping it instantly. He yanked his headphones off and rammed an earpiece under the door. Sometimes it pays to buy quality. He gave it a kick to wedge it firmly in place. It held. The guy began shoving the door violently in the opposite direction, and he was pulling out something from under his suit jacket. Curtis didn't wait to see what it was, he needed another wedge. Now. He pulled off his sunglasses and folded one side in. He just hoped his Randolphs were strong enough to hold. Just for a few seconds. As he jammed them under the other door, they bent outrageously out of shape. But they held.

Curtis saw the other Suit heading towards the outer doors, the non-revolving ones. He had about two seconds, max. The Suit stuck in the doors was dialling his cellphone. Curtis was relieved — he'd been expecting a gun. He quickly searched the hotel forecourt for an escape route — a couple of taxis were parked further back from the entrance, but the drivers were out of their cars, smoking. He was running out of options, but anywhere was better than here. Curtis noticed a black four-wheel drive parked over to one side. It had to be theirs. As he ran past it he got an idea. He pulled his swiss army knife out of his jacket, and opened it as he ran. As he went past the suitmobile, he bent down and rammed it up against the front tyre. The blade jammed up into the rubber, as he firmly wedged the handle into the ground with his foot. Time to move on. He kept low, trying to keep the four-wheel drive between him and the doors to the hotel, running stooped around the side of the hotel to the carpark, and jumping down behind one of the parked cars. His heart was racing, and he was breathing heavily. He had to get out of here. Anywhere.

He searched the carpark for a way out. Nothing. He leaned around from behind the car's bumper and checked out how far away the Suits were. They were scanning the parking lot for him. Maybe he'd bought himself a few seconds. He ducked back in. But just as he did, he spotted a cab pulling up outside the entrance. In the back seat was a head of blonde hair. It was Sam. Maybe there was a chance. He stood up.

'Hey!' he yelled, ducking down instantly, and running hunched over behind a row of parked cars around to the other side of the lobby entrance. When he next looked up he saw that the Suits had taken the bait. It had maybe given him another five seconds. No more. He darted across to where Sam was paying the cab driver, still in the back seat. He jumped in beside her, pushing her along none too gently, and closed the door.

'Hey!' said Sam, realising in the same moment that it was Curtis pushing her along the seat.

'Driver,' said Curtis, 'change of plan. Head back out and I'll give you 20 on top if you can do it without those guys stopping you.' The driver looked back to Sam, who was still throwing Curtis a what-the-fuck? look.

'He with you?' he asked Sam. She nodded, suddenly realising Curtis wasn't fooling around.

'Just go!' she said to the driver. To his credit the driver responded instantly. The promised tip must have really worked, because as they went through the lobby driveway, one of the Suits ran out in front of the cab. The driver floored it, the Suit moving out of the way just in time to save his other shin.

'Friends of yours?' asked the driver.

Curtis watched out the rear window. 'Just get us out of here. You'll get your 20.' As they pulled out into the traffic, Curtis just saw them climb into the four-wheel drive. He just hoped his MacGyver trick with the pocket knife would work. He kept watching behind them, waiting for the four-wheel drive to appear, as the driver looked back at him through his rear-view mirror.

'All right, that's enough excitement for me for one day. Where're we heading?' asked the cabbie.

'Oasis Hotel,' said Curtis, without taking his eyes off the hotel exit. As they turned a corner, the four-wheel drive still hadn't appeared. Only then did he allow himself to relax a little.

'Who were they?' said Sam quietly.

Curtis shook his head. 'Fill you in when we get there.'

'Get where? What's at the Oasis? Have you still got the … it,' she said, noticing the driver was listening-in on their conversation.

'Yes and no,' said Curtis. Which was kind of the truth, but that was all he was saying for now.

He was too busy trying to work out how the suit brigade had found him, why the FBI operation had been called off, and why Gina had told him it was still on, even though she must have known it wasn't going to happen. Curtis's heart dropped as he realised it must have been Gina who'd led the Suits to him. Unless the Feds had been pulled off by the Suits. This was getting more complicated by the minute. It was too much for his tired brain. He was also pissed about losing his headphones and his Randolphs. No matter, though. He'd get payback. That was for sure.

When the cab dropped Curtis and Sam out at the Oasis, Curtis started walking away from the hotel.

'Where we going, hotshot?' asked Sam. She had her camera with her, but it wasn't on. Yet.

'Somewhere we can talk,' said Curtis. Sam followed Curtis along the block and around the corner, where he stopped at an internet café. 'We can talk in here. Just don't eat anything. Hate to think what you'll catch.' It was the same coffee house he'd gone to a couple of days ago. But when he went inside, it was unrecognisable from the dirty grease-trap he remembered. The counter was clean, and the grease had been cleaned off the printer under the fryer. Even the keyboards on the old Macs out back looked like they'd had a wipe. But it was too good to be true. The same filthy FUB'er was behind the counter, still reading a magazine as he smoked.

'What happened to this place?' asked Curtis as he passed the FUB'er. 'It actually looks like somewhere you might want to eat.' The FUB'er looked up from his magazine. He gave no clue as to whether he remembered Curtis or not.

'Wife came back,' he said, and with a drag on his smoke went back to reading his magazine. Curtis shook his head in wonder as he headed out back to the computers. Sam sat next to him down the back, and as he logged onto the net on one of the machines, she cut to the chase.

'All right, Curtis. If you don't tell me what's going on right now, I'm outta here. Being with you isn't good for my health.'

Curtis was ready for it. In fact he was surprised she'd waited this long. He decided to start from the top. He told her everything. From the night he'd played Gonad over the net, the works. At one point Sam got up and ordered coffee from the FUB'er. She obviously liked to live dangerously. When it arrived she pulled out a cigarette and listened intently as Curtis talked, like she was memorising it all. At least the camera was off. After about 20 minutes, he was finished. Sam sat back in her chair, and lit another cigarette. Yep, she liked to live dangerously.

'Wow,' she said, blowing a cloud of smoke out in front of her. 'That's quite a story you got there, Curtis.' Didn't he know it.

'That's why I need to film everything from now on. It's insurance. I don't know who to trust anymore. It might get risky. And your camera might end up being the only thing keeping me alive. I need your help, Sam.'

Curtis looked at her. She appeared genuinely concerned for him. But so had Gina.

'What are you going to do?' she said.

'You don't need to know that. For your own safety. The less you know beforehand the better. If you lend me your digital, I'll feed you what I get over the net. How's that?' Sam sat silently considering this for a moment.

'OK,' she said, 'on one condition.' Curtis might have known this was coming. Seemed like everything this woman did had strings attached.

'I want to see what was on the disk first,' she said eventually. So that was it. The disk.

'Small problem,' said Curtis. 'The monkeys in the suits took it.'

Sam shot him a hard business-like look, stubbing her butt out at the same time. 'Sorry, Curtis,' she said. 'No deal. If you can't give me anything to go on, I'm not sticking my neck out again. I have a strong sense of self-preservation, and getting shot at isn't my idea of fun.' Curtis looked at her. He couldn't argue with that. He probably would have done the same under the circumstances. Time for the ace up the sleeve.

'That doesn't mean I haven't got what was *on* the disk,' he said carefully.

Sam's eyes lit up immediately. They were electric. And very blue. He hadn't noticed that before. She probably had a great future on TV. 'Where is it?' she asked.

Curtis swivelled round back to the Mac. 'Here,' he said, clicking open the attached list of files on his email. The ones with dates for filenames. Sam watched as he opened the file he'd watched earlier, and hit play. And it was just as bizarre as the last time he'd watched it. She didn't say anything when it finished. So he played it again. As much for himself as her.

'Show me the others,' she said. The way she said it meant she found it as freaky as he did. He clicked on another file. 670212. 12 February 1967. It was just as weird. It started out black, but as the camera angle pulled back it was clear it was being filmed from some type of space vehicle. The black became speckled with stars as the focus was adjusted. The edges of a window were clearly visible, and so were the round glowing shapes the camera was aimed at. Suddenly a burst of static hissed from the Mac's speakers. Curtis adjusted the volume to a lower level, as they listened to one of the strangest conversations he'd ever heard. It was an astronaut.

'*Bogey at 10 o'clock high.*' The camera zoomed in again on the objects. It was shaking a little.

A thin emotionless voice responded. '*This is Houston. Say again, Seven?*'

The astronaut sounded a little more edgy this time. '*Said we have a bogey at 10 o'clock high.*'

'Gemini Seven, *is that the booster, or is that an actual sighting?*' There was a pause. The reply didn't come until another wild zoom was completed.

'*We have several, looks like debris up here. Actual sighting.*'

'*Estimate distance or size?*' The objects became clearer as the camera adjusted focus again. It looked like the objects were saucer-shaped, and flying in formation.

'*We also have the booster in sight,*' came the reply, as the camera swung over to a large cylindrical object spinning slowly miles below the Gemini vehicle. And below the booster was the unmistakable cloud-covered image of earth. Then the video finished.

'They were the same type of UFOs that were in the other videos,' said Sam.

'Yep,' said Curtis, opening another file. They sure as hell were. 'Thing is, what are they doing flying through space in 1967?'

The next video was dated 690721. 21 July 1969. Curtis knew that date. Everyone did. It was *Apollo 11*. Neil Armstrong and Buzz Aldrin. The day they set foot on the moon. The footage was filmed in colour this time. It was the surface of the moon, the American flag clearly visible on a pole a short distance from the camera, which seemed to be set at a higher angle. Maybe it was being filmed from inside the lunar module. The speakers burst into life with a hiss of static.

'*What's there? Mission Control calling* Apollo 11.' An astronaut appeared at the bottom right of the camera. His back was to the camera. He was looking out at something.

'*These babies are huge, sir, enormous! Oh God! You wouldn't believe it …*' The camera panned across to the left, and it appeared that the module was in the middle of some sort of giant flat crater. As the camera continued its arc, two large, mysterious objects came into view on the lip of the crater at its furthest edge.

'*I'm telling you, there are other spacecraft out there … lined up on the far side of the crater edge … they look like they're just watching us!*'

The astronaut was unable to hide the shock in his voice. Suddenly the player window went blank as the video footage ended.

'Wow' said Curtis, 'you know who they were, don't you?' Sam shook her head. 'That was *Apollo 11.* The great step for mankind.' They sat in wonder for a moment.

'So these flying discs were on the moon before NASA?' She was as incredulous as he was. 'Is that what this means?'

Curtis shrugged. 'Well if they could get to Mars in 1962, I guess they could get to the moon.' This was outrageous. If it were true. If.

'Do you believe this stuff?' said Sam, looking at Curtis.

'I'm beginning to,' said Curtis. 'What do you know about Alternative 3?'

Sam shook her head. 'First time I ever heard of it was from the Odd Squad in the back of Jim's pick-up.'

Curtis sat thinking for a bit. 'So if NASA didn't even know about these things, who did? They had to come from somewhere?' Sam looked wired. It was scary stuff all right. Curtis scrolled down to one of the files towards the end of the list. 970218. The nineties. He started it up.

'*What was that flash?*' said a voice suddenly, as the screen filled with lots of white. As the screen returned to normal, Curtis realised he was looking at the interior of a space shuttle.

'*I don't know,*' said another voice. A head turned towards the camera, up close, at a crazy angle that could only happen in zero gravity.

'*That light flashed possibly just here ... and again!*' The astronaut was commentating for the camera.

'*I see it ...*' said the first voice, as the camera panned out the window and began zooming towards a fading flash of light. '*Thought it was just my imagination ...*'

'*I saw it too,*' said the other astronaut. '*So it's not. There were two of them.*'

Suddenly the screen flashed with white again. It was a similar light to the one Curtis had experienced himself. The light from the flying disc. Except here there were two of them.

'*There's another one ... what* are *they?*' said the astronaut. There was a long silence as the camera filmed the bright lights. They dazzled directly at the camera.

'*I wonder if they're taking pictures?*' said one of the astronauts.

'*What* is *that?*' said the other one.

'*This thing's passing in front of us!*' There was no mistaking the fear in his voice. There was another pause and suddenly the light went dim as they passed away from the window and over the rest of the shuttle.

'*I dipped surveillance for a second, but I had that one the whole time.*' It was the cameraman, his voice loud and blurry.

'*Yeah, I got that one too!*' said another voice from further away. Then the player window went blank. End of movie. Curtis didn't move. Neither did Sam.

'This is big, Sam,' he said. 'And I'm going to blow it open. Whatever it takes. You just make sure you're ready to air what I find. Straightaway. If you hold onto it without the public seeing it, you'll make yourself a target. Just like I am now.'

'Curtis, you don't have to do this. You won't be able to change anything. If it's that big, what chance do you think you're gonna have? You'll just end up getting shot at again. You might not be so lucky next time. It's not worth it.' Curtis couldn't believe she was actually trying to talk him out of it. Sam of all people, he thought, would want to blow it open. Even if it was just for a scoop. Maybe he'd misjudged her.

'I'm doing it,' said Curtis. 'With or without your help.'

Sam put her hand on his arm. 'Don't do it, Curtis. I'm not going to stand by and let you get yourself killed. I'll have to tell someone. I couldn't live with myself if I didn't.' Curtis took her hand off his arm and placed it back on her leg. His turn to call the bluff.

'Then we're finished here,' he said, getting up and switching the computer off. Sam grabbed his arm again, harder this time.

'OK,' she said reluctantly. He stopped his pack-up routine. 'I'll help you. Might even end up saving your scrawny ass.' She smiled as she talked. Curtis softened like a pound of butter in the desert sun. He sat down again.

'Thanks Sam. I mean that,' he said. He did mean it too.

'But I'm not helping in any way unless you tell me first what you're planning to do.'

Curtis shook his head. 'No way. If I'm doing this then it's by my rules. Or the deal's off.' Curtis could sense Sam's frustration. She desperately wanted to know what he had planned. But he'd trusted too many people with too much lately. It was time to play it safe.

Finally she nodded. 'All right. Your rules.'

'I need your digital camera, your lappie and a cellphone. Set up a satellite account from your other computer at work, and I'll download the goodies to you over the net.' Sam obviously wasn't used to taking orders. Giving them was way more her style. But she nodded anyway. 'And I'll need your cords for the lappie and phone. I may need a bit more than battery juice.'

'Can you at least tell me where you're going?' she asked.

'Sorry,' said Curtis. Nice try.

'All right,' she said, standing up, 'if you're not going to tell me anything, we might as well get on with it. My stuff is still back at the hotel. If you come back there with me you can grab what you need to do your thing.'

'Thanks, Sam,' said Curtis. She smiled back, in a caring sort of way.

'Doesn't mean I don't think you're completely nuts, you know.'

Curtis smiled too. 'You're not the only one,' he said. He'd been wondering that himself a lot lately.

14

After leaving Sam at her hotel, Curtis went back to the Oasis and packed his things and checked out. Then he took a cab to a car-hire company. A different one. He wasn't sure how long he'd have before the Hummer-hire man called the cops, maybe a couple of days. This time he picked up a different car completely. He found a tired ex-company fleet car. Beige, unremarkable and inconspicuous. On his way out of town he stopped and bought some fuel and a few essentials, including a chocolate toffee bar and a lighter. He drove the car across the apron to the air pump and made as if he was checking his tyre pressure. But while he was crouched down behind the car, he used the lighter to drip melted toffee and chocolate over the plates. Permanent dirt. The rest of the car was filthy enough to make it look realistic, from a distance. He bought a new pair of sunglasses too — Bono glasses, like Turk used to wear — and a new pair of headphones. Priorities.

Soon he was back in the car, heading towards Rachel, working on the rest of his plan. There were big gaps in it, that was for sure. He'd have to improvise. As the dirtmobile hit the ET Highway, Curtis pulled the plastic off his new phones and plugged them in. 'The Fly' — his song. Bono captured his mood exactly. He was feeling reckless. He was a burning star all right. And this one was going to light up the sky.

It was only when Curtis saw Rachel in the distance that he stopped thinking about Turk. He'd driven slowly past the truck stop, and saw that the burnt-out Hummer carcass had been moved away, the black marks on the asphalt the only reminder of Turk's fate. They had even started using the park again. But he couldn't see any marks on the road where the two flying discs had buzzed them. It was hard to visualise them in the daylight. They had been like apparitions. But it was almost a relief to finally see Rachel up ahead. He hadn't been followed or tailed, he was sure of it. He pulled in to Maggie's back door, and made sure no one was watching him before he went inside. The place seemed a lot quieter. Unnaturally so. Maggie was in the kitchen, baking. She jumped when she saw Curtis.

'Hi Maggie,' he said. 'I need a room and telephone line. Make sure no one sees you, and come into my room in 10 minutes. We can talk there.' Maggie just nodded. She went out front while Curtis stayed in the kitchen. She came back with the key to room three. Sam's old room.

'Have the cops been here?' asked Curtis, taking the key.

Maggie shook her head. 'No, but the Cammos were all over here a few hours back. They've gone now.'

Curtis left her in the kitchen and went back to the room. It was exactly as he remembered it. Minus Sam. He connected up the laptop and phones to the wall sockets. He didn't want to find a dead battery in the middle of anything. Maggie came in with her own key about three minutes later.

'Where's your girlfriend? Is she OK?' she asked.

Curtis nodded, deciding not to correct her on the girlfriend thing. 'She's fine. And so is the reporter. Has anyone heard from Jim?' Maggie shook her head.

'Curtis, there was no body and no pick-up. And he hasn't gone back to his trailer. I was out there just an hour ago.' So they'd cleaned up after themselves. No loose ends. Except him.

'Maggie, I have to find out who did this to Jim. I think they killed someone else as well. He was a good friend of mine. The best.'

'I'm sorry,' said Maggie.

'Which means I have to get inside the base. I need to get inside their systems so I can expose this shit. As soon as people realise I'm showing them what's really going on behind the shadows, they won't be able to touch me.' Maggie was a believer. He could see it in her eyes.

'You know, Jim and I didn't know each other for that long — maybe a couple of months — but I miss the grumpy S.O.B.' Curtis could see her fighting down the emotion. She was a tough old girl. When she looked back to Curtis, her gaze was steely cold.

'Anything you need, you just ask. You understand?'

Curtis placed his hand on hers. 'Thanks Maggie.' She left the room, and as she closed the door behind her, Curtis started up the lappie and connected to the web. Sam's homepage was News2U2day.com. Her name was under a teaser title called, 'A walk on the wild side'. Curtis clicked the hyperlink and the full story appeared, complete with still frames of video footage. They were pictures from the back of Jim's pick-up. Curtis scanned the story quickly. She had pitched it as a tongue-in-cheek story about the hikers and quoted some of the more far-out stuff they'd given her. It had them talking about Alternative 3, but the name itself was never mentioned. Just about everything else was though. It may have been good journalism, but Curtis couldn't help feeling for the people she'd conned into spilling their guts. He was watching the second video attachment when there was a knock at the door. He clicked out of the story and opened it slightly. It was Al, the Dweeb and the Greek woman. They looked hyped. But they just stood there.

'You guys looking for me?' asked Curtis. They nodded.

'Can we come in?' said Al, looking back down the corridor. Curtis opened the door up and they came into the room.

'What are you guys still doing here?'

'Maggie told us,' said Al. 'We decided to hang around for a bit. We want to help.'

'Got that right!' said the Dweeb.

'I'm not sure I need any help …' said Curtis, stopping as Al held up his hand.

'Look, Jim was our friend too. He would have wanted us to help you expose them.'

'Yes, but I'm not sure how …'

'Just because we're believers doesn't make us idiots, you know,' said the Dweeb. 'John here's an engineer, I'm a cycle mechanic, and Rita is an astro-physicist.' Wow. He never would have guessed that one. Curtis looked them over. Maybe they could help.

'Hi,' he said. 'I'm Curtis.' He shook their hands. They were very serious, but Curtis could sense their excitement. They were looking forward to this. Big time. But he wasn't sure how they'd be able to help him. Not with what he was planning. He needed to find something for them to do that would keep them out of his hair for a while. A good while.

'OK,' said Curtis, 'I'll give you a problem I need solved. At some point later tonight I have to get inside the base. I have to avoid waist-high optical lasers, motion detectors triggered by anything bigger than a cougar, and ammonia sensors that can smell my sweat. And I need to be able to move fast.'

The Dweeb was nodding wildly. 'We can do *that*, man!'

'We'll have something for you,' said the Greek woman, Rita. She looked like the intelligent one of the bunch.

'Thank you,' said Curtis. 'Jim'd be proud of you.' OK, maybe he was overdoing it, but it struck the right chord with them. As they all looked away, he realised they were genuinely cut up by Jim's death. Curtis was heartened by that. He had been too.

'I'll be here most of the afternoon,' he said. 'I have a few things I need to do, and I really need some sleep. Warn me if the Cammos come back. And keep out of the satellite photos.' The Dweeb and Al tensed at that. The Cammos must have really freaked them. They left the room and Curtis closed the door firmly behind them. At least it was one thing he didn't have to worry about. He sure wasn't looking forward to walking and crawling on his belly for hours in the dark. He just hoped they could come up with something effective. Otherwise he was on his own.

He turned back to the laptop, and typed in the UNA3 access code. In seconds the website was onscreen. He had a vague idea of what he needed to do, but he was really going to have to make it up as he went along. First things first. He needed access to their low-priority area, and in particular, the base network. He knew he wouldn't be able to run a worm, that was for sure. He was after much more than video this time, anyway. And it had to be done a hell of a lot more discreetly. Curtis had done some high-security programming in his time at Trident, so he had a general idea of what he was up against. He knew that if this was a general portal, as long as he behaved like a normal user he probably wouldn't arouse any suspicions. His movements would be logged — he knew that — but if he didn't trigger any alarm bells, his movements would go unnoticed until the system administrator checked the log later. It gave him a small window. Big enough. He clicked on the US flag. The base had to have been connected somehow to the website. They had arrived too quickly when the worm jammed Jim's system. He did a quick search for any links. There were none. He didn't dare spend any longer online than he had to, so he clicked out and sat thinking for a moment. Maybe he was approaching this from the wrong angle.

He got up off the bed and went out to see if Maggie was still around. She was in the kitchen. Al, the Dweeb and Rita were sitting around a table drinking coffee. On the table between them was a pad with rough sketches and diagrams on it. They were deep in hushed conversation. Curtis decided not to disturb them. And he made sure he didn't scare the living daylights out of Maggie this time.

'Maggie, I need your help,' he said.

Maggie wiped her hands on a towel. 'Anything.'

'I need you to think hard. I need the name of any suppliers you've seen going out to the base. Have any of them ever come in for a coffee? Can you remember the name of the company they were with? Maybe something on the side of a car door or something?'

Maggie thought for a moment. 'Yes, I remember we had a guy out here just a few days back. I saw the name of his company when he opened his wallet to pay. Wasn't very talkative.

That's why I peeked. I don't normally do that, you know.'

Curtis smiled. 'Of course not.'

'Anyway, I think it was GE&S. Something like that anyway,' she said.

'Thanks Maggie. That's great,' said Curtis. 'Might be just what I need.'

'Anything I can do, Curtis, you just holler, you hear?' said Maggie.

Curtis threw Maggie a thin smile as he returned to his room. GE&S. Time to do some searching. He found it in two minutes flat. An electrical systems supplier in Vegas. He did a check on their system, and found a number of backdoors. Within minutes he was inside their network on a NULL profile. He couldn't touch anything, but he was invisible to the system administrator, which suited Curtis just fine. He looked for any name resembling Area 51, but there was nothing. It must have been coded.

Then he noticed a series of drives that had been passworded. He looked at the system-log files to see which employees had accessed the drives recently. There were several. He wrote down the names that appeared, and their titles, and then entered the password directory and copied the complete list of passwords to Sam's laptop. Then he logged back on using one of the names, and entered each password. It only gave him three attempts before it closed out, so Curtis wrapped the list of passwords into a small driver programme, which forced the passwords to match without shutting him out. Within seconds, he was in. He went back into the passworded drives and accessed them. A list of sub-files appeared, and he clicked on one titled Emergency Procedure Documentation, and crossed his fingers. Inside the file was another list. They looked like client names. Among them was the name Groom Lake.

Curtis remembered Jim mentioning that Area 51 was also referred to as Groom Lake. Jackpot. He opened the file and looked inside. There seemed to be a vast number of electrical systems emergency manuals. He scanned through each of them. It wasn't until he was working his way through the fifth manual that he found something useful. A remarkably detailed amount of information on the base procedures in the event of an electrical failure. They were computer-controlled systems, with a separate backup, and a manual override backup behind that. But what interested Curtis most was the documentation outlining who should do what in the event they lost power.

Curtis looked through the documentation for a reference to the outer buildings. He wanted something close to the border. He found the topside maintenance supervisor. The information was accompanied by handy diagrams showing where the supervisor's office was — near the perimeter of the base — and where the emergency power control substation was. It looked like it was about two minutes walk from the office. The manual detailed a number of actions and tests the supervisor had to perform in the event of an outage. Maybe five to ten minutes worth of tests. It was enough. Just. Curtis memorised the diagrams, making note of the location of the supervisor's office. That was most likely where his network connection would be. He saved all the manuals he could find to the desktop of Sam's lappie.

The next thing Curtis looked for was any information on the base's power supply. Chances were that if it was computer-controlled, there might a remote access from GE&S. That way they could do network maintenance without needing to visit the base — usual practice for a high-security facility. Curtis searched through the network for any clue to an access number or drive. There was nothing. But he did find some drives that his current profile didn't have high enough security to access. Curtis went back through the list of names until he found one with a suitably impressive title. Soon he had access on the profile, the password driver programme getting him in instantly. He found a Remote System Maintenance Connection and brought up the access code to Groom Lake. This was it. He wrote down the information he needed to access this connection again, and logged off. There wasn't much more he could do now until dark. He just hoped the Odd Squad were going to come up with something useful. He was just closing down when Maggie came in again. She carried a tray with a plate of hot food and a coffee.

'Thought you might want a bite to eat,' she said. Curtis looked up at the food, and as he caught the aroma his stomach cartwheeled. He hadn't realised how hungry he was.

'Thanks Maggie. You're a sweetheart.' She placed the food down on the bed.

'Funny … that's what Jim used to say.' Curtis realised that Maggie and Jim must have had a thing for each other. No wonder she was so keen to help. 'Anything else you need?' she said, going back out the door.

'Just a few hours' sleep,' said Curtis. 'Can you wake me at six?'

Maggie nodded as she closed the door. 'You get some sleep. I'll wake you.'

Curtis eyed the food she had left him. It sure looked appetising. He made sure the door was locked before he sat down to eat, and in seconds it was gone. He sipped on the coffee and thought about what he was going to do tonight, but was too tired to think clearly. He needed to push it out of his brain for a while, and get some z's. As he lay on the bed with the curtains pulled, his mind went back to Gina. He was still thinking about her when he fell asleep.

The gentle knock on the motel room door woke him. It took him a few seconds to remember where he was. The motel. Room three. The knock came again. This time Curtis got up and stood behind it.

'Who is it?' he said.

'Curtis, it's Maggie.' He opened the door. 'Did you get some sleep?'

Curtis rubbed his eyes. 'Yeah … a bit.'

'Come out to the kitchen when you're ready,' she said. 'We've got something to show you. She looked pretty pleased with herself.

'Yeah, OK … thanks,' said Curtis. He closed the door and took a quick shower, but it did little to shake the weariness. He hid his things under the bed and tidied up. It wasn't his normal practice to be so houseproud, but he figured the less evidence there was of his presence, the better for Maggie. Especially if the Cammos called again. He examined himself in the mirror. He looked tired, like he'd lost weight. But his eyes were crystal clear, just as he was, about how far he might have to go to get some answers. No doubt about that. For Turk. Curtis ran his hand through his hair and looked at his watch. 6.15. Time to party.

Maggie was waiting for him in the kitchen. The diner was busier now, but he couldn't see any sign of his three fellow conspirators. Maggie waved him out another door, and took him across the road to a house. She headed towards an old makeshift aluminium garage. The lights were on inside. She took him round the back and in through a door, where he found Al, Rita and the Dweeb standing over some sort of contraption in the middle of the garage floor. There were papers and plans strewn over a workbench behind them.

'You guys been busy?' said Curtis, closing the door.

The Dweeb was beside himself with excitement. 'Have *we* got something for *you*!'

Al wiped his hands on a cloth and threw it on the bench. 'It might not be conventional,' he said, 'but you've got yourself some transport.' Curtis checked out the bizarre-looking, three-wheeled go-kart contraption in the middle of the garage. He had to admit, it looked intriguing.

'OK, let's see what you got,' he said, perching on the end of the workbench. He could see the pride in their eyes. They were obviously pleased with the result of their afternoon's work. Must have been a nice little team effort. Al couldn't have been more Al-like if he tried, as he explained the brilliance behind their DIY penetration vehicle.

'We had some limitations to work within ... the composition and weight of the materials, the height and speed of the vehicle, and of course, stealth properties.'

Curtis almost smiled. 'Stealth properties?' Al nodded.

So did the Dweeb. 'Yeah, man! This is something that fits between the cracks! You know what I mean?'

This time Curtis did smile. 'OK, maybe you better give me the dummies' version. What does it do?'

Al continued. 'Well basically we have a golf-cart chassis —'

'Hold on — a golf cart? Out here?'

'Came with the motel.' That was Maggie. 'Old guy who ran the place was a golf nut — even had plans for a nine hole course out in the desert. I use it to deliver the linen and room service. Don't worry, it's going to a good cause.'

Curtis couldn't help but shake his head at their ingenuity as Al got back into the spec-talk.

'It's low weight, with a non-metallic body and it's electrically powered,' All continued. 'So it's silent,' he added helpfully.

Curtis nodded. 'OK, got that.'

'We trashed the body and made a new one that will hold you lying down, to keep you under the opticals.' Curtis realised the tangle of pipes and canvas was a seat. He would basically be luging in this thing.

'We welded together, thanks to Vaughn here,' Al dipped his head to the Dweeb, 'aluminium pipes, around which we wrapped black canvas, which will hold you in position.' Yep, a luge, thought Curtis. Great.

But Al wasn't finished. 'We've also removed the two front wheels and welded the axles onto the support for the single wheel in front. The tyres were too small for our purposes. So we trashed them as well and installed mountain-bike wheels. Except for the front wheel — that's a high-pressure racing wheel. Very light and very hard. Vaughn had a whole heap of bike parts in his van.'

'How do I steer?' said Curtis.

'With your feet,' said Al, pointing to the two foot pedals either side of the front wheel. The accelerator is down here.' He pointed to small lever down the side. The contraption was basically an aluminium and canvas hammock with an electric engine underneath it, on bike wheels. It did look mean though. Every component had been sprayed black.

'OK,' he said, running through things in his mind, 'so it's small enough not to set off the motion sensors, and it's low enough not to set off the optical sensors ... what about the ammonia sensors? And don't forget it's going to be pitch-black out there. If this thing goes too fast I'm gonna end up face-planting.'

'We thought of that,' said the Dweeb. 'Rita came up with the answer right away, and we couldn't think of anything that would work better.'

'Well, what is it?' Curtis could sense that he was about to experience the masterstroke.

'A wetsuit!' said the Dweeb, lifting up a black neoprene bodysuit. Of course. A wetsuit. The Dweeb must have picked up Curtis's scepticism. 'It'll be cold out there, so you won't need to wear much else. Covers your whole body, and even has a hood and booties.'

'You mean one of you actually bought a wetsuit all the way out here into the desert?'

The Dweeb nodded proudly. 'I scuba dive, man!' Curtis shook his head in wonder. These people were almost as surreal as everything else that had happened to him over the last couple of days.

'But this isn't just any wetsuit,' said Rita. 'This one will be lined on the outside with tinfoil, and then painted over black.'

Curtis understood instantly. 'Infrared cameras. Body heat,' he said. 'OK, what about vision?' They all looked over at Maggie. As Curtis turned to look at her, she held up a set of night-vision goggles.

'Maggie,' said Curtis in mock surprise. 'Are they yours?'

Maggie nodded, somewhat embarrassed. 'Jim and I used to go on night hikes together.'

'I can't imagine where to ...' said Curtis. He looked at the butchered golf cart on bike wheels. Then he looked at the Dweeb's scuba suit. Finally he looked at Maggie, still holding up her garden-variety night-vision goggles. This might just be crazy enough to work. Not that he had any other options.

'All right,' he said finally, 'I'll give it a go.' The Dweeb, Al, Rita and Maggie looked so excited Curtis thought they were going to burst. They were like proud parents getting the thumbs up on their baby.

'I'll need to take it for a practice run after dark,' said Curtis. 'Let's meet back here at nine. I can fill you in on the plan over dinner in my room if you want to join me.' They nodded in agreement. 'You guys have done an amazing job — if it works! I'm blown away. Thanks.'

'You're welcome,' said Rita. Al and the Dweeb — Vaughn — beamed with pride.

'OK, I'm in room three. This is it, people. I'll see you there soon.'

Curtis walked back to the motel with Maggie, leaving them to finish tweaking their baby.

'You sure you're up to this?' she said as they closed the garage door behind them.

'No, I'm not,' said Curtis. 'But it's the only option left. It has to work.'

'You be careful, Curtis,' said Maggie. 'I don't know what you're up to, but I don't want to lose another customer. It's really bad for business.'

Curtis smiled. 'Yeah, you must have a whole cupboard full of beans waiting to be eaten.

Maybe I should have some tonight. Just to keep the snakes away!'

Maggie smiled for the first time since Jim's death. But deep down Curtis knew he could be next. If he gave them the chance. And he had no intention of doing that at all. No way.

Curtis had time to rearrange the motel room to accommodate his visitors, and Maggie brought in some extra chairs. Eventually the group arrived, and judging by the armfuls of equipment they carried, they'd been busy preparing for the night's adventures. Al and the Dweeb turned up carrying a whole bunch of electrical equipment. Rita came in carrying rolls of tinfoil and several bottles of spray-on deodorant anti-perspirant.

'Figured we may as well set up your room as our HQ,' said Al apologetically. Made sense, Curtis figured. What the hell. Maybe including them in on the plan had been his stroke of genius. They were clearly very smart people. Unorthodox, yes, but there was no questioning their enthusiasm or commitment. They were here for business. Just like Curtis.

'What the hell have you guys got there?' said Curtis.

'Radio gear mainly, and a few scanners and sensors,' said Al, dropping them onto the bed. 'We raided Jim's trailer a while back. Figured he wouldn't mind the stuff going to a good cause.'

'OK,' said Curtis. 'Maggie will be in with some food soon. Let's get started, shall we?'

Soon they were all seated around the tiny table in the centre of the room, discussing the plan of attack. They questioned every aspect of Curtis's plan — much of which he was making up as he went along — not that he told them that. But it was worth the effort. By the time 9 p.m. rolled around, they all knew exactly what they had to do, and what would happen if any of the huge number of what-ifs they'd gone through ever eventuated. Curtis was satisfied it was the best plan he'd be likely to come up with. This was it. Show time.

'Let's go and test this thing,' said Curtis, getting up and stretching. He could tell they were nearly as tired as he was and, he had to admit, they'd put everything into helping him. He realised he'd been way too quick to judge these people back in Jim's pick-up. What he'd written off as their paranoid speculation was turning into reality before his eyes. Curtis could never have imagined that Alternative 3 was more than something concocted by a demented mind. He was having trouble believing it himself. But he had seen the proof. Even the FBI were investigating it. It was time for people to know. Curtis was going to blow the whole thing so far out of the water they wouldn't know what hit them.

15

The practice was a complete disaster. They'd wheeled the cart down a side street to the edge of the desert without using any light in case they got snapped by a satellite. Al reckoned he could see to adjust anything using some special black light he'd picked up somewhere. Goodness knows what he'd bought it for. But it was lucky he had because once Curtis was buckled in he slid the throttle up and the cart bounced forward so hard it slammed straight into a tree, the front wheel riding up and making the cart flip backwards, end over end. And Curtis ass over tit. Al and the Dweeb rushed over, as Rita stood watching in the distance. They helped to unbuckle him, and he helped them as they heaved the cart back on its wheels.

'Nothing wrong with the gas,' said Curtis. 'Not sure about the steering, though.' Al was looking at the cart like he'd hurt a friend.

'This is a fragile structure, Curtis,' he said. 'It's made for speed, not strength. Give us a few moments, will you, and we'll try again.'

Curtis stood watching as Al and the Dweeb got stuck into the motor. They were in fix-it heaven. Rita got sick of watching, and went back inside. After a while Curtis started feeling like a spectator too.

'Hey, I need to go get ready,' he said. 'Is it fixable?'

Al wore a grave face. 'It'll be ready. You get suited up.'

Curtis waved and left them in the dark. When he got back to the motel room, he found Rita using Sam's laptop. She looked embarrassed when Curtis entered.

'I'm sorry ...' she said. 'I was just reading the manuals. Thought it would be more use than standing out there in the dark.' Curtis looked at the screen. She'd been reading the manuals Curtis had downloaded from GE&S. He'd meant to read them, but had run out of time.

'Anything useful?' he asked, taking the wetsuit off its hanger on the window curtain-rod.

'Plenty,' said Rita. 'This is very detailed information. Where did you get it?'

Curtis just smiled. 'If I told you, I'd have to kill you.' The look in Rita's eyes said she didn't find that all too funny.

'Or are you just trying to kill yourself?'

Curtis did a double take on that one. 'What do you mean by that?'

It was Rita's turn to shrug. 'Either you're

crazier than the rest of us, or you're very brave and noble. Which is it? Why are you doing this?'

Curtis stopped and looked at her. 'You guys think *I'm* crazy? Now that's one for the record!'

Rita held his gaze. 'Whatever the reason, Curtis, it's not worth your life. Don't take risks out there. This isn't a game.'

'I know,' he said. Curtis was a little dumbfounded at first, but he soon made up ground. 'Rita, look, I've never had someone close to me die before. Not like that. It's for them. I don't care about all that Alternative 3 shit. They're all bastards as far as I'm concerned …'

He was getting on a roll, when Al appeared with the Dweeb in tow effectively ending the conversation. 'Hey, we're smokin'!' said the Dweeb.

Curtis picked up the suit and went into the bathroom. He left Rita reading the manuals as Al and the Dweeb nanoo-nanooed to each other over the radio gear. When he'd closed the door, he stripped in front of the mirror. His body looked like he felt. Shit. He picked up one of the sprays Rita had brought in. It was some sort of extra-strength odourless stuff. Some people must be really serious about body odour. He sprayed his body from head to foot, the spray stinging cold on his skin. Then he climbed into the wetsuit, amazed at how much effort it took to put on. But it fit well enough. Next he put on the booties and the hood. When he looked at himself in the mirror, he couldn't help but laugh. Turk had always been the crazy one, but now here *he* was, dressed from head to foot in a wetsuit, at night, in a motel in the middle of the desert. And it wasn't fancy dress. Yep, he thought, and who was the crazy one now?

When he went back out into the room, he found Rita had been busy preparing the tinfoil. She wrapped the foil around his legs, torso, arms and head, holding it in place with seams of duct tape, like a tailor. If he didn't look enough like an alien before, he sure as hell did now. Even Rita found it funny. He put on an old robe and slippers, and a wig over his head that Maggie had magically pulled from nowhere. Curtis had to wonder about that woman. Then they walked him over to the garage. It must have made a great sight for the satellite cameras. ET meets Priscilla, Queen of the Desert. When they were inside, the Dweeb started shaking two cans of spraypaint and walking towards Curtis with intent.

'Outside?' he said. Curtis dropped his Priscilla look, and went with him out the door and round the side of the garage. He stood with his arms and legs splayed out as far as he could go, as the Dweeb sprayed the tinfoil black. It didn't appear like normal paint to Curtis, because it dried almost instantly and stuck well to the foil. When he had finished, Curtis held a towel up to his face as the Dweeb did his head. By the time he was back inside, Al was ready to buckle him in. Curtis carefully climbed into the canvas frame, and the Dweeb put a radio microphone on a tiny headset around his head, positioning the little microphone in front of his mouth. When he tried to test it though, the Dweeb nearly blew one of

Curtis's eardrums clean in two. The look Curtis shot him helped him understand the problem.

When he was buckled in, Maggie handed him the night-vision goggles which he put on, but left sitting up on his forehead. Rita handed him Sam's digital camera as Al duct-taped a cellphone to Curtis's arm. It was a back-up. The calls would be traceable, so it was for emergency use only. As Curtis was familiarising himself with the camera, Al began taping something else to his leg.

'What's that, a splint?' It was a long black plastic rod.

'Not quite,' said Al. 'It's a high-intensity cattle prod. Just think of it as insurance.' Curtis looked at Al accusingly. This guy was seriously weird.

'Hey! It's nothing to do with me!' he said, holding his hands up in mock defence. 'That one was Rita's idea.' Al finished taping the long black device to his leg, and stood back admiring his handiwork.

'Now you're sure both these batteries have been totally charged?' asked Curtis, patting the battery pack under the cart.

The Dweeb nodded. 'Checked and triple checked.' He held up a small sac, like a hot-water bottle with straps. 'And this is a mountain biker's drinkpac — just suck on the straw.' He put the harness on backwards, so the sac rested on Curtis's chest.

'Make sure you take different routes back to the room. I'll wait for the signal … just make it look good.'

Al put his hand out to him. 'Good luck, Curtis. You're a brave American.' It was embarrassing. Al seemed to think he was going to be doing something significant. Something almost patriotic. He didn't have a clue.

'Yeah, dude! Sock it to 'em!' said the Dweeb. Yeah right.

'Play it smart, Curtis,' said Maggie. Rita didn't say anything at all. That said plenty.

'Hardest part's to come, so keep focused,' said Curtis. 'You know what to do.'

'We'll be fine. Godspeed Curtis.' said Al, turning off the light and opening the garage doors as the others left. Curtis hadn't realised Al had such a hidden penchant for dramatics. He was good at it too.

Once they were gone, Curtis sat in the Dweebmobile and waited in the dark. After a few moments he pulled his goggles down and switched them on. He practised using his hands and feet on the controls, getting used to the way goggles made his body seem further away than it really was. They were amazing things. His ability to see in the dark — at least the bit he could see through the open garage door — had increased 20-fold. Now he just had to wait. He gently slid the lever backwards and brought the cart up close to where he had hung his robe. He pulled his MP3 player from the pocket and unplugged the radio phones and put them into the player. He needed a song for the moment. One to help get him in the zone, and forget about his nerves. 'Zoo Station' — the song fitted the bizarre sight through the goggles perfectly. He waited. He was ready for the shuffle, and he was ready for the deal. Yes, indeed, he was ready for the crush.

After what seemed an age of waiting, Curtis finally saw the signal. Brilliant flashes of white, red and yellow lit up the foreground outside the garage door. Fireworks. It must have taken a while for Maggie to convince the regulars to join her in a fireworks party in the parking lot. But it was the perfect diversion. Bright enough to obscure Curtis's departure from the satellites and spectacular but harmless enough to get the Cammos out and keep them watching for a while. That was the plan, anyway. He was sure they'd send out whoever was on duty to check it out. Being so close to a secret military installation and all.

He edged the cart forward tentatively this time. It jerked into life. He guided it out of the garage and pointed it at the darkness at the end of the street. He tested out the gas on the asphalt. It actually worked, and Curtis was surprised at how quick it was. He slowed as he hit the rough terrain of the desert where the asphalt ended, and concentrated on dodging the tufts of wild vegetation and Joshua trees that seemed to spring out of nowhere. By the time the next few songs had ended and Curtis had plugged his phones back into the radio again, Al was calling him.

'Bart, you there?' he said. He sounded panicky. The nicknames were Al's idea, so no one could work out who they were if they were listening in. It was a sobering thought, and no one had argued. Curtis got to choose them.

'I'm here, Homer,' said Curtis softly.

'You OK?'

'We're out of the blocks,' said Curtis. That was what Al had been waiting to hear. The transmission ended. They had to keep any talking to an absolute minimum. Even though they were using some obscure channel, and scrambling their transmissions with one of Jim's toys, there was a high chance they were going to be eavesdropped on.

Curtis checked his bearings again. Maggie had given him detailed instructions on what route to take to the base. She had obviously put the goggles to good use on her 'walks'. As he slowly got the knack of steering with his feet, and his eyes adjusted to the terrain, he began to speed up. It was just like a computer game. Except real. He knew he'd be in the saddle a while, so he sipped on the drinkpac, which was filled with iced water. He needed to keep his body cool. A couple of times he got stuck, running into small outcroppings of vegetation. But with the reverse gear he was able to back away and keep going.

Curtis was surprised at how easily the tricycle handled the desert floor. In complete silence. Soon he was lost in concentration, focusing all his attention on negotiating the terrain, keeping on course and gradually increasing his speed. He would be there way ahead of schedule. He wound his way through two large valleys, and over a small ridge. Eventually he could see the lights of the base making a silhouette along the top of the next rise. He was close. He reduced his approach speed, found a large tussock outcrop and parked behind it. He slowly looked around. There was no movement he could see.

'I'm at the gate,' he said into his microphone.

'You're early. System check's not for another 30. Sit tight,' said Al.

Shit. Sitting out here dressed like this in a moonbuggy wasn't Curtis's idea of fun. He hadn't realised how fast the thing was. There was nothing he could do except wait.

'Call me in 25,' said Curtis. The line went silent. He lay back and tried to lie as still as he could, lifting the hood of the wetsuit back past his ears. He needed to be able to hear now as well. His ears were more useful than his eyes out here, and he hoped his heat signature would be mistaken for a cougar's butt. But after a few nervous stares into the dark, he got used to the sounds of the desert at night and started to relax a little. He gazed up at the stars. They appeared in unfamiliar shades of green through the goggles, but in the crystal clarity of the lenses and the night-time desert air, they stopped being stars and became planets. Suns and moons and planets. They lost some of their mystique.

Curtis indulged in a little daydreaming. He had plenty of time to kill, his mind was racing, and he sure as hell wasn't going anywhere. As he looked up at the night sky, he wondered if it was possible. Alternative 3. If it was, then that meant that out there, not too far away, humanity had sprouted a colony. Perhaps. The moon sure seemed close enough. Mars was not far beyond that, though he couldn't pick it out of the hundreds of dazzling dots in the sky. Curtis shook his head in wonder. Because if it *was* true, then it had all been done in secret. He still had trouble with that. He knew how quickly a secret could travel, and how far. That was how they'd been busted all those years ago. Because Roly couldn't keep a secret. He'd started bragging about their exploits on the net, trying to impress the chicks.

Curtis needed to make sense of it all. He took a deep breath and chilled. He needed to start from the beginning. To put things into some kind of order, and to piece them together to see if they stacked up.

First, if the hypothesis was right, the Nazis had invented an aircraft so radically advanced, even for them, that they kept it secret after the war. It was so superior to conventional technology that they knew they'd be able to turn World War II into a sideshow. They used it to escape from the Allies, and hid out in a base they'd constructed during the war down in Antarctica. At the end of the war, the Allies somehow found out about the base, and went down there with guns blazing but instead they got their own asses kicked by aircraft so advanced they could fly from pole to pole in less than 30 minutes. The Nazis must have realised they'd end up getting nuked, especially going on Truman's track record. They obviously came up with some way to ensure their survival long enough to make a whole airforce out of these things. Maybe Jim was right and they cut a deal. That's what he'd have done under the circumstances. Technology in return for survival. Drip-feed the know-how to the Allies in return for them turning a blind eye.

But something else must have happened. They'd discovered the planet they'd been fighting over was dying. Suddenly the goal posts were moved. To space. And the clock was ticking. Maybe they overcame their differences and decided they needed to cooperate to succeed. Alternative 3 would have required the most advanced technology ever developed to make it a reality. Flying-disc technology. But it must have been expensive, even by the scales of the richest banking dynasties. It would have soaked up the equivalent of the GDP of a medium-sized country every year. A public space programme would have been the perfect cover. While most of mankind were celebrating what they thought were our first few tentative steps into space, flying discs were probably ferrying people and equipment to the growing colony on Mars.

Curtis took another long slow breath. He pictured in his mind the huge craft they'd seen from the Hummer. They were flying discs all right. No wonder there were so many reports of sightings in recent decades. And not just by drunk sheriff's deputies. They'd been seen by pilots and air traffic controllers, policemen and astronauts. Even US presidents had gone public that they'd seen what they thought were UFOs. And all along they were man-made. Curtis wondered if the President really thought they might be alien visitors, or whether he was part of the charade. Part of the most preposterous PR campaign ever, involving aliens, *Men in Black*, abductions, Blue Book, and maybe even ET. He lay there trying to work out some of the outrageous implications of all this, when Al interrupted with his five-minute warning signal.

'Five, Bart, good luck.'

'Thanks, Homer,' said Curtis. That got him hyped again. He could feel his pulse start to quicken. He wheeled the cart out from the tussock and headed up towards the lights. He could hear the soft gentle hum of machinery over the rise. It wouldn't be long now. As soon as the system check had ended, it would register on the programme he'd shown to Rita, who was monitoring Sam's lappie. Then she'd follow the instructions Curtis had given her over dinner. First, she'd kill the main topside lighting, flicking it on and off a couple of times to make it appear like a malfunction. Then she'd block the automatic computer-controlled back-up lighting. That would mean the supervisor would have to make the walk from his workstation to the emergency power system's control shed, the substation with its own generating system. Curtis figured he had about eight minutes.

As the cart crawled slowly up the rise, he got a strong whiff of something bad. It grew stronger, like the hot stench of freshly decaying meat. Like roadkill. As he neared the top of the rise, he had to catch himself from gagging. He spotted through his goggles what looked like a small dog lying in front of him. That was the smell all right. But as he started to move around the dead animal, he noticed a thin wire stretching across the ground directly in front of him. He stopped and looked at it for a second. It must have been some kind of sensor. But for what? Then Curtis realised what it was … and how the dog had been killed. There was a series of wires. And they must have been electrified, to keep wild animals and other unwelcome visitors out of the base. They were spaced out low to the ground, low enough for him ride over with the cart's rubber tyres. He tried not to think about how much current they might be firing. Enough to stop a stray dog in its tracks, though, that was for sure.

He negotiated the cart over the wires, hoping they flexed low enough for the wheels to clear. Soon he was through the barrier and almost at the top of the ridge. He stopped the cart and as quietly as he could began unbuckling the straps holding him in. Then he slid down to his belly and crawled up to the lip of the ridge, and as he carefully peered over the top, the base came into view ahead of him. It was enormous. Big just didn't come anywhere near it. Some of the buildings were bigger than anything he'd seen at Cape Canaveral. There was no sign of movement. No people, no vehicles and no flying discs. The outside lighting was limited to door entries and what looked like some security lighting. The whole complex was formidable.

He switched on Sam's camera and got some good footage. The 'before' shot. He'd just finished filming when without warning, the whole base fell into darkness. Curtis watched closely through his goggles for any movement. The lights flickered briefly a couple of times, and then died altogether. It was time to move.

16

Curtis jogged silently across the sloping hill towards the base. There were no perimeter barriers he could see, but he kept a close watch on the ground in front of him just in case. As he neared the outer ring of the base, he gently lowered himself to the ground. He was still in the shadows, but through the night goggles he felt like a fairy on a Christmas tree, so he flattened his body as hard as he could against the ground, just as a door opened. A man in uniform had left the large building on Curtis's left, and was walking out towards him, to a small building separated from the others. The supervisor. It had to be.

Curtis pulled his goggles up to reassure himself he was hidden in the blackness. The night took on a completely different reality without them. It made him feel safer. There had been no sirens or warning beacons, and the way the supervisor was walking suggested it wasn't the first time they'd had a power cut out here. But Curtis still felt himself starting to sweat, despite the cold air and remembering he'd left the drinkpac with the cart, he picked up a handful of cold, sandy dirt and rubbed it over his face, just to be sure. As soon as the supervisor had reached the substation and closed the door, Curtis got up and readjusted the goggles. Once he had his bearings again, he moved in a slow jog across a large expanse of asphalt towards the building the supervisor had just come from. He stopped and crouched down beside the door and listened. There was no sound of movement, so he chanced a quick examination of the door security. It was a single card swipe with a keypad. That meant a PIN. Shit. He crouched back down again and thought furiously. He had to come up with something. He couldn't stop now, not after getting this far. But he was way out of his depth. It was the sort of moment where the heroes in thriller novels suddenly drew on their SAS or CIA training. Fat chance. Curtis had to do it the old-fashioned way, with brains.

He realised he was running out of time. The supervisor would probably be finishing up soon and returning from the substation, and the lights would be back on. He needed a swipe card and PIN number, since Rita wouldn't be able to hack into the base security systems with the limited remote access she was using. He was on his own.

The only thing he could think of was the supervisor. He'd be back any moment, with his swipe card, and he'd have to use his PIN to get back in. Curtis felt for the cattle prod Al had taped to his leg, and pulled the tape off. It was as long as his forearm, thin and black, with two contacts at one end. Curtis figured that was the business end. He looked for a trigger, and found a button under the grip. There was also a dial sitting flush with the handle. He flicked it round to MAX, and looked for somewhere to hide. But there was nowhere close enough to the door he could find to wait. He was still searching when the emergency lighting came on. It was incredibly bright through his goggles and totally freaked him. He quickly lifted them up and readjusted his eyes to the light. He was surprised to find that the lighting was actually still quite dim. Only the door lights had come on, but he was right under one of them.

He ran back to the substation building and hunched next to the door. He could only think of one way out of this. He banged quickly on the door with his fist, and then darted around to the perimeter side of the building, away from the lights. He turned on Sam's camera again, flipping the LCD screen around so he could watch it from a 90-degree angle, and carefully placed it down at the corner of the building, facing back towards the substation door. It wasn't recording, but he could see along the side of the building through the screen, and just hoped it was small enough not to be noticed. A few seconds later the door opened, and the supervisor's head peered out. When he didn't see anyone outside the door, he walked outside and looked around. Curtis crouched into a sprinter's position, grasping the cattle prod firmly in one hand. He'd only have one attempt at this.

He pulled off the goggles and placed them against the wall in the dirt. The door swung shut behind the supervisor, who was now talking into a radio. Curtis couldn't hear his voice, but after a few seconds he nodded his head and hooked the radio back onto his belt. He looked about him again, and then walked back to the substation door. This was it. Curtis tensed as he watched the supervisor swipe his card and begin punching his PIN into the keypad. He had only seconds before the door swung shut behind him.

Picking up the camera as he went, Curtis walked as quickly and silently as he could towards the closing door. He was ready to break into a sprint the moment he needed to, but he'd judged it perfectly. As the door swung back into place, he jammed the end of the cattle prod into the closing gap, and quickly read the PIN on the keypad display. 9040. Gotcha. He pulled the prod out and crouched back down against the building. He had the PIN, now all he needed was the card. That was going to be easier said than done. Curtis examined the prod. It looked pretty harmless, but he figured that anything strong enough to ward off a charging bovine would be more than enough for a human. Maybe even enough to kill. He forced the thought out of his mind. They hadn't thought twice about killing Jim and Turk.

He readied himself. It would have to be quick. As soon as he lost the element of surprise he was dead meat. He knocked on the door again, louder this time, and crouched down and waited, the prod charged and ready. When the door didn't open immediately, Curtis thought the supervisor couldn't have heard his knock. Just as he was deciding whether to knock again, he heard the handle being turned, and the door opened directly in front of him. Curtis didn't stop to think. He rammed the prod inside the opening door and felt it hit something soft. The prod kicked in his hand as it sent who knew how many volts into the supervisor's body. Curtis held his breath as he listened to the sizzling sound from just inside the door. Then it stopped, and he heard a loud thump. He stood frozen for a second, the prod ready for another burst, but there was no more movement from inside. He pulled open the door and saw the body of the supervisor sprawled just inside. He looked unconscious. Or dead. Curtis went inside and closed the door firmly behind him, taking a deep breath as it locked shut. So far so good. He started to shake again, but found it easier to ignore this time. He was getting used to being scared shitless. He knelt down and listened for any sign of life. The supervisor was breathing. Just.

Curtis pulled the body back from the door and searched through pockets till he found the swipe card. It was only when he realised that he didn't have any pockets to put it in that he came up with an idea. He climbed out of the wetsuit. Most of the tinfoil ripped as he fought to free himself of the neoprene suit. As soon as it was off, he started undressing the supervisor. He was shorter and bigger than Curtis, but the uniform would do at a pinch. He looked for any other lines of outside communication from inside the small building, which was filled to the brim with walls of electrical equipment. There was nothing he could see. He found a screwdriver in a tool box under a desk, and put it in his pocket. Then he looked for some way of disabling the supervisor — he had no idea how long he would be out, but didn't want to take any chances. He went back to the wall of equipment and turned off everything he could find, wrestled one large machines with dials and monitors on it out from the wall, and yanked every wire and cord he could find from it, using them to tie up the supervisor's hands and feet. He couldn't find anything to gag him with though.

He went back to the door, fighting to keep his nerves under control. After a couple of deep breaths, he opened it and stepped outside. Everything seemed normal, despite the booming sound of his pulse in his ears. As soon as he was sure no one had seen him, he closed the door and jammed the screwdriver under the lid of the keypad, pulling off the cover to expose the button contacts and internal wiring. He jammed the cattle prod into the jumble of wiring and circuitry. It sizzled and smoked, as the LCD display flickered and went blank. No one would be getting back in here for a while.

Curtis tucked the prod under the supervisor's jacket and into his belt, and started walking back towards the main building. He tried to walk casually, as though it was something he'd done a million times before, fighting the urge to run with every step. After the longest few seconds of his life, he reached the door to the supervisor's office, swiping the supervisor's card the way he'd seen him do, and punched in the number he had memorised. 9040. The door lock clicked. He was in. The tension made him nauseous with fear, but he swallowed hard to fight it down and pulled on the door. It opened, and he walked inside. As the door swung shut behind him, he stood for a moment, half-expecting sirens and flashing lights to announce his entrance. But it wasn't at all what he had been expecting. No white walls and floor or harsh fluorescent lighting. The corridor before him was dimly lit, in a trendy underground bar sort of way. Hushed and business-like. And empty.

According to the floor diagram, the supervisor's office was three doors down on the left. As he walked along the corridor, he noticed that on either side were large internal glass windows, through which he could see walls stacked with some serious computers. In one room, a techie-looking guy was monitoring a set of displays at a control station. He had his back to Curtis, concentrating intently on the monitors. Curtis walked quickly past him, to the third door on the left. He swiped the card and punched in the same PIN, and went inside and closed the door, letting out the breath he hadn't realised he'd been holding the whole way down. He scanned the room — it looked like a normal office, but he decided to film it anyway. He did a quick pan of the room with the camera, then sat down at the desk, waking the supervisor's computer from standby. A system password request appeared. OK, thought Curtis. Here we go. He typed in the superviser's PIN number. *Access denied: incorrect username or password attempt #1* appeared on screen. Curtis searched through his pockets for the ID card. It was a security-clearance pass with a photo of the supervisor's head, and his name directly below it. Curtis typed in the supervisor's last name. The same message appeared, except this time it said *attempt #2*.

Curtis realised he would only have one more chance at this before he set off a system alert. He sat in front of the screen for a few moments, just thinking, drawing on all his experience of system-password configuration. He had learned the hard way that usually the most obvious solution was the right one. He decided to give it one more go, and prepared himself for inevitable system shutdown if he was wrong. And a hasty exit. He carefully typed in the supervisor's first initial, followed by his last name, checking three times that he'd spelled it correctly. Just as he was about to hit Enter, he stopped himself. It looked too easy. He just felt it in his gut. There had to be numbers involved, because alphabetical passwords alone were just too easy to crack, but it could have been anything from the guy's birthday to his licence plate or even his social-security number. At a whim, he decided to add the supervisor's PIN directly after the name, and then hit Enter and prayed. This time the machine took longer to respond. Curtis tensed as the hard drive whirred under the desk. Something was happening, that was for sure.

Suddenly a new message appeared. It was a log-in code. He'd cracked it. He was in. He wiped his brow and shook the tension from his hands, turning Sam's camera on again and setting it up on a filing cabinet directly behind him, zooming it in on the computer screen so it would film over his shoulder. Then he got down to business, bringing the main network menu up on screen. He was definitely in. First things first. He needed to familiarise himself with the system. The network structure was unusual — probably something purpose-built specifically for the facility. But it was connected to AURORA.UNA3 all right. No doubt about it. He scanned the directories, looking for something — anything — that he could use as evidence there was more going on here than national defence. And to somehow prove they'd murdered Turk and Jim and God knows how many other innocent people. He clicked on any link he could find that might reveal what was really going on. He tried directories with names like BATCH CONSIGNMENTS, NETWORK COMMAND, STRATEGIC DEFENCE and LOGISTICS. Each time, though, he was denied access. The supervisor's clearance wasn't high enough to access anything other than the local infrastructure-support systems.

He'd have to try and tweak the supervisor's security profile if he was going to be able to access anything useful. No system was invincible, but lifting the hood on an unfamiliar one would take time, the one thing he didn't have. Curtis looked at his watch. He'd already been inside for seven minutes. He got up and went over to the door, resting his ear against it. The corridor was still quiet, so he decided to risk a couple more minutes, and then he was out of there. He accessed the shared network drive, and brought up the registry coding, scanning quickly through it to see if he recognised anything that might give him access to the root structure. But as he did, he was hit with a powerful sense of *déjà vu*. He recognised the network structure. And the coding. In fact he knew it like the back of his hand. It was identical to a top-secret project Curtis had worked on at Trident a while back. It had been his first big project, and he'd worked his butt off to prove he was back on the straight and narrow, and that they could trust him with that sort of work. He also remembered it because it had a network architecture with the most paranoid security parameters he'd ever seen. Bells-and-whistles stuff. He had wondered at the time what it was going to be used for. And by who. He'd figured it had to be military. And here it was.

Curtis's pulse was racing. He knew this was way too big a coincidence to ignore, but the why and how of it was something he didn't have time to consider. Besides, he knew the system coding better than anybody on the planet. It was his baby. He knew its strengths — and they were formidable — but he also knew its weaknesses.

One in particular. Every software engineer leaves a back door to a newly developed system, to assist with the acceptance tests. The pressure to finish this one had been tremendous, and he remembered working almost 20-hour days in the final weeks before its delivery. And so Curtis had deliberately left a back door to this system as well, because he knew that during the site-acceptance tests, he'd be sure to need remote access to sort out the normal teething problems once they got it up and running on site. But the extreme secrecy around the project had excluded him from that part of the process. He'd meant to mention the back door to his team leader at Trident at the time, but in the mad rush it had slipped his mind. And since he was the only one who knew about it, and he had absolutely no idea where the system was going to be installed, he'd figured it wasn't important.

Curtis checked his watch again. Nine minutes. He didn't dare access the back door from the supervisor's profile — all his actions would be recoverable by a half-decent computer-forensic expert. His best bet was to make sure he'd be able to remotely access it from outside, using the supervisor's computer as a portal. If he made it. He opened up the computer's communication port log, and identified the one Rita was using from Sam's lappie. It would be spotted instantly if he left it open. But it gave him an idea. He fired off a series of coded commands, re-creating a little programme he'd developed years ago to hide his first furtive attempts at accessing secure networks. Its secret was its simplicity. All it did was trick the computer into believing that its com ports were shut and locked, when actually it left one open. He focused all his concentration on remembering the correct coding. When he was satisfied it was accurate, he installed it into the computer's root directory, where it would be almost invisible. As soon as it was installed, he removed all trace of the programme, and then removed all trace of his use of the computer. He was just finishing when a voice cut in. He hadn't even heard the door open.

'Hey, where's Errol? We need some lights back on out here ...'

Curtis looked up from the screen. It was the techie from the windowed room down the corridor.

'What happened to your face?' he said, instantly suspicious. Curtis didn't understand him straightaway. He sat staring at him like a deer caught in a pair of headlights. Then he clicked. *Shit*. He'd rubbed dirt on his face in the desert. He couldn't believe he'd forgotten about that. But he'd paused long enough for the guy to realise something was up.

'Do I know you?' he said, coming in. He was a busybody all right. As he came over to the desk, Curtis switched the monitor off and tried to come up with an explanation.

'I'm from GE&S. Got called in to fix the power backup,' said Curtis, beginning to sweat. 'I was on an underground job when I got the call ...' The techie looked at Curtis for a moment, sizing him up. It was pretty obvious he wasn't from GE&S, because he was wearing the supervisor's uniform. Eventually the techie nodded.

'Well, you'd better get a move on,' he said, going back out the door. 'We'll go into emergency lock-down in a few minutes and we'll be stuck here for ages.'

'Uh, yeah, I'm onto it,' said Curtis. The door closed behind him, as the techie's words sunk in. Lock-down. Fuck! He had to get out of here. Now. But there was one more thing he had to do. He switched the monitor back on, and brought up the screensaver programme. He activated the password-security option and chose a password. *Turk*. They'd never guess that in a million years. He was just finishing up when the door burst open, scaring the shit out of him. It was a security guard. So the techie hadn't bought the line after all. With a sinking feeling Curtis realised the game was up.

'Can I see your identification please, sir,' said the guard. Curtis saw he had a gun holster on his hip. The flap was undone, and he was keeping his distance.

'Uh, sure,' he said, reaching into the supervisor's pocket for his ID card. As he did though, the guard suddenly drew his gun out and pointed it at him.

'Two fingers, please, sir … very slowly.' The guard must have thought he might be pulling a gun on him. This was going from bad to shit. Fast. The sight of the barrel pointing between his eyes was the clincher. Time for the bullshit to end.

'Look,' said Curtis, slowly pulling the ID out from his pocket, 'I'm not from GE&S. If you'd just let me explain ...' But his request fell on deaf ears.

'Just hold the card out in front of you where I can see it, sir,' said the guard. Curtis found his use of the word 'sir' ironic under the circumstances, but obeyed him just the same. It only took one glance for the guard to realise that the photo on the card didn't match the face in front of him.

'Get up from the desk and stand with your hands flat against the wall.' The guard had dropped the 'sir'. It was probably significant. 'And keep your hands out where I can see them at all times,' he added. Curtis did as he was instructed. Like he had a choice in the matter. As he got up, he saw that the door had closed. It was just him and the guard in the small office, but there was no way he was going to try and do anything foolish with a gun aimed at his head. But it went against every survival instinct in his body to turn his back on it. Curtis couldn't help wondering if he was going to shoot him in cold blood, the way they'd done with Turk and Jim. Maybe they'd take his body out into the desert and make him just disappear, like they'd done with them.

'OK, OK!' said Curtis. 'Just take it easy!' He got up from the desk and faced the wall. As he did he realised he still had the cattle prod tucked inside his belt. The business end was down against his thigh, hidden by the supervisor's jacket.

'Are you alone?' demanded the guard. But Curtis had been through this sort of thing once before. This time he knew his rights.

'I'm not saying anything until I've got a lawyer.' Curtis heard the guard snort a laugh. Then he heard him talk tersely into his radio.

'ATTC 3 to Central. Intruder apprehended Sector Six. Suspect may not be alone.' The radio squelched, then an authoritative-sounding voice came through in response.

'Roger, 3. Commencing lock-down, and full grid search.' The next instant a siren burst into ear-splitting life from outside the office door. He was really fucked now. As Curtis leaned against the wall, he saw that the camera was still recording. The guard came over behind Curtis, and began frisking him, running his free hand down one side of his body. It gave Curtis an idea.

'You know you're on "Candid Camera"?' he said, nodding at the camera. The guard stopped frisking for a second and noticed the camera for the first time. In that same instant, Curtis reached down with one hand and switched the cattle prod on, lifting the upper end tight under his armpit to keep the contacts away from his body. He felt the heat of the charge against his thigh, but it was still hidden by the supervisor's coat jacket.

'Don't fuck with me, boy,' said the guard, resuming his body search. The manners had definitely gone by the wayside. He ran his hand up Curtis's leg where it eventually made contact with the prod. The guard pulled his hand back with a short yell of surprise, looking at his burned hand, a stunned look on his face. He dropped his guard, and his gun, for a split second. In that same instant, Curtis rammed the prod behind him hard into the guard's stomach. His whole body shook violently for a moment, and then dropped to the floor. The small room filled with a sharp burning smell, and there was a black hole in his uniform where the prod had made contact. It was smoking like the barrel of a gun.

'Don't fuck with *me*, man!' shouted Curtis. He realised he was acting way out of character — it was the sort of thing Turk would have said. Maybe fear did that to people. Curtis started to panic as his elation at overcoming the guard started to subside. In less than a minute, everything had turned completely upside down. He looked at the inert body of the guard sprawled on the floor in front of him, swearing out loud, repeatedly, not caring who heard him. Even over the piercing shrill of the siren, he could hear running footsteps outside in the corridor. Short of a miracle, he was doomed. It was only a matter of time before they searched the office and found him. Another faceless victim of Alternative 3.

Curtis ran through his options. He could stay put and wait to be captured, or he could risk escaping. At best he'd be caught. At worst he'd be shot trying. He fought to control his panic and think. The guard's radio burst into life.

'Sector Two clear!' someone shouted through the static. Curtis ripped the radio from the guard's belt clip and listened. Maybe he had a chance. If he could put them off the scent long enough to get back outside. He pushed the transmit button and shouted into the mike.

'Suspect now in Sector Three!'

The response came instantly. 'Roger. All units proceed to Sector Three.' Curtis listened nervously by the door and heard more footsteps in the corridor. They faded into the siren. Maybe they'd fallen for it. Maybe they hadn't. He couldn't hang around to find out. He ripped the supervisor's uniform off and began pulling the guard's clothes from the body. Time for disguise number two. He clipped the radio to his belt, but left the gun inside a drawer in the supervisor's desk. Guns weren't his thing, and he didn't want to risk getting shot if he got caught with it. He went back and put his ear to the door. He couldn't hear any movement over the sound of the siren. He had to risk it.

He swiped the super's card and punched in the PIN, slowly twisting the door handle to take a peek outside. But the door didn't open. He tried the card and PIN again, making sure he'd typed it in correctly. Still the door wouldn't open. He leaned on it with his shoulder, but it wouldn't budge. The lock-down. With a sick feeling he realised the doors must have been locked centrally when the alert had sounded. And now he was trapped inside the office. He leaned with his back to the door and slowly sunk to the ground. It was time to face facts. There was no way out of this. He'd failed. Maybe he'd been foolish to even try. There was nothing he could do but wait for them to arrive.

17

As he sat hunched against the door, Curtis felt the fight ebb from his body. He'd had enough. He resigned himself to the inevitable. He couldn't believe he'd come this far, to be beaten by a fucking door. He pulled out his radio and headphones from the supervisor's pockets.

'Homer, you there?' he said.

'Curtis?' Al sounded worried. He'd even dropped the nickname.

'Al, I'm fucked,' said Curtis urgently. 'You guys better get away while you can. Forget about me and disappear for a while. Thanks for everything.'

'What do you mean?' said Al. 'Calm down and talk to me.' Curtis took a deep breath.

'I got busted by a guard. I've zapped him but I'm trapped inside the super's office. They've locked the whole place down. I can't get out.' Al took a second to absorb all this. Curtis was sure he could hear the siren in the background.

'Are they outside?' said Al.

'Don't think so,' said Curtis. 'I used the guard's radio to send them searching somewhere else. But it's only a matter of time. It's no good.' But Al wasn't giving up so easily.

'Did you find anything?' he asked hopefully.

'Plenty,' said Curtis. 'But it's no use to me now.'

'Now listen. You have to focus. Tell me what sort of lock mechanism they've got on the door. How did you get in?'

Curtis shook his head in frustration. 'They use a swipe card and a PIN number. I used the super's to get in, but it's not working now. They've locked the doors centrally.'

'Try it again, and walk me through it as you go. Take it slow ... one step at a time.'

Curtis sighed. 'I told you, it's no use. I've tried it.'

'Try it again!' demanded Al. 'Do it! Now!' Curtis slowly got up and went through the whole process again, talking Al through it as he went.

'OK ... swiping the card ... it's asking me for the PIN. I'm typing it in, four numbers, nine-oh-four-oh, now I'm turning the handle ...' Again, the door handle twisted, but the door remained shut. 'It's not going to work.'

'Check for some other sort of locking mechanism. Does it have a key lock? Are there any locks on the door? They probably go to a higher security level when they lock down. There has to be something.' Curtis checked again for any other sign of a lock.

'Nothing,' said Curtis. 'I've got the guard's gun. I could shoot the door handle?' Yeah right.

Thankfully, Al didn't think the idea was too hot either.

'No … they'll hear it straight away,' he said. 'What about around the doorframe? Tell me what you see.' Curtis checked the doorframe carefully.

'There's some sort of lens thing built into the wall … but it's not anywhere near the keypad …'

'What sort of lens? Where is it exactly?' said Al. Curtis examined it more closely.

'Just a little black glass lens, like the peepholes they have in hotel doors. Can't see anything through it, though. Must be shut from the other side.'

'That's not right,' said Al. 'If it was a peephole it wouldn't be in the wall. How high is it?'

Curtis estimated its height. 'About level with my eye … same as a peephole.'

'Now listen, Curtis.' Al was starting to sound excited. 'Swipe the card again, and punch the PIN in. But before you touch the handle, tell me what the keypad display says.' Curtis had just about had enough of this. It was fine for Al to waltz through all this from the comfort of the motel room. But the siren was driving Curtis crazy. He checked the guard again. He was still out cold. He'd give it one more go. He swiped the card and punched the PIN in again. But this time he noticed that the display had in fact changed. He'd been so intent on getting out that he hadn't bothered to read the display before he tried the handle. Maybe Al was onto something.

'It says "scanning",' said Curtis. 'Nothing happening though.'

'Listen carefully, Curtis,' said Al. He was getting really excited now. 'It's not a peephole. It's a retina scan. It reads the iris ... it's like a fingerprint ... everyone has a different —'

'OK,' said Curtis. He felt a faint finger of hope rise inside him as he realised what Al was saying. 'I don't need the details. I've got the picture. I'll give it a go.' He had the guard's swipe card, and he might just be able to lift him up to the eye scanner, but he didn't have his PIN number. There was no way he could find the guard's PIN, unless — he remembered that the supervisor had used his PIN as part of his password. He was sure it wasn't a random coincidence. He sat down at the computer and brought up the network again. This time he chanced accessing the backdoor to the network — it was pointless trying to hide his actions now. As soon as they found the guard they'd know he'd been here.

Chances were the guard would also have a profile on the network. Curtis accessed the root directory and brought up a list of users. There were thousands of them. He scrolled through the list until he found the guard's name. Bingo. Then he brought up the system-user profile and there it was. Name and number. Curtis couldn't believe it had been that easy. But the hard part was to come. He dragged the guard's body over to the door, and propped him up against the wall underneath the scanner. He was a heavy mother all right. And since he was now wearing only his T-shirt and boxers, there wasn't much Curtis could use to get a good hold of him. This was going to be interesting.

He swiped the guard's card this time, and punched in his PIN. The keypad display said 'scanning', as for the super's card. Curtis squatted down like a weightlifter, wrapped his arms under the guard's armpits, and heaved him up to a standing position. Except he was facing the wrong way, and a thick line of spittle oozed from his mouth onto Curtis's neck when his head flopped forward. With a huge effort, Curtis got him facing round the right way, wrapping one arm around his midriff as he pulled the guard's head back by his hair. But he still had to get the guard's eye open, and close enough to the scanner for it to read his retina. As he tried to swing his arm up over the guard's head, the body slid through his arms and back to the floor with a sickening thunk. Ouch. This guy was going to wake up with a few bruises, that was for sure. He lifted him up for a second time, only to find that when he was in position, the keypad display had gone blank. It must have been on a timer. He'd have to go through the whole card-swipe, PIN-punch process again.

Curtis couldn't believe how hard this was. He vowed never to become a serial murderer — he would never be able to hide a body in a trunk. He lowered the guard, positioning him more carefully this time, and did the swipe-punch thing. Practice made perfect. This time he lifted the guard with both arms under the armpits far enough to get his hands up to the head, lifting his chin with one hand and spreading his eyelids apart with the other. With a huge final effort, he jammed the guard's head up close to the scanner. The display flashed and went blank, and Curtis held his breath. Moment of truth. He lowered the body and tried the handle, while gently pushing the door — it opened. A wave of relief surged through him, but he wasn't out of the woods yet.

He checked the corridor. It was deserted. Time to exit, stage left. He grabbed Sam's camera and the prod, and without really thinking why, decided to leave a pen on the floor so the door would remain slightly ajar. Maybe it was his sense of self-preservation. Maybe he'd played too many computer games. But the office was his only sanctuary if he saw someone approaching before he had time to get out.

He walked quickly to the door he'd entered only minutes earlier — even though it seemed like hours — and pushed hard. But again, he found himself with a door that wasn't going to open. He spotted the keypad, and was busy wondering why on earth they would want to lock people *in*, when his heart sank. Above the keypad was another retina scanner. There was no way he was going to be able to drag the guard's body down the corridor without getting caught. Curtis decided to go back to the super's office while he worked out a way through this. It was so unexpected but so obvious, that he kicked himself for not realising every door in the whole place probably needed an eye scan to get through. That was what they'd meant by a lock-down. More like a lock-up, Curtis though drily. At least he'd left the office door ajar. When he returned he shut the door firmly behind him. He leaned back on the door and wondered whether it was worth risking trying to drag the guard's body down the corridor. Even if he made it, he still had to go through the swipe-punch routine. He shook his head in disgust. To come so close, and yet still be so far away was almost soul-destroying. Maybe Al could think of something.

'Talk to me, Al,' he said into the mike.

'It's Rita,' came the reply. Where the fuck was Al?

'Rita,' he said urgently, 'where's Al?'

'He's not here,' she said. 'They've gone to the base to find you. Are you out?' She sounded very matter-of-fact. Curtis began to wonder if anything got this woman excited.

'What do you mean, coming to find me?' said Curtis.

'You're gonna need some help. We're in this with you, remember. Where are you?' Curtis shook his head in wonder. These people were incredible. Maybe even stupid.

'I'm still in the office. I got the retina scan to work OK, but there's another one on the outside door. I think every door's got a scanner. I can't drag his body down the corridor. It's just a little too obvious, don't you think?' The frustrated sarcasm wasn't lost on Rita.

'I understand, Curtis,' she said. 'Give me a second.'

'I'm sorry, Rita. I gave it my best shot ...' Curtis let his head drop into his hand. He was at the point of just giving up.

'There is an alternative,' said Rita finally.

Curtis waited for her to explain. 'Yeah ... well ... are you going to make me guess?'

'It's not an attractive one,' she said after a short pause. What the hell was this woman up to?

'Rita, I don't have time for games. Either you tell me or I'm finished.'

'OK, Curtis, I understand your situation perfectly.' She sounded a little indignant at Curtis's impatience. Not that Curtis gave a fuck. 'If you can't take the guard's whole body with you, why don't you just take his eyeball instead?' She said it so deadpan, it took Curtis a couple of seconds to realise what she was saying.

'You've got to be fucking joking, Rita!' He shook his head in disgust. 'I can't believe you're even suggesting it.' But he couldn't help looking at the guard's closed eyes as he spoke. The very thought of it was repugnant. It would make him no better than them.

'Listen. If you can think of another way out, then go for it. I just want you to understand it's an option.' Curtis sat in silence for a moment. He was wondering if he had the balls to do it. Nope. No way.

'Sorry, Rita,' he said finally. 'Nice idea in theory. But I couldn't do that to someone.'

'Even someone who would shoot you without a second thought? For all you know he could be the same guard who killed Jim.' She did have a point. A completely repulsive one, but a point nonetheless.

'Do you think it would work?' he asked finally. 'Hypothetically speaking.'

'Yes, I do, but you'd have to move fast. The iris dilates once the blood supply is removed. Once that happens it probably won't be recognised by the scanner.'

'How long would I have?' he said.

'I'd say two minutes. It's not as bad as it sounds. The eyeball is connected to the brain by a nerve stem. It's long enough to let the eyeball hang from the socket once it's removed. It's just like pulling a hard-boiled egg through a doughnut. You can use the cattle prod to separate and cauterise the stem. He'll have a hell of a headache, but you'll seal the wound so he won't bleed to death. It won't kill him.'

'Yeah, right,' said Curtis sarcastically. 'Just blind him in one eye for life.' He found the whole conversation surreal. He'd never had the stomach for blood and guts. Even TV hospital docu-dramas left him squeamish. But that was before all this. Things had sure changed.

'OK, I'll give it a go,' he said finally. 'I can't stay here much longer, that's for sure. Are you in touch with Al?'

'Only by cellphone,' said Rita.

'Tell him I'm heading back the way I came, and not to do anything stupid. No point all of us getting arrested.'

'I think that's the least we've got to worry about,' said Rita. 'Good luck, Curtis. You can do it. I know you can.'

'Thanks. If you don't hear from me, it worked.'

Curtis looked again at the guard's face. He was so vulnerable in his underwear. Sure, he was a big boy —and probably a mean mother when he was conscious —but his pale white skin made him look helpless. Losing an eye was just an on-the-job hazard. He'd have a good medical plan. Curtis realised he was talking himself into it — drumming up his courage.

He went over and knelt down beside the guard, tilting his head back and opening his left eye. It was remarkably blue. At the same moment he was admiring Blue Eyes, he heard someone run down the corridor outside. It was all the incentive he needed to stop procrastinating. He extended his forefinger and gently lowered it into the corner of the guard's eye socket. The eyeball flexed under the pressure, making a wet sucking sound as it separated from the socket lining. It was too much for Curtis. The rising nausea in his stomach sent a shot of bile up into his mouth and he gagged on it. He quickly withdrew his finger and coughed it through. It made him angry that he was such a wimp. Fucking guard — it was his fault he was in this situation. He fought down the nausea and steeled himself for the disgusting job ahead.

The anger helped. This was for Turk. He rammed his finger in hard, up to his second knuckle. It looked gross. He curled his finger round the back of the eyeball and pulled, the guard's eye seeming to swell in size, pushing his eyelid open into a surprised expression. Curtis pulled harder. He could feel the tissue tearing underneath, and the hollow eye socket suddenly filled with bright red blood. He'd broken a blood vessel. The sight of the blood filling the guard's eye was completely obscene. Curtis tried to ignore it and pulled again, even harder this time, forcing down his repugnance with a loud shout of disgust. Suddenly the eyeball plopped out of the socket, dangling limply from a thin red stringy tube. That was the clincher. Curtis let go of the eyeball and promptly vomited onto the floor. It was a hard, gagging vomit, his eyes watering over with the effort, and he had to wipe away the puke from his chin with his sleeve. He felt another pitching in his belly as his stomach contracted for a second time. This time there wasn't anything to bring up, but it left him coughing and gagging up green bile.

Curtis looked up to the roof as he sucked in a few breaths of air to recover from the effort. He chanced a quick look back at the eyeball. It was still hanging out, staring at him. He had to finish it. He lifted the cattle prod in one hand, and held the eyeball delicately between two fingers with the other. When the stem was between the contacts he zapped it, and it instantly separated, burning both ends into small, black, congealed stumps. If he hadn't already thrown up, he would have now. Two minutes and counting. Time to get the fuck out of there. He got up and wiped his mouth again, forcing himself to look at the guard's face for the last time. It wasn't a pretty sight. Curtis felt sick to his soul. But as Rita had said — it was his only option.

He swiped the guard's card and punched in the PIN, holding the eyeball up to the scanner. He tried the door handle and pushed. The door opened. It was going to work. He checked the corridor again — it was empty, but he didn't know for how long. He walked through the door and closed it firmly behind him, and walked briskly to the exit. Again he swiped and punched, and again he held the eyeball up, and with his heart in his mouth, he pushed on the door. It opened. He was so relieved at finally getting outside that he momentarily relaxed. He didn't see the guard on the other side preparing to swipe his card to get in, until it was too late.

'Hey!' said the guard, almost as surprised as Curtis. Despite wearing the one-eyed guard's uniform, Curtis could tell this one wasn't fooled for an instant. He reached for his gun. Without thinking, Curtis threw the eyeball up in front of his face. The guard recognised what it was instantly, forgetting his weapon for a second. There was no mistaking it was the real thing. It looked gross, the little stem swinging wildly from the back. As the eyeball rose and fell in front of the guard's face, Curtis barged past him, heaving him backwards onto the ground, and sprinted off in the direction of the substation, round to the far side where he'd left the night-vision goggles. He stooped and picked them up without stopping, and continued his mad dash for the safety of the darkness at the base perimeter. As he reached the edge of the base where the asphalt turned back into desert, he allowed himself the luxury of imagining he might just make it.

He'd started to slow up a little when he heard the pounding of the guard he'd just slammed into, just behind him. Curtis picked up the pace until he was sure he was no longer lit by the lights from the base, and crouched to put the goggles on. Now he had the advantage. He could see the guard running towards him, and he wasn't wearing goggles. He did have a gun drawn though, and he looked like he was prepared to shoot first and ask questions later. Curtis thought about trying to overpower him — this guard was the only witness to his escape, but he decided discretion was probably the better part of valour for now. It was time to disappear.

Curtis waited for the guard to pass him, and then began quietly moving towards where he'd hidden the cart. He just hoped he'd be able to find it again. He ran doubled over, as quietly as he could, all the time keeping the guard in his sights. He was only about 50 feet away, but he had his back to him, and was walking slower now. Curtis approached as close as could without risking the guard hearing him. He could see the cart through the goggles, past the guard. He chanced a look back towards the base, and froze. He could see a black four-wheel drive being driven madly across a wide asphalted area. He watched as it slowed to a quick stop where three men ran towards it, and jumped inside. He could see another vehicle approaching from further back. The guard must have radioed for back-up when he'd first seen Curtis. Fuck! Curtis realised he wasn't going to be able to play cat and mouse here all night with the guard. The four-wheel drives would be on him in minutes, and he was sure the drivers would be wearing night-vision goggles too. He turned his attention back to the guard, judging the distance to the cart. With a sinking feeling he realised he'd left the cattle prod back in the supervisor's office. He was on his own.

Curtis looked back to the base to see the two four-wheel drives speeding across the asphalt apron towards him. He'd have to chance it. He walked as silently as he could towards the guard, ducking each time he looked his way. The goggles were a huge advantage, and he could see the guard clearly, his weapon stretched out in front of him, swinging it back and forth in wide sweeping arcs. In between each swing of the gun, Curtis managed to get up to within 10 feet of him, then he rushed him. The guard heard him instantly, spinning the gun around to meet him, but Curtis arrived before he could take aim. He threw himself at the guard in a vicious shoulder charge that sent them both sprawling. The impact knocked his goggles askew, but he managed to keep sight of the guard's gun as it dropped just feet from him. He crawled over to it, and heaved it away into the darkness, just as the guard rushed him from behind, sending him spinning back into the ground. This time the goggles were knocked off completely, and in the split second it took him to adjust to the darkness, he felt his head explode as the guard punched him in the face, the blow glancing off the bone under his eyebrow. The pain was unbelievable — he'd never been hit like that before, ever. And he knew that he probably wouldn't survive another punch if it really connected.

He extended his arm and felt for the goggles in the sand. His fingers touched the strap, and he instinctively gripped it in his hand, swinging them up and over him with every ounce of strength he possessed. They found their target. The blow threw the guard to the ground, as Curtis jumped to his feet and sprinted towards the cart. He could hear the guard getting to his feet behind him. But he could also hear something else — it was the growl of two big diesel engines being pushed hard. He didn't look back. He didn't have time. He grabbed the cart, swung it around, and climbed into it in one single movement. Maybe luging was his thing after all. He shoved the throttle lever forward and started putting the goggles back on as he went. He was still adjusting the strap when the left wheel rode up over a small mound of vegetation, throwing him out of the seat.

He got up and readjusted the goggles. He could see the guard sprinting towards him, and the bright headlights of the two four-wheel drives not far behind. He climbed back in and hit the throttle for a second time. Being able to see made a huge difference, but the guard was still gaining on him. As he wove the cart desperately through the random islands of desert vegetation and rocks, he smelt the same pungent odour he'd encountered on the way in. The dead dog. He must be close to the electric wires. He wondered if the guard knew about them. The way he was charging after Curtis suggested he might not. Curtis had no idea how far away the wires were, but they had to be close. He risked opening up the throttle again, as the guard closed in. If he got thrown out again he was a goner this time. A white object flashed by under the wheels of the cart — he'd nearly hit the dog's carcass —the stench becoming almost unbearable for a moment. He looked down and realised he was crossing the wires. The guard was so close he could almost reach out and touch Curtis, and through the goggles Curtis could see the look of triumph in his eyes. He was just beginning to wonder if the guard had somehow missed the wires when he heard a loud crash behind him. Curtis swung his head round again and saw the guard falling directly behind him. He'd caught his foot on one of the wires, and had fallen across two more. His body was convulsing and jerking, and Curtis could see smoke beginning to rise from the prone figure.

Not far behind, the headlights were still approaching. He wasn't out of this yet. Not by a long shot. He edged the throttle forward, focusing all his attention on dodging the islands of scrub, sending the cart hurtling forward at a ridiculous speed. He now had the knack of steering the careering cart through tight gaps in the rocks and vegetation, constantly looking for a route the big vehicles wouldn't be able to follow. He fought to keep the cart under control as it flew through the darkness. Several times he was nearly thrown out of the seat — he hadn't had time to do up the straps to hold himself in — but somehow he managed to keep himself, and the cart, intact and the right way up. After a while he risked slowing up enough to look behind him, and saw the drivers of the four-wheel drives were having just as much trouble as him negotiating the maze of rocky outcrops. They were keeping up with him, but the wildly bucking headlights didn't appear to be any closer than when he'd last looked.

He forced himself to keep going hard, pushing the crazy contraption to the limit, eating up the ground with every minute. He knew it would only be a matter of time before they'd scramble the choppers, and since his infrared signature would be a dead giveaway, they'd find him in minutes. He forced the thought from his mind and kept going. The chase continued for what seemed like forever through the cold desert night. Curtis felt himself tiring, his mind numbing with fatigue, but every time he felt as though he couldn't go on, he chanced a quick look behind him. The sight of the following headlights kept him going.

Eventually he approached the top of a small rise at the end of the huge valley, and as he rounded the crest he was surprised to see more lights heading in his direction. They were car headlights. At least a dozen of them, coming straight towards him. They lit up the desert like a casino, and he couldn't for the life of him understand where they'd come from. They had to be guards brought in from patrolling the base perimeter. He realised he'd have to swing in a wide arc to avoid them, but still he kept going at the same breakneck speed, knowing the other four-wheel drives were only minutes behind him.

As he began to veer away from the new threat ahead, he noticed the vehicles were bunched up in an unusually haphazard way. If they were guard vehicles sent to intercept him, they should have been spaced out in a line, setting a trap which the guards following would drive him into. But there didn't seem to be any order to their formation. He kept watch on their approach as he steered away from them, and as they gradually came into profile, he could make out the features of the lead vehicles, which were lit up by the headlights of the ones behind. With a surge of elation, he realised that they weren't black four-wheel drives at all. They were a motley assembly of cars, vans, pick-ups and even a couple of motorbikes. It had to be Al. The cavalry had arrived.

Curtis vowed to give Al a big wet kiss when he saw him, as he aimed the cart back towards the convoy, on a route that would hopefully intercept with theirs before the Cammos caught up with him. He was dead tired, but the flicker of hope burned stronger now, giving him new energy to keep the cart racing through the desert towards them. As he closed the gap between them, he saw that the four-wheel drives had crested the hilltop and were also racing towards the convoy of vehicles. Curtis wondered if the sight of their lights had given the Cammos as big a surprise as it'd given him. They were probably wondering what the hell was going on. But he was sure it wouldn't take them long to put it together. Then the convoy would become a target too. He just hoped Al had thought of that.

That's when he heard the music. It was faint but increasing rapidly in volume as he approached. They were playing rock music — he was sure of it. He could hear the throb of a drum and bass. Curtis figured at least one of the vehicles must have had a boom box. It had to be Al's way of telling him that they were friendlies. Smart thinking. Maybe he'd have to give him two wet kisses.

He saw that the Cammos were forced to weave like crazy, and they were having as much trouble keeping the big vehicles under control as he was with the cart. As he approached the convoy the glare of their lights became too strong for the goggles. But he had no way of signalling to them that he was close. He was sure they could see the two Cammo vehicles being pushed wildly through the undergrowth. He just hoped they realised he was in between them and the lights. He lined up the cart between the two lead vehicles and ripped the goggles off with one hand. But in the instant it took for his eyes to adjust to the darkness and the searing brightness from the oncoming vehicles he lost control, tipping the cart over on its side. He tipped and rolled with the cart, pushing himself to his feet and sprinted, waving his arms. Suddenly the air was split by one, two and then at least a dozen car horns, tooting excitedly. They'd seen him.

The convoy slowed as they approached him, and he could see people hanging out of windows yelling and cheering for him to hurry. The scene quickly turned to chaos, as they all circled him from both sides, turning around ready to head back to safety. Curtis searched for Al among the faces extended from every window. Through the cheering he heard him.

'Curtis! Over here!' It was Al's voice. He stopped and tried to find where he was. Then he saw him — leaning out an open door of a four-wheel drive utility. He didn't need another invitation. Curtis ran over and climbed in. The Dweeb was driving, and Maggie was in the back.

Al patted him on the shoulder, beaming from ear to ear. 'Good to see you, Curtis!'

Then he turned to the Dweeb. 'Let's go!' The Dweeb finished his U-turn and floored it.

18

'Who are these people?' said Curtis, looking at the strange collection of vehicles whose owners had risked imprisonment to join in the rescue mission.

'Just about the whole township!' said Al proudly. 'When they heard from Maggie about your situation, and what we were up to, we couldn't stop them.'

Curtis turned back to Maggie, who was pale, but also grinning proudly. 'Thanks, Maggie. I owe you one.'

Maggie shook her head. 'I think we owe you, Curtis. I was worried sick about you.'

Curtis turned back to see how close the Cammos were. 'Well, we're not home yet,' he said. 'I reckon we've only got a few minutes before the helicopters arrive.' That sure changed the mood. No one needed reminding of what had happened to Jim out here in the desert. 'What's the plan for them?'

Al and the Dweeb looked at each other. Curtis realised they didn't have a plan.

'Every car's got someone with a handicam. If they start shooting at least one of us will get through and turn the tape over to the media.' It was Maggie from the back seat.

'Somehow I don't think cameras are going to stop these guys. It might buy us some time, but …' He shook his head.

'Well, it's all we've got,' said Al. 'Let's do it, Maggie … the sooner they see them the better.' Maggie picked up a handheld radio and spoke into it.

'OK, we've got the parcel. Time for the cameras!' she said. 'And don't forget to light them up with the torches. We have to make sure they see them!'

Curtis watched the vehicles around them light up from inside, as torches and interior lights were switched on. He could see at least one person in each vehicle leaning out a window, holding a camera pointed behind them, back towards the chasing Cammos.

'Let's hold it together, people,' said someone over the radio. It was truly a bizarre sight. Curtis wasn't sure whether the ploy was working or not, but the Cammos seemed to be holding their distance. He was sure they were probably just biding their time waiting for the helicopters to arrive. Suddenly a loud bang came from their left.

Someone was shooting at the Cammos. Maggie responded instantly.

'Ivan, if you don't put that rifle away right now, you'll never be served a hot meal again, you hear me?' she shouted angrily into the radio. 'You want to get us all killed?'

'Sorry, Maggie,' came Ivan over the radio. 'Just having some fun, that's all. Wasn't even aiming at them.'

'Get your kicks another way, Ivan,' she replied. She turned the radio off. 'Crazy Russian,' she said under her breath.

'I have to get to a computer,' said Curtis. 'If I can access their system I might be able to find a way out of this.'

Maggie lifted up a laptop from behind the back seat. 'Thought you might need this,' she said. 'Even brought a freshly charged cellphone and connection.'

'You're wasted in that kitchen, Maggie,' said Curtis, taking it from her and plugging in the connections. Maggie beamed from ear to ear.

'Now if we can just keep this thing level,' he looked at the Dweeb, 'I might be able to find a way to keep these choppers from blowing us to kingdom come.' He switched on the laptop, and telnetted to the port he'd left open on the super's computer. He just hoped they were so busy chasing him they hadn't yet discovered his handiwork.

In a few minutes, Curtis was back inside AURORA.UNA3, and this time he was really in. No permission issues to deal with now. He opened the security directory, not really sure what he'd find, but nevertheless determined to discover a way to keep them all alive. He saw a huge number of directories with complicated names and coded acronyms. He began clicking through them one by one. There had to be something there. Some way to make them call the dogs off. But the list was endless. It would take forever at this rate. He was going about it the wrong way. He decided to prioritise his search by security level — since he had complete access to the entire system, he was able to locate the security parameters for each sub-network, and eliminate all but the areas requiring the highest clearance.

Now the search became interesting. His attention was instantly caught by a network subsystem link — Satellite Command. It looked serious. He entered the network through his backdoor programme, and was met by a complicated structure of acronyms and indices. He opened one of the submenus, and the screen burst with information. A rotating three-dimensional blueprint image of a satellite appeared above a series of coordinates. They were positioning systems for orbital satellites. Real Star Wars stuff. He realised now why they had insisted on the paranoid security. They were running their whole operation on the system. He could cause some major problems for them if he wanted to, but he had no intention of doing anything he didn't have to. Unless they forced him into it.

Curtis opened up another screen and searched through the maze of network menus for a name or contact number of someone important. Al and Maggie were silent, letting him concentrate on the laptop bouncing around on his knees. The Dweeb was doing the best he could to keep the vehicle level, but it was an impossible job, and several times he almost lost it as the vehicle rode along the rough desert floor. Suddenly Maggie shouted behind him.

'The choppers are coming!' Curtis turned and saw that three brilliant cones of light had risen over the horizon, and were rapidly eating up the ground between them and the fleeing vehicles. It was going to be close. He clicked through the system user menus and prioritised them by security level. At the top of the list was Network Command Control. And a name. Elias Godwin. There was no title or rank identification that he could see, but it would have to do. There was a single cellphone number under his name in the Emergency Procedure Manual. Time to say hello.

'I need another cellphone,' said Curtis, without lifting his eyes from the screen.

'Here,' said Al, reaching into his pocket. Curtis dialled the number on the screen and waited. It seemed to be going through. And then he heard a ring tone. Wherever and whoever Elias Godwin was, he was in for an unpleasant surprise. It answered on the third ring.

'Yes?' said the voice at the other end. It sounded impatient. Authoritative.

'Elias Godwin?' said Curtis.

'Who is this?' asked the voice, instantly suspicious.

'It doesn't matter who I am. Listen carefully …'

'How did you get this number?' demanded Godwin.

'That's not important,' said Curtis. 'Just shut up and listen. Unless you call off the security choppers chasing a group of vehicles in the Nevada desert right now, you're gonna lose control of one of your satellites. You've got 30 seconds to comply.'

Curtis killed the call and went back to the screen. The others were silent, watching him intently. He activated a security procedure within the system that locked out all other access to the network. It was a contingency installed within the system to prevent outside penetration and capture by unwanted trespassers. That's hackers for the uninitiated. But since Curtis had SuperUser access he was the highest level security clearance using the system. So it effectively locked them out of their own system. Touché.

'Are they still coming?' he shouted back to Maggie. He saw Al and the Dweeb also nervously watching the approaching cones of light.

'They're still coming!' said Maggie. Curtis looked at his watch. Forty seconds had passed. He dialled Elias Godwin for a second time. This time he was waiting for the call. He answered on the first ring.

'Look, I don't know who the fuck you are, or what you think you're playing at …' Curtis shut him down. He had to keep the calls short to avoid the risk of them being traced.

'Save the bullshit, Elias. You're going to have to make some quick decisions. You have failed to comply … Are you at your computer?' There was a short pause. Curtis waited impatiently.

'Yes, I am,' said Elias eventually.

'Bring up your satellite number XZ405,' said Curtis. 'You no longer have control of that satellite. You'll notice that its orbit characteristics have been altered, and it is now armed. If your choppers from Area 51 come within half a mile of the vehicles leaving the base perimeter, it will begin firing its laser attack beam at the rest of your satellites …'

'That's impossible,' said Elias. 'No one can access those systems.'

'Well, that's where you're wrong,' said Curtis.

'Now listen here, son —' interrupted Elias.

'No, you listen to me, you murdering son of a bitch,' said Curtis angrily. 'This is just the start if you don't do as I tell you. Think of it as payback.' He killed the call.

Up ahead, Curtis could see the faint lights of Rachel. They were nearly there but, under the circumstances, it provided little comfort.

'They're still coming, Curtis!' said Maggie. She sounded worried. And for good reason. The choppers had split up. One was tailing them while the other two had moved into position on either side of the convoy. They were tightening the noose and positioning themselves for the kill. Curtis shook his head in disgust. He'd been left with no choice. It was time to show Elias and Alternative 3 he meant business. He set the coordinates for the satellite so it was aimed at exactly the same coordinates as the one immediately below it on screen. Then he activated the automatic tracking mechanism. A red 'locked' button began flashing. He moved the cursor over the 'execute' button and waited. The choppers were still closing in. Fuck. He had no choice. He hit the button, and instantly the coordinates for the target satellite went blank. Something had happened. He couldn't help looking up into the night sky as he dialled Elias again.

'I hope you know what you just did, son,' he said. He sounded real pissed. Curtis lost it. He didn't want to screw around with their hardware, but the idiot had given him no choice. Maybe he wasn't making himself clear enough.

'I told you, you fuck! *Call them off!*' he shouted. '*Now!*'

Elias paused. Curtis decided to give him five seconds. Before he'd counted to four, he responded.

'OK, son, calm down. They won't come any closer. Why don't you tell me who you're working for?'

'I'll calm down when they're gone,' he said, ending the call. Al and the Dweeb were watching him closely as he sat fuming.

'Keep going. I think it's working,' he said finally. He was close to losing it, and he knew it. He took a few moments to pull himself together. They were relying on him to get them out of this. The ragtag collection of vehicles was making good progress, but it felt frustratingly slow to Curtis. He could hear the deep throb of the choppers as they hovered at a distance. The

Cammo vehicles had backed off too, but still followed them at a distance, like coyotes waiting to close in for the kill.

'What do we do when we get there?' asked the Dweeb. Curtis shook his head.

'I can hold them out for a while, but as soon as they figure a way to cut me off, that's it. They'll probably have to risk closing down the entire system. As soon as they think we're a greater risk to it than doing that, we're history. I have to figure out a way to make them keep it open. I just hope I've bought us enough time to work out how to do it.'

The seriousness of their situation had replaced the earlier adrenaline rush and excitement of rescuing Curtis with an unspoken uneasiness. Curtis could feel their nervousness. It was their turn to rely on him. He concentrated on the screen. He needed to find a way to threaten their whole system without destroying it, but in a way that meant they had to leave it open. But there was nothing he could see that would do it. He was flying blind, scanning through directory after directory.

'We're nearly there, Curtis,' said Al. Curtis looked up. The lights of Rachel were close.

'Head for the 'Inn,' he said. 'It's me they're after. I'll grab my stuff and then I'm heading back to Vegas. Hopefully that'll take the heat off everyone here.'

'Where will you go?' asked Maggie.

'If I can make it back to Vegas, there's someone there who'll post my video and everything I've saved off here onto the net. It's a news site. I'm going to expose everything.'

'The reporter woman,' said Maggie. Curtis just looked at her. His eyes told her she'd guessed right.

'OK folks!' said the Dweeb, pulling in to the park outside the motel. Most of the other vehicles had followed them there too. People were starting to climb out, still searching for the Cammos and the choppers.

'Where are they?' said Curtis, climbing out of the Dweeb's four-wheel drive.

A guy looking towards the sky pointed them out beyond the township. 'They've landed I think. One at each corner of the town.' Curtis looked to where he had been pointing, but couldn't see anything. They must have turned all their lights off.

'Let's go inside ... bourbon's on me!' shouted Maggie.

The people who'd driven out into the desert were hyped. Some were laughing hysterically, patting each other on the back. Some looked pale. The Dweeb came rushing up to him. 'Curtis! There are Cammos all over the place. They're surrounding us.'

'Get the cameras on them!' said Curtis, rushing inside the restaurant. He could see two groups of men in black vests positioning themselves at the corners of the buildings on either side of the 'Inn. They were shining thin red lights through the large restaurant windows.

'Get away from the windows!' said Curtis, realising instantly the significance of the lights.

Laser sights. They were probably just waiting for back-up before they stormed the place. The few people inside ducked down below the sills, and hid under the tables. Curtis knew he had to act now, or he'd be responsible for more deaths. It was something he didn't even want to consider. He ran back to the room with the laptop and knocked.

'Who is it?' said Rita through the door.

'It's me, Curtis. Open up.' The door swung open.

'Curtis! Are you all right? Is everyone OK?' She looked anxious. 'What happened to your face?' Curtis walked past her into the room.

'It looks worse than it is ...' He stopped mid-sentence, his heart skipping a beat. Sitting on the bed was Gina.

He stood looking at her. 'What are you doing here?'

'Hello Curtis,' she said. Her smile was thin and short-lived. She looked uncomfortable. 'No one knows I'm here. I came back for you.'

Curtis decided he didn't have time to debate it. She was here now, and that was that. But he was concerned for her safety. It wasn't good for people's health to hang with him for too long. 'You really shouldn't have come ...' he said.

'Rita filled me in while you were gone. I know what's happened. I've come to help you escape. My car's out back.' Curtis looked at Rita. She was willing him to take up Gina's offer. But as much as he wanted to, he couldn't trust her completely. Not any more.

'How do I know you're not just setting me up?'

'Curtis, we don't have time for this,' she said. 'We have to get you out of here.'

'Not just yet,' said Curtis, opening up the laptop on the bed. It was still on, and connected to UNA3.

'I have to find us some life insurance first.' He forced his tired mind to think, ignoring the commotion going on around him.

'What are you going to do?' asked Rita nervously.

'There must be a weakness,' he said, flicking through the network. 'There must be something I'm missing.'

'You're inside the network!' said Gina, unable to hide her surprise.

'Believe me, it wasn't easy. And it's not much use to us out here.'

'What are you trying to do?' she asked.

'I don't know … Let me think for a minute.' He remembered the conversation he'd had with Gina beside the pool. It gave him an idea. They had to be synchronising such a monster system somehow. If they were running satellites, space-communication links and who knew whatever else on the system, it would all need to be perfectly synchronised. He scanned the registry files. With a surge of elation he found what he was looking for. They were synching their system with their own independent atomic clock. Very accurate, and impossible to access. But its weakness was the fact that its timing was translated into computer code before being directed to all their systems.

Curtis thought for a moment, remembering a story one of the techies had told him at Trident. The guy had been travelling, and had set his work email to forward to his remote email address. But he'd inadvertently forgotten to turn off the forwarding on his remote address as well, so the emails just bounced back and forth between the two addresses. As they collected a new header each time they bounced, they increased in size, until after nine days the system collapsed under the weight. Such a simple thing, but with disastrous consequences. Maybe he could use the same concept.

He scripted a small executable programme. He wasn't sure it would work, but if it did, it would be nearly unnoticeable. Curtis installed his programme into the same directory they were using for the atomic clock. It was like setting up a mirror that would reflect the signals being sent from the clock back to itself. Almost insignificant, but potentially very effective. And the only chance they had. He activated the programme, and dialled Elias Godwin.

'Yes,' said Godwin on the second ring.

'A virus has been planted in your atomic clock,' said Curtis. 'If my finger leaves the keyboard, or the signal is jammed, it will activate itself. Do you understand what this means?'

'Give me a second ...' said Godwin. Curtis could hear muffled talking in the background. 'I understand. What do you want?'

'Are you in contact with the helicopters?'

'Yes, I am,' came the reply. Cold as ice.

'You tell them to let us pass through. Make sure they understand what will happen if my finger leaves the button,' said Curtis. There was silence from the other end. 'If any of them even looks like shooting, your system is history. I'll give you three minutes to call them. Then I'm coming out.'

'Listen to me —'

Curtis ended the call.

'What have you done?' asked Gina, as Curtis started packing up his things.

'Don't you worry about it,' said Curtis. 'The less you know the better … and I need your cellphone.' He held his hand out, waiting for her to give it to him.

'Sure,' she said, handing it over. He pocketed it.

'Now stand over there and turn around,' said Curtis. She looked confused.

'What's going on?'

'Just do it, or you stay here,' he demanded. The time for pleasantries was way gone. Gina looked over at Rita, who gave no hint of what she was thinking. Finally Gina walked over and placed her hands on the wall. Curtis bent down behind her and began a quick body search, starting from the feet up. When he was satisfied she wasn't wearing a wire or any sort of location device, he stepped back.

'OK, you can put your arms down,' he said.

'Curtis, what's going on? Talk to me!' She was pleading. Too late for that.

'Let's go,' he said, turning to leave. 'Thanks for everything.'

414

'Take care, Curtis,' said Rita.

Curtis looked back to Gina, who was still standing where he'd frisked her. 'Well, are you coming or not?' he said. He could see that she was forcing herself to get over the indignity of the search, but she decided to go with him all the same. A part of him was glad that she had.

'Where's your car?' he said, as they walked along the corridor towards the back exit.

'I told you, it's out back. It's a rental.' At the exit door, Curtis pulled open the laptop and activated the trigger programme, and then held it up, holding a finger on one of the keys.

'You lead the way,' he said and followed her out to a small hatchback.

'Check underneath before you get in,' he said. That sent Gina's eyebrows skyward. But he wasn't taking any chances. Not after Turk. He watched her check round underneath the vehicle. She shook her head when she was done. 'Nothing.'

Curtis nodded at the front of the car. 'Now get in and open the hood and boot. Don't turn it on yet.'

She did as she was told. Curtis lifted the hood with his elbow, and satisfied himself it wasn't rigged. He did the same with the boot.

'OK, let's go,' he said, climbing into the passenger's seat. 'Back to Vegas.' Gina started the car, and with no small relief, no bombs went off. As she inched the car forward, Curtis noticed a red light dancing across Gina's face. It flashed off before Curtis could decide whether he needed to call Elias again. Just a little reminder that his exit was being observed. Gina pulled out onto the dirt road that led back to the highway. He kept watch as she drove, but the Cammos were holding their distance. He was half-expecting to be shot at, but Elias was holding to his end of the bargain. Their route out wasn't blocked, and he allowed himself to breathe a little easier as she turned onto the highway leading back to Vegas.

'Curtis,' said Gina eventually. 'This isn't what —'

'Save it,' he said. He didn't want to hear it.

'You have to listen to me,' she said. She really wasn't getting the message.

'I don't want to hear it. Just shut up and drive. I need to think.' Gina pouted and turned back to the road. Maybe she was starting to get as angry with him as he was with her. He was way past caring. He took Gina's cellphone from his pocket and dialled Sam's number.

'Sam,' she said on answering.

'It's me,' said Curtis. 'I'm on my way. Everything ready?'

'We're all set. I've got a cameraman and a sound guy. Room 1405. Where are you?'

'Just leaving now,' said Curtis.

'Any problems?' Curtis laughed to himself. His whole life had become one big problem.

'No, it was a piece of cake,' he said. 'Like stealing candy from a baby.'

'If you say so — see you soon,' she replied.

'Bye,' said Curtis, ending the call. At least something was going right.

They sat in silence, Gina fuming and Curtis fighting to stay awake. His head hurt and his eye had puffed up, and he was covered in scratches and bruises from the tumbles in the cart. But nothing was going to distract him from what he needed to do. The rest of the journey was a constant struggle to stay awake, and stay alive.

As they approached Vegas, Curtis noticed a patrol car pulled up at some lights. As they drove by, the car turned to follow them two cars back. Another joined in behind a few streets later. Someone had got the cops involved. It had to be Elias. Now they were using local law enforcement to handle their dirty work.

'At the next lights,' he said, 'I'm going to duck down and open and shut the door. From that time on, don't look down at me, OK?'

Gina looked at him. 'Curtis …'

'From that time on, don't look at me,' repeated Curtis.

Gina went back to driving, refusing to back down. He decided he'd try it anyway. He killed the trigger programme and stuffed the laptop under his arm. As she approached the set of lights, he ducked down below the seat, scrunching his legs up on the floor. When the car had rolled to a stop, he swung the door open, and then quickly shut it. He watched Gina's face. She hadn't looked over yet. He willed her not to. Finally the lights went green, and they were rolling again. Neither of them said a word, Gina not taking her eyes off the road, and Curtis not taking his eyes off Gina. When she braked at the next set of lights, he swung the door open again, this time getting out in a crouch, and shutting the door firmly. Gina still hadn't looked at him.

He turned and crept past a parked car, then straight into a casino lobby without looking back. He'd chosen this place because of its size and all the people, and he did his best to mingle with the crowd milling around outside, where he could watch the street. Only one police car passed by. The other must have fallen for the feint, which meant it'd still be a block back, and the one that had just gone past would probably follow Gina for a while longer before stopping her. But not too much longer. He darted back through the lobby of the casino to another lobby entrance, and went back outside onto a side street. He was two blocks from Sam's hotel, but far enough away to survey the scene before he walked into something.

He was glad he did. As he entered the forecourt, he saw that two black four-wheel drives were already parked up on the curb to one side. They were both empty. Which meant they were probably all inside. They must have traced his call. But to do that, they would have had to have known what number to scan for. Gina's number. He shook his head in disgust as he entered the hotel lobby. There was only one guy, standing over by the concierge's desk. He was wearing sunglasses. Inside. What a doofus.

Curtis waited as a group of Japanese tourists swarmed through the door in front of him, and headed over to the elevators. The guy still saw him though. As he was pressing for the 14th floor, Curtis saw him radioing into a lapel mike, looking him straight in the eyes as the elevator doors closed, but he was too far away to stop them shutting. Too bad. Curtis lifted the laptop up and activated the trigger programme again, holding his finger down on the space bar and leaving it there. The numbers flicked up to 14 and the lift slowed. He had no idea what to expect. Maybe he was expecting the worst. And as the lift doors opened, his fears were realised. Two men were hustling Sam and a couple of hip-looking dudes down the corridor. Sam looked up and saw him in the lift. So did the two guys.

'Run, Curtis!' she shouted. She turned to the Suit holding her. 'Our rights are being violated!' Curtis immediately hit the close button, as the Suits ran towards the lift. He hit the top-floor button, and waited. After a few agonising seconds the elevator doors slid shut, and began to rise. But he was caught. He knew there'd be no way out of this now.

When the elevator doors opened he made his way to the fire escape, and went up a short flight of stairs. He pushed the emergency doors open onto a neon Vegas night. As he walked across the roof the wind tugged at his hair and whipped about his clothes. So this was what it had all come down to. He squatted down against the far wall, pulled Gina's cellphone out and dialled. It was time for Elias to come clean or face the consequences. He was no longer just bargaining for his own freedom. He was bargaining for the freedom of everyone. The right to know what the fuck was going on. He would slowly paralyse their system until they came clean. Alternative 3 was history. The call hadn't even finished ringing once, when it was picked up.

'Curtis,' said Elias on answering. How the fuck had he learned his name? Not that it mattered any more.

'Listen to me, you son of a bitch,' he shouted into the phone. 'Don't make me do it. If my finger lifts off this keyboard, your whole system goes into meltdown. Permanently.'

'Curtis, you've made your point,' said Elias calmly. 'It's over.' He sounded different. No longer angry. Maybe even relieved.

'Not for me it's not,' said Curtis. 'Not until you call the gorillas off, and I want a recorded account of everything to do with Alternative 3 sent to every media outlet in the country within the hour. I'm closing you down.'

As he spoke he saw three men climb out of the emergency-escape door and split up, taking positions around the roof, boxing him in. They were holding weapons, but none were pointed at him. Yet.

'Curtis, it's finished. If you won't listen to me, then hang up — there's someone you need to speak to.'

'You're not getting the point, Elias,' said Curtis. 'I'm not negotiating here, I'm telling you. Call them off. Now!' But Elias's voice remained calm.

'They're under orders not to shoot. They're just keeping you where we can see you.' As Elias was speaking, he heard and then saw two choppers appear from behind a tall hotel. They slowed to a hover on either side of the roof. Inside he could see men hanging out the doors, dressed in black. They were strapped in, watching him through the sights of high-powered rifles.

'I'm hanging up, and you've got 30 seconds,' he said and hung up. This was bullshit. He was close to ending it, and he was past caring how. If they couldn't be forced to expose their audacious conspiracy, he'd be forced to shut them down. And he was prepared to die trying.

'Curtis!' He looked back to the doorway. It was Gina. Somehow she'd tracked him up here, and managed to slip past security.

'Gina, get out of here!' he yelled across the roof. 'There's guys over there with guns!' But she didn't seem to have heard him. She just kept walking towards him, oblivious to the men around her. They seemed to be ignoring her too. He couldn't understand why, but he was past caring. Past everything.

'It's over, Curtis,' she shouted as she approached him. 'Come back inside. Please!'

But he wasn't going anywhere. He shook his head as the phone started ringing in his hand. 'I can't, Gina. I can't let them get away with this. It's too big. People need to know what's going on.' He answered the phone. 'Who is this?'

'Hey, Curtis!' The voice sounded familiar, but he couldn't place it. 'Congratulations, man! You've done it! I don't know how the hell you did it, but you've made history.'

'Who is this?' repeated Curtis. The person on the other end of the line sounded like he knew Curtis well. It was unsettling him. What the fuck was he talking about?

'It's me, man! Roly! Gonad! Take your pick!' Roly?! What the fuck?

'What's going on, Roly?' he said, unsure of how to handle this development. He sounded so relaxed. Happy even.

'You've just made yourself a very rich man,' said Roly. 'And us of course! They thought their system was invincible. You showed them, man! You sure showed them!' Curtis's mind was spinning. Rich? Us? Them?! This wasn't making any sense.

'Roly, I'm not in the mood for this bullshit. You're supposed to be fucking dead!' Gina was standing beside him now, listening intently to the conversation.

'I knew if there was one person in the world who could crack their system, it would be you. This was the big one, Curtis. Awesome!'

Curtis was starting to lose his patience. 'Roly, if you don't tell me what the fuck is going on right now, I'm ending this call.'

'Hey dude! Chill out. You just won us the security contract for Alternative 3. We had to convince them their system was penetrable, that's all. We sure showed them, man. You showed them!'

Curtis didn't like what he was hearing. 'Who's we?' he said. He felt his world coming apart. This couldn't be true.

'Me and Prometheus. It's just business, man. Sometimes these bozos think they're too clever. So we prove them wrong, and we pick up the business.'

'What business?' said Curtis quietly. The awful truth was starting to dawn on him. Prometheus's hacks into the most secret security systems were legendary. He had figured they were probably just myth. Urban legend. Maybe they weren't.

'Security, man!' said Roly. 'All we had to go on was those mpegs and rumour. I thought I could do it, but they were too good. I had to disappear. I knew you'd click about the game. That access code was all I could retrieve when they closed me down.'

Curtis was getting angry. At Roly, at Gina, at Alternative 3, at everything.

'Roly, you *fuck*! People got killed helping me crack this system. You're no better than them. You'll go down with them too.'

'Hey whoa, man! You mean Jim and Turk? They're not dead! Turk's right here beside me!' He heard him asking Turk if he was dead. 'See, he's not dead, and neither am I, and neither is Jim.' Curtis reeled as though struck by a physical blow. He shook his head, dazed and confused.

'Let me speak to him,' he said.

'Sure,' said Roly.

'Hey dude! I always wanted to burn out and not fade away!' It *was* Turk. He was as upbeat as ever. It just made Curtis angrier.

'Turk,' he said. He was struggling to find words that could adequately convey his emotions.

His disgust at being used like this. Manipulated. By his friends.

'I was really looking forward to seeing what that Hummer could do,' said Turk. 'What a waste, man!'

'You're dead, Turk,' said Curtis.

'Well, if being dead means a new identity, no more parole, and lots of money, I'm dead and loving it, man! Means I won't ever get to star in my own Hollywood movie, but hey … it's a small price to pay.'

'Put me back to Roly, Turk,' said Curtis quietly.

'Enough proof of life for you?' said Roly, coming back on.

His mind was still catching up. Still trying to piece it together.

'But what about Jim? I saw him die.'

'You thought you saw him die, just like you were supposed to, man,' said Roly. 'Amazing he's still alive after that one — he was so set on making it look authentic he nearly did end up barbecuing himself!'

Curtis's mind was racing. He thought back to his first meeting with Jim, looking for clues. Anything — a giveaway sign he should have noticed. But it was a convincing act. He was good all right — he even fooled Maggie.

'So Ollie and Styles aren't Feds, are they?' he said.

'Feds! No way, man! They're actors too,' said Roly. 'We knew you'd never go for a job like this without some incentive. We figured we'd just make it more attractive for you. Don't worry, man. Your cut of the contract will be way more a mil'. We can retire on this one!' Curtis slowly dropped the phone as he turned to look at Gina.

'You too,' he said. It was a statement, not a question. She nodded slowly. Curtis sat back on the lip of the wall and shook his head and laughed. A long slow wry laugh. This was too much. He'd been used. Completely. Like a pawn in a chess game. He couldn't believe it. Fucked over big time. He deactivated the trigger programme and lifted his finger from the keyboard. Then he picked up the phone again. Roly was still on the line.

'Keep your money, Roly. I don't want any of it. Give it to the poor bastard spending the rest of his life with one eye. You're no better than they are. I can't believe you know about Alternative 3 and you're just going to let them get away with it. I'm sorry, but I can't do that. I won't do it.'

'Hey man ...' said Roly, but Curtis cut him short.

'I thought you were my friend,' he said quietly. 'See ya round, Roly.' And without even killing the call, threw the cellphone out into the night sky as hard and far as he could, watching the lights reflecting off it as it spiralled out into the darkness. Before it had hit the ground, he was walking back towards the stairwell. He hadn't even looked at Gina. One of the men had rushed up and was closing down the laptop, and putting it into a bag. They didn't try to stop him.

'Curtis! Wait!' she shouted after him. He kept going.

'Don't leave me, Curtis. Not like this!' He didn't look back. Fuck her, fuck Roly, fuck Alternative 3, fuck everything. He was finished. And so were they. All of them. He went straight to the elevators, and took one down to the lobby. He noticed a few Cammos, and they noticed him. He kept walking, heading directly for the doors. They didn't try to stop him either. He walked out into the early-morning air. It would soon be dawn, he realised, as he headed out into the city. Anywhere, but here.

Curtis walked the streets in a daze. His world was unrecognisable. So much had changed. The truth wasn't about who or what. It was simply about why. Everything he knew — about the world, history, and even his friends — had been twisted into a bizarre reality that made his head spin. It hurt too. He just walked, not knowing or caring where he'd end up. When the sky began to glow with the pale light of dawn, he realised how tired he was. Hungry. He found himself heading back to the diner. He didn't have anywhere else to go. The FUB'er was serving hot breakfasts to lonely gamblers who looked like they'd been up all night too. He looked up when he saw Curtis enter. He probably didn't look too good, the way the FUB'er did a double take.

'Your lady friend's been asking for you,' he said. 'She's out back.' He motioned with his head towards the computers. Curtis followed the nod. Gina was the last person he wanted to see right now.

But it wasn't her, it was Sam. She looked relieved to see him. 'Curtis,' she said, checking the door, 'you made it!' He sat down beside her. He was beyond tired. He was close to collapsing from exhaustion.

'You OK?' he said.

'Bastards took all my equipment,' she said, 'but I'll live. What happened?'

'Long story.' He shook his head. He was having trouble accepting it. 'You still up to trying it?' he said. Sam looked surprised. 'Of course. But are you? You look like shit.'

'I'm OK,' he said wearily. 'How do we do this? I don't have access to the network anymore. We'll have to use what we've got.'

'Shit!' said Sam. 'I was counting on you. They took all my film, everything.'

'We've still got the stuff from Jim's disk. It's not conclusive proof, but it'd get people asking questions,' said Curtis.

'I'm keen if you are,' said Sam. Curtis opened up the internet connection on one of the Macs and logged on to his email account. But when he entered his username and password, it simply said *User not recognised*. He tried it again, making sure he was typing correctly. He was so tired he could hardly concentrate. But again, the same message appeared.

'It's gone too,' he said finally.

'What do you mean, gone?' asked Sam.

'They've locked me out,' he said. 'It's finished.' But Sam wasn't giving in that easily.

427

'Look. It's your word against theirs. We can interview you, and at least get your story out to the public.' But Curtis shook his head.

'Without some sort of evidence, I'm going to look like a headcase. They'll deny it the whole way.' Sam sat in silence. She looked as dejected as he felt.

'But that doesn't mean I'm going to give up trying,' he said finally. 'Somehow I'll get it out there. I don't know how, but ...' He was too tired to worry about it now. There'd be plenty of time. He could wait.

'I should really get going,' he said.

'Where are you going? How will I contact you?'

'I'm not sure,' he replied, getting up. 'Don't worry, I'll be in touch.' Sam gave him a hug. It was a close hug, full of emotion. Curtis was surprised to see tears forming in her blue eyes.

'Take care,' she said as they pulled apart. He looked into her eyes and smiled back, reassuring her he'd be OK. And then he turned and walked out the door.

19

As the Greyhound bus lurched into motion, Curtis couldn't help wondering if he'd ever see Vegas again. Or Gina. That was what had hurt him most. But even she would soon be just a memory. He'd slept for nearly 14 hours straight at a shelter for vagrants he'd found next to a church. The lady running the place had woken him, worried he'd overdosed or something. The meal she'd served him wasn't spectacular, but it was hot and nutritious. He'd had two servings, before collapsing on the cot. He looked down at the 10-dollar note in his hand. That and the bus ticket were all he had left in the world. He'd tried using his ATM card at a machine, but it had been swallowed, telling him he was accessing an unauthorised account. The same thing happened with his credit card. He'd gone back to the diner to check once more that he'd been locked out of his email account. Just to be sure. But it still didn't recognise him, and as he had sat at the computer he wondered what else they had erased.

He checked everything he could think of — his online bank accounts, his social security number, the works. But they'd been busy. And extremely efficient. It was like he'd never existed.

They'd thought of everything. Every trace of him had been erased. Even his high-school photo had been replaced with someone else's picture. So this was how they worked. The final straw was the FBI database. When he'd searched for his name, his request had come up blank. He was a non-person. All he had was in his bag. A few clothes, a useless wallet, his old cellphone and his MP3 player. He put his headphones on as the bus threaded its way through the city towards the freeway. Bono was reading his mind. 'So Cruel'. He was right about one thing though. He sang about how in love there were no rules. No rules at all. As the song ended, he hunkered down in the seat and drifted off into a fitful sleep.

He wasn't sure how long he'd been sleeping, but the shrill tone of a ringing cellphone dragged him back to consciousness. He heard another cellphone ring. He just wanted to sleep. But two more phones began ringing, and with a start, Curtis realised that they were all ringing from the back of the bus. He opened his eyes and looked around. At least six phones were ringing now, including the woman sitting right behind him. Then his own phone rang. It couldn't be. He answered, looking about the bus. It had to be Gina. She had to be here somewhere.

'Hello?' he said.

'Look out the window.' It *was* Gina. Curtis sat up straight and did as he was told. He got the surprise of his life. Gina was driving alongside the bus in a convertible Hummer, just like the one they'd hired to go to Rachel. She was holding her cellphone and driving with one hand, keeping the Hummer level with his window. She looked fantastic.

'How?' He was lost for words.

'Look down in the passenger's seat!' she said. Curtis leaned up to the window and looked down. In the seat next to her was a large aluminium suitcase. On top it had a sheet of paper taped to it. It simply said $.

'It's your cut. Mine's in there too.' Curtis was dumbfounded. Too many raw emotions were fighting to get out.

'Well?' she said. She was smiling at him. 'Fancy a ride with a rich chick?'

'Where you heading?' asked Curtis.

'Somewhere with lots of sun and no taxes!' she said, beaming from ear to ear. 'Oh and the Hummer's a present from me. It's yours.'

'What about the driver?' asked Curtis. 'Does she come with the car?'

'Comes standard with this model. If you want her, that is.' She glanced up at him. Curtis felt some of the bitterness fade as he smiled. It felt good.

'You've got a deal, Ginger,' he said. 'Just give me a second.'

'Take as long as you like, Fred, I'm not going anywhere.' Curtis ended the call and got up, threading his way forward to the driver.

'Can you let me off, please,' he said. The driver did a double take.

'Here?' Curtis nodded.

'Here's great,' he said as the driver signalled and pulled over to the edge of the freeway. 'Here's just perfect.'

He stepped down out of the bus, and began walking to where Gina had pulled over just ahead. And as he approached the Hummer, he couldn't help thinking that maybe, just maybe, things weren't going to be so bad after all.

EPILOGUE

Cut to a tropical paradise. Blue skies, blue seas and white sand. And Curtis's bright red body stretched out on a recliner. The regulation shades and headphones are still present, but the sea air and sun, and especially Gina, has speeded his recovery. Most of the scratches and bruises have faded, but the shades still hide a bright red scar above his left eye. A permanent memento from Alternative 3.

The scars inside are going to take a little longer to heal. He knows that, but he's in no hurry. He and Gina aren't pushing things, just taking each day as it comes. Sometimes he wonders about the security guard facing the rest of his life with one eye. But as each day passes, the burning desire to somehow get his message out to the world grows. He knows that while he remains discreet, Alternative 3 are going to leave him alone. He is a non-person. He doesn't exist. It'll just end up being his word against theirs, with any evidence or proof forever erased. And despite what Roly and Turk have done to him, he doesn't want revenge. Just to be left alone. He's vowed never to contact them again. Maybe he will one day, but that day is a long, long way off.

In between dozing at the beach and spending time with Gina, he's taken to going for long walks. Just himself, the birds, and Alternative 3. He can't let it rest. After a particularly long walk, he'd come back with an idea. He'll write a book. Gina encourages him. Maybe she doesn't think he's serious. Maybe she thinks it will help him deal with stuff. So for two days now, he's sat on the recliner with a new laptop on his knee, bought specifically for the purpose, while Gina reads thrillers and sunbakes. Her skin is quick to tan, and she's looking great. They've had a few talks about things, in their beachfront bungalow cottage, late at night. She actually laughed out loud when he told her that he thought she was a Fed. He's started calling her Clarice, and making that lip-smacking Chianti and fava-bean sound. She keeps ordering him martinis, shaken not stirred, and calling herself his Bond girl. The stupidity helps. They have a lot to work through, and though neither of them are pushing things, they're both keen to put it behind them.

He watches her as she walks up the beach towards him after a swim in the sea. She's ringing her short hair out. Even now, his heart skips a beat when he watches her like this. The same way it did back in the train. Before Alternative 3.

'Waitress!' he says, as she sits down beside him, shaking his empty glass.

'What did your last slave die of?' she smiles, with no intention of getting back up off the recliner.

'Service is shocking out here,' he mumbles under his breath.

'How's the book going?' she asks. She's noticed there are some words on the previously blank screen.

'OK, I think,' he says, lifting the laptop over to her. 'Have a read while I'm gone. Tell me what you think.' Curtis threads his way past the pool to the bar, basically a little thatched shed with coconut leaves for a roof. Very 'Temptation Island'. He waits for the barman to notice him, and pushes his glass forward.

'Another lime and soda, please,' he says. He turns back to the pool and soaks up the scene. He's still pinching himself every day, afraid it will all disappear and he'll find himself back in Vegas. Or worse. But time is everything. They haven't made any plans. They're living for the moment. He's earned it, he figures.

As he turns back to pay for the drink, the barman signals that someone else has paid for it already. He looks over to the other side of the bar, where a man is sipping on an iced tea, his sunglasses and wide-brimmed straw hat obscuring his face. As he lifts his head, Curtis realises he knows the man. It's Terry Hay. What the hell is he doing out here? And more importantly, how did he find them? With a sinking feeling he walks around to meet him.

'Don't tell me you're here on vacation,' says Curtis.

'Nice place,' says Terry. He looks over towards where Gina is sunbathing. 'Nice view too.'

'What do you want, Terry? You come to take me back?' says Curtis. But much to his surprise, and considerable relief, Terry just shakes his head.

'No, Curtis, this is a social call. I've resigned from the force.'

Curtis blinks. 'You've resigned? Did it have something to do with me?'

'It had a lot to do with you,' says Terry emphatically.

'I'm sorry.' That's about all Curtis can think of to say. He'd had no idea that Terry had put himself so far on the line for him.

'Don't be. I'm working for myself now. I just came to tell you that as long as you don't return to the States, you'll be left alone.'

Curtis snorts. 'Be a long time before I'd even want to go back.'

'There's another condition though, Curtis,' says Terry. Seriously.

Curtis's eyes narrow behind his Randolphs. Wait for it.

'Let's just say it concerns issues of confidentiality,' says Terry, sipping his drink. Curtis understands immediately. As long as he keeps his mouth shut about Alternative 3, he's safe. Maybe that's all that's keeping him alive.

'They'll leave us alone?' asks Curtis warily.

'They'll leave you alone, and so will I.'

'What's happened to Turk and Roly?' Not that he cares. Just curious.

'Oh, they're fine,' says Terry. 'Just fine. They send their regards.' Sure they do. Assholes. 'What are your plans?'

Curtis shrugs. 'Don't have any yet.' Of course they've been talking about places they want to visit, and things they want to do, but at the moment it's all pie-in-the-sky stuff. Daydreaming.

'You'd have a hell of a future in computers,' says Terry. There's a sparkle in his eye that Curtis doesn't quite understand. 'You're something else, you know. I knew you had it in you. Pity no one will ever get to hear about it.' Curtis watches him silently. What's his game?

'The money won't last forever. Have you thought about that?' he asks.

Curtis shakes his head. 'Haven't thought about much, to be honest.' He's getting better at lying now.

'Of course, if you were ever inclined to go back to the computer-security game, you'd give me a call, wouldn't you?' It's the way he says it, as much as what he's said. But he's said enough. Curtis blinks. The realisation dawns on him.

'You're Prometheus,' he says. And suddenly it all makes sense. Roly and Turk. They could never have masterminded something like that. No way. And they wouldn't have just used him like that. Terry looks away. That says plenty.

'I'm someone who understands you,' he says. 'Don't do anything stupid, Curtis. It's not worth it.'

'You'll go down with them,' says Curtis. 'What you did was wrong, Terry.' Curtis shakes his head in disbelief. Roly, Turk. They had all been supervised by Terry. He had fostered a gang of computer-security 'consultants' from the very hackers he was supposed to be turning around. All except him.

'Forget it, Curtis. Forget me, forget the job, and forget Alternative 3. It doesn't exist. It never did, and it never will. If you know what's good for you, just walk away. You've got money and your life. Don't push it.'

'Are you threatening me, you asshole?' says Curtis. Fucking nerve.

'I'm watching out for you, you stupid son of a bitch,' says Terry. 'Someone with your ability will always be a threat. Don't make them nervous, is all I'm saying. Use your head, be grateful for what you've got.'

'You're no better than them,' says Curtis. 'You're a fucking psycho. Do you know what you put me through? Do you know what you made me do?' He jabs his finger into Terry's chest to punctuate his sentence. He should be grateful it isn't a fist in his face. Or a finger in his eye.

'Must be time I was heading off,' he says vacantly. 'You're a smart kid, Curtis. Don't do anything dumb.' Terry gets up off the bar stool and holds his empty glass out for the barman. Curtis's mind is still reeling. So much finally makes sense, but it's hard to swallow. And hard to fathom.

'You look after her,' he adds, nodding over towards Gina. Curtis follows his eyes back towards Gina. She's oblivious to their conversation. 'She's a good kid. You both are.' He gives Curtis a wink, and then lowers his hat back down over his eyes, and heads towards the hotel complex. Curtis stands leaning against the bar for a few moments. He draws a deep breath and forces himself to relax, then takes his glass and heads back to Gina.

'They got you squeezing the fruit now?' she says, without looking up from her novel.

'Huh?'

'You were gone for ages,' she says, lifting her sunglasses. 'I was about to send out a search party.'

'Oh ... just catching up on things,' he replies. 'Still can't believe it, really.'

'I read your writing,' says Gina. 'I think you need to make it more interesting.'

'Yeah? What do you mean?' says Curtis, lifting the laptop back onto his lap.

'Well, for starters, any book that starts with "My name is Curtis Hatch, and this is my story" would put me straight off. You have to make it more involving or you're just going to end up sounding like another wacko conspiracy theorist.'

Curtis re-reads his intro. She's right. He needs to make people live what he's lived. Feel what he's felt. Only then will they understand what has happened. And why.

'Yeah,' he says finally. 'Maybe you're right. Back to the drawing board.' Gina goes back to her book, as Curtis deletes what he'd written. The cursor flashes at him, daring him to try again. He sits lost in thought. And as the sun slowly creeps across the cloudless sky and the waves lap at the shore, his mind goes back to where it all began.

To the start. To the mpegs. His fingers begin to flick across the keyboard ...

Berlin, April 1945

```
The Russian soldiers aren't taking
any risks. Their progress into the
heart of Berlin's central district is
slow, deliberate and cautious ...
```

AUTHOR'S NOTE

Alternative 3 is a new breed of thriller genre I call 'fact-shun'. I've done what conspiracy theorists do best — taken some facts, and shunned the rest. Enough to make any true conspiracy theorist proud. None of the conspiracies in *Alternative 3* were of my invention. All actually exist and most can be found on the net. All have elements of plausibility — the Nazi's *did* invent a working flying disc. A UFO *was* spotted over LA during WWII. President Truman *did* order a huge military expedition to Antarctica in 1946/47. Cheat codes *are* available on the net. Hackers *can* do everything Curtis and Gina do.

Ken Mitchell, 2003

ACKNOWLEDGMENTS

To the fabulous team at HarperCollins — Tracey, Vanessa, Rod and Shona — thanks a bundle for your patience, guidance and support. And to Lorain —— it probably wouldn't have been finished without you!

To Lisa — see what I was up to all those nights in the study? And I bet you thought I was just surfing! Thanks for your wonderful loving support, cups of tea, honest criticism and incredible patience in putting up with the mad ravings of an overactive imagination.

To Joanne and Paul — every writer needs a personal fan club while they're writing, and you're the Pres and Vice-Pres of mine! Thanks for your help, support and encouragement.

To Mark — damn fine matchmaker and bloody good mate. Your positivity is truly contagious. Thanks for everything.

To Steve — this is to make up for all those nights when all you wanted was a few quiets, and all I did was talk UFOs and conspiracy theories. Next one's on me.